PRIME

BRIAN BEACH

Copyright © 2013 by Brian Beach

All rights reserved. Printed in the United States of America. No part of this book may be used or reproduced in any manner whatsoever without written permission, accept in the case of brief quotations embodied in critical articles and reviews.

Special thanks to Kendra, Donna, Billy and Heather.

Grateful acknowledgement goes to
Stephen, Ken, Jesse, Darrel, Dan and Emil.

www.ThePrimeNovel.com

facebook.com/ThePrimeTrilogy

First Edition: 2013

ISBN: 978-0-9889818-4-3

This book is for anyone
who has ever dreamed of being a hero

and

For my friend Jon
You are greatly missed

Prologue

"Perfect! Absolutely perfect," Shava said. Utra smiled through her mask of concentration. The times were rare indeed when her mentor, Shava, gave anything more than just a nod of approval. Today, however, was different. Instead of using her powers for a single purpose, like a protective aura, which was relatively easy, today she was using the power of transmutation...and not on an inanimate object like a cup.

Today they were using a rare albino peacock. As far as the young student was concerned, this was multitasking at its finest. Shifting her weight onto her haunches, with outstretched arms, she opened her consciousness and tipped her head back. Utra could feel everything about the bird. It seemed that when she did, a cup full of knowledge poured into her mind. She was filled with impressions of the majestic creature's home, its weight, and even an impression of a crafty red fox that had stalked it the day before, but had left unfulfilled.

"Do not get lost in the whirlpool of knowledge," the warrior said, shaking his head. As he brought his arms to his chest, all traces of the previous praise erased from his face. "You just want to lightly touch the bird's consciousness. Any more than that and you might get pulled in. Remember, this is a beautiful animal, but a wild one nonetheless."

Utra drew in one full, complete breath, stood erect and swept her arms upward towards the heavens. As she did so, she caught a glimpse of the fully-eclipsed suns that were showering the palace courtyard with purplish rays of light. In one fluid motion, the teen spun on her toes and forced her energy downward. Her arms swept down from the upright position to her sides. When she did, the bird began to rise off the soft purple blades of grass. It now hovered two feet in the air. At first, its feathers ruffled. It let out an involuntary squawk. But soon it settled down, as Utra focused on the stillness of her mind.

Shava gingerly walked up behind her. He placed his calloused, warrior's hands on the teen's shoulders. "Now, separate the bird's soul from its body." Utra grinned.

"Child's play," she thought. And indeed it was. She had done this simple trick countless times in the two years of training with Shava. It was fundamental physics; mind over matter. The albino peacock immediately spread out its magnificent wings and tail feathers, as if preparing for attack. But with one firm tug from Utra's dominant will, the bird's essence was separated from its body. It reminded her of a magic show she had seen when she was younger.

A street performer had a table set with fine antique handcrafted plates, resting on a tablecloth of luxurious linen. With one swift jerk, the performer stole the linen from under the eating utensils, without so much as disturbing one place setting. At the time, she was impressed. Now, a decade later, she saw that it was nothing more than a parlor trick compared to what she could do.

"Be careful," said Shava. "Do not sever the thin cord that binds the soul to the body." Beads of sweat were forming on Utra's forehead. She was glad she had tied back her long, black hair. She didn't need any more distractions.

The exquisite bird barely paid any mind to its weightless state. It bobbed up and down in the air, free from the confines of gravity. Directly to its left was a miniature starburst of glowing energy, tethered to the bird by a slender umbilical-like thread of soul energy.

"Very nice. We are almost done," said Shava, his brown face looking anxious, as if a tower of cards were about to fall. "I want you to molecularly change the bird's body into glass, and then reinsert the bird's life force."

Utra closed her eyes and visualized the royal bird in attack mode, full of fury, defending its nest. Its tail feathers and wings outstretched, it was suspended with its fierce talons ready to scratch her face. She then thought of brilliant, multifaceted glass sprouting from the soil. It reached upwards in a spiral to hold the glass bird aloft, still in all of its fury.

The teen opened her eyes, only to see her mentor shaking his head in disbelief. "Aren't you forgetting something?" Utra knew immediately that she had forgotten the most essential step. Poised in front of the young trainee's eyes was, in fact, the fiercest crystalline bird ever seen. A thousand artisans could never capture the sheer detail that Utra had infused into her creation. However, by its side still floated the vibrant life force.

"Many apologies, my friend," Utra said. She inwardly gave a mental tug, and instantly the large statue began to shine with utter brilliance, casting a rainbow of colors in all directions. The young god, finally relaxed, took in the radiance of her completed work. "I created this," she said, with an astonished look on her face.

Chuckling, Shava stepped forward. Standing side-by-side again with his student, he explained. "Yes and no, child. Your conscious mind alone could never have done this with such fine detail. Only by cooperating with your subconscious can you access the infinite knowledge which resides in us all."

"I apologize. I didn't mean to sound proud," Utra said, bowing at the waist as a sign of humility.

The tall warrior stepped forward, tossing his long, gray hair over his right shoulder. Standing in front of his student, he spoke. "Utra, I cannot emphasize this enough. You are royalty. You are no longer required to bow to anyone except the Creator. To do so would be seen as a sign of weakness by others." He brought his voice down so it was a low, hushed tone. "Not even the Royal Guard would understand. I know your heart, child. You mean well. But you are no longer the little orphan that I met living on the streets long ago. You are the Prime. You are the single most powerful being under the three moons." Utra couldn't help but feel slightly embarrassed by the statement. As a result, she dropped her gaze to the ground.

"Seven Lords!" Shava exclaimed. "This is exactly what I'm talking about. You have to stop doing this. Look me in the eyes." She slowly looked up to meet Shava's gaze. The eyes of her master were intense and focused. Even though he was fully relaxed, his eyes gave the impression that he could attack at a split second's notice, a fact that she had witnessed on many occasions.

"Listen to me, child. When two lions meet in the jungle, the first test of dominance that takes place is the locking of their eyes. The first to lower its gaze does so in submission. After that, the hierarchy is established. They don't need to fight, because the end is no longer in doubt." Shava put his long arm around his young student. "You are possessed of the strongest force in the universe. Act like it! Not so much for the other lions of this palace, but for the hyenas that unfortunately live here as well."

Smiling, Utra met her mentor's gaze. "I do not bow before your power. I bow before your wisdom, mighty Shava."

"There is the sly little beggar that I met in the streets of the bazaar." Master and student both turned to admire the courtyard's newest decoration. "I will say this, Utra. If you only learn one thing today, I want you to realize that we are constantly changing. Like the light shining from this work of art, we too are fluctuating and shifting. Even though you are a god, you must continue to change and grow. In the future, when obstacles arise, it is your responsibility as the sovereign to adapt, overcome, and persevere for the good of the people that depend on you." He turned once more to face Utra.

"We, as people, inherently fear change," he said. "Even if the situation is not dangerous, people are wary because it takes comforting familiarity and replaces it with imposing newness. In these next few months as a ruler, you need to be a light to shine the way for your people. But that's enough for one day. Let us get lunch."

Utra smiled from ear to ear. "Finally," she said, stretching her arms out. "I'm starving. But what of the peacock? Shouldn't we change it back?"

The warrior looked back with disdain towards the bird. "No. Leave it. Another lesson for today is never bite Shava on the leg." They both chuckled and began walking across the large courtyard towards the temple.

Utra had to admit, she was surprised that the bird had even gotten close enough to tear Shava's silken pants. The dried blood around the torn fabric suggested that the bird had ripped into more than just his tunic bottoms. Though, even if he was hurt, Shava would never say so. He was not only the finest warrior in all the land, but the most stoic as well. She couldn't help but wonder if today's incident was an indicator that he was slowing down in his old age.

Utra tried her best not to pry. However, being omniscient, she knew that the fearsome instructor, a brown-skinned Lycuran, was the oldest of his warrior race. The Lycurans were the original race on this earth. Utra's people had only come here four thousand years ago, and she knew that Shava was at least six thousand years old. She'd often wondered what secrets her instructor held in his head, but she'd promised herself that Shava's head was off limits. Still, there were so many things to have borne witness too; particularly, the rise of the Royals. The sixty-six year war had seen Utra's people, the Hermarions, rise up against the tribal system of the Lycurans, to establish a caste of ruling Hermarions.

Utra was not necessarily tall. She was a full foot shorter than Shava, who stood a commanding seven feet. To see them side-by-side might seem comical. He was large and imposing. He walked with a purposeful stride that said, "If you're in my way, get out of it or suffer the consequences." Across his back were his weapons of choice; two black, telescopic riot batons that he had fashioned on his own.

When she had first met Shava, she'd thought he was insane. The preferred weapons for most everybody, including the Royal Guard, were tempered steel blades. But, after witnessing the warrior's deadly proficiency with the two sticks of death, she knew his weapon was superior in every way. Since that time, he had also upgraded them, adding a power source built into the handles. With a flick of the switch, his alloy metal clubs coursed with energy. The combination of energy and sonics gave the twin batons pulverizing strength.

Utra, in comparison, was lean and athletic. When she walked, she moved like water; twisting and turning. Her years living as a thief in the marketplace had taught her that. She felt an odd, sort of nagging guilt, when she thought of where she came from, even though she had never stolen for sport or out of spite. She stole out of necessity. It was something that she didn't like to dwell upon, as if thoughts of the past could somehow bring about the reversal of her fortune. In the long run, she preferred not to tempt fate. If there was one thing the fledgling god had learned, it was that her mind was incredibly powerful. Even when her will wasn't engaged on anything particular, random stray thoughts would manifest in her everyday life.

As they made their way across the lush grass, Utra noticed the blades were cool to the touch and still covered with the dew of the morning. This was quite possibly because of the week-long eclipse of their three moons. In fact, everything in the courtyard was bathed in a faint purple-hued twilight. The metallic palace, with its high minarets and ornate pillars, while absent its usual sheen, was impressive nonetheless.

In her opinion, the palace was ridiculously huge. Seven stories high, it stood as a testament to her people. A whole generation of workers had labored most of their youth away on this project, and for what? She thought it was hideous. The only reason the Prime hadn't changed it was out of respect for the people, who would surely take offense if she had. As it was, even though the coming of the Prime was prophesied for millennia, when Utra was proven to be the Chosen One by defeating the Demon Lord Shaitain, the general public protested when the Royal Family was removed from the palace. It seemed to her that politics was a very tricky arena. Even as a god, it was nearly impossible to make everybody happy.

As they neared the large metal doors, two of the Royal Guards stood at the entrance, each bowing their head as Utra and Shava entered the palace. The inside was lavishly decorated. The shiny metal of the upper walls was ornately carved by sonic blades, telling the long history of the Royal inhabitants and how they came to the desert planet from far away.

"Temple, please adjust the temperature to 95 degrees."

"As you wish, Lord," the monotone voice of the temple's artificial intelligence replied.

"Aaaah, much better." Utra sat down on a couch and turned to Shava with a quizzical look. "What do you feel like for food?"

"Hmmm," Shava scratched his head. "Now that is a topic worth meditating on... Something healthy."

"I agree with you, old friend. Perhaps fruit and cheese."

"Excuse me, Lord," Temple interrupted. "But there is an Ambassador Bavir to see you."

"Thank you, Temple. Send him in," replied Shava.

Utra sighed, staring at the ground and rubbing her forehead. "I guess I won't be eating anything. Feel free to dine without me," she wearily said to her mentor.

The look on Shava's face was grim. He didn't like politicians, no matter how friendly they seemed. "I will stay, Utra. I'd like to see what the wolf has to say."

Utra chuckled, "Do you not like him as a person? Or is it because you are a soldier, and he's a politician?"

"Both. I don't trust him."

The ambassador walked in with two Imperial Guards flanking him. Even though Shava loathed Bavir, Utra found him to be pleasant. He was a distant relative of the Royal Family and was highly educated. In fact, when the Royal Family left, it was Bavir who offered to stay and facilitate the transfer. Everything Utra knew about the Royal Temple and the Royal history was due to the Hermarion's kindness.

"Welcome!" Utra stood and gestured to a bottle of wine to her right. "Refreshments?" she asked the politician. Bavir bowed fully at the waist. He was dressed in a purple tunic with ornate gold thread woven in.

"I hate to be abrupt, Lord Utra, but I'm here with a message from Division."

With a sweeping gesture of her hand, Utra placed a chair behind him. "Have a seat. I insist."

"Thank you." Bavir looked cautiously behind him and sat slowly, as if the chair might disappear at any moment. Smiling nervously, he took a deep breath. "As I'm sure the two of you are well aware, the Monarchy is waiting for Shaitain's replacement to be appointed. The last time I was here, we had gone over some names of possible candidates."

"Ahem," Shava raised a finger. "If I may be so bold, I'd like to remind you that the last time you were here was only two days ago." He rocked himself off the couch and stood at full height. "We had a confidential conversation, which somehow ended up on the news later that night. I don't know who could've done that. Do you?"

Bavir bowed his head and folded his arms. "I'm sorry if you feel that way, but I'm of the opinion that the people have a right to know what's going on with their government. Now, let me get back to my reason for coming. On behalf of the Monarchy, I humbly request that an appointment be made. It's tradition that when an opening comes up it's filled immediately. Shaitain was the head of the Demonic Branch, and you defeated him over three months ago."

Pulling up both of his sleeves, Bavir began to raise his voice, but remained seated. "The Monarchy hasn't been fully functioning in three months. They're understaffed, and the angelic Host has been business as usual."

"Shava, please sit down," Utra ordered. She then turned her attention to Bavir. "I made my position very clear two days ago. I follow the light. My allegiances lie with the Host. I know the tradition is to automatically appoint a replacement. However, it is not written in any of the holy books."

She looked at Shava, who was staring with disgust towards the politician. She then directed her gaze at Bavir, locking eyes. "Since defeating the old serpent, a new golden age has come. We finally have a time of plenty. We have very little sickness or death. And under my rule, we no longer have need for war."

"You are correct," Bavir sighed, as he folded his hands. "But there is a downside too. Offspring continue to be born, yet none of the elders have died. We are out of balance. Your people are frightened that the Department of Death will raid their cities and take what is owed. Your people are--"

"Superstitious, Bavir," Utra interrupted. She stood up in one swift motion, not breaking her gaze with the Ambassador. "I believe superstitious is the word you're looking for. The week-long eclipse is a natural phenomenon, yet the people of the cities have flocked here in droves. There are thirteen thousand, four hundred and sixty-two people praying at the rear of the temple right now, and I can hear every single one of them. Half of them think the world is going to end. The only way I've kept my sanity is because my room is lined with psychonium."

"Then end this, Lord Utra. Restore balance and calm your people's fears. Please, I am begging you."

"No, Bavir. What I will do is let them see for themselves. The eclipse is halfway over, and everything so far is uneventful. No harm will befall my people. I'll make sure of that. But I need them to see that the Department of Death is impartial. They don't even really care about our concerns. It's not like they have a quota to fill. Now, I have entertained your suggestions, but my opinion remains the same. I am the Prime. I alone defeated the Demonic Branch in open battle, and the throne is mine. I appreciate your opinion. However, it pleases me that the Monarchy is weakened, and I am in no hurry to restore the darkness."

"Well, then you are a fool, my friend, because we are surrounded by darkness." Bavir got up with a look of unease, glancing toward the warrior. Bavir bowed politely. "As always, your bluntness is a rare treat."

"You're most welcome, politician." Walking over to the couch, Utra watched as Bavir made his way towards the door. The Prime couldn't help but notice that Bavir's pleasantries and finesse were all but absent on his exit. On top of that, despite feeling that she'd done the right thing, she felt like she'd made her first political enemy.

"Oh, and... Bavir, should you ever come back, make sure you're not wearing that color. As you know, purple is the color of the Royal Family. And you are no longer royalty." Shava lifted his wine glass to his lips and swallowed what remained. Then he slammed the glass down so hard that the stem broke. Bavir stopped dead in his tracks, but he didn't turn around. It was at least ten seconds before the Ambassador resumed his pace.

"Thanks, Shava," Utra said shaking her head incredulously. "Are you trying to make enemies?"

Leaning back with his hands behind his head and slapping his feet heavily on the shiny metal table, he sighed. "I don't know what to tell you. I waited through the whole conversation for you to say something about it. You know the rules, and so does Bavir. He taught them to you!"

There were times in her life when Utra felt that being the Prime was not worth it. Today was quickly becoming one of those days. "I know that, Shava, but Bavir was royalty. He used to live here."

"Still, he can't continue doing this. I'm avoiding any further confusion on his part," Shava said, getting up to stretch. "Now, can we put this behind us and eat?" Shava laughed as he grabbed his sides. "I just might die of hunger."

"And then I would have to resurrect you," Utra gave a sly wink as she also got up. She was in a decidedly better mood now that Bavir had gone, and she was looking forward to finally relaxing. "I have an excellent idea. How about a feast in my room?"

"I agree," replied Shava. "Go upstairs and unwind. I'll prepare lunch and come up in a bit."

The teen began to trudge up the seven flights of stairs, until she was certain that Shava couldn't see her. Then, with an inward blink, she phased up to the seventh floor, which was all hers. Shava was of the opinion that Utra should stay as grounded as she could, and that included walking the flights of stairs to her bedroom. But today, she just didn't feel like it.

At first she thought it was odd to be eating in the sleeping quarters, but by now it had become routine. As far back as a week, the travelers began arriving. She didn't mind at first. They had come to pray. That was normal. But four days before the onset of the eclipse, what started as silent prayer requests in her head had turned into a constant wailing. This prompted Utra to install the psychonium walls in her room.

Psychonium was a radioactive material. The waves that it emitted effectively neutralized all forms of brain waves, from Alpha to Delta. This form of safe housing wasn't exactly appealing to Shava. He was against it. His reasoning being that Utra was the Prime, and the planet's defender. He felt she had to be receptive to all danger. The young god agreed with her trainer, in theory, but after the first day of a nonstop typhoon of emotions wreaking havoc in her brain, even Shava could see that his student was showing signs of psychic wear and tear.

Once in her own space, Utra began to relax. She fell back into the comforter and felt its form-fitting edges around her. She stared up at the vaulted ceilings, trying to remember what it felt like to be normal. It was such a distant memory. In reality, it had actually only been a couple of years ago. Kicking forward, Utra used the momentum to rise up out of the bed. The last thing she wanted was to fall into the seductive embrace of sleep. A nap at this time of day would surely bring her trainer's unwanted criticism, and that wasn't on her agenda for the afternoon.

"What to do, what to do?" she wondered. Scanning the large room, all the Prime could see were more ways to fall asleep. She glanced at her books on philosophy. The whole eastern wall was filled with shelves of books. Just now, though, reading wasn't what she needed.

She instead headed in the opposite direction, to the armoire. The mirror was a lovely shade of metallic black, in the shape of a teardrop. Since coming to the temple, this was where she had spent the majority of her time. It gave her some measure of comfort and escape just to stare into the black mirror. Lowering herself onto the black, crushed-velvet stool, the teen stared at her reflection. Glancing at her light blue-colored skin, she reveled that everything about it was perfect. There was not a blemish to be found. She grinned. For the most part, she liked the way she looked. Her matching hair and eyes were both as black as the sand at Black Rock Beach.

She had only seen pictures of it, but the Black Rock Beach was somewhere she had always wanted to go. Clear on the other side of the world, it was the most desirable vacation destination for the rich and the famous. It was said to be a lush paradise of relaxation. She smiled into the mirror. It would be so nice to leave the desert plains for a while. She had always told herself that, as soon as she was able, she would go and see the water. It was ironic that now she had infinite wealth and power, but no time to go.

Utra found her silver brush and began running it through her shiny black hair, breaking it free of its snags. "How did my hair get so knotted?" she pondered. Looking back at her life, Utra could see the divine paradox that was her existence. Before, she was as free as a bird, but a relative commoner. Nobody paid her much mind, but inside she always knew that she was special, and destined for a purpose.

That's why she felt being discovered by Shava wasn't mere chance. It was wheels within wheels that brought them together. Two short years later, on her eighteenth birthday, Utra faced the inevitable clash with her adversary, Shaitain. The battle was epic, spanning three days and three nights. When the suns arose the next day, Utra stood victorious over the many-headed serpent. It signified the dawn of a golden age for everybody. Everybody except for her, that is. It seemed that while everybody else was released from bondage, she was now the one who was shackled.

There was no victory feast. There was only meeting after boring meeting with the two Divisions that worked under the Crown, which was founded by the Creator. According to angels in the Host, even though the Prime was a million times more powerful than any being, the Creator was still infinitely stronger than the Prime. Utra stared into the mirror and wondered. If being the Prime was this unpleasant, how much worse would it feel to be the Creator?

"Who wants lunch?" announced Shava, as he briskly entered the room. In his hands was a tray covered with fine cheeses and meats. Utra quickly banished her thoughts and set her eyes on the tray. The contents looked delicious. She stood up and crossed the room to her bed, sitting down gingerly so as to not disturb the tray.

Utra looked at Shava. "May I ask you a question, my friend?"

"Of course. Is everything okay?"

"Oh, the food looks great. I just wanted to know if, after things with the eclipse settle down, maybe we might be able to go on vacation?"

"Anywhere in particular?"

"Black Rock Beach."

"I don't see why not. We may be able to squeeze a quick trip in. I must say, the calendar is pretty well packed though."

To her, that didn't sound like a yes or no. Yet, given the circumstances, she would take what she could get.

"Lord, there is a phone call for you on line one."

"Go ahead, Temple," the teen shouted, looking up.

"Hello, Lord Utra. This is Bavir. I know I just left the palace, and I don't wish to disturb you; but there is a situation brewing on the news. Have you seen it?"

"I've not, Bavir. What is it?"

"There are two reports of missing children, both from the lower region. The people are getting anxious and congregating in the streets. It's as I feared. They already feel the Department of Death is responsible. I'm on my way back to your palace, with resources from the Royal Guard, just in case things get out of hand."

"Good idea, Bavir. We shall see you shortly." Utra terminated the call and sighed heavily. "Can anything else go wrong today?"

Shava chuckled and leaned forward, patting Utra on the back. "It could be worse, my friend. I'm going to take the food downstairs before the guests arrive. I trust you will need no help in finding the missing children."

Utra removed her tunic top so that she was wearing only her bottoms and a sports bra. She looked in the mirror as she walked to the vanity. She was impressed. Her physique was looking better every day. She reached over, past her silver brush, and grabbed a black band to tie her hair back. Pulling her hair into a ponytail, she leaned into the mirror, smiled at herself, and gave a wink.

The pillows on the bed were messy, but there was no time to straighten up. Utra sat down, cross-legged and closed her eyes. If these children were freshly missing, the trail would be hot. All she had to do was isolate the parents' thoughts, the kidnappers' thoughts, and the children's thoughts. She could possibly have the children at home and the kidnappers in Royal Guard's custody before Bavir could get to the temple to aggravate Shava.

"I can't sleep. I'm scared."

The realization that she wasn't the only one in her room shocked the teen, causing an involuntary flinch. Eyes wide in disbelief, the young god could barely believe her eyes. Before her stood a youngling. It was a small, pallid child unlike anything she'd ever seen before. Completely gripped by shock, Utra reached out with her mind and screamed for Shava. There was no doubt her mentor had heard her, because there was the clatter of crashing plates, followed by the sounds of heavy feet running up the palace stairs.

"Who are you?" asked Utra, the shock and disbelief still gripping her.

The child looked back through bleary, tear-soaked eyes. Stepping forward, he rubbed one of his damp eyelids with his pajama sleeve. "My name's Josh," the child replied, immediately sniffling afterwards. Embarrassment began to wash over Utra as she began to realize there was no threat here. The child was young and small, and wearing clothes fashioned out of a fiber that she didn't recognize. In the child's hands was a doll of some sort.

"What in the seven hells is this?" exclaimed Shava, both telescopic batons charged and crackling with energy as he stood in the doorway.

"Stand down. I overreacted a slight bit." Utra's hearts were still racing as though a threat existed, even though it was plainly obvious this child was no danger to her or her Master.

"Who is this strange, alabaster child?" the warrior asked, his face changing from extreme rage to complete confusion. The child stared at Shava, eyes wide with fear, saying nothing. Then, without warning, the child quickly darted to the bed, hiding behind her right side. Pins and needles danced over Utra's skin, just having the strange child so close. But the young Lord remained calm and fought the urge to jump off the bed.

"Shava, this is Josh," she stated, her voice sounding stressed. "And I am Utra," she said, looking at the child.

The child's frightened form peeked around the teen's athletic frame. Cautiously, the child held up the plastic doll and said, "This is Wolverine. He protects me."

Letting loose with a hearty laugh, the warrior turned off the charged batons and looked quizzically at his student. "This is what you were screaming about?"

"I was meditating and I was caught off guard," stated the flustered teen. "Besides, it wasn't exactly the child that scared me. When I opened my eyes, the face on his tunic scared me."

Shava chuckled, walking around the bed to get a closer look at the uninvited visitor. "Utterly phenomenal," he said, shaking his head in amazement. "This child is not from this dimension." Stepping towards the wall, he gasped, "Amazing! The child entered through this door way."

Taking her eyes off the peculiar child, Utra could see that her bedroom wall, which was fairly plain other than the fireplace, now had a new doorway. It was open and led to a decorated living quarters, which was rather dark. It had no lights on, except for a small nightlight plugged into the wall.

"The other side of this wall is the courtyard. And we're hundreds of feet in the air!" Shava gasped. "This is impossible! The only two people that can open a doorway are the Prime and the Creator."

Utra was glad that he was enthralled by the discovery. It would hopefully divert his attention away from the fact that the child had caught her off guard. Having calmed down now, the child was sitting right next to her. One hand was holding the Wolverine doll, and the other was loosely holding a portion of the Prime's pant leg.

"Josh, how did you get here?" asked Shava.

"I was asleep, and I had a nightmare. Two bad men were hurting my dad." The child looked at Utra with pleading eyes. "You've got to go help him."

"We will, Josh. But we can't just charge into another dimension unprepared. Forgive me, but I'm going to touch your head," the teen said, moving so she could face the child. She placed both of her index fingers on the child's temples. She felt slightly wary touching an alien child. Though it was obviously in trouble, and somehow it had found its way to the temple. It had to be the will of God.

Images began to flood her mind. "Oh, my!" Utra exclaimed with alarm, as she released the child and sat up. "Shava, a word please."

Shava came up, eyes trained on the young alien. Arms crossed protectively over his broad chest, he asked "What is it?"

"It would appear our visitor, Josh Michaels, is a human boy."

Shava slowly shrugged his shoulders. "What's that?"

"Well..." Utra sighed, and looked back at the boy, "Josh's dad is his guardian, but there is also another called a mother."

"Fascinating," Shava's eyes widened. "What would he need two for?"

"It seems that in Josh's dimension certain characteristics have been separated from each other. One half is called a male, and the other is called a female. They need each other to reproduce. This little traveler is called their son."

The look on Shava's face was a mix between fascination and confusion. Utra was wondering the same thing. This was unheard of. Of all the different beings on this earth, angels and demons included, none of their essences were split at birth. Like the Hermarions, the Lycurans were born with both essences in full expression. Usually, during adolescence, they could choose their own gender, much like the angels and demons did. This was unimportant regarding creation of offspring. A mature Lycuran or Hermarion reproduced without coupling. For some reason, quite possibly because of the unforgiving terrain they were brought up in, most Lycurans chose the masculine essence, sending their female essence into regression. Being a male allowed a person to become a warrior, which was a highly honorable position. Those that chose to exhibit the female essence not only raised their own children, but also the orphaned children of the dead warriors. With this unique upbringing, these children were often enlightened adolescents who frequently chose to become the men of the priesthood.

"One question remains," Shava pointed out. "How did Josh get here? Even if he were a Prime, he's not old enough to have any power. Even the angels and demons combined, as powerful as they are, could not create a portal. Only the victorious Prime and the Creator have the power to do this. So how did Josh get here?"

Utra shrugged her shoulders and grinned sheepishly, saying, "I don't know how, but I created his universe." Utter bewilderment was all that she could read off of her friend's face. She didn't blame Shava.

"This isn't possible. I haven't even remotely begun to train you to think these things, let alone to do them."

Utra stood up and placed her hand on her friend's shoulders to comfort him. She didn't understand this either, but her energy signature was in the bio matrix of the child. "It seems that the doorway was made by me as well. I know my energy well enough to spot it from a mile away."

Shava stood rooted near the doorway, staring at the young boy. Finally, he looked at his pupil. "What you say is true, but you haven't the training to do this. That can mean only one thing, my friend. Your unconscious did this."

"But to what end?" Utra asked.

"I don't know," her mentor replied, "but this is highly disturbing in itself, not to mention ominous. Your inner self doesn't interfere unless it's absolutely necessary."

"Your Excellency, Ambassador Bavir is here with members of the Royal Guard."

"Let them in, Temple," shouted Utra over her shoulder. "My apologies, Shava. I didn't locate the children. I was sidetracked by the boy."

Speaking in a hushed tone, he motioned for his student to come forward. "In all my years, I've never heard of anything like this happening. Let me take care of Bavir while you watch the child. When I get back, we can go to Division headquarters. The Host will help us figure this out." With that said, the massive warrior slipped past his student and looked down at Josh. "You be good for Utra."

"Okay," the pale little boy smiled at Shava. "I will." Utra watched Shava exit the room and close the door behind him. Then she turned back to Josh. The small boy had walked over to the mirror and was now sitting on the black stool, facing her. "Utra, when will we go help my dad?"

"Soon, Josh. When Shava returns, we can take you to a special place called Division headquarters. The angels will give us everything we need." The boy nodded and looked downward at his feet, and then back at Utra, but he did not speak. "Is there something else, Josh?"

"Ummm, are you a lady or a man?" the youngling asked.

Utra grinned and let out a chuckle, "I guess on your world, technically, I'm both."

The child said, "That's kind of weird."

Grinning at the Josh, Utra looked up into the teardrop mirror and smiled at herself. "I suppose where you're from it may be strange, but on this world we are considered very normal," the teen assured the young traveler.

***

Shava hurried down the hallway towards the main foyer. He could already hear the sounds of multiple guards downstairs. He really didn't feel like dealing with political matters right now, not that he ever did. If it was up to him, he would disband the government. He liked the old Tribal Council much better. It felt much more personal. Heading down the first flight of steps, the tall warrior cursed himself for deactivating the elevators. But he knew it was one of those things that had to be done.

Part of Utra's training was to remind her that, no matter how powerful the young god became, she was still part Hermarion.

Daily activities, like housework and walking stairs, kept the young god grounded in humility. Despite his best efforts, she was still a handful.

Her progression as a Prime was slowing down. Two years ago, his student was learning way ahead of the curve. Unfortunately, Shava noticed that lately she was slow and absent-minded. He knew the underlying cause. Utra was at that age. She was discovering herself. Every now and again, more so in the past few months, Shava would look up to catch the teen staring at herself in the mirror. In fact, last week the warrior had walked in on Utra twirling her hair and flirting with her own reflection. His student was somewhat embarrassed when he'd caught her. He knew that sooner or later this would happen. The Hermarion culture and customs were well known to him.

It was a no-win situation. On one hand, he knew full well that Utra was entering childbearing age. This was fueling the outrageous vanity that she was exhibiting. Shava could not feed into it though. He knew, once the Prime sired a child, most of her powers would pass to the offspring. Because of this, Shava had been working nonstop to set up the teen's foundation as the new ruler. He knew the young god needed a break. However, for the sake of the future, he would have to push her to the breaking point and beyond. He knew it sounded unfair, but she'd thank him later. Coming down the fourth set of stairs, Shava could see the foyer.

It was completely filled with Royal Guard. There were way too many just to search for two missing children. Instinct stopped the veteran warrior in his tracks, and he silently moved into the shadows. Something wasn't right. He carefully peeked through the temple window and scanned the courtyard. By the light purple hue of the eclipse, he could see that most of the pilgrims were still busy praying. However, some of them were donning riot gear and heading up to the temple in groups.

Crouching low, Shava could feel the heat rising to his face, as his hearts began to beat faster. He could feel the adrenaline heightening his senses and the old, familiar queasy feeling, as his body pulled the blood from his stomach, diverting it instead to his muscles. His body was preparing to do the one thing Shava did best: kill.

Dropping to one knee, he silently drew out the twin telescopic riot batons from their sheaths. He couldn't help but smile. They were relatively new, and he'd never used them on maximum setting. He swallowed hard and bowed his head. It was a shame Utra was babysitting upstairs. But as soon as the fight broke out, Temple would alert her. Shava just wanted a head start before the Prime came down and put a stop to it.

He stood up to take a head count. There were probably close to two hundred. He looked over the carved banister for Bavir. He found, much to his surprise, the little snake had actually come in with the troops. He was armed to the teeth, and in full riot gear, like anybody who was unaccustomed to combat. At least he had come. He lowered down to his stomach and placed his head near the edge of the railing.

"Listen up, everybody. We have new orders. We are not to engage."

Shava could distinctly make out the voice of Tikril, the head of temple security. He winced. These were his own people. What was going on here?

"They both should have been down here by now. Something's wrong," Tikril said. "Our new orders are to set the bomb and evacuate."

That was all Shava needed to hear. Rising up to full height, he set the riot batons to maximum power and jumped the banister. Pulling off a three-story silent drop towards the marble floor below, he came down behind Tikril. As Shava landed, he drove both charged batons through his unsuspecting prey's skull. The force of his weight and the sonic vibrations exploded Tikril's head cleanly off his body. Using his momentum, he brought the batons down the traitor's back, one on each side of the spine. All that was left of the head of security's lifeless body was pulp, shattered bones, and his dislodged spine.

Nearly sixty of Shava's former guards stood slack-jawed, as the warrior rose slowly to his full height again. His whole upper torso was painted by a splattering of Tikril's blood. Locking eyes with Bavir, he cackled sadistically. The politician's legs began to shake so violently that he fell into the guard behind him. Shava extended the batons out in front of his powerful body. As he did, his sweat showed off every scar he'd ever received in battle.

"I'm going to say this one time, for those of you who don't know me. I just killed the man who taught you everything you know. Leave now, and there will be no more bloodshed. Stay, and I will escort you to the home of your ancestors." One by one, the sounds of dropped swords began to echo through the great room. Shava stared mercilessly across the sea of astonished faces, his gaze driving away even the strongest of wills.

"N,n,n...No," Bavir stammered. "Do not break formation! Remember why we're doing this."

Turning towards Bavir's voice, Shava growled, "Good idea, traitor. Why don't you remind them why they're doing this. Because I would like to hear it as well."

"They are fighting for freedom. Freedom from the tyrant Utra, the so-called prophesied one who promised a better life. But here we are three months hence, and what do we have? Half of the Royal Guard was let go because there is no Royal Family to protect. Surely, the rest will be let go as well. What do we need a guard for, when we have the Prime to protect us? Soon nobody will have a job. The tyrant can do them all.

"I asked you earlier, Shava, to give a glimmer of hope and to honor the proud people's traditions by filling Shaitain's position.

But you laughed at their request. Treatment centers are shutting down because there are no people to treat. The places of worship are all empty because Utra says she does not want their money. She just wants the public's love. But I'm sorry, love does not pay for the luxuries that we've grown accustomed to under the reign of the Royals. Look around you, warrior. These aren't the faces of traitors. They're the faces of the disillusioned and the disenfranchised."

Shava had heard enough. To the left and the right of him he could tell that swords were being picked up. Bavir was no longer trembling, as he had mere minutes before. Instead, the corners of his lying mouth were curling up in a sneer.

"Outside these temple walls are throngs of people, who eagerly await the return of the Royal Family. If Utra was smart, she would have killed them. But she didn't. Now she'll see what a mistake that was. A little advice," the politician said to the warrior. "Next time, teach a little less philosophy and religion, and teach the Chosen One how to play ball in politics." Lifting his sword over his head, Bavir screamed. "Arm the bomb! Death to the tyrant!"

Unimpressed, Shava cracked his neck, first to the left and then to the right. He looked Bavir in the eyes one final time. "You know she's only a teenager, right?"

Bavir smiled and spoke more softly, "I don't care how old she is. She's standing between me and what I want." Before the sentence was completely out of the greedy politician's mouth, the warrior struck him so quickly that the movement was nothing but a blur. Then a jab to his throat exploded both his jugular veins. The next movement was a vicious uppercut. The baton found its way under the protective chest plate and into Bavir's lower stomach, immediately exploding his hollow organs. The last thing Bavir saw, as he fell to the ground, were eyes filled with anguish, hotter than the three suns, burning his very soul.

The Guard stared in horror as their leader's body hit the ground, and then the solitary warrior began to paint the walls with their traitorous red blood.

***

"Why is Elmo red?" Utra asked, laughing.

"Because he's a monster, silly!" Josh chuckled. The face on the boy's pajamas was the first thing that she'd seen when she'd opened her eyes. Truth be told, it was the face on the child's pajamas that had given her such a fright. She had never seen anything like it before. Tunics with print and images were forbidden by law in the realm. The more she looked at it though, the more Utra saw it was harmless. What was most peculiar to the young god was how the boy referred to the shirt as if the Elmo were real. Reading the boy's mind earlier, she had learned that it was actually a puppet that spoke in the third person.

"Why do you think Elmo speaks weirdly, Josh?"

"I don't know. He's my friend, and he teaches me stuff. Besides, you and Shava talk weird too. Are you guys monsters?" the boy asked.

"I hope not! Why do you ask?" Utra queried, cocking her head to the side.

"Because you have blue skin. And Shava's way taller than my dad. He's like a giant." As he said this, the boy stretched his arms out above his head and made crushing noises as he stomped around her bed.

Watching the boy pretend to be Shava, Utra was overcome by a warm feeling of joy. It was something she so terribly missed. Fascinated, she watched as Josh scowled and did his best impression of the warrior's glare. The Prime's joy was pushed out by remorse when she realized that she had never known what it was to feel so free and uninhibited, even as a child. She wondered if she ever would feel that way. Everything in her life now revolved around meetings and responsibility.

"That was a performance worthy of applause. I think perhaps you should show Shava on his return." Josh flashed a huge smile and was about to speak when the sound of a scream and the clashing of metal startled them both.

"What's happening?" cried Josh, as he quickly took refuge under the black, metal vanity.

"Temple, status report!" shouted the blue god.

"Sire, there are multiple aggressors engaged in hostile activities towards Master Shava," the voice replied.

Utra was perplexed, "Why was I not notified, Temple?"

"All warnings have been suspended by your Highness." The comment struck the Prime like a slap in the face. She looked over at Josh hiding under the vanity table. The boy had pulled the black stool in to protect him, and he was peering around it.

Trying not to reveal the storm of emotions that were rising in her, she smiled at the child. "Listen to me, Josh. You stay right there. I will return. I promise you." A frantic nod was all the boy could manage, as he clutched the Wolverine doll to his chest. "Temple, deactivate psychonium shielding," Utra commanded as she slid her purple tunic over her head and cracked her knuckles.

"I'm sorry, Lord, but…"

Utra did not even bother listening to the rest. She turned to the temple wall that led to the courtyard. With one thought, the metal wall folded and wilted downward like the petals of a flower scorched by the triple suns' heat. As soon as it did, the weight of the situation fell upon the young god.

There were no missing children, of course. However, the reporters and the public thought there were. It was all part of Bavir's plan to destroy her, and it was working. Utra stretched out her mind. She could feel Shava's unbridled rage, as well as the angry thoughts of a large group of protesters heading towards the temple. They had already started two large fires that were burning out of control outside. The air began to crackle as the teen's energy began to expand outward. Her pure, white aura began to shine forth like a candle in the dark. Just a thought was all it took to extinguish the fires. She then sent the pilgrims home, out of harm's way. Utra glanced up at the three solar orbs and cursed under her breath. No doomsday predictions would come to pass as long as she was alive to prevent them. Shaking her head, she turned back towards her room.

"Temple, what is the status of Ambassador Bavir?"

"Deceased, Lord."

Utra smiled. She already knew this, but she wanted to test the boundaries of the temple's artificial intelligence. Crossing her arms, she lifted her eyebrow. "Execute protocol 211. Lock down all doors and windows." There was no reply, but Utra could hear the slamming of all the devices. Even the storm shutters had closed. "That's what I thought," exclaimed the god. She looked over at Josh, who was still on his knees. She gave him a wink, and then she was gone.

Phasing through the floor, she dropped seven stories straight down. She hit the foyer floor like a lightning bolt, cracking the marble and sending shards onto the unsuspecting anarchists. It only took the blink of an eye for the Prime to survey the scene and see that things were actually a lot worse than she'd believed. There were bodies scattered everywhere. She broke into a run towards her mentor, who was in a corner, fighting off a large section of the guard.

Utra knew there was a bomb from the instant she dropped the psychonium shields. The only problem was locating it. Although she could read the minds of the terrorists, she couldn't sense where it was. All explosive devices, along with guns, had been outlawed by the Royal Family two generations ago. In fact, the only bomb Utra had ever seen was in a picture in the museum.

Utra splayed out her fingers and sent a ball of fire rolling over the guards standing in her way. There was a fury rising inside of her. She was trying to maintain her calm, but something wasn't right. As she back-flipped over a blade aimed at her head, she figured it out. There were more people in the room than her senses were telling her. Something was definitely out of the ordinary, and she wasn't waiting for the extra players to tip their hat.

Summoning the energies within, the young god teleported Shava to her side and yelled, "Get behind me!" as she held out her arm and snapped her fingers. Immediately, thirty-eight necks broke. As their lifeless bodies all hit the ground, the commotion ceased. Utra scanned all around her. The foyer was silent now. According to her senses, they were the only two beings in the large room. But she knew that wasn't true. Looking past the one hundred and forty-four bodies that surrounded them, there were still more people to be dealt with. A group of twenty people were in front of them, and a group of twenty people were standing against the opposite wall, just watching. They all wore black robes and had metallic skull caps on their shaved heads. She was guessing they were plated with psychonium. As they started to walk towards her, Utra went back down into a battle stance.

"Are you all right, Master?" she asked, without turning around.

"I've never felt better," he replied, facing the other twenty. His student knew this was not true, though. She could feel that Shava's right wrist was broken, and he had lost one of his riot batons. Utra extended her energy around both of them and mended the warrior's wounds.

"You have my gratitude. You're a fine friend! Look through my eyes for a second, if you would." Expanding her awareness once again, Utra could see that the twenty robed figures on her side were advancing as well. Unfortunately, the bomb was still nowhere to be found.

"Where is Josh?" asked Shava, as he began to charge his remaining baton.

"Upstairs, locked in my room," She answered, wiping her forehead on her sleeve.

"I don't want to alarm you," her Master said with his mind, "but there are two angels here. They are both cloaked. Without a doubt, they are aiding our enemies. Every now and then, I see the light bend off of them. They're hidden amongst the wall carvings."

Utra watched as the twenty cloaked figures approached. She glanced upwards to the wall. She wasn't too surprised to find that Shava was right. There, among the scenes carved in the wall, was an extra figure. Its skin matched the metallic wall. Yet, unlike the carvings that were engaged in the story of the Royal history, this figure was looking straight at her.

It was deathly quiet in the large temple hall, except for the sound of Shava's weapon. As the figures on her side came into view, Utra was shocked to see she knew most all of them. They were all members of the priesthood. They stood thirty feet from her, in a uniform line. Then the black-robed figures began to fan out as they started to chant in low voices.

"What do you want?" shouted the teen, her voice echoing in the vast temple. A cloaked figure stepped forward slowly, its hands hidden in its black sleeves.

"Calm yourself, Prime," said the figure in a soothing voice. "There's no need for violence. We come to talk."

"Save the lies. We're far past that. What do you want?"

"Well, Shava, I'm impressed. Your prodigy has a temper." The cloaked figure moved closer. As it did, Utra reached out to touch it and watched as her hand slipped right through the clergyman.

The priest smiled, "You didn't think we would engage a person of your power unprotected; did you?"

"Then you're aware of what I can do?" Utra asked, backing her words with her conviction.

"Oh, of course. I knew, when you were but a small child, that you were the Chosen One. Even back then, your aura was a song unto itself." The robed figure waved his hands, as if he were conducting a symphony. Then the smile faded from his face. "I know everything about you. You are the long-awaited prophecy fulfilled. The part that pains me is that, since coming to the priesthood forty years ago, I've been hoping and praying you would come." The priest's face looked absolutely crestfallen, and a tear descended down his cheek. Utra expanded her awareness yet again, but she still did not feel anything. It was as if they were ghosts. All she needed was for one of them to become tangible.

"The day you were revealed as the conqueror over Shaitain, I rejoiced. However, I wasn't quite prepared for what happened next." His face immediately went from sadness to anger. "For forty years, I was admired. My congregation loved me." His eyes narrowed, "On occasion, I was even feared." The robed figure stepped to the side, motioning to his chanting companions. "We all knew our order would be disbanded. That was also not the painful part."

"Then what was?" asked Shava, his voice filled with impatience.

"After I left, I walked through the bustling market. It was filled people that I had delivered, baptized, and counseled. They all paid me absolutely no mind. I got not so much as a greeting." His calm voice was nearly a scream now, and Utra could see the veins standing out on his neck. To compensate, the other robed figures chanted all the more loudly. "I am sorry, child, but I am not going to fade into obscurity after being worshiped and adored my whole adult life. I just cannot accept that."

Utra was completely dumbfounded. She had no idea that so many people had been adversely affected in the past three months. She breathed in a deep breath. "I'm sorry. I didn't know this was happening. What do you want to be done about it?"

The cloaked figure longingly stared into the teen's eyes. "I am sorry. But the only way I can be whole again is if I become the Prime."

"You can't. There is but one Prime, and that is me." Utra brought her hands up, and electricity jumped from palm to palm. Her eyes glowed an iridescent shade of blue. The cloaked figure scowled.

"Hit a nerve; did I? He reached down and touched the silver cord wrapped around his waist. His long finger flickered over it.

Utra could feel the power growing within her, begging to be released. She locked eyes with her adversary as the ground began to shake underneath her feet. She had heard about all she was going to take. She stomped her left foot on the marble floor, creating a series of cracks that spread outwards. When the young god opened her mouth, what came out was not so much a voice, but a vibration. "I AM THE PRIME."

In response, the chanting became louder. The cloaked leader wrapped his skinny fingers around the cord. He looked at Utra with eyes devoid of reason. In them was only fanaticism and anticipation. "Oh, yes. I always knew you were the Chosen One, and I recognize your legitimacy to the throne. But this knowledge does nothing to quell the hunger within me that wants to take it for my own." With that, the silver cord dropped, and the cloak parted open to reveal the explosives underneath.

"Now, Shava!" Utra shouted as the young god dropped to her knees. The warrior's large frame spun around, and in one motion quickly threw his riot baton with all his might. It flew past the intangible priests, piercing the camouflaged angel in its shoulder, pinning it to the wall. The angel shrieked violently and went limp. Utra smiled and fired off a bolt of lightning at the metallic mural on the opposite wall. It absorbed the energy. When it did, the angel, who had been sitting there disguised, became visible and fell to the ground like a swatted fly. Then exactly what she had expected would happen took place.

One by one, the robed priests began to register with her senses; and just as quickly, she was disabling them. She turned two to ice before they could even move, and the next one to amethyst. She had a pretty good lock on them when the zealot materialized and went to activate his explosives. To his surprise, all that was found on his chest were bricks of cheese. The look on his self-righteous face was priceless when Shava ran up and headbutted him, breaking his fanatical nose.

Utra couldn't help but smile before she moved on, transforming the next three into salt. They were coming faster now, rushing forward in threes. So she dropped the flair and went back to freezing them. From the corner of her eye, she could see Shava viciously attacking any figure that went to remove their cloak and detonate their own explosives. There were only a few more left when Utra wheeled around to see the stunned angel had not only gotten up, but was glaring murderously at them. There was no time to sort things out. The Prime opened a black hole behind the angel's back. The look of homicidal rage instantly became one of horror as the black-winged angel was yanked off of its feet and sucked into the swirling, black vortex.

Then all hell broke loose. The first bomb detonated near Utra. She crouched down low and instantaneously threw up a containment field around the blazing fury. She had never felt so much unrelenting resistance. She leaned in and spread her arms wide, her energy flowing forth, pushing against the raging ball. To make matters worse, the vortex was still open, and the hungry black maw had created a vacuum in the large temple. Everything that wasn't bolted down began to move towards it. This included the lifeless bodies of Shava's victims. Fear began to creep up on

Utra. Things were quickly spiraling out of control, and she had never faced anything like this. The only thing that came close was her battle with Shaitain, but that was one-on-one.

The wind whipped at her face and tunic, as it rushed into the inviting whirlpool of dark energy. Pushing the ball of explosive fire towards the vortex was taking all her concentration. To push the explosion back, counter the vacuum, and not give in to the feeling of impending doom that she was feeling was testing her very fiber. Thankfully, all the fanatics were too busy holding on for dear life to have to deal with them too.

Shava had anchored himself by holding onto the banister. He was repeatedly shouting something to Utra, but whatever he was trying to say was lost in the roar of the vacuum. "Heavens help me," Utra thought to herself, as she guided the ball of destructive energy towards the black hole.

The corpses of the Royal Guard were being sucked past Utra, their arms and legs flailing like rag dolls as they whirled in the air. Absolute horror gripped the teen as the first of the old priests gave in to fatigue and simply let go. The clergyman went cartwheeling into the void, but not before he detonated his bomb. The blast shook the temple violently, but only momentarily. The concussive force had been lessened by the vortex. Its fierce might hovered at the entrance, like a dragon threatening to crawl out, and then imploded into the hole.

And then she felt it; a fear so crippling it almost sent her to the floor. And it wasn't coming from her. It was coming from Shava. Utra looked to the banister and found that he was no longer there. His massive form slid along the marble floor towards the hungry nothingness. Utra's concentration buckled as dread began to squeeze her like a vice. She took her attention off of the rolling ball of energy that was the initial explosion. Its fury began to slowly blossom, but the young god could not lose her Master. If she lost Shava, she would be truly alone.

"Enough!" the young god screamed at the top of her lungs. "Enough!" The teen pushed as hard as she could with her mighty will, sending wave after wave of pure energy forth. The ball of fury shrunk down to a grain of sand, which was then jettisoned through the black hole. Utra was blazing like the suns. Shadows danced off the walls, cast by the young god's light. With one final push, it was complete. The torn fabric of reality was woven shut. Utra stood in the center of the large foyer. For one small second, the only sound was the ringing in her ears.

Shava's voice broke the stark silence with one powerful command, "Run!" The warrior was on his hands and knees, gasping. He looked exhausted. He pointed frantically behind the teen and repeated the command. Spinning around, Utra was met by the fiercest set of eyes she'd ever seen. There, before her, was the other angel. It was hunched over, its long black hair drenched in sweat. This didn't look like any angel she'd seen before. Its long wings had feathers as black as coal. It just stood there, staring at her with hatred. With its left hand, it gripped the riot baton impaled in its right shoulder. It looked like it was struggling to say something, as it shuddered in pain.

"Run, child, please! It's an agent of Death!" Shava said weakly.

The angel parted its blood-coated lips and snarled, "Kill you." Utra's eyes widened with horror as she felt her mentor's life force disappear. The angel's eyes bulged in pain, but it still managed to smile with its sharp, bloody teeth.

Utra heard Shava's lifeless body hit the floor behind her. A numbness washed over her like she'd never felt before. She didn't feel like holding back any longer. What was the point? The heretical priest smiled, as he slowly limped up to the bloody angel's side. A trail of blood was still flowing from the zealot's broken nose that Shava had given him earlier. In his hands, he held a detonation device. One by one, the broken remains of the fanatical order began to converge on Utra. The numb teen looked into the cold, uncaring eyes of the angel. Then the Prime watched the hands of the zealot find their way to the detonator, turning everything to fire.

The young god felt the impact, and she was ready for it. What remained of the zealot in that first tenth of a second couldn't fill a thimble. She could feel the confused, disembodied souls of the heretic order. Most likely, they had been promised immortality. The tears that streamed from Utra's face were instantly evaporated by the intense heat that flowed throughout the room.

She stared into the angel's eyes for what seemed like an eternity, neither one looking away. At three quarters of a second past the blast, the angel reached into her mind and said mockingly, "So have we had enough, stubborn little god? Are you ready to die yet?"

"Why are you doing this?" Utra asked, numbly.

"It's just your time to die. Accept it," the Angel of Death said.

"No! Only I decide that!" the teen screamed. At nine-tenths of a second after the detonation, she was gone.

When she entered her bedroom, she didn't even dare to look in the mirror. There was no time. The temple foyer was big, but once that was filled with flames, the explosion would have nowhere to travel but upwards. The temple was made completely of metal, and the storm doors were all in place. The only way out was through the bedroom wall she had opened earlier, but the teen had no intent on using that as an exit.

As gently as she could, Utra grabbed Josh. The child was sobbing hysterically. His eyes red, he grabbed onto her neck and pressed his face into the purple tunic. Utra ran to the portal the small boy had come from. She stopped right at the opening, not knowing what to expect. Looking down at Josh, she took a deep breath, closed her eyes, and crossed the threshold into the unknown.

***

The first thing Utra noticed was the vibrational bandwidth. It felt so foreign. But most of all, she noticed that Josh was not with her. There was nothing but blackness surrounding her. "What was the meaning of this?" she thought.

Frantically, she felt her chest and all around herself for the small boy. It was so black that Utra couldn't see her hand in front of her face. She called out to Josh, but her voice had no sound. She was seized by an indescribable fear. The vibrations of this space were completely different from not only hers, but also from the space that she'd just come from. She looked in every direction possible, hoping to see some small fraction of light. She searched for any indicator she could head to, but she couldn't see a thing. She was completely alone. So at that moment, Utra did the only thing she felt capable of doing. She drew her knees up to her chest and cried. She truly had nothing. Totally alone in the darkness, the young god sobbed.

By the time she stopped crying, Utra had no idea how long it had been. To be truthful, she had no idea if she was infinitely large or infinitely small, nor if she was right side up or upside down. At one point, a question had entered her mind. How long had it been since she had taken a breath? All she knew was that she didn't feel like she needed to. So she didn't.

By now she had her fill of confusion. Utra decided it was time for some well-deserved order. If the world without was undefined, she would just have to go within. Closing her eyes, the young god found the landscape of her own mind. Amidst her inner consciousness was the answer that she had been hiding from all long. The god opened her eyes and said, "Now I remember."

She willed herself to vibrate, slowly at first, and then faster and faster. Soon the molecules emitted sound, then light, then heat, then electricity. It was a spectacle to behold. For days, or maybe it was years, this went on. The higher she vibrated, the farther her molecules stretched. And finally, when she had stretched out as far as she could possibly go, there was a loud bang. Suddenly, Utra was no more.

But a new universe was coming together. It had order and direction. Most importantly, it would eventually have a little boy named Josh, and he was destined to be the greatest Prime in existence.

***

Back in Utra's home world, Death sat up against the metal wall in the foyer of the temple. The heat inside was finally dying down. Eventually, everything did. Death knew this better than any mortal. He looked up at the metal walls where the Royal Family etched their version of history. "What a bunch of lying assholes," Death chuckled. It didn't matter now. The walls were slagged, and not a shred of story remained. It really didn't matter what the true account of history was. Sooner or later, every one of those self-righteous me-first pricks got up close and personal with him. After that, it was all inconsequential.

He hadn't moved since the conflict earlier. The way the whole thing went down made him take pause. It wasn't supposed to happen like that. By all accounts, this was supposed to be a simple job. It was predestined that under the eclipse Utra's number was up. Yet somehow, some way, she had cheated Death. That much was certain. The angel shook his head. He knew he was in deep shit. A simple tag 'em and bag 'em ended with an agent of death missing in action, and a high-profile target giving him the slip.

"Oh, well," he thought as he chewed on his fingernail. It wasn't a total loss. He claimed forty members of the old priesthood, a gang of Royal Guards, and a prominent politician. Not too bad. He began to get up, his shoulder fully healed. Somewhere on the floor was a puddle of molten alloy that used to be a riot baton. Rising up, Death stretched and said, "Shava, my friend, you had a good run. But in the end, you have to dance the dance, just like everybody else."

Crossing the gigantic hall, he ran his fingers through his black hair, and threw on his usual visage. Instantly, he was clothed in a black tunic with silver thread woven in; and his wings were obscured from mortal sight. He looked backward more time. He didn't usually get nostalgic, but on any given world he knew that there were only one or two people like Shava at any given time. Now, with his passing, it wouldn't be too long before the jackals ran this planet into the ground.

Phasing through the wall, Death looked up at the three suns. Goddamn, they were beautiful when they were eclipsed. This shade of purple light only came around with the eclipse. It was a rarity to be sure, unless you were immortal. In a few days, it would be gone; but one day it would be back. Eventually, everything comes full circle. In awe of the damage the blast had caused, the angel looked around the private courtyard. The grass was scorched from the heat of the fire, and the trees and bushes were still burning.

Looking at one burning bush in particular, the Angel of Death couldn't help but notice the fierce glass bird. Poised to attack, the life force within it was held in perfect stasis. Death marveled at the detail. No ordinary artist had crafted this. The flames danced around the glass bird. It called to Death's memory another bird, called the Phoenix. He chuckled and nodded. "How befitting, Utra. Well played." But Death knew, as surely as the suns would come full circle, that so too would Utra, in one form or another. And when that day came, Death would be waiting.

Chapter 1
Beginnings

"Try to keep up, mom!" Josh called backwards as he worked through the crowded airport. "The sooner we grab our bags, the sooner we can get out of here."

"I'm right behind you, hon. Slow down just a bit though. If I spill this coffee, I'm gonna kick your ass all the way to Milton. Papa won't even have to give you a ride!" Josh turned and winked at her, noticing the uncomfortable look on her face. He knew his mother, Samantha, hated crowds, but what could he do? It was Easter Sunday, and Logan Airport was completely swamped with holiday travelers.

"See, we're the first ones here," Josh said, as he stepped up to the shiny baggage carousel. Sam sighed and shook her head at her son.

"It's not even moving, dork. You ran me over here, like I was Seabiscuit. It isn't even on." Trying his best to stifle a chuckle, Josh threw his arms around his mother and gave her a calming hug.

"We're almost out of here, mom. Try to relax," he said, putting his chin on top of her head. "Did somebody wash you in hot water?" he teased. "I'd swear you're shrinking."

"Excuse me," she replied, pushing him playfully away. "I decided to wear tennis shoes for the flight. And besides, don't think that just because you're taller than me I'm going to stop calling you Little Bear."

Even though he didn't mean to, Josh flinched at the mere mention of his childhood nickname. "Mom, don't call me that," he said, in a hushed tone. He nervously looked over both of his shoulders. The woman arched an eyebrow in response.

"Don't worry, loverboy. I'm sure none of the girls on our flight heard. As it is, they're probably still exiting the plane." As she said this, Sam took her coffee cup and held it out to him. "Be a good son and hold my caffeine infusion. I'm going to call your grandfather and make sure he's on time." Josh took hold of the cup and watched, as she walked away. As soon as she was out of sight, he sat down on the metal lip of the carousel. He could feel the waves of heat coming through the thin cup, warming his hands, but he paid it no mind. He had more urgent thoughts to tend to. Even though his mother tried her best to pretend everything was okay, Josh knew it might not be.

For the past twelve years, since his father passed away, it had been just the two of them. She was pretty much his best friend. Sometimes he swore he knew her better than she knew herself. In fact, he often wondered whether it was the crazy dream or his mom's emotional pain that woke him up the night his father died. Josh looked down at the shiny metal rail and checked his face. His blue eyes were barely visible under his straight, blonde hair. He brushed his bangs back and let them fall forward before he checked on his mom again. It always cracked him up to see her in regular shoes.

After his father died, his mom went back to school and got her broker's license. Since Samantha Michaels Realty was born, there was rarely a moment of the week when his mom didn't have high heels and a dress on. For him, it was a large part of her persona. It was the one thing that never changed. He had watched his mom, as she rose to the top of her profession. A single mother who had made good, she was bringing in six figures a year. It was absolutely heartbreaking to watch her struggle as the market collapsed over the past few years. It was a long, hard ride that had ended in bankruptcy for her company and the foreclosure of their home in Santa Cruz, California.

He grew up in that home, which was two blocks from the

ocean. He could literally see the boardwalk from his bedroom window. Now they were in Massachusetts, moving in with his grandparents. They weren't the only family they had, but his grandparents were the only ones who could take them in. Sam's parents lived in Phoenix, Arizona but lived in a small two-bedroom condo. Josh didn't know how he'd fair living in Arizona. His mom always said it was hotter than the devil's armpit out there. He was okay with Massachusetts though. He'd been coming here for most of the summers since he was five. "Okay, Larry, we'll see when you get here," Sam said, ending the call.

"Don't tell me he forgot."

"No," said Sam, "he had to stop and get gas." She sat down, taking her black scrunchy off of her wrist and pulling her shoulder-length blonde hair into a ponytail. Cocking her head towards Josh, she added, "For some reason, he's bringing the Green Machine."

"Of course," mused Josh. "The guy has a brand-new Audi, and he's bringing his '99 Cadillac Deville." Josh stood up, and a second later the carousel began to move.

His mother smirked, "What are you getting up for?"

"Because my bag's going to be the first one to come out."

"Oh, no, you don't. Go sing that song to Schrödinger, because..." Her voice trailed off as she watched her son's bags appear immediately, tumbling off the conveyor belt and onto the carousel. "You have to be kidding me, Josh. How do you do that?"

"Ancient Chinese secret," Josh mocked, as he scooped his bag up and kissed his mom on the cheek. "See ya out front, mama san."

Since there was a sea of cars out front, Josh thought it would be best to move to either of the farthest ends. He couldn't get over the mob. The place was a madhouse. For a second, Josh wondered if it had been a good idea to leave his mom alone at baggage claim. Then he spotted her making her way towards him, through the crowd. Coming up next to him and leaning on the light post, Sam took in the last bit of her coffee before she spoke. "You know, you really didn't take too many pictures at the going away party last night."

"Yeah, I know," Josh said, tapping his fingers on the pole. "I just wasn't that into it." That was a lie, of course. Josh had invited a handful of friends. They all showed up to say goodbye, but they soon took off for a house party. Josh was left to sit and talk with people he barely knew. It was almost physically painful.

"You seemed to have a long conversation with Dale. That must've been interesting," his mother said, coyly.

"Ugh!" just thinking of his mom's fifty-year-old coworker made him cringe. Josh had been trapped at the dinner table for forty minutes while Dale viciously ear-raped him, extolling the virtues of how the new Lord of the Rings was going to kill at the box office. Josh wasn't disputing that. He knew it would. He just couldn't understand why it took forty minutes for Dale to get to the point. Holding onto the pole with his left hand and his bag with the right, he kicked the concrete with his Chuck Taylors. "Hey mom, did you know that Dale has every James Bond film on Blu-ray?"

Sam frowned. "No. How did that come up?"

"I told him that we're both big 007 fans just to switch the subject up."

"What did he say to that?"

"Oh, he went right back to telling me about how hobbits are the ideal pick to carry the ring," Josh said, shaking his head.

"I'm sorry, babe. I should've jumped in and helped out."

"Epic fail, mom. Epic fail."

"There are twenty-three Bond films Josh, and I've seen every one with you, but I don't know if I could talk for forty minutes on any of them."

Josh chuckled. "Maybe if it was Diamonds are Forever."

They both laughed. It had been his father's favorite movie. His mom had seen it more than any other. At that precise moment, a yellow checkered cab maneuvered out of the pack of cabs and eased up to the curb next to them. The windows automatically came down, and the driver leaned over.

"You guys have been standing here for a while. Do you need a ride?"

Josh bent down. "No, it's cool. We've got somebody on their way, but have a nice night." As he stood upright, he glanced at the advertisement perched on top of the cab's roof. The picture automatically grabbed his attention. It was a photo of a beautiful set of diamond earrings. Even though he didn't need to, he read the caption anyway; "Diamonds are forever." He knew it was a common slogan, but his mom probably wouldn't see it that way. Glancing over, it was just as he thought. His mom had immediately looked down at the sidewalk, like she hadn't noticed.

"Whatever," Josh thought to himself, as he sat on the curb. He didn't know why, but for some reason, these occurrences were happening more and more frequently. Sometimes he would talk, and whatever he spoke would somehow show up. At first, it seemed his mom was just as fascinated as he was. However, as these instances became a daily occurrence, it seemed to Josh that his mom was more upset than fascinated. He couldn't understand why.

After two minutes of silence between them, Josh saw the enormous green behemoth speeding towards him. His gray-haired grandfather, Larry, was at the wheel, waving. Josh's grandfather had been a pretty well-known trauma doctor in the military. He was long since retired now. It was weird to Josh that, while his grandfather never talked about the military or being a trauma doctor, his grandmother, Claire, would tell you everything you need to know about nursing and then some.

"There he is! How's my grandson?"

"Good, Papa." Josh stepped off the curb and hefted his bag into the back of the Cadillac. His grandfather kept it in really good shape. The forest green paint was sparkling. He'd had this car as long as Josh could remember. It was odd, because his grandfather bought a new car every four years. Josh wondered why he loved this particular car so much.

"How was the flight, Sam?"

"Oh my God, Larry, a lot longer than I remember." She looked at Josh and bit her lip before yelling, "Shotgun!" and pushing her way past him.

The ride to Milton was easy-breezy. Josh leaned back against the huge leather seat, watching scenery as it passed by. "We got a large package in the mail yesterday, Josh. Do you know what it might be?" Larry asked.

"Oh, thanks. It's my skateboard. It's the only transportation I'll have until I find a job."

"Well, your grandmother and I were talking about that," his grandfather said. "We decided that if it's okay with your mom, we want to give you the Cadillac for your sixteenth birthday."

"Are you kidding me?" Josh asked, his eyebrows raised.

"I wouldn't kid my favorite beach boy."

Josh smiled and laced his fingers behind his head. "Looks like I'll be getting around in style. How's the radio in this thing?"

"Fine, I guess," Larry replied. "Fire it up, Sam." His mom reached over and turned on the radio, which Josh knew would be oldies. Sound pumped through the speakers, and Josh wasn't surprised to hear the Beach Boys sing, "I Get Around."

His grandfather looked at the radio and gave a chuckle. "That's one hell of a synchronicity. Do you have any idea what the odds are of that happening?"

"It happens more than you'd think," Sam groaned. Josh flashed a broad smile, as he lowered himself back into the leather seat and thought, "Maybe Milton isn't going to be so bad after all."

***

"Oh, Sam, my dear, you look lovely!" Josh hung onto the door frame as his grandmother wrapped her arms around her daughter-in-law. It wasn't every day they got to see each other. By his count, it had been at least four years. As they embraced, he noticed his grandmother's hair. Last summer, it was salt and peppered. Now it was almost completely gray. She smiled at Josh. "Come here, Little Bear." She looked him up and down. "My God, you're getting tall. Look at you."

"He's only 5'10," Claire. You're going to inflate his ego," Sam said, as she sat down and began thumbing through the TV Guide. Josh gave his grandmother a hug. As he did, a familiar sense of safety washed over him. It was the same feeling he got every time he came here. Ever since he was a child, there was a strong, palpable feeling of security around her. It was as if somehow this small, older woman, could hold back an army. It was perplexing to Josh, if only for the reason that his grandfather stood 6'4" and spent the first half of his career in the military. Yet, for some reason, Josh just didn't feel the same level of safety he felt with his grandmother.

"I never thought the day would come when I could say welcome home, Josh."

Sam turned in her seat. "I really appreciate this, Claire."

"Oh, nonsense, Sam. You're family. You know we've wanted you guys to move to Milton since Alex passed." As she said this, Josh couldn't help gazing at the living room walls. There were pictures of his dad everywhere, at all stages of his life. Josh's favorite was near the kitchen. It was of his dad in his fire department turnouts. On the back of his helmet was his nickname, Sugar Bear. He was carrying his paramedic bag on his shoulder. Everybody in the picture looked panicked, except for his father.

Like his grandmother, his father exuded an other-worldly confidence. The look on his face basically said, "Stand back, I've got this."

Josh knew it must be hard for his mother to be here. Back in Santa Cruz, there was only one photo of Josh's dad in the whole place. It was Josh and his parents at Disneyland. He was four years old, riding on his father's back, wearing his mouse ears hat. It was only three months after that when his dad died. He was fighting a fire, and a section of the ceiling came down on him. He died doing the job the Michaels family was famous for; saving other people's lives.

"Your room's just the way you left it," stated Claire, as she stepped down into the living room to join Sam. "There was a box that came for you. I put it on the bed."

"Thanks, Nana," acknowledged Josh. If it's okay with you guys, I need to run over to Charlie's and figure out what time he's going to pick me up."

"In that case, you might want to grab your class schedule off the table there," his grandmother said, motioning to the console table next to the front door. Josh grabbed it and stuck it in his back pocket.

"I'll be back in a bit," Josh said, as he headed out the front door. Instead of walking down the driveway and out to the street, he quickly cut across the large lawn. He noticed that there was a vast difference in lawns between the two states. In California, the yards were smaller. There was also a kind of a definable border that said, "This is my area. Stay out of it." Massachusetts lots were big, to the point that his grandfather purchased a riding mower. The only thing that separated his grandparents' house from their neighbors was a distinct line of pine trees that you could easily walk through, that basically said to Josh, "Come on over."

Halfway across the lawn, Josh noticed it was getting kind of cold. The sun had just set. By the look of the ground, it had rained earlier that day. He was accustomed to rainy, cool weather, since he'd grown up near the ocean. In winter, Santa Cruz had fog and smelled of seawater. Out here it was a stark cold, and he could see every star in the night sky. Fighting the urge to throw his black hoody over his head, he gingerly stepped around a puddle on the neighbor's front walk and rang the doorbell. By the sound of the footsteps, Josh could tell it was Charlie's mom, Sue, or, as his grandmother called her, Big Sue. Sue was one of the nicest ladies Josh knew, but she looked like a lumberjack. She was just big, which was even more pronounced when she stood next to Charlie's dad, who was short and skinny.

"Mr. Michaels. As I live and breathe. Happy Easter!" Before Josh knew it, her big arms were wrapped around him. It almost felt like he was ten years old again. "Claire said you guys were coming," Sue wailed as she ran off into the kitchen, emerging with a box of wine. "It's time for the welcome wagon to put a smile on your mom's face." The large woman smiled, tucking the box under her arm and brushing past him. "Charlie's in the basement playing his video games," she said over her shoulder. And just like that, she was gone.

Josh chuckled. Sue was like a force of nature or a large puppy. She had too much energy for him. Josh slowly turned around, pausing in the hall to look at the wedding pictures of Charlie's parents. It killed him every time he saw them. In fact, he was glad Sue wasn't there to see him laugh. There they were. Sue, as big as a truck, was wearing a Cheshire cat grin, like she just won the Massachusetts state lottery. Next to her was Charlie's dad. With his glasses and bald head, he looked perpetually nervous. Over the past ten years, Josh had only seen Charlie's father a handful of times. He was in the export business, and he was always on the road. Josh wondered what brought people like them together. Sue looked to Josh like she should be married to a linebacker, or the guy on the Brawny paper towel wrapper.

Navigating his way down the hall, Josh found the door to the basement and walked down the steps. "Jumpin' George Michael! Look what the cat dragged in!" shouted Charlie, grinning. "I thought you'd never make it." Josh pounded fists with the redhead, and then made for the sofa by the concrete wall.

"What's up, bro?" Josh asked, throwing his shoes up on the old coffee table.

"Nothing much, man." The teen swiveled his chair around and shut down the computer screen he'd been working on. Then, just as quickly, he turned back to Josh. "So tomorrow you're the noob, huh?" Charlie grinned, his red eyebrows arching. He had the same smile as his mother, but somehow his was always laced with sarcasm and a touch of neurosis. "Let me see what classes you're in," he demanded, reaching out with his long arm. Fishing it out of his back pocket, Josh handed over the unopened letter. As Charlie tore open the envelope, Josh scanned the room. It was basically the same as he remembered it, with a few new additions.

Josh knew from his grandparents that the basement was given to his friend, not as a gift to him, but as a buffer zone for the rest of the family. There was no two ways about it. Charlie was high-strung, and he was driving the rest of the family insane. In the ten years they had been hanging out, Josh could recall numerous times when his friend's demeanor had gone from hilarious laughter to a full-blown venomous rant, with the speed of a striking cobra. So Big Sue gave him his own room, or more appropriately, his own cement-lined, soundproof room. Josh vaguely remembered a time when the basement was a play room, but they quickly transformed it into a second living room, containing all of Charlie's parents' old college furniture. The boys had spent a lot of their pre-teen summers playing video games down here.

The latest incarnation came two years ago, when Charlie moved his bed in there. He put it up against the concrete wall, opposing the couch. Now he rarely went in the house anymore. The whole left side wall across from Josh was dominated by Charlie's dad's old business desk that the boy had converted to a computer workstation. Hanging over the desk was a poster of Johnny Cash glaring at the camera with his middle finger extended. Each year Charlie's taste in rock became louder and harder. Last year was punk. This year was metal. Josh noticed he still had the red fauxhawk, though. Perhaps there could be a new development.

"Jesus, Josh, you're in AP statistics!"

"Don't hate," Josh chuckled, placing his feet back on the table. "It's one of the few things I got that matched my old school schedule."

"It kind of sucks low-hanging donkey balls, Michaels. Come slum it with me in beginning algebra."

"How you know so much about computers but know nothing about math is beyond me," said Josh. Charlie didn't answer. Instead, he steamrolled onto the next topic.

"At least we have a few classes together. You'll dig it."

"So what were you doing when I came in?" asked Josh.

"I don't know if you can appreciate this kind of thing, seeing as you come from California. You're all a bunch of godless heathens out there," teased Charlie. "But check this out," he said, as he grabbed his phone. "I'm at church with moms, and the singer is revving us up for the Word like usual, with Happy Clap and the Funky Bunch doing their thing in the background. Everybody's feeling good and getting into it, when all of a sudden, this lady in front of me pitches forward and nails her forehead on the pew in front of her. She totally knocked herself out and put a big gash on her forehead," he said excitedly.

"So, let me get this straight. You were in an actual church?" Josh asked, while nodding his head and grinning. "I've known you for ten years. The only time you've ever mentioned the word God is when it's directly followed by the word dammit."

"Do you want to hear this story or not?" snapped the redhead, looking annoyed. "So she's bleeding all over the place, and then she passes out cold," Charlie emphasized with his hands. "Then somebody screams to call 911."

"Well, did you?"

"No, I was busy recording this," Charlie said, holding up his phone. Staring intently, Josh watched as the lady was lying unconscious on the ground. He could see blood was streaming out of a one inch wound on her forehead.

"Vicious laceration," Josh said, nodding.

"Yeah, well, hold on. Here comes the good part. Watch the Mexican girl."

"Get out of my way," said a girl's voice. "Charlie, put that away!" she said, pushing the camera away.

"She's kind of a bitch," added Charlie, still staring at the screen.

"I don't know why she'd have a problem with you. You're so easy to get along with," chuckled Josh.

"Zip it, Michaels. Look!" Charlie commanded, pointing at the screen. Josh watched as she bent down, ripped part of her white dress, and applied it to the unconscious woman's head. All of a sudden, the camera angle shifted to her hands. "What do you see?" asked Charlie.

Josh stared at the grainy footage. "Well, if your phone wasn't such a piece, I might be able to see what's going on." Just then, Josh saw what looked like light in the girl's palms. Then the older woman was sitting up with her back to the camera. "Big deal," exclaimed Josh. "She passed out. It happens. I saw it all the time working as a Fire Explorer."

"Would you shut up and watch the video?" Charlie insisted, his eyes getting bigger.

Josh looked at the phone and watched as some people helped her up. She looked unsteady on her feet. She took two steps, wavered, turned, and came towards the camera. In Josh's opinion, she looked dazed. All of a sudden, the bloody dressing that was on her head dropped to the floor. Her forehead was clean, and the cut was gone. Josh was caught off guard. "What the hell?"

"See, I told you," giggled Charlie. Josh didn't know what to think.

"There is no way this could be real. This has to be a hoax."

"Well, it's not," said his friend. "I was there, and it was very real."

In the background, Josh could hear big Sue repeating over and over, "It's a miracle." Sitting back, dumbstruck, he tried to rationalize what he'd just seen.

Looking up at Charlie, Josh blurted, "There's gotta be an explanation."

"Bullshit, man. I would've thought that, if anybody understood this stuff, it would be you."

"It's impossible," Josh said, as he stood up and clasped his hands, bringing them to his mouth.

"It's impossible for you to have powers. But you do."

Josh sat back down quickly. "Nothing like this."

"What you can do is serious stuff, Josh. You enter other people's dreams."

Josh really didn't want to get into it. He could tell Charlie was getting excited. So he just agreed with him and shrugged his shoulders. Charlie shook his head. "Listen, I'm sorry. I know you have mixed feelings about this stuff. Hell, if I hadn't experienced it firsthand, I would think it was bullshit too. Go home. Get some sleep, and I'll pick you up bright and early."

"Yeah, you're right," Josh agreed, as he yawned and stood up. "I'm dying for sleep. I've been up way too long, and the flight is catching up to me." Josh high-fived Charlie and headed for the door. "I'll see you in the morning."

***

Josh snuck in quietly and made a beeline for the stairs. As he passed by the kitchen, he could see his grandfather had already gone to bed. He stopped silently at the stairs and listened for a second. He could hear his mom laughing as Sue vividly recanted the details of her first time in Las Vegas. It was good to hear his mom laugh. He knew she had reservations about moving here. In the past, Sam had said that she and Claire didn't always see eye-to-eye. Josh didn't know what happened, but his grandmother had never mentioned it either.

"More box of wine, ladies?" Josh heard his grandmother say, followed by giggles.

"Whatever their differences," he thought to himself, "a box of wine made it all better." After he showered, Josh trudged to his room and laid on his bed, replaying the thoughts from earlier over and over. Something had obviously happened on the video, but Josh couldn't figure out exactly what it was. Whatever it was though, he didn't feel like arguing with Charlie. He'd been down that road before, and it never led anywhere good. He's learned through experience that tact was something his friend didn't possess.

At the very least, his demeanor was abrasive. At times, he could even be possessive. Unfortunately, he'd only gotten worse every year. Now that he was in his teens, if he felt like somebody was trying to cheat him, Charlie wouldn't walk away like Josh. He would openly engage the person and throw out a finely spun web of conspiracy theories. There were times Josh questioned why he put up with it, but he knew the answer. It was always the same reason that kept Josh coming back for more, when a sane person would normally walk away. Despite all of his faults, Josh was attached by the hip to Charlie, seemingly through destiny. The two had dreamed of each other, before they had ever actually met.

Josh didn't remember much of his childhood. It especially pained him that he really couldn't remember his father. But his mom said that, for his age, that wasn't too uncommon. For instance, Sam had told Josh when he was younger that her first memory was her initial day of kindergarten. His was a bizarre dream about a blue-skinned god that he had on the night his father died.

As he stared up at the ceiling, he couldn't help but wonder how cruel could God be? Josh's first memory put him a day late and a dollar short of remembering his father, the one person he'd lost. He didn't know how many times he'd stared at the photo of him at Disneyland, the one where he was on his father's shoulders. Each time, for the life of him, he couldn't remember it ever happening. Unwelcome tears filled his eyes and ran down his cheeks. Josh paid them no mind.

After the accident, Josh began coming to Massachusetts, mainly because Claire had badgered Sam until she relented. Before he'd come out here for the first time, Josh didn't know what to expect. He was apprehensive, because he didn't know anybody; or so he thought. During his first day in Milton, when he was a child, Josh immediately recognized the neighbor boy's face from the dream he had in California a week before. He knew it was weird, so he didn't say anything. Much to his surprise though, Charlie recognized him too, and introduced himself to Josh. They had been friends ever since.

In the dream, Josh was running through a plateaued field near a mountaintop. A cool breeze was blowing, sending ripples along the light green blades of grass. His backpack bounced up and down as he ran towards the brilliant sun in front of him. In the dream, it's springtime; and life is wonderful. Looking to his right, Josh sees another boy running with him. Using both his hands, the boy performs the most magnificent cartwheel. He laughs as he catches up with Josh, his red hair tussled every which way.

Continuing on their path, the boys find a little white terrier pup. Then the games begin as they alternate between chasing and being chased by the dog. It was so wonderful to feel so happy and alive. Side by side, the friends raced on through the dogwood and azaleas that were in full bloom on the mountainous landscape. It looked to him like the field went on forever. That was fine with the boys. They were both young and vibrantly alive. So much so that Josh felt the urge to pounce. He ran to the left. The red-haired boy followed, laughing and giggling the whole way.

    Josh climbed a small set of rocks, let loose a roar, and pounced on the boy. They rolled with the momentum and sprung back up, covered in wild flower petals. One more ferocious roar and they were off again, with the little white terrier nipping at their heels. Josh was overcome by how beautiful the landscape was. The rich sounds of nature flooded his ears, and butterflies danced around him, vying for his attention. But then, he saw her. Josh stopped running and stared in amazement at what was before him. It was a girl in a white dress. She had long, black hair and the kindest brown eyes he'd ever seen. Walking up to her, he bent down, picked up an azalea, and gave the beautiful flower to her.

    The young girl beamed at Josh, and then walked off towards the forest behind her. Josh couldn't help but smile too. As he watched her, she turned and shot him one more smile before she disappeared. It was then the terrier grabbed his attention once more. The small white dog jumped up against Josh's leg, barking and running off. Tearing off in hot pursuit, Josh was eager to catch up with his friend, but he noticed the sky had grown ominously dark. Clouds were rumbling and beginning to blot out the sun's rays. Wondering what could have caused this, he ran, more determined than ever, towards the speeding dog. The wind began to pick up, threatening to wash out the urgency in the small dog's yelp. Suddenly, without warning, the dog came to a screeching halt on the side of a huge rocky cliff. Josh was startled to see the red-haired boy was hanging on to the ledge; but he was beginning to slide off. The boy stared at Josh, terror-stricken, barely able to hold his head up over the ledge.

Knowing he was the only one who could save his new friend, Josh grabbed onto the boy's arms and pulled as hard as he possibly could. All he had to do was get his friend over the lip, and they could both fight through this. But the boy was kicking frantically, and the contents of the bag were weighing the boy down. As the sky grew darker, the wild barking of the dog increased. Josh was filled with urgency. He had to act now, but his strength was quickly dissipating. The boy was just too heavy.

"You have to get your bag off," he screamed, as the wind howled louder. Josh hung on for dear life, as the rusty-headed boy tried to loosen the book bag. But it was on way too tight. It seemed his fate was sealed. In one last attempt, Josh pushed with everything he had. But it wasn't enough. His body was weakening. He slipped to his knees, getting a closer glimpse at the abyss below.

Then all of the sounds, from the terrier's barking to the howling of the wind, drowned out as the boy pleaded, "Don't let go, Josh." But it was way too late. With his energy gone and off balance, Josh pitched forward, as they fell into the abyss together.

Chapter 2
An April Fool

In Josh's opinion, there was nothing more annoying than being woken up out of a dead sleep. It was the crack of dawn, and it sounded like there was a bird party going on outside of his window. "Seriously?" Josh said, his eyes wide open. "You've got to be kidding me." Throwing off the comforter, Josh looked at the clock through bleary eyes. He wasn't supposed to be up for another hour. Flicking on his light, Josh opened his bedroom blinds and let the morning rays flood his room. Expecting there to be fifty birds, instead he found there was just one. It was an ugly, old bird with a brown head and beady little eyes. Josh listened as it sang nonstop for five minutes, until he finally decided he was over it and went downstairs. By the sound of things, he knew his grandfather must be up. The smell of coffee hung in the air while the news echoed from the kitchen.

Josh rubbed his eyes and yawned as he walked in. "What is that godforsaken thing outside of my bedroom window?"

"I see that you've met Mr. Thrasher," Larry said, looking up from the daily newspaper.

"Is that what that bird is?"

"Yeah. There's a nest of them under your window."

"What is that thing doing up so early?" asked Josh.

"Boasting to anybody that will listen about how great it is," his grandfather replied.

"I'm not impressed," he snorted. Reaching into the cabinet, Josh grabbed a coffee mug and filled it up with orange juice. Leaning up against the counter, he looked at his grandfather and asked, "How long do you think it will take for the moving truck to get here?"

"A few days, maybe longer," his grandfather replied.

"Your mom couldn't find anybody who would drive the car out here until after Easter. Why? Is everything okay?"

"Oh, yeah," assured Josh. "It's just that all my extra clothes are packed in the car. I only have about four days' worth in the suitcase."

"That could be a problem," Larry said. "But, if you really need them, there are some of your dad's old clothes in the attic."

"Thanks, Papa, you're the best."

***

"So, basically what you're saying, Michaels, is that your own mother thinks you're a mama's boy," Charlie said, with one red eyebrow raised.

"No, I didn't say that," moaned Josh. I'm just saying that I wouldn't have necessarily applied for the fire department Explorers on my own, but my mom felt that I could benefit from some male interaction."

Charlie grinned. His left hand on the steering wheel, he ribbed, "And, finish the sentence, Josh. She picked up the application and filled it out for you." As he said it, Charlie used his right hand like he was teaching an ESL student how to enunciate.

"Whatever." Josh shook his head. "It was a good experience. I got to see a million things I never would've seen otherwise." He nervously tapped his fingers on the Jeep door while he twirled his Saint Michael's necklace with his other hand. The necklace was one of the only things he had that had belonged to his father. His grandmother had a similar necklace she always wore. Saint Michael was the patron saint of the medical field, so it made sense to Josh why his grandmother had one. But his dad never wore jewelry.

In fact, when Josh's dad married his mom, he immediately

took off his ring. His mother said that, on the night of his bachelor party, his father, Alex, was picked up by forty of his closest friends. There were police, fire and medical personnel from three different counties, all present and cheering as he walked into a no-name tattoo parlor where he had his wedding band tattooed on his ring finger. According to his grandmother, Josh's father carried the necklace with him in the chest pocket of his uniform until the day Josh was born. Then it then became his.

"So let me ask you, Josh. What kind of things have you seen?"

"Well, I've seen people who were alive one minute and dead the next. I've seen babies being born. I've seen enough car accidents to know that this old Jeep of yours is about as safe as juggling chainsaws with Crisco on your hands."

A grin spread across the redhead's face. "Well, it's the only thing we have. And it's free. And free is my second favorite four-letter word that starts with 'F.'" Rolling his eyes in response to the comment, Josh silently drank in the hot mess that his friend had picked him up in earlier. It was a definite workhorse, and it was tougher than most cars, but it had seen its fair share of damage. There was no roof, just a roll bar; and both of the small doors were removed. As hazardous as it was though, it was their only option until Josh got his license. Pulling into the mini-mart parking lot, Charlie gunned it, put the Jeep in neutral, and cut the engine. The brown Jeep silently coasted across the asphalt towards its unsuspecting victims, a group of ninth graders standing in a circle by the payphone. In his mind, Josh could practically hear the theme to Jaws as the metal land shark propelled forward toward its prey. At the last possible second, Charlie screamed, hit the horn and slammed on the brakes. The only words that could describe what happened next were "deer" and "headlights." Five teens tensed up like they'd been caught stealing. One boy squeezed his bottle of water so hard it sprayed the girl next to him full-on in the face. Josh watched as the shocked girl looked at her wet clothes and then to the boy. It was obvious he was sorry, but she slapped him in the chest anyway.

One of her girlfriends walked over to the Charlie's side of the Jeep and glared at him. "Smooth move, dingus. Has anybody ever told you you're psycho?"

Charlie looked at her and slowly nodded his head. "Yeah, my therapist. Now beat it," he said, abruptly dismissing her. He slowly swung his long legs out of the Jeep, rose to his full height, and proudly strolled into the mini-mart.

"So this is how the school year's going to play out," Josh thought to himself, as he exited the Jeep.

"Why do you hang out with that idiot?" stammered the girl in the wet tee shirt.

"You wouldn't believe me if I told you. But for what it's worth, I'm sorry," Josh replied, as he made his way past them.

Charlie was still cracking up when Josh got inside. In his hands he had his usual choice snack of beef jerky and a soda. "Did that girl really call me a dingus?" asked Charlie. "I don't even think that's a real word," he said, paying for the food.

"It is. I've heard my mom say it, but I forget. You'll have to Google it." For a small moment, Josh thought how unwelcome the whole ordeal was for the ninth grade boys. He remembered how, when he was in ninth grade, he just wanted to be left alone. Josh didn't necessarily see Charlie as intimidating. In fact, even as aggro as he was, Charlie always reminded Josh of a lanky skeleton he had seen in a movie when he was young. But he could see why younger people who didn't know him would think he was threatening. He was over six feet tall. To them, he was a giant.

Exiting the mini-mart, Charlie took a good long swig off his soda. "Excuse me. Can you spare some change?" Josh looked over his shoulder. Standing behind them was a homeless guy. He looked like he'd definitely seen some miles. His tan pants were ripped in both knees, and his white tee shirt looked like he'd used it to wipe his hands.

"I don't have any," Charlie immediately lied.

The man laughed. As he did, his dreadlocks bounced up and down. "Well, it's a good thing I wasn't asking you." Josh could pretty much tell this wasn't just some guy looking to scam the teens. He had broken leaves in his hair. He looked genuinely homeless.

"Give me just a second," Josh said, as he dug into his pants. He pulled out the only money he had. It was the five dollar bill his mom had left him for lunch. he looked at it and then held it out to the homeless man.

"Ahhh, hell, no! What the hell do you think you're doing?" cried Charlie, a look of horror on his face.

"It's my money," explained Josh. "I can do whatever I want with it."

"No, Michaels, it's not your money. It's your mother's money that she gave to you for lunch. And if you think I'm going to let you give one dime of it to this dumpster pirate, you've got another thing coming." The man pulled back his hand like Charlie had slapped it. Much to Josh's surprise, the look on the homeless man's dark, weathered face wasn't shame or humiliation. It was pity for the very person who was staring him down.

Josh folded his arms on his chest. "Listen, Charlie, I'm not getting into this with you. You know that we both probably ate more this weekend than he ate all week. I slept in a warm bed, and he slept on the ground. Not having lunch at school today won't kill me."

"If you give this guy your money, he's just going to use it for drugs," Charlie objected.

"Okay, you win," Josh agreed, and threw up his hands in defeat. He knew Charlie couldn't be reasoned with, and being late to his first day of school definitely wasn't on his to-do list.

Turning to the transient, the young boy shrugged his shoulders. "I tried." The Rastafarian smiled and winked at Josh.

"I know you did. Your parents would be proud."

"Hurry up, Michaels," barked Charlie, as he slid behind the steering wheel.

Heading to the battered, brown Jeep, Josh inconspicuously crumpled the five spot in his hand and dropped it to the asphalt as he walked. The only indicator that the homeless man caught the secret drop was the Rasta's chuckle, followed by the words "Right on, right on." Sliding onto the cracked leather seat, Josh buckled himself in. He really hoped Charlie would ease up as the day progressed, but he knew that the odds of this happening weren't in his favor. The first half of the day was a pleasant surprise for Josh. Milton High School seemed pretty nice. It was a newer building, built in 2004, and everything was kept really clean. When he walked the halls, he noticed that the big difference between Milton and the school he had come from was an air of purpose. There didn't seem to be stickers on the lockers, and the teachers were more formal than he was used to. Josh immediately noticed how, when the warning bell sounded for class, everybody was seated and ready to get started. All in all, he was glad that his first and second classes were on his own. It gave him a much-needed break from Charlie and his caustic nature, which wasn't all that bad, usually.

He remembered when they had first met. Charlie was a handful, but he was always funny. The boy loved to entertain and to have the spotlight on him. His views on reality, in general, were unique. But he would always point out something that Josh seemed to overlook. That's what he liked about Charlie. On the other hand, Josh knew that, with each year that Charlie ventured into his teens, his redeeming qualities seemed to regress, only to be transformed into darker traits. His unusual, quirky insights had blossomed into rants, and his everyday, jokey mentality had somehow mixed with an inflammatory kind of demeanor that Josh tried to avoid at all cost. He'd seen in the past, that when Charlie said something aggravating, he was usually doing it on purpose. And those that chose to engage him, hoping to sway his opinion, quickly wished they hadn't. Josh sincerely hoped his friend would be different in a school setting. "Who knows," he thought to himself, walking into his third period English class. Maybe under the watchful eye of the teachers, Charlie could keep it together.

"So how's the day been so far?" Charlie asked, grinning ear to ear.

"Good," Josh replied, as he took the desk next to him in the far right corner. As he did, he couldn't help but notice that students were rapidly pouring in and filling the seats. Yet the seat in front of the redhead went unfilled.

"Look at my 2:00," instructed Charlie. Josh casually glanced up to see an Asian girl with long, black hair, walking through the door. She was dressed in a red and white cheerleading outfit that said Wildcats on the front. He had to admit his buddy had good taste. "That's Vivian. She doesn't know it yet, but she's gonna be my wife someday," boasted Charlie in a whisper, like it was already a done deal.

Josh smiled, "Go big or go home, man." He scanned the room to see if he recognized anybody from his first two classes, but it was unfamiliar faces from front to back, all except for one. He recognized her instantly as the girl from the video the evening before. She was sitting five desks to his left on the other side of the room. He could have sworn that she was looking at him, but now her face was looking down into her English book.

"Mr. Michaels," the teacher's voice boomed. Josh's face suddenly got hot as he noticed everybody was looking at him. In his first two classes, he'd introduced himself no problem. This time, however, was a little different. He'd just gotten caught staring at a classmate.

"Lovely," he muttered under his breath, as he turned forward in his chair.

"Let me be the first to introduce myself," the teacher said, seated behind the desk. "I'm Mr. Douglas. It's nice to meet you."

"Thanks. Likewise," Josh replied, taking note of the immaculate manner in which the young teacher was groomed. His dark pants were pressed, and he had a forest green dress shirt under a dark sweater vest. He smiled and ran his hand over his dark, shaved head.

"Come up to the front and tell us about yourself."

He could feel his face getting flush with embarrassment, as he stood up and walked to the front of the class. Even though he had already introduced himself today, Josh noticed he felt a little lightheaded. "Well, my name is Josh. I'm from Santa Cruz, California. I've lived out there all my life. I just moved out here with my mother, who pretty much single-handedly raised me after my father passed away when I was four. He was a firefighter-paramedic, and he accidentally got trapped in a burning building." When he said this, Josh watched as everybody made the obligatory "Oh, my God" face. He'd seen enough of it in the last two classes that he knew it was coming. The girls were much more animated than the guys, sometimes putting their hands to their chest or mouth. "Ever since I was old enough, I've been a Fire Explorer, doing training with the fire department. In fact, next weekend I'll be doing a ride-along at a station near my house," Josh announced, feeling his confidence come back. "I'm hoping one day to work in emergency medicine."

"Good, Josh. Any other talents? Do you play sports?" the teacher asked.

Feeling recovered from the earlier embarrassment, Josh shrugged his shoulders. "For the past two years I've done parkour." As he suspected, the faces in the class went blank. "It's also called free running," he added, "but I'll just show you guys real quick."

Turning away from the class he approached the wall. Jumping up, Josh slapped the wall and flipped backward in the air. Bringing his knees up tight, towards his chest, and orienting himself to the ground, Josh came down in a kneeling position, facing the class. At first, he could tell everybody was stunned. But by the time he rose back up, the classroom was filled with applause.

"Very good, Josh. I'm impressed," Mr. Douglas said, with a grin on his face. "However, I'm sure the school has some kind of rule to protect students from harm. So since it's not sanctioned, you might want to keep the acrobatics for when you're off-campus." Josh grinned sheepishly and shrugged his shoulders as he made his way back to his seat.

"Show off," Charlie whispered, from the desk in front of him.

"That may be," thought Josh. But in the end, he didn't regret a thing. As he'd come up to the applause from his classmates, Josh snuck a look at the beautiful girl from the video. The ear-to-ear smile told him everything he needed to know. His first impression was a good one. To him, that was all that mattered.

***

Lazily making his way to sixth period, Josh's only thoughts were resting on how much he seriously needed a snack and a nap. It was odd, but the flash of energy he had enjoyed in third period, seemed to be just that. Since then, the wind had definitely left his sails. It all started in fourth period gym class, when they'd gone on a mile run.

In retrospect, if he had kept a steady pace, he probably wouldn't have burned so much energy. But much to his astonishment, his running partner, Charlie, ran pretty slowly for a tall guy. In fact, the tall redhead started out okay, but soon fell into an awkward, clumsy pace that devolved into what looked like half-hearted speed walking. So Josh slowed down to match his friend, which only caught the eye of the P.E. teacher, Mr. Clark. For the rest of the mile, the teacher blew his whistle every time Charlie slowed to a walk. So, for the rest of the run, Charlie screamed and cursed as he doggedly pounded the ground with his lanky legs.

Charlie's bad mood gave way to glee though, when he guessed that Josh actually had surrendered his lunch money earlier on in the day. "I'm doing this because I care about you, Josh. You had to give away your lunch money. Now you're going to watch while I bite into this amazing sandwich." The look on his face was filled with satisfaction as he moaned after every bite, "Oh, so good."

Josh couldn't help but shake his head and chuckle at the over-the-top acting his companion was pulling. "Look at this," Charlie said, as he held up the apple and polished it on his shirt. "I've never eaten an apple, but I'm gonna eat this one, just to prove a point." Biting into it, he nodded, "So that's what they taste like." He then tossed it in the trash. "Delish."   "Whatever. It was my money," declared Josh, defiantly. Unfortunately he could definitely feel the growing hunger in his belly, a hunger that only increased in his metal shop class. Now, an hour later, he could really feel the effects of the run and the skipped meal. He felt drained, which was a shame.

***

He had actually been looking forward to sixth period. It was American History, and it was taught by Mr. Douglas. Out of all of his new teachers, Josh had found that he definitely liked him the best.

Josh strolled into the classroom with his American History book tucked under his arm. It was the last period of the day, so he'd decided to leave his backpack in the locker. Quickly scanning the room, Josh headed for the first available desk. As he sat down, he breathed in deeply and gazed at the clock on the wall. Only one hour left. It struck him as odd how the last hour of school also felt like the absolute longest. He actually considered himself lucky that Mr. Douglas was the teacher. He had a straightforward, mellow manner. When he asked a question, he didn't ask for a volunteer. He just picked at random, keeping all the students on their toes. Josh was lost in thought, admiring the pictures on the walls when the girl from third period, came in.

    She'd taken off her sweater from earlier, and now she had a light blue top on. It seemed to him that every time she moved, her long, raven hair danced, practically casting off its own light. It was funny to Josh that he didn't even know her name yet, but she had been running through his mind all day. Just looking at her made sixth period worth it. She sat down near the door and began to talk with the girl next to her. Josh didn't know what fascinated him more about this girl. Was it her raw beauty, or was it the possibility that she actually did have healing powers? And if she did, could she be the key to figuring out his abilities? Whatever the reason, Josh knew he couldn't stop thinking about her. And even though this girl quite possibly had the kindest, most compassionate brown eyes Josh had ever seen, he still felt there was a chasm of the unknown separating the two of them. He was too nervous at this point to breach it. If he introduced himself and she shot him down it would wreck the whole day.

    Looking around, Josh could see Mr. Douglas at his desk. The teacher had been watching him, as he was watching her. Josh knew he should've felt guilty, but the teacher smiled and nodded his head and approval. Josh smiled back. He knew he liked him, for some unknown reason. There was something about Mr. Douglas that just exuded knowledge. It was everything from the way he talked, to the way he dressed. It wasn't just book knowledge either. Josh knew it was definitely life experience knowledge, even though he didn't look a day over forty.

"Hey, hunger strike," chided Charlie, as he swung into the open desk next to Josh. He looked like he'd just run water through his hair and brushed it forward into a fauxhawk. The top of his head looked like two red waves had collided against each other.

"Let me ask you a question," Josh asked. "How old you think Mr. Douglas is?"

"Hmmm," pondered Charlie. "I'd say he can't be any more than forty-five. His 'fro doesn't have any gray hair in it."

"I don't think it's called an afro when it's as short as he has it." Josh said, shaking his head. "It looks like he shaved his head bald and maybe has a few days growth on it."

"Josh, he's Black. I'm not an expert in the field, but I think afro's a blanket term. If you really want to find out though, ask him."

Josh immediately shot Charlie the evil eye. "Are you high?" he whispered. "From what I've seen, he's my favorite teacher. I don't want him to think I'm an idiot. I'm no barber; but technically, I'm pretty sure it's called bald."

"And I'm just saying I disagree," mumbled Charlie.

"Okay, class, rein it in," Mr. Douglas said, as he clapped his hands together. "You know I'm not a big fan of videos, but this documentary is a good one. It points out some of the many factors that precipitated the Civil War. I feel that it's a little more multifaceted than the book we're studying out of this year. I have to warn you guys. The DVD runs about fifty minutes. So this is going to take us up to the bell. If you have any questions, write them down. We can talk about them tomorrow."

The teacher shot a finger at Josh. "For those of you who don't know, we have a new student all the way from California." Josh smiled and waved as everybody turned their gazes towards him. He was just about to introduce himself, but Mr. Douglas rolled right on. "Due to time constraints, we'll meet Josh tomorrow. Dianna, if you would, dim the lights."

Josh watched as the girl he had been eyeing leaned forward and turned off the lights. As his eyes adjusted to the dark, Josh could make out the outline of an extended middle finger and Charlie's grinning face. Josh chuckled and shot one back and then turned his attention to the video. He tried to take as much of the video in as he could. Although halfway through, his eyes were getting heavy. The only thing that was keeping him from falling asleep was the pit in his stomach from not eating all day. His attention found its way back to the screen, and Josh saw that there was a discussion about the difference between muskets and the new technology of rifles.

"So when these rifles were introduced, they were a lot more accurate and had a range four times longer than the muskets?" "You're right," the other commentator chimed in. "And the newer rifle had less of a kick and a fraction of the fumes."

And then it happened. Josh felt as if somebody was driving a car through his lower intestine, and his stomach wanted everybody to know. It let out a growl so loud, it startled even him. "Shit fire," Josh thought, feeling embarrassed. Sitting deathly still, he pushed against his angry stomach in an attempt to muffle the growling sound. "Please don't do this, please," Josh pleaded frantically in his head. But it was no use. The next one sounded like somebody pulled a table across a wooden floor. Josh sat there with his eyes wide, not a touch of drowsiness left in him. In fact, he felt like running out the door. Charlie was leaning over the top of his desk, with his eyes shut tight, hands clasped around his mouth like they were an iron mask. Filled with dread, Josh clutched the sides of his seat and prayed that it would stop, but no such luck. The next wave hit, and this time it actually sounded like somebody was talking gibberish. It lasted about three seconds. Immediately thereafter came an explosion on the TV, lighting up the dark room. He was mortified to see half of the students were looking at him and giggling.

Stricken with the realization that this was bad, but it could get infinitely worse, Josh looked over at Charlie. His friend's eyes were now wide open, like he was in the front car of the roller coaster about to go over the edge. His body convulsed with silent laughter each time he heard Josh's rogue stomach cry out. Then, silence. You could actually hear a pin drop in the classroom. Josh looked up at the TV to see it was the same guys walking over to a different gun. "That was impressive, Bob. But wait until you hear what this Gatling gun can do.."

As if on command, Josh's stomach lurched and made a sound like a steel ball rolling across a dinner table. Unable to hold it in any longer, Charlie let two grunts through his nose and then exploded into laughter. Within a matter of a second, the whole room was in hysterics. Hanging his head low in the dark as his classmates laughed, Josh silently begged, "Please, God, kill me now."

Searing white light erupted from the fluorescent bulbs overhead, revealing Mr. Douglas standing at the doorway. By the stern look on his face, Josh could tell he wasn't pleased. He scanned the room while he paced his way over to the TV. Sighing, he shut off the DVD player, leaving a blank, blue screen. "What's going on here?" he asked.

"Why don't you ask musket boy?" chuckled a girl in the front row. Josh noticed she was from his Spanish class. Almost the whole room was laughing now. Josh could feel his heartbeat pounding in the back of his head. It was a strange sensation. One that would warrant further thought, if he didn't have the overwhelming urge to crawl under a rock.

"Josh, are you okay?" Mr. Douglas asked, his face turning to a look of concern. Josh didn't know what say. He wanted to look up, but his eyes wouldn't move from the desk. "Josh, are you alright?" repeated the teacher.

"I think he's gonna cry," came a male voice.

"Hold on." Charlie laughed and held out his hand, waving it around. Josh looked over Charlie's desk to see that his face was beet red. "I can explain," assured Charlie, as he wiped both his tear-soaked cheeks. "Mahatma Gandhi here thought it would be an excellent idea to give all his lunch money to a homeless guy at the mini-mart before school." Charlie looked towards Josh and chuckled again. "I told him not to, but he did it anyway. That sound is his stomach growling because he hasn't eaten since last night."

Josh's first attempt to speak came out as a dry cough, so he cleared his throat and retorted, "It was my money. He needed it more than I did." Looking around him, Josh could see that some of the kids were still giggling. But nothing prepared him for the kick in the chest that came when he saw Dianna. She was staring at him, her cheeks streaming with tears of laughter. Josh slumped down in his seat and clenched his jaw as he fought back what he knew would happen next. If he didn't get out soon, he'd cry. Not out of sadness or pain, but out of sheer humiliation. "How the hell did this happen?" he thought to himself. "Is this what I get for helping someone? It's my first day of school, and already I've got a derogatory nickname."

"Charlie, why didn't you share some food with him?" Mr. Douglas asked. "Or lend him some money?"

"I couldn't," Charlie sniffed and dabbed the corners of his eyes with his shirt. "He had to learn his lesson. That hobo basically took advantage of his gullibility. So tomorrow, when he sees him again, Josh won't fall for it. Lesson learned." Charlie then reached up, took in a deep breath and chuckled one more time before he brought his hand straight down, slapping the desk of the boy next to him. Startled, the boy jumped and looked to see the redhead's face morph into a sneer. "Mark," he said slowly. "The only person who is going to cry, if you make fun of my friend again, will be you." With that, he withdrew his hand.

"Enough!" demanded the teacher, as he folded his arms across his chest. "Josh, I have a question for you," the teacher asked thoughtfully, stroking his black goatee. "Knowing what you know now, would you do it again?" His ears ringing and face on fire, Josh lifted his glassy eyes. He knew that he couldn't speak. So with his jaw clenched, he slowly nodded. "Well, Charlie, that settles it," Mr. Douglas exclaimed as he turned off the TV. "You officially can't tell the difference between gullibility and determination."

Josh glanced over at Charlie. The look of shock on his friend's face was priceless, which gave him a small measure of satisfaction. He knew Charlie wasn't at fault for what happened. He was just doing what he thought was right.

"Excuse me, Mr. Douglas," Josh recognized the voice as the girl from his Spanish class.

"Yes, Elizabeth?"

"Does this mean we can't call him musket boy?" Josh sighed as the room began to erupt into new waves of laughter. It seemed that even the teacher was amused, as he shook his head and smiled. But then, just as quickly, the smile was replaced with a look of disappointment. As he looked out over the classroom, the laughter died as quickly as it started.

"I can't tell you how much it hurts to see this side of you guys. Before today, I never thought you'd let me down like this. And to a brand-new fellow classmate, no less." He dropped his head down and then brought it back up again. "For your homework tonight," he said as his face became stoic, "we're going to have a little competition," he said as he began to pace the room. "I want you guys to go home and list as many people as you can, both male and female, who have given of themselves. It might be a king or queen or maybe even a Fire Explorer. Even though this person has given more than enough of their time, they might feel that they should give even more, often times bringing hurt and scorn upon themselves."

Mr. Douglas looked up and then continued, "These people do it anyway. It's ingrained in their nature, as evidenced by certain characteristics. They're brave and slow to anger. They nurture. They know the pathways from knowledge to wisdom, and they understand the difference between the two." The teacher stopped and paused for a second. "It's always the same. Unfortunately, the hardest part for these people is not the obstacles and the sacrifice they have to make, because they accept that it comes with the territory. The hardest part is the lack of understanding that others show when they carelessly mock and ridicule the very people that are trying to help make this world a better place."

"Surprisingly enough, when asked if they would do it all again, even knowing the humiliation and the pain, they always say the same thing: yes. So anybody who might fit that description, you can put them on the list. To start you on your way, I'd like to make a suggestion. When you do a Google search, the aforementioned people usually go by the titles of Lady, Prophet, Teacher or Mother." At that point Mr. Douglas paused to scan the room from left to right, to make sure his students were paying attention. Then, in a loud voice he slowly said, "Messiah."

"Umm, Mr. Douglas, what does the winner get?" Dianna asked.

"The winner gets to leave here tomorrow after sixth period and not sit in detention with the rest of the class." As gasps filled the room, the teacher took two deliberate steps backward and sat on his desk for what seemed to Josh to be an eternity. Then he looked right at Josh. "What do you say, Mr. Michaels? Is one hour of detention enough?" Josh was floored by the presentation he'd just seen, but even more so by the request of the instructor.

"Well," Josh said, swallowing hard. "I mean, if it was up to me, I'd say this whole thing was an accident. I'd kind of like to put it in the past and forget it ever happened." The teacher smiled at Josh and stood up from the desk.

"Ladies and gentlemen, it seems that I had forgotten to mention one of the hallmark traits that denote these remarkable people from the norm. It's the uncanny ability to forgive. You can thank your lucky stars that Mr. Michaels possesses this trait." As he said this, Mr. Douglas began smoothing out his facial hair with one hand. Then he started again, "This is my classroom." His voice reverberated off the walls. "I'm not going to tolerate bullying of any kind, at anybody's expense. I am your teacher. I have a responsibility to guide you down the path to knowledge, a responsibility that I'd like to think that I perform rather well. But don't think for one second that I won't end your individual learning experience in order to preserve the group learning experience. Are we clear, Charlie?"

Startled, the redheaded boy perked up. "What?" he stammered.

"I understand that you were standing up for your friend, however misguided your intentions may be. But the next time you engage a fellow classmate in an aggressive manner, you and I will be taking a trip to the principal's office. Are we clear?"

"I'm sorry, Mr. Douglas. I wasn't thinking," said Charlie.

"I appreciate that," said the teacher, as he sat down, running his hand over his bald head. After a second, a smile crept back on his face. "I know that you all heard what I was trying to say today. When the time comes, I know you'll remember this. Whether or not you decide to follow it is always up to you. Your homework tonight is to go home, enjoy a good dinner and come back well-rested for tomorrow. I know there's ten minutes left, but class is dismissed."

***

"Holy crap, son, did you see that?" howled Charlie as they

walked to the parking lot. Josh grinned. He was starting to feel better just knowing that Mr. Douglas had turned a horrifying experience into something totally different.

"Hey, punk ass," Josh directed towards Charlie. "Next time, remember I'm your friend. Keep the laughing to a minimum, okay? And, at the very least, cut down on the tears."

"Dude," Charlie answered, "there was no way I could keep a lid on it while your stomach was playing bombs over Baghdad. But enough about your untamed colon. Charlie grinned, "How about my crazy display of testicular fortitude? I totally wanted to slap the taste right out of Mark's mouth," chuckled Charlie, as he threw his book bag into the open Jeep and slid onto the seat.

"Oh, you mean when you could have gotten expelled?" Josh said under his breath, heaving his bag into the back of the Jeep and buckling the seatbelt over him.

"I've never seen Mr. Douglas act like that before," Charlie mentioned, as he pulled out of the entrance.

"Really?" asked Josh, surprised. "He seemed pretty comfortable in the situation."

"I know," agreed Charlie. "All I can say is, before you showed up, he'd always given me the impression like he was laid back. His demeanor is usually like the guy on the Allstate commercials, but today he got all riled up. He's officially my favorite teacher now."

"Oh, really? This wouldn't have anything to do with me saying he was my favorite teacher; would it?"

"Not at all," replied Charlie. "I'm just saying I see him in a new light."

"It's cool," Josh said, as his blonde hair blew back and forth in the wind. "Get your geek on."

"Hell, no, Michaels. I may be many things, but I'm not a geek."

"Oh, I'm pretty confident the geek gene is in full

expression. Charlie, you're the only person I know who, when he gets off the couch, stretches and screams 'There can be only one!' while he shakes his arms and legs."

"Loving good television and movies doesn't necessarily make you a geek," insisted Charlie, as they pulled up to the stoplight. "But since we're on the subject, look up, man."

Josh took a look above him and snorted, "Oh geez, we're on Highland Road. What are the chances of that?"

Charlie grinned. "I was wondering when the old Josh would make an appearance. I think he was just waiting for the first day of school to be over."

Josh smiled. "Hey, did I mention my grandpa is giving me the Audi for my birthday?"

An astonished look crept over Charlie's face. "Shut the front door! You're kidding me!" he said, as he put his hand on Josh's shoulder.

"Yeah, I am, you dork. April fool's," laughed Josh. "Now get your hand off me. But in all seriousness though, he is giving me the Green Machine," Josh added with a big grin.

"He's giving you the Dragon Wagon?" Charlie shouted, his eyes lighting up. "That's even better! Do you know how cool we're going to look? It's a certified pimp-mobile."

"Really?" Josh asked, sounding a little skeptical.

"No, seriously. Back in the day, Cadillac was the official sponsor of pimps everywhere." A horn blasted out of the background, waking Charlie out of his daydream.

"Light's green," said Josh.

"Uh huh," Charlie mumbled, his lips turned up in a huge smile as he held his middle finger up over the roll bar. Stepping on the gas, he screamed out loud, "There can be only one!" as they sped off, down Highland Road, laughing.

Chapter 3
Trinity

The return trip from Milton High School was always longer than the initial trek in the morning. But for some reason, today it wasn't long enough for Dianna. While most of her classmates that didn't have a driver's license rode the bus, she preferred to walk. It was less than a mile to her house, and she loved the scenery. Today, however, she was lost in thought as she walked down Canton Avenue. Inside of her, a sea of emotions was swelling and crashing, attempting to overtake her. She stopped walking and looked up at the sky. When she woke up today, she was nervous about going to school, after what had happened in church Sunday. In Dianna's opinion, it was just a careless mistake.

She was obviously getting a lot stronger in her healing abilities. So much so, that just by touching Sister Beverly, instead of just checking to see if she was okay, she'd actually healed her in front of a whole group. The problem was that it wasn't just the usual church people that knew her. It was Easter Sunday, and the church was packed with people who didn't usually go. Much to her surprise though, nobody at school really said a word about it, which was great, Dianna thought. But there was a boy from her school who had videoed what happened, and that's where the problem began. Her father, Ramon, wanted to go with her to school to ask the boy to erase it, but she told him she would handle it. And she would have, when she got to third period. She not only saw the boy, Charlie, but there was a new student, a boy named Josh.

He seemed oddly familiar to Dianna, and it was hard for her not to stare at him. Then when he introduced himself, he said he was into the whole 911 rescue thing. It caught her attention immediately. Was it possible that this was the boy from her dream?

Just thinking back on it caused Dianna to feel lightheaded. So she took a deep breath and continued walking. Dianna had planned to talk to Charlie at the end of the day, but there was a huge commotion in class. Josh, who had been so confident and playful in English, even doing gymnastics, seemed silent and withdrawn in American History. Then the whole class ganged up on him and teased him for something so stupid Dianna could barely believe it had happened.

Through the whole ordeal, Josh never backed down. Even though Dianna knew he must have been mortified when Charlie told the class what happened. The look on his face broke her heart, causing her to cry. She couldn't believe she had cried in class, especially when she barely knew him. But for Dianna, the most confusing part was when class let out. She'd stayed seated at her desk, waiting to talk to Charlie. When he came up with Josh by his side, Dianna noticed the Saint Michael necklace around Josh's neck. She froze.

It was true. He was the one that had saved her in the dream. He was the paramedic. He had to be. Thinking back on it, Dianna knew the whole realization was kind of heavy, but she really couldn't forgive herself for blowing it. Josh and Charlie walked out the door, and she didn't even get up because she was just so stunned.

As she turned the corner onto Taylor Road, Dianna could see that nobody was home. The driveway to the white two-story home was empty. She pulled her phone out of her pocket and, at the same time, let her book bag slide off of her shoulder. It hit the front porch with a dull thud. "God, I can't wait 'til I get a car," she thought. Dianna typed:

Where are you? I need to talk to you ASAP

She sent the text off to Nina as she unlocked the front door.

Right now Nina was the only person who could understand.

Dianna went into the kitchen and stood with her back up against the cool, stainless steel refrigerator. Her mind was still racing. Her phone chirped and lit up. Dianna looked at it:

    I'M JUST LEAVING THE SALON DOWN THE STREET. I'M ON MY WAY.

Nina was basically Dianna's best friend. She could tell her anything. She wasn't family, but she may as well be. Nina had rented a room from Dianna's dad for the past few years. In a lot of ways, she filled in after her dad had kicked her sister out.

    Dianna loved her father with all her heart, but he was stubborn and strict. Her sister, Camille, was just plain wild. It almost pained her to admit it, but Nina was the sister Dianna had hoped Cammy would be, but never was. One night, after Cammy came home drunk and holding her bra and panties in her hand, Ramon snapped and sent her off to live with her grandfather at the Indian reservation. Less than six months later, she was gone from there too.

    Dianna looked up as she heard the door open. In walked Nina with a concerned look on her face. "Are you okay, child?" she asked.

    "Umm, I guess," Dianna said slowly, as she pushed herself off of the refrigerator. "I seriously dropped the ball today at school though, and I don't know what to tell dad. He's going to be so mad."

    "Don't worry," Nina said, smiling. "If it's about the video, it's not that big of a deal. Your dad just wanted it deleted because he doesn't want anybody to see it online. If the media did come here to investigate, along with every jackass skeptic trying to prove it's false, it would be a circus. He doesn't want you involved in that, and neither do I." Nina walked over to the kitchen table and set her purse down. Then she added, "I hate to say it, but your dad's already dealt with one major church scandal. He doesn't need another."

Dianna almost cringed as Nina mentioned it. It was a constant reminder of her dad's shortcomings in his early life. Back when Dianna was four and Cammy was ten, their father was a prominent pastor in Boston. Their life was great, until allegations of an affair surfaced, along with pictures of her father with one of the women from church. After that, her father was asked to step down. But being stubborn, Ramon refused. So the congregation ran them out of town.

"Yeah, I remember," Dianna said. "You don't have to remind me."

"Yes, I do, Dianna!" exclaimed Nina, as she stepped forward and put her hand on the young girl's shoulder. "You're almost sixteen. It's time for you to start gaining your own independence. The first step is realizing your father's not the Superman you've built him up to be. He's a good man and a great father, but he does have flaws."

Dianna smirked at her friend. "I know, but even Superman had a weakness. That didn't stop him from protecting the ones he loved."

"Touché, child," her roommate said, as she walked around the tile counter to grab her purse. "So that was the big emergency you texted about?"

"No," admitted the girl, "but sooner or later, dad's coming home. I don't want to lie to him about the video footage, but I can't tell him the truth either."

Nina rummaged through her purse and pulled out her compact mirror. "I have no idea how Ramon could have two children so completely different. One's a fierce hellcat. The other," she looked at Dianna, "is an angel who wouldn't say shit if she had a mouthful of it. So, what could be so bad that you can't tell your dad?" Dianna walked over to the oak dinner table and sat down silently next to Nina.

"Remember the dream I had right before you moved in?"

"Of course, I do," answered the woman, her demeanor suddenly serious, as if somebody had flipped a switch inside of her.

"A new boy came to school today," Dianna said, leaning closer to Nina.

"And you think this boy might be the one from the dream?" she finished, her face full of concern.

"I do," said Dianna. She paused for a second and continued, "He looked like him, and he had the necklace."

Nina narrowed her eyes, "Okay. What's his name?" she asked.

"Josh Michaels."

Nina gasped and dropped her purse to the floor. Sitting up, she said, "That's impossible."

"What's impossible? Is everything okay?" asked Dianna hesitantly. The woman didn't reply. Instead she just sat there, fluttering her eyelids, like she couldn't comprehend what she'd heard.

"Are you sure, child?"

"Yes, I'm positive," answered Dianna. "You just said it's not possible. What's not possible? Do you know him?"

"Oh, no, not at all. I know his grandmother. We talk at the supermarket every now and then," Nina explained with a distracted look on her face. "The last she told me, he was in California."

"Santa Cruz," Dianna clarified. "Are you sure you're okay? I've never seen you like this."

"I'm fine, child. I'll be back. I have to make a quick phone call."

Dianna watched as Nina wandered out of the room. It was uncharacteristic of her to show even a small portion of outward emotion. She was always cool and calm. "Maybe she was having a bad day," thought Dianna. Bending down, she picked up the spilled contents of the purse and placed the bag on the kitchen counter. She couldn't explain what had just happened, but she hoped Nina was okay. Dianna needed her help with this difficult situation. Dianna really didn't know what she'd do if it weren't for her father and Nina. Together they were like the Three Musketeers. Nina came in a peculiar time in Dianna's life. After the scandal at the church, Dianna's mother divorced Ramon. After a lengthy custody battle, he was alone in a new town with two daughters.

Dianna was pretty proud of how her father immediately picked himself up and began a new career as a bus driver for the school district. It seemed like everything would be okay. Unfortunately, as Cammy got older, her rebellious nature had Ramon at the end of his rope. That's when Nina showed up. She had filled the position of church secretary and posted a room wanted ad on the bulletin board. It was funny to Dianna that Cammy was originally the one who brought up the idea of renting a room to Nina. After a month of living together, Cammy found out that Nina had a response for every one of the rebellious eighteen year old's comments, tricks or lies. It seemed Nina could unflinchingly anticipate everything Cammy served up. It was only a month later that Ramon sent her to live with Dianna's grandfather.

Since then, Nina had really stepped up to the plate both as a sister and a friend. According to her dad, she was like his own Ukrainian Mary Poppins. Dianna seriously hoped not, because Mary Poppins left after everything was fixed. She really hoped Nina would stay, even though she knew her housemate had a husband in the military. According to Nina, he was in the Middle East, serving out the last of his four-year contract. Dianna wondered what would happen when he came back home. She hoped they would find a house in Milton and stay. She couldn't bear it, if Nina had left.

She had grown to love her housemate, with her copper hair and what Dianna jokingly called her midnight tan. The woman's skin was milky white with hardly a blemish. Ramon always joked that, when they went places together, even the White people looked at her like she was strange. The thing that Dianna loved most about her though was that Nina didn't freak out about her power. Dianna was always self-conscious about her abilities. In fact, she knew, even though she had acquaintances at school, none of them would ever understand the situation she was in. It was because of her powers that Dianna never really made any friends. It just seemed safer to hang out with her family.

"Your dad's home," shouted Nina from upstairs. Dianna took a deep breath and pulled her long, black hair into a ponytail. In the background, she could hear Nina amble down the stairwell, trying to get down the stairs before Ramon came in. She heard the sharp slam of a car door and then saw Nina come around the corner. Her lips pursed and copper tresses bouncing, she slid into the seat across from Dianna. Her small frame was clothed in her usual black yoga pants and a purple top. "Just act natural," whispered Nina, as the door opened and then slammed shut.

Both girls sang in unison, "Yay, Ramon's home," and then chuckled.

"How are the two most beautiful women in the world?" he asked, stepping into the kitchen, with both arms loaded up with grocery bags.

"We're amazing, as always," replied Nina in a melodious voice. She watched him as he walked over to the white kitchen counter.

"I got some steaks for dinner tonight. I was thinking I can grill them up, if you guys can handle the potatoes and corn in here."

"I can do that," replied Dianna, her hands folded in anticipation on the table.

"So, how did school go today?" her father asked, as he pulled the groceries out of the paper bags. "Did you ask the boy to erase the tape?"

"He didn't go to school today," Nina lied, as she stared

directly into Dianna's fear-filled eyes.

"He didn't? That's strange."

"Not really," Nina countered. "It's Susan Bernacki's kid. They're Polish, and they celebrate Easter Monday in their culture."

"Yeah, I guess that's true," said Ramon, shrugging his shoulders as he disappeared into the backyard.

Dianna stared in amazement as Nina blew on her fist and pretended to polish her knuckles on her purple shirt. "You can thank me later," she bragged.

"Oh my God, Nina, what were you thinking?" Dianna blurted out, completely shocked at what just happened.

"Relax," Nina said, twirling her finger in her hair. "You said you couldn't lie to your father, but that doesn't mean I can't."

"Well, the coals are lit," Ramon announced, strolling back into the kitchen and leaning over the counter.

"Ramon Imperial, are you flexing your arms?" giggled Nina, as she peered over to look at him.

"No, no, not at all," stammered the forty-two-year-old, standing up and looking at his arms self-consciously. Dianna knew Nina was just giving him a hard time because he'd just started going to the gym with her on a regular basis. Holding the back of her hand to her forehead, Nina pretended to be fainting.

"Why, I do declare, Mr. Imperial. What could a little ol' girl like me do to earn your favor?"

"I don't know. How about getting started on the corn?" he chuckled.

"You're a real charmer, Ramon," Nina said sarcastically. Dianna looked at her dad and smiled. He was a good-looking guy at his age. He had a great head of hair, and women were always checking him out. For some reason, though, after her mom left him, Ramon never really jumped back on the dating bandwagon.

Wiping his hands on the black kitchen towel, Ramon walked over to the kitchen table and sat at the head of it. He looked at Dianna and in a serious voice said, "It's really very important that you talk to that boy tomorrow when you see him. Okay?"

Dianna nodded. "I will, dad. Don't worry."

"It's a weird world we live in. People wouldn't understand what you can do. Hell, I can't understand what you do," he said, as he shook his head.

"Dad, I've talked to grandpa before, when I visited Cammy. He said you had the gift," Dianna pried, as she gazed intently at her father.

"That might be so," he said, as he cocked his head to the side and folded his arms. "When I was young, I spirit-walked and could glimpse the future. But that's gone now. These days my only power is the ability to locate the slowest line of traffic on the freeway, and somehow I can always pick the worst check-out counter at the grocery store."

"Ramon, your daughter's being serious," Nina said sharply, as she rose from the seat and grabbed the corn. "The only person who can answer these questions is you."

"I told you guys that I parted with that path a long time ago. When I met your mother, Dianna, I converted. And when I did, it put a wedge between your grandfather and me. He couldn't understand why I did what I did, and I couldn't understand why he chose to stay on the reservation after your grandmother died."

"Why wouldn't he? It's his heritage," Dianna exclaimed.

"Not to burst your bubble, honey, but your grandfather didn't have enough Native American blood in him to fill a shot glass. The Imperials were Spanish royalty," said Ramon, as he folded his arms over his chest. "There was an uprising and most of the Royals fled. They had to leave their homes and wealth behind. That's how they came to America. First they settled in Virginia, and then they spread out to Kentucky."

"What?" cried Dianna. "I don't understand. He said he

grew up in a tribe."

Ramon drew in a deep breath and chuckled, "I really didn't want to tell you this until you were older. However, since you're turning sixteen soon and we're on the topic..."

"Please don't tell me grandpa was a liar," said Dianna, hesitantly, as Nina reached over the table and put her hand in Dianna's.

"No, not exactly," Ramon started, his face grimacing, "but he did have a knack for stretching the truth. Your grandfather was born in a Melungeon settlement in the Appalachian Mountains." Dianna looked at Nina. The woman squeezed her hand and smiled. Ramon continued, "The Malaysians were the actual first melting pot in American culture. They lived on the outskirts of society, and the residents ranged from Native Americans and freed slaves to the French and Portuguese."

"I think your grandfather maybe went to school until he was twelve. He never really talked much about the outside world. In fact, I really don't know if he'd ever been to a big city. At any rate, he met my mom at seventeen. She was visiting family in the area. She had come all the way from Oklahoma, where she lived on the Shawnee reservation. According to her, it was love at first sight. One weekend quickly turned into a month, until finally she had to go home."

"How did he end up living on the reservation?" asked Nina, totally engrossed.

"Well, it wasn't easy," Ramon sighed. "But if you've ever heard the term silver-tongued devil, that described your grandfather perfectly. It was just part of his persona. Mary Jo took him home to the reservation, and he's lucky they didn't beat him black and blue."

"Why didn't they?" asked Dianna.

"It's possible," said Ramon, "and I'm just assuming, but your grandfather might have scared them."

"No way," Dianna insisted.

"Yes, way," her dad replied. His eyes narrowed, "This wasn't happy, laid-back grandpa. When this happened, my dad was seventeen. He used his skills of persuasion to win over her parents, but the council wasn't biting. So he threatened to leave and take Mary Jo with him. Now, at the time, she was the most gifted healer the Shawnee had seen in generations, not to mention she was descended from Native American royalty. They couldn't let her leave."

"So what did they do?" asked the young girl.

"Well," said Ramon, "according to your grandmother, a few of the core group who'd objected called a meeting. Mary Jo begged your grandfather not to go. She thought they would beat him to death if they got the chance, and she was probably right."

"What happened next?" Dianna inquired, leaning in.

Her dad chuckled and shook his head. "No one really knows, but your grandparents were married the next day."

"Wait a second. You're holding back, Ramon. I know you you're hiding something," Nina teased.

"Don't you have corn to tend to?" Ramon teased back, looking at the unshucked corn lying on the counter in front of Nina's right hand.

"Come on, dad, she's right. You're not telling us everything."

"Oh, all right," Ramon reluctantly said. "My father was a very strong-willed individual, but persuasion and fascination were the least of his talents."

"Go on," urged Dianna.

"I saw him do stuff that literally defied the laws of physics. He used to carry an old Zippo-type lighter with him. When I was a kid, he'd sit in a chair and flick it out. He'd hit the little metal wheel and, I swear, as impossible as it sounds, he could make the flame do things. I would sit there and watch as he would cause the flame to grow and jump up. He could even form shapes. At any rate, it was always rumored that my dad could spirit-walk before he ever lived on the reservation. Nobody knew how he learned, and I never asked. When my grandfather was alive, he told me the story of what really happened that night between my dad and the Tribal Council."

Ramon paused for a moment and swallowed. "He said that my father didn't show up to the meeting with the elders like he said he was going to. Instead, he hid in the forest." Stopping, Ramon looked at them both. Dianna could see the indecision in his eyes as he looked at her. "The core group held a celebration that night while my mom cried, because she thought my father had run off and abandoned her." Shifting in his seat, Ramon cleared his throat. "My mother waited all night, but he didn't come back. And then, in the deepest, darkest part of the night, as everybody slept, my father entered a trance and single-handedly pulled every Shawnee man, woman and child onto the astral plane. Nothing like that had ever been heard of before. Then, in front of everybody, including my grandparents, my father told them how much he loved Mary Jo and how he'd go anywhere, do anything just to be near her. He begged the elders to give him her hand in marriage. But even still, they just laughed and told him that he was a fool. They warned that, if he didn't leave the reservation immediately, they'd use their combined might to trap him forever in the spirit world."

At this point Ramon stopped, like he wasn't sure what to say next. But then, an epiphany must have fallen from on high because his eyes lit up like he could see for miles. "And so, my father, seeing no other choice, summoned all of the fury that he'd felt when he walked into the forest that night. He drew on the unbridled hate that had burned within him as they taunted the woman he loved. As he glared at them, he filled with an unquenchable rage. Just when he didn't think he could take it anymore, he pulled out his lighter and flipped it open. What jumped out was so horrific, so terrifying, that three generations of witnesses refuse to even speak of what they saw that night. As soon as the sun came up the next day, your grandparents were married. And no one ever dared to challenge your grandfather again."

Chapter 4
A Not-So-Square Deal

"I'm serious, Josh. Serious as a heart attack. Did you not learn your lesson last time?" screamed Charlie from behind the steering wheel.

"It was just a buck," Josh said, as he jogged up to the dingy brown Jeep. "Besides," he said as he slid into the seat and buckled the seatbelt, "didn't you hear a thing Mr. Douglas said Monday?"

"Oh, I remember," Charlie mused as he drove out of the parking lot. "I have a mind like a steel trap."

"Oh, do you?" Josh laughed, sliding his black sunglasses over the bridge of his nose.

"I do. And I don't remember professor super fly saying at any point that you should continue giving your money to that feral human."

"And I don't remember you thanking me for getting you and the whole class out of detention," Josh said, raising his eyebrow.

"Whatev. That hobo probably lives a better life than we do anyway."

"Are you high?" blurted Josh. "I seriously doubt that." Pulling into the students' parking lot, Charlie looked at Josh. "Seriously, I think they do. I see that guy. Despite living on the street, he seems fine to me."

"Your point?"

"My point is that years of being white and over-privileged has destroyed whatever defenses my genetics had built up from our time in the wild."

"You're seriously retarded," Josh replied in amazement. "Please tell me Sue dropped you on your head as a baby."

"I'm not done yet, Michaels," continued the redhead. "The

average homeless person has one pair of socks, which they never change. His socks were yellow, Josh. I can't even shower barefoot after gym class on a Tuesday without having a Tinactin party by Thursday." Josh chuckled.

"Okay, I'll give you that one," he said, grabbing his backpack and sliding out of the Jeep.

"And that's not all," added Charlie. "He eats stuff from out of the dumpster. If I eat day-old refrigerated leftovers, my stomach is straight up Jackasaurus Rex. It's bullshit. I mean, seriously, you've never once wondered how homeless people sleep outside in the dirt next to dog shit, drinking from each other's bottle of hooch, and day after day, they're fine? Meanwhile, I touch a doorknob, and it's TheraFlu time."

"I don't know," Josh answered skeptically. "I'm not saying you're not right, but, statistically, if the doorknob you touched was at school, you gotta figure thirty kids per class, six periods a day. That's a lot of different germs."

"Yet still a small amount, compared to the dirty coins and dollars that that bum handles every day. You could take an average quarter, and I guarantee it has more bacteria on it than a doorknob."

"So what are you saying, Charlie? The key to the fountain of youth is hidden in the genome of the homeless population?"

"No, jackass, that's not what I'm saying. But there is some kind of built-up defense and adaptability in people. Whatever it is, my family lost it a long time ago."

***

Josh walked into English class and took a seat all the way in the back. As much as he loved Mr. Douglas's class, he really just wanted to go home. Big Sue and Charlie's dad were gone for the weekend. It took some serious ass-kissing, but Josh convinced his mom to let him sleep at Charlie's Friday and Saturday. It had been about a year since they'd hung out in the basement, ordered a pizza, and played video games. That's why he was looking so forward to it. To get ready for the all-night tournament, Charlie decided to bolt out and grab some munchies. He texted after first period that he was headed back to the mini-mart, and then during second period texted to say that he'd never made it back to school. He was at home about to take a nap, and then he would pick Josh up after school.

The whole week had been dominated by homework and reading. Josh didn't even have time to go through the box of stuff his grandpa had brought down from the attic.

"Is this seat taken?"

Josh didn't even have to look up to know it was Dianna. "No, feel free," he said, trying not to sound too enthusiastic. He had to admit he thought after Tuesday she'd probably never talk to him again.

"I wanted to say I'm really sorry for what happened on Tuesday after school," she said, sitting down in the seat in front of him. "Everything I said was directed at Charlie."

"I totally understand," replied Josh. "I'd kinda be mad too. Last I saw, there were ninety thousand hits on YouTube."

"I know," whispered Dianna, as Mr. Douglas got up and walked over to the center of the room. "My dad asked them to pull it. They were cool about it."

"Not bad, Miss Imperial," Josh said, as he smiled.

"You'll find I'm full of surprises, Mr. Michaels," she said, smiling and turning around to face forward.

"Okay, class, let's get started. If you recall, I asked you all to do a one-page piece on who has impacted you the most in your life. Before you hand it in, I'm going to randomly pick a few people to give a quick, bullet-style presentation, starting with you, Garrett. Josh looked over at the Milton High School quarterback.

As Garrett started his presentation, it couldn't have been more than ten seconds, Josh noticed he could smell Dianna's perfume. He smiled as he breathed it in. A guilty pleasure, if ever there was one. He wondered if he'd ever work up the nerve to ask her out.

He really couldn't think of anything else lately. She didn't act like any other girl he'd ever met before. Weighing his options, Josh decided not to ask her today. It was hot off the heels of her arguing with Charlie. Come Monday, if they talked again, he'd ask for her number. To be honest, Josh couldn't go another week of her running through his head without being able to text her or talk to her.

"Hey, the teacher's talking to you," the girl to Josh's right said, poking him in the shoulder. Josh bolted to attention.

"What?" he cried, about three times louder than he'd intended."

"Please, Josh, save your daydreaming for one of your electives," Mr. Douglas said, smiling. "It's your turn."

Grinning, Josh stood up and laid his paper down. What he had to say he didn't need a cue card for. He scanned the class, took a deep breath and began. "The single most influential person in my life is my mother."

***

"Gentlemen, please be seated. We still have a few things on the agenda to discuss before we adjourn. If you would, please give your attention to William Hasden." Looking out on the board room, the imposing figure waited until all eyes were on him. Every one of the board members revered him, and he reveled in it. Drinking in the complex cocktail of emotions, he gave a tug on the sleeve cuff of his gray suit and then spoke.

"Thank you, Mr. Gregory. I'm going to have to ask at this time that anybody who is not a CEO of Hasden Corporation or an affiliate, please leave the room." He patiently waited as half of the suits in the room got up and filed out. Meanwhile, his regent, Deus Gregory, crossed over to the bar and came back with a crystal decanter of aged scotch. Bill watched as Deus poured a glass for him and one for himself. He looked out on the remaining crowd. There were just ten people in the room now, and only four of them were human.

"I'll dispense with the pleasantries. You all know me. I've interviewed all of you at one time or another. To my left is Deus Gregory. To my right, painstakingly recording all of this, is my personal assistant, Angela Mahvet. As of the last time I traveled out here, it was noted that Lifeline Ambulance, a subsidiary of Hasden Medical, was somewhat stagnant. The employees consist of a large majority of top level paramedics, which are gouging our profit margins. To add insult to injury, we have a higher-than-average number of on-the-job injuries. This is, to make it quite plain, unacceptable." He stopped momentarily as the faces all nodded in agreement.

"Some of you have voiced the opinion that we should turn up the heat a bit and make the climate a little more inhospitable so that these tenacious top level leeches and chronic disability abusers might fly off and nest somewhere else." He reached down and grabbed the sweaty glass of scotch on the rocks and took a swallow. "I think I have a much better solution. Angela, if you would." The young woman opened the laptop in front of her. Within seconds, the slideshow was on the wall. "As you can see, the numbers show that Lifeline is no longer viable as a company. Since it's at the end of its life, I propose that we stage our own funeral."

"Starting next month, Mr. Bell will be leaving us to set up shop within our also near-death competitors, Vita Ambulance. Mr. Nix will be taking control of Lifeline. The first thing I want to have done is to create six new administrative positions, preferably as supervisors. From there, I want you to promote the top six most obstinate sons-of-bitches that Lifeline has and get them out of the field. Now, when you get there, Nix, you will be glad to see that our usual bloodhound, Phyllis, has already been there for three months, compiling a list of anybody who could possibly interfere with the plan. From that point on, we start dumping our shares. Mr. Nix, it will be your job to run Lifeline into the ground. I want every political bridge burned, late response times, skeleton crews; the works."

Drawing in a sharp breath, Bill swallowed down what remained of the expensive scotch and set it next to Deus, who immediately refilled it. "Come December, when the 911 contract comes up, Lifeline, bloated and overstaffed, will outrageously overbid. That leaves the newer, leaner Vita, that everybody in this room should have sunk most of their money into by October at the latest, to come into town and take the contract with an all new, bright young workforce. By the end of the year, Lifeline will have shut down, losing all of its contracts. After a short dismantling and redistribution phase, Mr. Nix will take a year off, vacationing on the beaches of Thailand for playing his part, only to return as the Regional Director of Nightingale Medical." Hasden smiled as the sounds of applause filled the room.

"I have a question real quick, Bill." Peering to his left, he could see one of the human CEOs, Gerald Iblis, had his hand up. "Looking at the breakdown packet for Lifeline, the budget allotted for company functions and barbecues is a little high, don't you think?"

"Not really," Hasden explained. "All it takes is one strong-willed pain in the ass to stage an uprising, alert the media, and rally the public behind them. We could lose so much more than what it costs to have a few barbecues. There are two ways to remove a problem tooth, Gerry. You could punch someone in the mouth and hope that did the job, but then they'll never trust you again. However, if you give them anesthesia, it might cost a little more, but the tooth comes out quickly, and the person has no complaints after. Now, if you don't mind, Gerry, I'd love some ice in my scotch." Deus took the glass of scotch and walked it over to Gerald. The older man's face looked flustered as he stared at the glass. Finally, he looked at Bill's personal assistant.

"Angela, honey, could you please get some ice for Bill?" The young woman didn't even bother acknowledging him. She just continued scribbling and erasing in her notepad. Hands shaking, the gray-haired gentleman gripped the cup with both hands and turned to Hasden. "I'm sorry, Bill. I didn't mean to--"

"I don't give two figs and a fuck what you did or did not mean to do!" barked the director, his eyes filled with disdain. "Just get the ice!"

"Angela, please document that this meeting was adjourned at 18:45." Angela smiled at him. Bowing her head, she stood up and filed out of the mahogany double doors with everybody else, leaving Hasden and Deus alone in the room.

Deus ran his fingers through his gray hair and frowned from his leather seat. "I'm so tired of the shit," he moaned. "I remember a time when being a demon was so much more fun." Having a seat at the head of the table, Bill scowled.

"You'd rather hang out with the angels at division headquarters?"

Immediately shaking his head, Deus laughed. "I'm not that tired. I just mean we haven't had any fun in years." Hasden nodded in agreement.

"Leading the sons of man astray is a full-time job in itself. While it's one that I relish, I do agree that this mortal coil has grown kind of stale." Interrupting them, Angela came in from the adjoining door, carrying her laptop. "Something wrong?" Bill asked.

"I don't know yet. I'll let you decide," she said. As she rolled a leather chair over and sat down, she opened the laptop.

The screen glowed, casting pale light on her olive colored skin. "This video was taken Easter Sunday in Milton, Massachusetts. The girl is a fifteen-year-old named Dianna Alexa Imperial." Tapping his pen on the ornately carved wooden desk, Bill sat in silence, watching the screen. Finally, Angela spoke, "Is there anybody that you want attached to this?" Ignoring her, Bill hit the play button again and stared in silence. "If I may be so bold, Bill..."

Looking at Angela first and then Bill, Deus nodded his head at the screen. "I've seen some powerful humans in my time, but this shit is ridiculous. I wouldn't trust this to anybody."

"She's obviously powerful," Hasden interjected. "Her name alone indicates that she's descended from one of the most powerful bloodlines."

"Shall I notify the Monarchy, or dispatch Phyllis?" Angela asked, her eyes gleaming. Hasden smiled and shook his head. Leaning back in his chair, the age spots on his arms began to disappear. Hasden grinned at Deus, as his regents' old, wrinkled skin firmed up and dull, gray hair gave way to vibrant brown with auburn highlights. Sitting up straighter than he had in months, Bill grinned at his assistant.

"Deus is right. This is too big to just be a fluke. Don't notify anybody. We'll handle this ourselves." Looking down at his teenage hands, Bill pulled at his gray sleeve cuffs. "Oh, and Angela, make the necessary arrangements. We have school on Monday."

***

"Here's a thought," Nina announced, as she lowered the magazine she was reading to her lap and glanced over at Ramon. "Maybe the next time I ask you to elaborate a story, you just tell me to keep my mouth shut." Ramon smirked from the recliner and grabbed the remote control at his side. Finding the mute button, he silenced the TV and turned to the woman lying on the matching leather couch, "Let me guess. Nightmares?"

"Tuesday and Thursday," she confirmed. "In the last dream, I was one of the children. Why do you think your father pulled them into the dream too?"

"Well," started Ramon, as he repositioned in the seat to see her better, "I know for a fact that he didn't want to do anything to the others. He just wanted to marry my mother. I can only assume that, once he decided there was no other choice, he went to the final option. I imagine he included everybody because he didn't want the children to grow up and challenge him."

"Has Dianna given you any feedback?" she asked, shifting over to her side.

"Not really," he replied, a look of uncertainty on his face. "She's really been beating herself up over the video being on the internet, so I haven't had a chance."

Nina nodded in agreement. "Still, it might be good to talk to her about her grandparents and the other side of her culture."

"I don't know about that, Nina. Most of what I remember are the legends, and I don't want to fill Dianna's head with that. My mother died of cancer when I was thirteen. I don't really remember that much about her." Scratching his head in contemplation, he continued, "My dad was thirty-nine when I was born. For all intents and purposes, he was pretty much the local celebrity that you met when you took Dianna to the reservation. For some reason though, we never really clicked. He was born in 1930," Ramon nodded, "It was a totally different time. Women had only been voting for may be three elections, and antibiotics and birth control weren't even invented."

"Insane," Nina grinned. "So how did you come about?" she asked.

"My father's pride, possibly, or pressure from the tribe. I have two older brothers and an older sister," he said, "but when none of them showed any signs of the gift, well, you get the point."

"I've got to say, I was impressed. He was a nice old man," observed Nina. "All of Dianna's cousins were nice too, given the circumstances."

"What? That a paleface escorted a deserter's daughter onto Indian land?" Ramon teased.   Nina smiled broadly and nodded, "Yes, something like that."

"I have a question," Dianna asked from behind them. Both Ramon and Nina jumped as they realized there was a third person in the room.

"I didn't hear you come in," said Ramon, looking flustered. Dianna stood against the doorway with her arms crossed, wearing her gym clothes.

"I have a question," reemphasized the daughter. "I can understand why you didn't take me to the reservation when I was thirteen. It would have been nothing but problems. But why did you lie to me when grandpa died?" Ramon hung his head in shame and didn't reply.

"When I told you grandpa came to me in my dream before he passed, why did you totally dismiss it and say it was a fluke?" Her father listened silently. "Why did you do that when you knew what he could do?" the girl asked, tears welling up in her eyes. Nina sat on the couch, not saying a word.

Looking at his daughter, Ramon softly replied, "Because your grandfather came to me that night as well, and he asked me to. After meeting you and seeing how pure of heart you were, he asked me not to tell you anything that could alter your image of him until you could handle it emotionally." Dianna stood against the door jamb, hugging herself, as tears rolled down her face.

"He was my grandfather."

"I know, babe," her father tenderly replied. "But he didn't want you to jump to the same conclusion that his son had." Dianna sniffled, looking at her father. After a brief moment's pause,

Ramon continued, "I thought the only reason he contacted you was because he knew Cammy didn't have the discipline to develop the gift. I thought it was suspicious that you had just turned thirteen, and here he was taking an interest in you. It turns out," Ramon added, "your grandfather already knew he was dying. He just wanted to see you face-to-face and tell you that he loved you."

"I don't see the need for all this secrecy," Dianna murmured, as she wiped her nose with a tissue.

"Now you don't, but I guarantee you," her father assured her, "it's been almost three years. Now you're a lot more mature and capable of understanding than you were at thirteen. This wasn't done to confuse you. It was done so that ten or fifteen years down the road you can remember him and know that he loved you, and not view the memory through jaded eyes, like I did."

"I guess," Dianna said as she sniffled again. "I really need to take a bath and go to bed. It's already been a long day."

"Good night, dear," her father said, watching her walk out of the room and up the stairs. When she was gone, he sunk back into the black leather recliner. Looking up at the ceiling, he sighed, "Well, that was awkward." To his right, Nina beamed at him.

"I couldn't have handled that better myself. Your father would be proud of you."

***

"I seriously hope those two boys don't burn the house down," Claire remarked, as she cleared the dinner table.

"Oh, come on. They're fifteen. How much trouble could they get into?" Sam asked.

Claire turned around and arched her eyebrows at her daughter-in-law. "I'm sure you have heard of the things Alex did when he was sixteen." Scraping the leftovers off of the plate and into the trash, she continued. "Josh is only a month away from being sixteen."

"I have confidence in your grandson. I think I raised a pretty level-headed kiddo."

"Oh, it's not him I'm worried about," Claire answered. "It's that redheaded child of Set he runs around with."

"Oh my God," Sam chuckled, "I'm so glad you said that and not me."

"Honey, thank you for another amazing dinner," Larry said, as he strolled into the kitchen and kissed his wife on the cheek. Sam noticed he'd returned with the dog leash in his right hand.

"How was the walk?" asked his wife.

"Oh, I think that will be the last time Flynn will need to go out for the night," Larry replied, sitting down at the table across from Sam. No sooner had Larry sat down than the little white Scottish Terrier pranced in and started sniffing at the ground for a possible nugget of fallen meat from the dinner table. "Did I tell you that damn bird under Josh's window swooped down and pecked Flynn the other day when we were in the backyard?"

"No, Larry, you didn't," Claire replied curtly, loading the dishwasher. Sam had seen that look enough to know that Larry was about to get an earful. "I told you, you silly old man, to take care of it when it started nesting. But you wouldn't have it. This is the exact same thing as the damn mice."

"I know, dear," Larry replied.

Sam couldn't help but smile. She knew that Larry had a heart of gold, but sometimes it backfired. Ten years ago, Claire spotted a mouse that had fallen into the backyard pool. Larry fished it out with the net and let it go on its way, much to Claire's dismay. Sam knew the man just didn't have it in his heart to kill the mouse. Two weeks later, Claire was fit to be tied when the scratching in the walls started.

It took an exterminator and a little bit more money than Larry would have liked to have spent to tackle the infestation. As

Claire read Larry the riot act, Sam was surprised by how the old man seemed to be oblivious. She knew Larry could hear Claire, but he paid her no mind. Instead, he reached down and picked up the small, white dog, winking at Sam, as he smiled and scratched the dog's ear.

"I sure wish big Sue were here," Claire said, as she came up to the table.

"Now, dear, you really shouldn't call her that," Larry replied, softly scratching the happy dog's belly.

"Why not? She looks like she could take on a whole football team. If you'd stayed up on Sunday night and listened to her stories, you'd know that she probably has taken on a football team, if you know what I'm saying."

"That's why I don't stick around when you girls drink wine," the old man replied.

"If Sue were here, she could take you out and show you the town. Girl loves to man watch," chuckled Claire, as she sat down.

"I don't know," Sam said, blushing.

"Oh, come now," chided Claire. "You have to go out sometime and have some fun. I'm sure Larry and I are a laugh riot. But how much Wheel of Fortune can you take at your age?"

Sam laughed at the obvious joke and shrugged her shoulders. "I guess your son just ruined me for other men," she replied.

"Listen, Sam," suggested Larry. "I know that Claire shares my opinion when I say that you've done an incredible job raising Josh. I mean, you've obviously poured your heart and soul into that boy. It's been over eleven years. We'd be happy if you found love again."

Sam fought back the tears. She'd expected that sooner or later this might come up. Even though it had been expected, she still felt slightly embarrassed. Claire grabbed her daughter-in-law's hand and gave it a squeeze, "We're here for you. Anything you need." Sam relaxed and took in a deep breath.

"I'm sorry, you guys. I'm just so stressed lately."

Claire smiled at her with sincere sympathy. "Don't worry, dear, you find another job."

"That's not what I'm worried about," Sam said, as she looked at her in-laws. "I have to ask you guys a question; a serious question."

Claire looked at Sam, "Of course, honey."

Sam took a second to compose herself, drew in a deep breath and spoke. "I don't really know how to say this. I knew, when I met your son, that he was unique, I guess you could say. But it wasn't until we started living together that I realized just how different he really was." Claire sighed as she stood up.

"If this is about what I think it's about, I'm going to need a good bottle of wine."

Larry stood up and handed the dog over to Claire. "No, dear, I'll get it. This conversation is all yours." Sam sat in silence as her mother-in-law slowly sat back down.

"So what exactly is this about, Sam?"

"Well, um, is Larry mad at me?"

Claire smiled softly. "Not at all. I can only assume you want to discuss my son's powers. He got his abilities from me."

Sam couldn't help but feel shocked at how unflinchingly the older woman had thrown it out. Larry resurfaced in the kitchen, carrying a bottle of merlot. "I take it I was correct on the topic?"

"What can I tell you?" Claire asked.

"Well," Sam began, easing up a little. "It started when we moved in together. He would have dreams of the future, and they were always right; births, deaths, even political stuff." Larry sat down at the table with three glasses. "Then," Sam added, "he began visiting me in my dreams at night. When he was pulling his twenty-four hour shifts at the firehouse, we would sometimes go on long, elaborate adventures that somehow seem to last for days.

In reality, it was hours at the most. Each one was so distinctly different and vivid. In one, we lived as dogs on a ranch. I swear, when I got up in the morning, I had to remind myself to walk on two legs. And through it all, Alex would come home in the morning and tell me about the dreams long after I had forgotten about them," Sam said, sounding confused.

Claire smiled proudly, "Alex was highly talented. Sometimes, I truly believe that the only limit he had was his imagination."

"Alex told us that you had some knowledge of his capabilities," Larry said, pouring the wine, "but we didn't know to what extent. It's a hard topic to broach." Claire grinned and took a glass.

"It's called dream bending. What you experienced with Alex was just the tip of the iceberg. He could do incredible things."

"I'm sorry, Claire. It's hard to believe that Alex could top the things I saw. There were things that, if I hadn't seen them with my own eyes, I wouldn't believe."

"I'll drink to that," said Larry, lifting his glass.

"Oh, shush, dear. You're used to me by now," Claire said, laughing.

"The problem is, while we were married, Alex had difficulties."

"What kind?" asked Claire, swirling the red liquor in her glass.

"Like separation of reality from fantasy. Sometimes he talked to people who weren't there. He had conversations about how the demons were trying to get to him." Looking over at Larry, Claire frowned and turned back to her daughter-in-law.

"Without getting too deep into it, a lot of that stuff is kind of normal. Alex always carried an incredible amount of power in his aura. As good as he was at reflecting negative energy, sometimes he would experience some side effects. You have to remember that the human brain and our moods are all just a mixture of chemicals."

"I'm just really worried, Claire."

"About what, dear?"

"Josh, of course."

Claire looked at Sam, puzzled, "I don't know what you're talking about, dear."

"I don't want Josh having the same problems as Alex, now that his powers are getting so strong." Claire sat in absolute, stunned silence.

"That's not possible," she mumbled.

"Then somebody needs to have a talk with your grandson."

"What Claire's trying to tell you, Sam, is that the power is passed from father to daughter and mother to son. It's not genetically possible."

Claire swallowed. "You'll have to forgive me for saying this, Sam. When Alex told us that he proposed to you, we searched your family tree. Your bloodline has never produced anything even remotely notable, other than healthy, happy individuals. If you don't mind me asking, Sam, what is it that Josh is doing?" asked Claire, her face etched with doubt.

"I don't know, Claire. How much time do you have? First, he dream bends, as you call it. Second, he says things, and they immediately happen. He can hold a twenty minute conversation with me and then flip on the TV or radio, and it'll be playing on either. Two weeks ago, we went to the movies. He told me a random story about how we should really go to Italy for vacation, just to see what real Italian food is like, and how we should rent a Jaguar to drive around in, just for kicks. Then, as soon as the previews started, the first advertisement is a movie about a boy who looks disturbingly like my son, who stows away on a boat with a girl, who looks surprisingly like me. They end up eating food in Italy, followed by a chase scene, where they steal a car and get away. Would either of you two like to guess what type of car they stole?" Sam asked, sounding very frustrated by now.

"I think I get the point," said Claire.

"No, I don't think you do," barked Sam. "My son, who I love more than life itself, is driving me bananas. Sometimes it's just mildly annoying, but at other times it genuinely frightens me," Sam admitted. Claire couldn't help but notice her daughter-in-law's trembling hands.

"Calm down, Sam. I'll handle this."

"I could barely wrap my head around Alex, and now it's happening to Josh." Sam began sobbing again. Claire reached over with her right hand and tipped the bottle of merlot onto its side. Sam gasped as the dark, red fluid spilled towards her lap. Jumping up, she pushed away from the edge of the table and waited for the fluid's inevitable cascade to the floor. Instead, much to her surprise, it stopped. Frantically, Sam looked to Larry, who was busy draining his glass. Sitting next to him, Claire didn't seem fazed in the slightest.

Sam looked back down at the table, as an invisible finger began to write in the merlot. She stared at the message in disbelief. "I told you. I will handle it," was written on the table. Then, as suddenly as it formed, the message disbanded and the merlot, as if drawn by gravity, ran right up the side of the bottle and deposited itself inside.

"That was impossible," Sam whispered, staring at the clean table. The old woman grinned back at her.

"Apparently the word impossible doesn't apply in our family."

Chapter 5
Everything

Looking up at the perfect, blue Massachusetts sky, Josh thought to himself, "This must be the good life." Then his bike went over the apex of the hill. As it did, he felt the extreme rush that only seemed to come from moving way too fast.

"Catch up, slowpoke," shouted Charlie from further up the trail. Josh wore a giant grin, as the trail twisted turned and attempted to buck him off. Catching up to his friend was a pipe dream, and he knew it. He was on his beach cruiser, and Charlie was on a mountain bike.

As the scenery buzzed by him, and the wind whipped through his hair, Josh gripped onto the handle bars for dear life. After a week of reading, writing and trying to adapt to the stress of being a new student, Josh finally felt alive. A full night of video games and pizza had led to waking up way later than normal. In his opinion, whoever invented sleeping in deserved a medal or something. Josh nodded at Charlie, as he rolled up near him. "This place is amazing!" Josh exclaimed, forcing his weight onto the pedals to gain some speed. Each year Josh came to Massachusetts to visit his grandparents and to give Sam a little break. And every time, Charlie and he spent most of it in the basement playing video games and watching TV.

But this year, Charlie was finally sixteen; and he had the Jeep. They could practically go anywhere they wanted to. It wasn't like they hadn't before, thanks to his grandparents. Josh and Charlie had seen all the zoos, museums and amusement parks the state had to offer. Last year Big Sue had even taken the boys to Plymouth Rock and the town of Salem. But this time, it was different. They were unsupervised. Just knowing that gave Josh a sense of freedom that was more precious than gold.

"So what do you think?" Charlie said, coasting effortlessly by Josh.

"This place rocks," replied Josh. "Let's head to the jungle gym over there." One of the only redeeming qualities of Charlie's Jeep was that it had a bike rack on the back of it, so they loaded up the bikes and drove to Dorchester Park. The place was enormous. They'd been riding an hour now, and they were still finding unexplored area. Charlie rode ahead, with Josh trailing behind lazily on his beach cruiser. Even though it wasn't built for this type of stuff, it was still Josh's bike of preference. It was a perfect day for a bike ride. There was a slight breeze, but nothing too big

Coasting on his bike, Josh could easily hear his phone playing the music app from the pocket of his board shorts. It was like his life had a soundtrack, as he meandered around through the occasional joggers and people walking their dogs. Riding up to the jungle gym, Josh swung his leg off the bike and laid it down in the grass. Charlie was slowly coasting around the perimeter.

"Hey, watch this, thumb dick" the redhead yelled, as he struck a soda can with his rear tire. The can pitched out into the grass. Charlie steered over toward Josh with a look of victory painted on his already pink face.

"You should really put some sunscreen on, guy."

"No, I don't want it to get in my eyes," he said, slowly circling around Josh like he was a redheaded lion and, the blonde boy was a helpless gazelle. He had blue jeans and a white tee shirt that read, "Sarcasm. It's what's for dinner."

"Well, if you need it, I have it," said Josh, patting the other pocket on his shorts.

"Is my face pink?" Charlie stopped and straddled his mountain bike.

"Not as pink as last night," teased Josh.

"You're an asshole, Michaels."

"And what did we learn last night, class?" Josh sang out, as if he were a teacher.

"Not to go poking around in our mother's nightstand," Charlie mumbled in return.

Josh laughed out loud. He couldn't help it, even though he knew Charlie didn't think it was funny. Last night, after they'd ordered pizza, Charlie decided he also wanted chicken wings and soda. This resulted in the two teens leaving the basement and going into the house to see if there was any extra cash lying around. After scouring the kitchen and living room, they ended up in Charlie's parents' room.

"I know mom has a change dish somewhere in here," the redhead said, as he stepped into the master bedroom and turned on the light.

"I don't know about this," Josh whispered. It was odd just being in the room. He felt like he had just hopped over a barbed wire fence and was standing somewhere he wasn't supposed to be, like Big Sue's room was private property. Charlie shot him a look of disgust and shook his head.

"I live here, remember? It's not like we broke the window and came in or something." Josh took a look around the room. It was clean. In fact, it was spotless. Charlie sat on the immaculate bedspread and opened his mother's nightstand drawer. Josh watched, as his friend sifted through the contents of the drawer. "I know there be gold in here." Charlie spoke in his best pirate voice. "Aaar, where be the gold?" Josh walked over and flicked on an extra light, while turning around to see Charlie sitting on the bed with a stack of contents on the bedspread.

"Cheese and crackers! What are you doing? Excavating the whole drawer?" Josh asked, walking around the bed and coming up to Charlie's side.

"What the hell is this?" Charlie said, pulling out a molding of a butterfly with straps attached to it. Josh followed the electrical cord to the black battery box on the other end and turned it on.

Immediately, Charlie jumped like a cat, as the butterfly sprang to life. The look on his face went from confusion to shock in no time flat.

"Why that's not gold at all," Josh chuckled, mimicking Charlie's pirate voice. "That be Sue's vibrator!"

Balancing on the bike pedals, Charlie shook his head. "Whatever, dude. I'm sure your mom has a tool chest full of those things."

"And big deal, if she does! She's a single mother," Josh pointed out. "Besides, I didn't laugh because your mom has something that half the women in the world own."

"Then what the hell were you laughing at?" snapped Charlie.

"Your face!" Josh snickered out loud. "It looked like a hot piece of glass after you pour cold water on it."

"What?" Charlie asked, his eyes narrowing with confusion.

"Shattered! Completely shattered!" Josh said, as he laughed out loud again. "I've gotta say this though. If the memory of finding your mother's vibrator is going to be burned into my brain, it might as well be as hilarious as possible."

"I guess so," muttered Charlie, sounding unconvinced. He leaned over his handlebars. "Know what kind of pisses me off?"

"I don't know, what?"

"My parents really didn't teach me anything," Charlie said, shaking his head. "I mean, you could fill a garage with the shit my parents never talked about."

"Is this about the vibrator?" asked Josh, perplexed.

"No, dummy. I know what a vibrator is. I'd just never seen that particular one before. What I'm trying to say is that my mom never told me not to go in that drawer." Charlie cocked his head, like he wanted to say something that was right on the tip of his tongue. "Ya know, my dad is always on the road. And me and my mom don't talk all the time." Josh could see that Charlie was fairly serious. So he decided to keep his mouth shut. "The sex talk in my house was ludicrous. It consisted of my dad coming into the basement, unannounced, with a box of condoms. Then he babbled for two minutes about sex." Charlie shrugged his shoulders and gave a WTF pose. "After he left, I was more confused than when he started. It's like he had written a map to China on a napkin using crayons and then told me to drive there."

"I guess I can understand that," acknowledged Josh, scratching his elbow. "The good thing about Sam is we're tight. So she kinda gave me too much information. Then she said if I needed more, all I had to do is ask."

"I mean, I'm not a dip shit. If I really wanted to, I could have asked my uncle. He'd hook me up. I guess what I'm complaining about is that I always feel like my parents are only doing the bare minimum. When I walk around school, sometimes I can't help but wonder, like, what kind of software is in the other kids' heads? I feel like I've got the stuff that came from the factory, but other kids have all the updates and extra software."

"I kind of feel like that sometimes," Josh replied. He felt conflicted because he didn't want to see Charlie get all manic on him. At the same time, he couldn't tell him that he knew his parents would feel a little more comfortable around him if he wasn't so high tension all the time.

"I'll give you an example," Charlie started. "All my life, my parents didn't tell me what to do in any given situation. They more or less just tell me what not to do. And if I do get an answer, it's the usual standard issue 'because' bullshit."

"Like what?" Josh asked.

"Last December me and mom get into it over Santa Claus, the Easter Bunny and the tooth fairy." Josh shook his head to show he was listening. "I'm one hundred percent on board with the idea of the holidays. They're good, but why do I feel like a goddamn idiot when I ask a grown woman why she lied to me about a man in a red suit? I mean, for centuries now, people have used these figures. Parents lie to their children about somebody they know doesn't exist. Until, one day, they just slap the child in the face and say, yeah, it's not real. What's even stupider is that the child grows up and pulls the same thing on their kids. All I learned from these three instances was that the people I trust the most had no qualms about deceiving me, and at a young age. At a time when I believed in fantastic things, I began to second-guess even myself because of this bullshit."

Josh didn't know what to say, "Um, I don't think anybody purposely tried to poison your mind."

"You're not listening to me," Charlie chuckled, as he threw his hands up. "I dig all these holidays. Nobody's more nostalgic than me. I watch every Christmas-related DVD in my collection every December. What I'm asking is why these people just aren't teaching their kids that the big pile of presents around the Christmas tree was bought by them in the first place? Parents should just tell their kids that the real reason they do this is not because of a man in a red suit, or Jesus, but because they love them. What's so damn wrong with saying they love their kids, and giving them presents? Anyway, what I'm trying to get at is, I posed that question to Sue. But instead of giving me an answer or saying 'Gee, I don't know, son. Let's figure this out,' she just shrugged her shoulders and said 'because.' And goddammit, Josh! I'm no longer okay with that word!" Charlie vented, shaking his head in disgust.

Josh sat there for a second and tried to take in what Charlie was saying. He was used to Charlie's odd form of laying the blame on others, while rationalizing his own actions. He also knew there was always a kernel of truth behind his friend's accusations. It was obvious that, despite wanting to live in his basement in solitude, he also missed the family life as well. "So what do you think, Michaels?"

"Well," thought Josh, "I think that I'm glad I moved here. And if this weekend is any indicator, then this summer's gonna be fierce. Oh, and I think you might be getting coal in your stocking."

"What?" cried Charlie, laughing.

"And," Josh added, "maybe an eye patch and a hook."

"Dude. Looks like somebody wants to walk back to Milton," Charlie ribbed and pointed his bike in the other direction. Josh got up and walked towards the beach cruiser. As he did he pulled out his phone and hit play on the music app, swinging his leg over the seat. Josh eyeballed the skinny redhead. "What do ya say, Cap'n?"

Josh goaded. "Charlie, how about we go plunder yer dad's drawer tonight?"

***

Nina stopped in the middle of the doorway, drinking in the moon. It hung there, perfectly situated in the window frame of the two-story home. From the hallway, it looked like somebody had punched a hole in the nighttime sky. How many times had she stared at that very same nighttime moon, in its various phases, searching for the answers to the questions that life endlessly threw at her? "Befitting," she mused, that it should be staring back at her tonight as she wrestled with whether or not she should go through with her plans. Glancing back at her own sleeping body, tucked serenely under the blankets, she wondered one last time, if this was the right course of action. She could just as easily jump back into her physical body, with just a thought, and be dreaming within minutes. But if she did, she knew that, when she woke in the morning, the questions would still be unanswered. She had to know.

Heading out of the room, she glided effortlessly down the hall. Her pale skin always seemed almost luminescent in her astral form. As she came to her friend's room she took an imaginary breath and passed through the door. There she was. The black-haired teen was deep in sleep's embrace, while her body secretly rebuilt everything her waking hours had so selfishly torn down. Nina stared at the beautiful girl as she slept. Her stunning features, her raven hair and beautiful brown skin, were only a thread hanging from a sweater when Nina looked at who she truly was and who she would one day become. She knew that, in all this world, there was no one quite like Dianna. She possessed a superhuman capacity for love, compassion, and trust. A trust that Nina knew she was about to betray. She sat at the head of the bed and considered what she was about to do. She was going to invade Dianna's dreams. It was something she'd never felt the need to do before today.

But the fate of the world was possibly hinged on this one dream. Lord knows, it hung on Dianna. That's why Nina had to do it. She had to know if this boy Josh was the one destined to be her other half, or if the girl was just being brash and impulsive. As Nina situated herself next to Dianna, she thought of the folly it would be for any other being to attempt this, no matter how skilled. The girl's defenses could decimate her astral form in seconds. The woman knew that. Whereas somebody else would try to pick Dianna's brain like a lock and therefore set off her mental shields, Nina didn't need a pick. She already had the key. The child loved her with all of her heart, and Nina loved her as well. Lying side-by-side, the woman uttered one simple, soundless word into Dianna's ear. As she did, the unconscious girl smiled in her sleep.

Walking amongst the memories in Dianna's mind was like actually living them. The woman knew from the many years of experience that all dreams were different. Some people's dreams lacked vitality. It was like watching ghosts flow through a dream. Others were so lifelike and vibrant, if you weren't trained well enough, you could actually forget you were in the dream to begin with. She knew people who had actually gotten lost doing this, and it always happened the same way. The dream bender forgot where they had come from and accepted the other person's dream as their reality.

Nina was hardly surprised that the interior of Dianna's dreamscape and memories were infused with an energy so vivid it could convincingly compete with the real thing. All Nina had to do was sift through a few memories, until she came to what she was looking for. At fifteen years of age, the girl hardly had any dreams as large-scale as this one. Nina stood, looking at the large monolith shining like a prism in the dark. It outshined all the other memories. Nina watched as Dianna's energy flowed into the memory and emanated a rainbow of emotions out the other side. The woman walked up to the monolith and admired the extreme detail carved upon it. Whoever cast this was a master craftsman, no doubt, she thought to herself. Now all that was left to see was if the boy inside was truly Alex Michaels' son. Nina took her palm and placed it on the glowing memory, and then she was gone

The smell of wildflower was so fragrant it was practically intoxicating. Nina opened her eyes to see the sun in all its glory. She looked at her arm and marveled at how she could feel the rays warming her skin. In an instant, she knew exactly where she was. It was Georgia in the springtime. There were dogwood flowers everywhere. Walking through the grass, she couldn't help but marvel at the detail. She could even smell the frost in the air from the white-capped mountains in the background.

"Raaar," Nina heard off in the background. The woman tried her best to blend into the scenery as two five-year-old boys raced towards her. Laughter filled the air, as they ran willy-nilly through the lush grass with their backpacks on and a small dog at their heels. Blonde and full of energy, the one boy giggled out loud, as he raced to catch his redheaded companion. Nina could actually feel the excitement. The boys' laughter was so infectious it made her want to laugh as well. With a dog yipping and the sun beating down on the rocks, it was so perfect that she wanted to go run and play with them too. To laugh and be free under the warm sun, that's what she really wanted most of all in that moment was just to play. Nina started to run towards the boys, and then she saw her; Dianna.

The realization hit Nina like a brick to the face. The barrage of sensation had almost lured her in. She'd almost been lost already. The shock of the realization was fading. She had to get out. Dianna was so close though. As Nina looked at the five-year-old, she could see her energy blazing like a star. Then, all of a sudden, everything slowed and stopped. Nina anxiously looked at Dianna, who was frozen between steps. The redhead was suspended in mid leap, with is mouth open and fiery locks flowing from his head. "What's going on here?" Nina thought to herself. That's when she saw the blonde boy was walking towards her, eyeing her curiously. He scanned her up and down. There was no doubt in her mind that he was the creator of this memory.

He stopped, and then precociously he took another step towards her. "Who are you?" the boy asked curiously.

"My name is Nina," she said. The boy's energy reached out and touched hers. His face broke into a smile. "You're one of the watchers," he said.

"I am," she said, smiling. "Can I ask you a question?" Nina said, as she bent down on one knee. "What is your name?"

He smiled with zeal in his eye. Then he enthusiastically threw his arms out and proclaimed, "I'm Josh!"

Nina giggled, partly because of how animated he was, but mostly because, when he said this, she suddenly became aware of the sun's brilliance again. As she looked up at the fiery orb and then back into the beaming eyes of the boy, she said, "You most certainly are, Josh. You most certainly are."

"It was nice to meet you, Nina. I'm going to go play now.

See you later." Before she could even register the words, the dream began to resume. The white dog pounced forward and was nipping at the redhead's shoe as he descended back down to the earth and continued to run forward.

  The small, blonde child stopped and looked back at Nina, smiling from ear to ear. Then he bent down and picked an azalea and gave it to Dianna. With just one look at the girl's eyes, it was no longer in doubt. He was the one. The curious part to Nina wasn't that the dream continued, but that Dianna didn't follow after the boys. She turned around and walked into the forest. Running up beside her, Nina watched as the girl walked into the surrounding trees. Making her way into the forest, it was actually so thick that at one point she thought she might lose sight of Dianna.

  And then Nina saw it. There was a thin, almost unnoticeable, bioelectric seam. This wasn't one dream. It was actually two dreams woven together. "Phenomenal," Nina gasped. Only the Creator had such a power. Nina ran after the girl. As Dianna walked into the clearing, her body was maturing with each progressive step, until she was twelve years old.

  Standing amongst the trees, Nina watched as the dream began to unfold before her. The landscape had changed. They were no longer in Georgia, but back in Massachusetts. The woman recognized this area too. It was the Neponset River, no more than a few miles from where they live. The memory was accurate in every detail. She could hear the river, as the water gently rolled through on its journey. She smelled the pine trees surrounding them.

  The girl stood motionless, seemingly entranced by the swirls and eddies in the river. Stepping towards the water, the girl shed off her dress and continued to walk evenly, almost sedately, towards the water. Nina pondered what could possibly be going through her mind just then. She seemed to be hypnotized. The girl, clad only in white bra and panties, stepped between two massive pine trees rooted on the shore of the river bank. Moving effortlessly, the watcher glided between the two wooden pillars, towards the girl. As she touched down behind Dianna, she couldn't help but be moved at the twelve-year-old image of the girl. She looked exactly the same as when she had first met her. Without hesitation, Dianna stepped into the river. Bit by bit, the water enveloped the young girl's body until it was at her shoulders. Standing alone on the riverbank, Nina couldn't help but be filled with dread for what she knew would happen next. She'd discussed the dream with Dianna before.

Nina braced herself as serpents began to descend from the treetops. The girl obliviously floated in the water so comfortably in the new habitat that you would think she was born in the water. The serpents were no longer than Nina's arm, but she knew that wasn't what made them dangerous. For a second, she was almost overcome by the need to protect the child. But she knew that this had to happen.

Slithering and sliding, the serpents on either side of the river entered the water. Nina didn't really want to watch the rest. The thought of Dianna's pain wasn't something she relished. Suddenly, the hypnotic veil that covered Dianna's vision was pulled away. Nina watched as recognition spread across the girl's face. She not only saw the serpents converging on her from all sides, but she also saw the ones that continued to spiral down the tree trunks. Bracing for the attack, the girl vigorously kicked and swung her arms. The first of the serpents closed in on her. Nina winced when she saw the look of shock on the child's face, as the first set of fangs pierced the skin of her abdomen.

Dianna's screams were so loud that Nina could swear they were shaking the trees. The child thrashed about in the water. She was bit again, this time in her upper thigh. Standing in solitude, the woman watched as crimson ribbons of blood began to flow forth from the young woman's wounds. She looked tired now and was barely able to tread water, when the inevitable happened. Two more razor-sharp fangs pierced her flesh. Dianna, raw with fear, grabbed the serpent and submerged. The watcher stood in disbelief at the graphic display that she had just borne witness to. Yet, despite the horrible event that just took place within it, the river paid no mind. It continued to roll onwards; concealing all evidence the struggle had even taken place.

Nina stared at the waters, waiting for Dianna to come up. She never did. Doubt began to creep into the woman's mind, that is, until the earth began to shake violently. Suddenly, an explosion of energy sent the river in every conceivable direction. The first wave of psychic energy ripped past Nina as water sprayed by her, taking with it branches, pebbles, and the superficial layer of soil on the shore. The watcher stood in awe of what was before her. In the riverbed, among the rocks and fragments of fish and serpents, stood Dianna. She was wild-eyed, with teeth chattering from the cold. In each of her tightly clenched fists was one half of the snake who had dared to attack her.

Total amazement washed over Nina. She could see the waves of energy had cleaved the water away from the shores, and it was being held back by the young girl's will. Dianna limped towards Nina and what was left of the devastated shore. Her blood stained the wet, white undergarments that stuck to her shivering frame. The watcher's relief at Dianna's victory was soon overshadowed, when she saw the indescribable look of agony on her face. Nina lowered to the ground and reflexively hugged her knees to her chest, gripped by the sense of sorrow her psyche was experiencing.

The young woman trembled and shook in agony as the venom coursed through her veins. Her face contorted in agony. Her eyes were bloodshot. The girl moaned with every step, until she finally collapsed on the ravaged riverbank. Nina stared at

Dianna, her baby, who was so delicate and yet so strong. As Dianna slipped into unconsciousness, the landscape became fuzzy and dark. So did Nina's vision.

"Charlie, get the rig ready!" commanded Josh. "IVs, blankets, and hot packs. She's hypothermic." Nina's vision cleared up to see Josh carrying Dianna in his arms. No longer the precocious five-year-old boy, he charged up the embankment with ease holding the young woman to his chest. "Stay with me. Everything's going to be okay," he assured her with a soothing voice. Nina watched as Josh sped by in his dark navy Class Two uniform. The only thing that divided the blue pants and collared shirt was his black leather belt and matching steel-toed boots.

"Get out of the way!" boomed Charlie, as he cut his way through the crowd. Nina watched how the medical bag on his shoulder bounced much in the same way that his backpack had only minutes earlier in the meadow. And then for Nina, the vision faded again.

"Code 3 to Beth Israel!" Josh shouted through the bulkhead.

"Not doing it, Josh. Milton's a lot closer."

"Not your decision," replied Josh, as he put the oxygen mask on the barely-conscious woman. "Israel's down the street from Franklin Park Zoo. So I'm pretty sure they'll have anti-venom handy. Now light 'em up and go!" he ordered. The gold-embroidered paramedic patch seemed to blur as Josh quickly assessed Dianna's vital signs. Reaching up towards the ceiling, he gave a tug on the tourniquet wrapped around the IV bag that was suspended from the ceiling hook. Nina noticed that Josh's movements were smooth and deliberate. Even though the situation looked grim, she could tell by the look on his face that Josh had every intention of protecting Dianna, no matter what problems arose. His determination and will were going to see them both through to the other side.

Placing the tourniquet on Dianna's arm, he swiftly reached

in to one of the Plexiglas cabinets on the wall. The man in front of Nina was confident and mature. The bright sun overhead and the smell of wildflowers around him had been replaced by fluorescent dome lamps and the smell of fear. Josh shined, nonetheless. Even though the road was rough in the back, the ambulance rose and fell with it. Josh started the IV. As he taped it down, Dianna's eyes fluttered. She groaned. Nina could tell, by the way she was gripping the handrails of the narrow gurney, she was still in a lot of pain.

She noticed something else, too. Dianna had aged. She had to be at least fifteen. "It burns," she murmured, clutching at her lower stomach. "Please make the burning stop."

"I'm going to do that," Josh reassured her. "Give me just a second." Turning to the front, Josh asked, "ETA?"

"We're lookin' at about four minutes," Charlie said, flipping the siren from yelp to wail. "Good, good. When you get a chance, hook me up with a ring down to the hospital." Once again, Josh reached into the cabinets. He pulled out a vial of medication and a syringe this time. He drew up the medication and then set down the vial upright, as Charlie slammed on the brakes. The glass container rolled off of the seat and onto the floor. Nina heard Dianna groan, as the force of deceleration pulled on her already burning abdomen.

Josh really didn't seem to notice when the ambulance stopped. His foot was wedged between the gurney and the bench. The only part of him that did move was his Saint Michael necklace, which Nina knew was not store-bought. The necklace hadn't even been forged by human hands.

Charlie screamed out the window, "The flashing lights mean pull to the right, not stop in the middle of the damn road!" As the ambulance pulled forward, a voice came up from the wall-mounted speaker.

"Emergency, this is Dr. Rosenblum." Josh grabbed the

gray microphone from its cradle and pressed on the black button.

"Hello, Dr. Rosenblum. Medic 847, inbound code 3 with an approximately nineteen-year-old female found unconscious near Ryan Park. She has multiple snakebites. Initially she was hypothermic, but she's warming up with blankets and heat packets. I have a 16-gauge catheter in her left forearm, and the IV is running at ten drops a minute. We have an ETA of less than three minutes. All her vital signs are stable at this time. I'll be treating her for pain as protocol allows."

The doctor's voice replied through the speaker, "Good job. We'll be waiting when you get here." Josh returned the microphone and grabbed the IV tubing. Cleansing the port with an alcohol swab, he pushed the needle in. Nina glanced over to Dianna, hair matted and face glistening with sweat. The watcher gasped, as she recognized the red and white medication.

Dianna asked, "What's in that?" Josh smiled, and as he did, Nina swore the whole back of the ambulance lit up.

He placed his thumb over the plunger and looked at the woman he loved more than anything in the world. "Everything," he replied.

Nina could feel the memory was coming to a close as everything in the ambulance started to vibrate out of sync with her. She saw Josh push the plunger. Then everything went sideways, as Nina was yanked out of the memory and thrown backwards. What followed was a feeling as if she was falling into darkness, accompanied by a cacophony of sounds. The last thing she remembered was hearing the cries of a newborn, followed by the doctor's voice announcing with pride, "It's a girl."

Shooting up in bed, Nina stared at her bedroom wall, disoriented. Her pulse was racing and she was breathing like she had just run a marathon. Collapsing back on her moist pillow, she put her hands to her forehead and thought about what had just transpired. One thing was for sure, the version Dianna had told

Nina really didn't do the memory justice. Although, the details didn't matter much. What she had just seen wasn't the future. It was just one of many possibilities mashed together, sent from the subconscious as a heads up. However, Nina wondered to herself, if the newborn's cries were coming from the future. Could it be a daughter? Or was it Dianna's first memory that Nina saw, as she was yanked out through the wormhole?

Swinging her legs over the side of the bed, she gave herself a second to readjust to her physical body. Nina sat up and looked at the collection of pictures, dimly lit by the moonlight. Most all of them were of her and Dianna. The woman stood up and walked over to the pictures hung on the wall. Even though darkness dominated the bedroom, she could still see one of her favorite photos in the light of the full moon. The picture was taken the night Nina moved in with Imperials, the day after Dianna had the dream.

That morning, years ago, Dianna had awoken to find she had become a woman, having started her first period. It was a tough, emotional day for everybody involved. With everything in her immortal heart, Nina wanted to tell Dianna that from that day out, the worst was behind her. Unfortunately, she knew better.

***

"I know this is going to sound strange. If it's not too much trouble, could you let me off in front of the fire station?" asked Josh. The older, balding bus driver looked over at him and then looked back at the road.

"You don't ride the bus much; do you?"

"Not all that often," admitted Josh, as he leaned forward to make eye contact. "Why?"

"Well, we don't normally drop people off anywhere but the designated stop. Since this is your first time though, I guess I can make an exception."

Josh gripped the pole in front of his seat, as the bus slowed down and then rolled to a stop in front of a brick building. "You tell the firemen Benny said hi," flashing his name tag at Josh.

"Any particular one?" asked Josh, as he stepped down onto the curb.

"Nah, they all know me," Benny said with a smile. "I've been driving this route for five years. I don't think a month has gone by when I haven't had to call 911 for a passenger," the older man said with a chuckle.

"Are you kidding me?"

"Not at all. Last week I called 911 three times. One was for a woman who was going into labor. The second was an asthma attack, and the third was for a fight between passengers. One guy got taken to jail and the other to the hospital. Later that night, after the hospital patched him up, I picked him up and dropped him off by his house."

"Would you mind if I mentioned you in my English report?" Josh asked. "It's called Heroes of Massachusetts."

Smiling ear to ear, Benny nodded at Josh. "You know what, kid? You just made my day."

***

"If they look over here one more time, I'm gonna lose it," Nina said under her breath, as she shot a stare at the next pew back. Dianna nodded, and her raven-haired ponytail bobbed up and down with her head. It was bad enough having to go to school and deal with the weird looks after the video hit the internet. But here, in their own church, she wasn't expecting this.

From the moment she walked in, she could see people pointing and staring at her. It was kind of a letdown, because this was the one place she felt she could go to escape this kind of thing.

She stood and pretended to sing along with the group, while straightening the sides of her black skirt. As she did, she couldn't help but feel like the choir was looking straight at her.

"This thing's riding up like crazy," she whispered to Nina.

"Would you guys calm down already?" Ramon said in a hushed tone.

Dianna knew her father didn't want to be here. After the reporters had started calling the house, Ramon recommended they lay low for at least a week. "But why should we?" she thought. It wasn't fair. Ramon had only come to church with her and Nina because they hounded him until he relented.

"Okay, okay. You girls are crazy," Ramon said, agreeing to go.

"He looks good in a suit," Dianna thought. Today he was wearing her favorite blue one, with gray pinstripes.

As she was looking towards her dad, a man in the pew behind her tapped on her shoulder. Dianna ducked her head down and looked at the young man. He definitely wasn't dressed for church. The unfamiliar man had slicked-back hair and a pencil-thin mustache.

"Yes, can I help you?" Dianna asked, trying to be polite.

"Hello, my name is Simon. Simon Glass. And I was wondering if I could ask you a few questions outside." Dianna was stunned. Who would be so brazen? They followed her into a church.

She was just about to answer when Nina leaned over and poked him in the chest, "Take a hike, Simon."

"You can't do that," he said, raising his voice for everybody to hear. As he did, he turned his shoulders towards Nina. Dianna could see there was a small bag under his left arm. The bag had been altered. She could see the camera lens poking out of it. Dianna glanced nervously over it, towards Nina. She could tell, by the look on the woman's face, that she wasn't fooling around.

"NO. Seriously, Simon. It's time for you to go," she said, raising her voice an octave and pointing towards the door.

"Are you threatening me?" asked the reporter. "I just want to ask some questions. There's no need to make threats."

"Nobody's threatening anybody," a voice behind Dianna said, calmly. The girl turned to see the pastor standing at the entrance of the pew. She felt like she'd die a thousand deaths. This was exactly what Dianna had hoped wouldn't happen. The whole congregation had gone silent. If they weren't staring before, they most definitely were now.

"I'm going to tell you one more time, paparazzi. Scram!" Nina barked.

"Now, now. Calm down," Pastor Kato said in a calm, soothing tone. There were few men in Dianna's eyes who could measure up to her dad, and Pastor Kato was definitely one of them. She'd never once seen him look anything but happy. "Would you mind if I asked what it is you're doing here?" the pastor inquired.

"I'm just an independent contractor, who came to ask Ms. Imperial some questions."

"Well, you do know we're kind of in the middle of service, right? Maybe you could come back another time?" suggested the pastor.

"Don't try to railroad me," Glass said. "I have a constitutional right to be here, and I'll sit here as long as I want."

"That's what I like to hear," the pastor boomed. "God loves a man with conviction." Up on the stage, one of the choir singers shouted out a hallelujah. Dianna grinned, even though she couldn't tell if it was sincere or if the congregation was just razzing the reporter. "You're right. You can sit here as long as you want," remarked the pastor. "I'm glad you brought that video recorder with you," he said, pointing at the concealed camera, "because there's something I think you're going to want to see. Or, as you reporters usually say, something the world has a right to see."

With that, the pastor looked at Dianna's dad. In a raised voice he asked, "Who wants to hear Brother Imperial get up on that stage and speak the Word?" Dianna's jaw hit the floor, when she heard what was just said. She looked over towards Ramon, who looked just as shocked as she was. This time, with a grittier tone and twice as much conviction, the pastor yelled, "I said, who wants to hear this man of God call on the Holy Spirit of our Lord?"

Dianna stood stunned, as applause resounded through the church. Nina stood there with both fists clenched. Dianna was shocked to see that she had tears in her eyes. "Amen!" Nina shouted.

Holding out his hand to Ramon, the pastor asked, "What do you say, Ramon? Do you think you can remember how to raise the Spirit?"

"It's been a while, but I'd be honored," Ramon said.

"Then bring your beautiful daughter up to the stage with you. She can sit in my seat, next to the pulpit."

"Are you sure?" Dianna asked hesitantly. She'd never seen anybody else ever sit in the luxurious seat. Pastor Kato was either in it, or it sat empty as he was up preaching.

"Yes," he assured her with a smile. "Now go take a seat next to my wife, and watch your dad do his thing." The pastor added in a loud voice, "Myself and Sister Nina will sit here with this fine young visitor to answer any questions that he may have."

Making her way out of the pew, Dianna could barely contain herself. She glanced behind her to see Nina sitting down on one side of the reporter. The pastor had already put his arm around the young man and was talking a mile a minute. Best of all was the look on Mr. Glass's face. As she walked away, she couldn't help thinking he looked confused, like he just realized he was scammed in a game of cards.

"Are you ready to do this?" Ramon asked, as he took her right arm.

"Yes, let's," Dianna said, trying not to sound too giddy. Anticipation soon overshadowed her previous memory of the reporter. She was finally going to see her dad do what he loved the most. Stepping up to the stage, Dianna let go of her father's hand. As he veered off towards the pulpit, she sat down next to the pastor's wife.

The smiling woman had her gray hair up in a bun. "Don't worry about that uncouth gentlemen," whispered the lady. "My husband has more than a few tricks up his sleeve to deal with his type."

"Thank you, so much," Dianna said, meaning every word.

"Well," the pastor's wife said, when you get to be my age, you'll realize that saving people takes many forms."

"Thank you, Pastor Kato." Ramon's voice boomed over the speaker system. Dianna turned to the pulpit. The sound up here was louder than she thought it would be. "This isn't really what I'd expected today when I woke up," Ramon chuckled. As he spoke, the microphone amplified his voice. Suddenly, the screech of feedback filled the room. "Whoa," Ramon sputtered, tapping the mic. The girl tensed up as she watched the faces of the congregation. The whole thing was starting to feel awkward. Dianna could see her dad's face, as he searched for something to say.

"Come on, dad," she thought.

"Take your time, Brother Imperial. You've got this," urged the pastor from the audience.

"Yeah, Ramon, do what you do best," screamed Nina.

In just the twinkling of an eye, Dianna saw the indecision on her father's face melt away. He looked over to his daughter and said, "I Love You." The girl had heard this a million times, but never quite like that.

"I love you, too, daddy" she stammered back, holding her shaking hands to her face.

He then looked at the audience and uttered one word into the microphone: "Expectation." He paused for a brief second before he continued. "It's what is in my heart. For soon my King shall return, bringing with him a love so pure, so refined, that even death will be conquered." Ramon paused for a second and gripped the podium. "As his foot touches the mount, war will be abolished. Hatred will be but an archaic, forgotten word. For just as my Lord hates these things, so too will his true children." Dianna's heart rose as she watched the packed audience all nod in agreement. "Until then," Ramon said, his voice rising, "I will wait with expectation in my heart." Dianna was pleased as the reporter stood up, a scowl covering his face, and walked out the door. It was a victory she relished, but she didn't know if she could smile any wider.

"Sometimes I truly wonder if an eternity could ever be long enough. God knows I would spend an eternity searching for him," Ramon said. "Come to me, my Lord. I will speak to you with the gentleness that was made for your heart alone. Truly, you must all be made in God's image, because this congregation has shown a sacrifice of love worthy of our Master. Even as the powers of this world crash down upon us, until we can bear no more," Ramon went on, shaking his finger, his voice rising in a crescendo. "Even when we cry out in pain, no one will heed our call, except for the Lord. He will lift us up, and he will renew us." Ramon hovered for a split second and then finished, "Truly, he is our betrothed."

Clapping and whistling exploded from the audience, along with shouts of encouragement. Dianna couldn't remember ever feeling closer or more proud of her father than she did at this moment. As she clapped her hands, she saw her dad look her way and wink at her. Looking out at the audience, she could see Nina holding out a thumbs-up of approval, while next to her sat the pastor with a huge smile on his face. Over the sounds of the applause somebody shouted, "Keep going, Brother. Preach it."

And so he did. And his daughter couldn't have been happier.

Chapter 6
Six Jars of Water

"How was your ride-along Sunday?" asked Charlie, beef jerky hanging half out of his mouth, while he talked and chewed at the same time.

"It was cool. I learned a lot," replied Josh. "They really didn't let me ride along because of my age, but I got to sit and talk with them about some intense calls. I even got to interview the Chief. They'll give me an application to volunteer when I'm old enough," Josh said, as he pulled his hoodie over his head and then ran his fingers through his hair. "How do I look?"

"Like you fell in a wheat thresher," chuckled Charlie, trying to rip the long piece of meat.

"I'm not amused," Josh said.

"All right already. You look okay, but your eyes look kinda tired. Did you sleep last night?"

"Barely," Josh yawned. "I had to get all my homework and reading done because we screwed around all weekend. Then I fell asleep for a few hours and got woke up by that crazy bird outside my window."

"Seriously, man, I hear that thing all the time when I come outside."

"He just doesn't shut up. That's why I shut the window on that side of the house."

"That's one of the perks of living in the basement," Charlie bragged. "I'm surrounded by cement."

"All I know is I need to get some sleep tonight," Josh mumbled, taking a swig of his chocolate milk.

Charlie nodded, "I can kinda relate. The neighbors on the other side of us had this giant Saint Bernard, and he had this choke collar made out of chain."

"What for?"

"I think the dog was too strong for a leash. He didn't look aggressive, but he was a giant dog."

"Oh, yeah. I remember him," said Josh.

"Well, anyway, the dog had this chain around his neck, and it had a few extra links that hung down. So, basically, he'd sit on the porch all day and do nothing. But when nighttime came, he'd prowl around the backyard like he was Lewis and Clark on an expedition. You could hear ching, ching, ching, ching and the sound of him breathing from a mile away." In his mind Josh could see the behemoth of a dog just breathing hard and slobbering everywhere.

"So what happened?

"I went to Sue and told her I couldn't sleep because the dog's chain was keeping me up," Charlie laughed. "Just ching, ching, chingin' all night long. But she blew me off and told me to sleep with my window shut."

"Okay," Josh said, trying to finish off the carton of milk.

"No, not okay," Charlie countered. "I went next door and told them that, because of their mobile spit factory of a dog, I couldn't sleep. So the owner, Mr. Davis, actually asked me what it sounded like. So, in front of his kids, I told him it sounded like the ghost of Christmas past was masturbating under my window all night long."

Josh didn't want to, but he seriously had to laugh. Unfortunately, he still had milk in his mouth. Swallowing hard, Josh tried to force it all down. He knew instantly that it was a failed attempt. Only half of the milk made it down his throat. The other half went into his windpipe. Josh choked and coughed into his black hoodie trying to get the milk out. The two boys to the left of Josh were laughing hysterically as Charlie crossed his eyes and made the chinging noise, while he breathed heavily.

More classmates joined in on the laughter as Charlie flared

his nostrils and spoke in a funny voice. "Ching, ching, ching. Why won't anybody play with me?" Josh coughed again and again trying to get the milk out of his windpipe. When he looked up again, Dianna was walking into the room. Why couldn't he get a break? His face had to be beet red right now. His nose was running, and he couldn't stop coughing.

"Are you all right?" she asked from two rows over.

"Stellar," croaked Josh, as he buried his face in the only part of his hoodie that was clean. Still coughing, he didn't know how this could get worse.

"Geez, Michaels, you look like you're going to blow a gasket," snickered Charlie. Wiping his face the best he could, Josh pulled off the hoodie and put it on the floor under his desk.

"I'm okay, really," Josh replied in a hoarse voice.

"Does anybody know where Mr. Douglas is?" Dianna asked.

"I saw him when I first came in," Nick told the others. "These two new students came in like they owned the place, saying they were in this class. So Mr. Douglas said there was more room over in Ms. Bailey's class, and they should talk to the principal about transferring them over there. Then the tall guy gave him attitude. So they all took off to hash it out with the principal."

"That doesn't sound too good," exclaimed Dianna.

"And get this," Nick said, excited. "They rolled into the parking lot in a silver and black Bentley GT with tricked out black rims."

"What?" Charlie cried. "You've gotta be kidding me!"

Josh coughed into his hand and thought to himself, "Great, this is all I need." The class door swung wide open. Mr. Douglas came in, followed by two boys. Josh noticed Mr. Douglas didn't look too thrilled.

He thought the first kid looked normal enough. He had black, spiky hair and seemed to smile a lot. The second one was a beast though. He looked as tall as Charlie, except he was insanely muscular with short, auburn hair. Something about his eyes didn't sit well with Josh. They were narrow, almost like he was continuously angry. He reminded Josh of a pitbull he'd seen once.

Charlie looked back at Josh with wide eyes, mouthed "WTF," and looked forward. Already Josh could hear the girls whispering around him. Michelle turned around to face Leah.

"Cute!" she said excitedly.

"Super cute!" Leah agreed.

"Well, boys, we're just going to have to make do with what we have. We don't have any more desks," Mr. Douglas said, as he removed all the books and equipment off of the extra lab table. "Are you sure you guys don't want to try another class? It would be more comfortable."

"I don't have a problem with being here. As the Principal pointed out, this class isn't maxed out," said spiky hair.

"Right," Mr. Douglas said slowly, as he turned towards the class. "I'm sorry for all the confusion. I know we're behind, but we have two new transfer students from California. Not too far from where you came from, Josh."

"That's weird," Josh thought to himself. These guys didn't look like they were from California to him. He did a double-take and saw they were both looking in his direction. Josh gave them a nod. Spiky hair saluted him with two fingers.

Mr. Douglas motioned to the class. "Boys, if you would introduce yourselves."

The pitbull spoke first. "My name's Deus. I'm from Orange County, California. I was captain of the football team, and I took the division championship for wrestling." Then, just like that, pitbull sat down. Josh jumped, as his phone vibrated in his pocket. Being as subtle as he could, Josh glanced down at his lap. Charlie had sent him a text. It read:

WHAT A TARD.

Josh grinned and looked up at the ceiling until the urge to scream with laughter had subsided. Spiky hair didn't just stand up. He walked straight to the head of the class.

"Hello," he said politely. "My name is William Hasden, III, but I like to be called Billy. This is my cousin, Deus Gregory," he said, pointing at the huge teen. "My father is the owner of Hasden Medical, which deals in a wide array of medical supplies, which is anything from fire trucks and ambulances to simple bandages. Basically, if it makes a profit, we sell it. We came out here because my father is trying to negotiate the transport contract for some of the surrounding areas."

Vivian raised her hand. As she did, she bit her bottom lip. "I just want to say sweet ride. How much did it cost?"

"Not a dime. It was a gift. A friend of my dad's gave it to me."

Mr. Douglas interrupted. "Thank you very much, Billy." Josh typed into his phone:

SPIKY HAIR'S NOT BAD

and hit send.

"If you'd please clear your desk and hand up the paper I assigned you over the weekend," asked Mr. Douglas, standing up. "I was going to have you read these out loud. However, since we're behind schedule and we have new students today, we're just going to briefly discuss the theme. This will be a great way for our new students to get acquainted with us. Both Billy and Deus can participate as well. We'll start from the left and work to the right." Walking to the middle of the room and picking up all of the papers, the teacher continued, "The theme was tell the story of an event in your life that you feel is unique, and nobody else has done. Rico, we'll start with you."

Mr. Douglas sat down and started to grade the papers on

the spot. Josh had to admit he was pretty impressed with some of the stories. Rico and his brother, Howard, both had walk-on parts as extras in The Bourne Identity. "I think I might have to watch that again," Josh thought. Scanning the room, he could see that only a third of the students were actively listening to the stories. Most were busy writing their homework for other classes or drawing in their notebooks. Yawning, Josh stretched his arms and pretended to crack his back. While he did, he tried to steal a glance at Dianna without seeming too obvious. She was busy writing in a journal. Josh glanced a little longer and noticed that she was smiling. She looked amazing today.

On the other side of her was Deus. Much to Josh's dismay, he was looking at her too. Sitting forward, he felt his phone vibrate again. He kinda wished Charlie could wait until lunch. What could be so important that he'd risk getting them caught? Multiple times in the last week, Josh had seen Mr. Douglas warn people about disrupting the class with phones:

> I DON'T LIKE RICH PEOPLE. THEY ALWAYS THINK THEY'RE BETTER AND HAVE TO ONE-UP EVERYBODY.

Josh looked up after reading Charlie's text to see if anybody was looking. Mr. Douglas was busy grading papers. Seizing the opportunity, Josh quickly replied:

> THIS WOULDN'T HAVE ANYTHING TO DO WITH THE FACT THAT VIVIAN'S BEEN CHECKING THEM OUT NONSTOP SINCE THEY WALKED IN, WOULD IT?

Josh didn't even need to ask the question. He already knew the answer. Charlie would probably take it personally, like he always did. Josh really didn't see the big deal. So they came from money and had nice things. The big guy seemed dumb as a post. They both probably already had girlfriends anyway. He'd talk to Charlie at lunch, for what good it would do. Hell, Charlie wasn't even remotely poor. He just had less money than these kids did, and Josh knew that's what bothered him.

Josh had a feeling the redhead would harbor some imaginary grudge against the new kids just because that's what he did. Josh didn't care though. He knew money couldn't buy happiness because he felt a hundred times better now that he lived here.

"Good story, JM," Mr. Douglas announced, not even looking up from the papers. "Deus, would you like to go next?"

"Yeah, sure," Deus replied, standing up and leaning on his desk. "Once I was walking down the beach in Rio de Janeiro and I saw this girl drowning. She'd been pulled out by the undertow. I called for help, but nobody came. I'm not really a strong swimmer, but I couldn't let this girl drown. So I threw off my shirt and shoes, and I swam out and caught her before she was pulled under. By now, I noticed that I was caught in the undertow too. We almost both drowned that day, but I fought my way back to the shore and saved us."

Josh didn't know if that story was true or not. Living by the ocean in Santa Cruz, he had heard stories of people who were washed out to sea. Out of those handful, he'd never heard of anybody making it back without the help of a lifeguard. The undertow in Santa Cruz was wicked. He was sure that if he checked the internet, there would be far more stories of drownings than of heroes who had done what Deus had just claimed.

Mr. Douglas looked up from the paper and nodded, "Good story, Deus. Billy, would you like to go?" Josh looked towards Billy. As he stood up to address the class, Josh noticed that, when Billy talked, he liked to emphasize with his hands. Kind of like the people on the late-night infomercials.

"Well, okay. I was on a ski trip once in Cortina, Italy. We headed out fairly early for this place where we knew there was virgin snow." Josh cocked his head to look at his vibrating phone:

AND HERE WE GO. THE CAVALCADE OF TALL TALES HAS BEGUN.

"When we got there," Billy started, "we were the first people around. I set out with my buddy. Both of us were on snowboards, and everybody else was skiing. We got only about a hundred yards before I heard the sound of cracking ice behind us. I looked behind to see a humongous wall of white coming up on us. It was an avalanche, and it was gaining fast. I knew, if I had any chance to beat it, I'd have to stop sweeping and stay straight. So I tucked down to reduce drag and friction. Even though I was easily doing over 100 mph, I barely made it out alive. My friends weren't so lucky." Josh couldn't believe what he was seeing and hearing. Billy actually shed a tear drop and wiped it away with his thumb. Josh looked around the room to see if anybody else had trouble with the story.

"Dude, you're high." Josh sighed and looked towards Charlie, who had both hands pulling his hair. "It's pretty much impossible to outrun an avalanche," stated Charlie. "On top of that, snowboards don't even touch the speed of skis."

"Are you calling me a liar?" challenged Billy. His face immediately turned red, and his eyes narrowed down.

"This isn't good," thought Josh. He saw Deus slowly stand up and glare at Charlie.

"I'm just saying, man, it's impossible."

"What? You got a better story, big man?" Deus taunted Charlie.

Josh looked over to make sure Mr. Douglas was paying attention. He was surprised to see, not only was he watching, but he was up and moving towards the front of the class.

"As a matter of fact, I do," sneered Charlie. "When I was five, I dreamed of somebody before I even met them. This person was three thousand miles away at the time." Josh heard a loud gasp and turned to see Dianna staring, not at Charlie, but straight at him. The feeling of ice being poured into Josh's veins came first, followed by a general queasy feeling as the room seemed to twist itself. "Oh, shit," Josh thought.

"That's enough, all of you!" barked Mr. Douglas. He was only feet away from Charlie when he shouted. Josh watched as Charlie jumped and flipped around. He'd obviously been caught off guard. The two boys, however, grabbed their book bags and walked out without so much as an explanation.

"What an idiot," Josh thought, as he looked at the back of Charlie's stupid red head. If it wouldn't get him suspended, he'd slap the freckles right off of his cheeks. Mr. Douglas didn't say anything about the new students leaving. He just stared at Charlie, like he was considering sending him to the school nurse for a psyche evaluation. "Good," thought Josh. "It'll do him good." Then the thought occurred to him that maybe he should tag along and get his head checked for hanging around with him.

***

Josh weaved through the crowd of teenagers, who were all trying to find a spot to sit down and enjoy their lunch break. He passed by plenty of spaces, but Josh wasn't so much interested in eating as much as he wanted to find Charlie and put his foot in his ass. Josh looked from one end of the cafeteria to the other and didn't see him. For a guy his height with red hair, you'd think he'd stick out like a sore thumb. Finally, he spotted Charlie through one of the windows, walking alone outside.

Josh sat the tray down and headed for the doors. "What were you thinking?" he whispered angrily. As he got closer to Charlie, he wanted to tear the redhead a new one. But his anger quickly vanished, as he saw his friend's glassy eyes. Charlie just shrugged his shoulders and didn't say anything. Josh wondered if the teen could talk, even if he tried. The look on his face was what you'd expect to see on a lost child.

Now Josh felt embarrassed for all the things he had thought

about him over the last hour. Charlie ducked out of class so fast at the end of the third period that Josh hadn't gotten to talk to him. "Look, the one thing we both agreed we should never talk about was the dream."

"I know," he mumbled, looking at his shoes. "I'm sorry, Josh," Charlie said. "I know that sometimes it's hard to be my friend." Josh stood there, speechless. He couldn't remember a time when they had ever had a disagreement and Charlie hadn't argued with Josh like his life depended on it. "It was the one sacred trust between us, and I threw it away. I'm sorry."

"It's not that bad," Josh said. Part of him wanted to revel in the victory. After ten years, he was finally hearing an apology from his obstinate friend. But the other half of Josh was screaming, "Stop him, before he cries!"

"It could've been worse. You could've said my name." Josh was trying to be consoling, even though he knew most people in that class could figure out that he was Charlie's only friend, and he was the only one who'd ever lived that far away. He sat down on the grass, and Charlie followed. Both of them sat silently, as they watched the crowd of students mill about.

"I just seriously don't like those guys," Charlie said, looking at the ground. "If my girl situation was bad before, it's gonna be impossible now that these guys are here." Josh could tell this whole thing was centered around the fact that Charlie was no longer the biggest kid in class. Add in a dash of his disillusionment with Vivian, who the boy talked about at least once a day, and that explained why he didn't like either of them.

"Look, guy," Josh said in his best Santa Cruz voice. "If you think Vivian's hot now, wait until summer, when we're hangin' around the lake and she's tanning in a bikini." Josh watched as his friend's eyes went from his 'have you seen my lost puppy' mode to his 'party over here' mode.

"Hell, to the yeah, man," Charlie came back to life, his eyes widening. "And then I'll step up and be like, did somebody call for a redheaded massage machine? And she'll be like, I did, Mr. Charlie Beefcake Bernacki." Josh was relieved. It was a little more than he'd hoped for, but it was better than Charlie's previous mood.

"Excuse me, do you guys mind if I join you?"

"There is a God," thought Josh.

"Have a seat, Imperial," said Charlie, totally drained of his enthusiasm.

"Hey, Dianna," Josh couldn't help but smile when she sat down on the grass across from them. "So what do you think of the new guys?" Josh asked, wishing Charlie would break out in hives and run off screaming.

"Boys will be boys," she said, smirking.

"What about their cock-and-bull stories? I can't be the only one who saw through that," complained Charlie.

"I know," Dianna agreed, biting into her sandwich. "Welcome to the female side of things, gentlemen. I can't make it through the day without some guy I barely know telling me a tall tale."

"You're kidding me, right?" Charlie blurted in disbelief.

"No. Sadly, I'm not kidding you, Charlie. My sister used to date a guy who swore he worked for the FBI. This went on for months. Then one day, my sister and I go to get her car washed. Just guess who's walking around with a towel in his hand." Josh smiled, as Dianna giggled and took another bite. He'd heard stories from his mom about male clients bragging about all kinds of things.

Charlie raised his red eyebrows and folded his arms over his chest. "Girls lie too, you know."

"I never said they didn't," she pointed out. "Don't get all defensive. All I'm saying is it's not a big deal that the stories were embellished. They're obviously trying to impress somebody."

"Yeah, but who? Josh asked. Dianna thought about it for a second.

"Could be the girls in class. Could be just one," she said, wiping her mouth and opening her bottle of water.

"I don't like him," complained Charlie. "That Deus guy looks like his steroids do steroids. And Billy says he got that car as a gift. As a gift?" Charlie yelled. "If that's the shit he's used to, he's not just rich, he's crazy-ass, stupid rich. And that's even worse! What I want to know is why these two spoiled brats are hanging around a public school."

Glancing at Josh, Dianna smiled and asked, "Is he always like this?"

"Some days are actually worse than others," admitted Josh.

"I've got another question," Charlie announced. "Why are you here, Imperial?"

"Geez, guy. Calm down. She just came to talk," Josh cried.

"I doubt that," Charlie grimaced. Josh looked to Dianna, but she was completely unfazed by Charlie's behavior. She almost looked amused. "Listen," Charlie told Josh, looking skeptical. "Me and Imperial have been going to school together since around the fifth grade. She never once spoke to me." Turning to Dianna, he snapped, "And I already told you last Wednesday, I deleted the video. So I'm gonna ask you again. What do you want?"

"Okay, since you put it that way, Charlie," Dianna said, looking annoyed, "I came over here with a request."

Charlie looked at Dianna, exasperated, and threw his hands up. "Well, let's hear it."

"I want you to go over by that tree there and pick me a flower and bring it to me." Charlie stared at her in amazement and snorted, "What do you think I am? A damned butler? You're crazy."

"Hold on," Josh said, getting between them. "I'll get it." As he stood up and started walking towards the tree, Josh thought to himself, "Holy cow. They fight like cats and dogs."

"Why do you assume everything is about you?" Josh heard Dianna ask Charlie.

"God," thought Josh. "Why can't Charlie take a hint and leave us alone?" He really just wanted to talk to Dianna, but it felt odd having Charlie around. It made him feel like a Judas if he played one side too heavy. He hoped he didn't get in trouble for doing this.

Marching over to the flower bed, he stopped in front of it and picked the most beautiful flower he could find before walking back. Upon returning, Josh was surprised to see the somber look on Charlie's face. Dianna must have put him in his place, because the wind had definitely left Charlie's sails. Coming up to Dianna, Josh smiled at her and handed her the flower. Taking it, she smiled back. She had the kindest brown eyes he'd ever seen.

And that's when he stopped, and the sound of ringing in his ears became noticeable. Josh wanted to take a breath, but found that he really couldn't do it. He looked over at Charlie for help, but all he got was a blank stare. For a split second, something became totally obvious. Then it was gone just as quickly. Looking back up at Dianna's face, the realization flooded back in.

"Now do you remember?" Dianna smiled.

Josh grinned back. "How long have you known?" Dianna twisted the azalea in front of her smile.

"I was only a hundred percent sure, when Charlie opened his mouth in English class." Josh looked over at Charlie and pointed to Dianna.

"I know. She told me when you went to go get the flower." His voice sounded less than enthused.

"How did you figure it out?" asked Josh, still amazed.

"My dream has two different parts. In the other part, we're older; and you have your necklace on. I don't think I could have figured it out without that. There is no way I could have matched you to your five-year-old face." Shrugging her shoulders, she continued, "Charlie and I have been going to church and school for a long time. Plus, he's one of only a handful of redheads at school. Still, I never in a million years would have thought he was the redhead from the dream. One of the things that I don't understand though, is why I was young in one part and older in the other."

"I don't know. I've never given it much thought. I was five at the time," Josh admitted.

"That's another thing that's odd. I was almost thirteen when I had the dream."

"What?" exclaimed Josh, stunned. "Charlie and I were five." Josh watched as Charlie stood up and brushed off his pants.

"Don't look at me. I totally forgot there was even a girl in the dream, until she reminded me." Josh could hear the cynicism in the redhead's voice. "I mean, all I remembered is me, you and Flynn."

Josh took in a deep breath when he heard the dog's name. "Jesus Christ, Josh. Seriously?" Charlie cried, obviously annoyed. "Don't you even remember your own grandmother's dog was in the dream?"

"It was a long time ago," Josh defended himself. "And the dog in the dream didn't exactly look like Flynn."

"Still," Charlie said, shaking his head in disgust. "He's still a small, white dog. Whatever. I'm done with this. I thought I'd analyzed this dream up and down over the past few years. But just in the past few minutes, I just found out from Imperial here that, even though we all had the same dream, somehow all three of us only remember what we want to. I don't remember her. She didn't remember me. You obviously don't know your ass from a hole in the ground. Maybe I just paid more attention to the dream because, unlike either one of you, it's the only thing that's ever been special in my life. So, if you'll excuse me, I'm going to go beat up the bathroom stall because I've had to throw heat since second period.

And then afterwards, I'm going to drop your silly ass off," he said, pointing at Josh. "And even though I could really use a snack and a nap, I'm going to ignore that feeling because I'm gonna drive across town and punch my therapist in the face!" Charlie said, storming off.

"Please tell me this is one of his bad days," Dianna asked.

"More or less," Josh replied. "I guess, since we grew up together, I just don't notice that much." It was at this time that he did notice that his wish had come true. He wanted Charlie to leave so he could talk to Dianna. Now he couldn't think of a single word to say. She sat there in front of him in silence, smiling. It seemed the more she smiled, the more he wanted to smile. "So, Mr. Michaels," she finally said, "I have a few questions for you."

He chuckled. "Really? Because I've got a few answers, along with a really tall tale of how I do side work protecting the President on the weekends. But I'll keep that one to myself."

Chapter 7
Earth and Sky

"Well, it's official. As of Monday next week, you'll be riding the bus home," announced Charlie, as he sat down at the silver lunch table and ripped into his slice of pizza.

"That's kind of what I thought was gonna happen," replied Josh. "Don't worry though. As soon as I can, I'll take my driving test. I get the Green Machine on my birthday. That's not far away."

"What's up, Imperial?"

"Why does Josh have to take the bus home?" Dianna asked, her curiosity peaked.

"Do you want me to tell the story?" Josh asked. Charlie pulled hot, melting cheese off the corner of his mouth. Josh shook his head. "Because, really, I want nothing to do with this fiasco. There are five witnesses that will place me at the Vatican at the time of the event."

Dianna pushed away her lunch box and leaned in, over the table. "Okay, now I have to hear this. What did you do?" she asked. Charlie threw up a finger while he chewed.

"Well, you know Ms. Hatch?" he started.

"Yeah, she's my girls P.E. teacher."

"Well, for some unknown reason, she was our P.E. teacher today," emphasized Charlie. "And for some reason, she hates me. I'm really not too wild about her, either."

"I don't know about that one, Charlie. I know her pretty well. Somehow I doubt Ms. Hatch sits at home and plots ways to take you down."

"I can pretty much vouch for Charlie on this one. There's no love between them," Josh said, wiping the pizza sauce off his lips with a napkin.

"R-i-g-h-t," Dianna said, as slowly as possible. "The teachers have better things to do, guys. Are you sure it's not because three times a day, every day, since the time I've known you, the phrase 'that's gay' falls out of your mouth to describe stuff you don't like?"

"Whatev," snickered Charlie.

"No, not whatev," Dianna sighed. Ms. Hatch is actually gay, you insensitive idiot.

"ANYWAY," Charlie shouted, cutting off Dianna, "for some reason, Mr. Clark wasn't there, who I actually do hate."

"Are there any teachers you like?" asked the girl.

"Mr. Douglas is kinda pimp, but that's it," he replied. "Mr. Clark is always on my ass."

"If I may," Josh interjected, looking at Dianna. "He runs like he's trying to get dog shit off his shoes."

"I do not!" protested Charlie.

"You do too. You run like you hate the ground. You're the tallest guy in gym class, and you come in dead last every time. I'm just saying."

"Sorry. I'm not a marathon runner. Geez," Charlie whined. "Anyway, dip shit's gone. Hatch has us running laps, which sucks, because we're supposed to be in the air-conditioned gym learning how to wrestle. But it's cool. She was out there running with us, which is more than Clark does. Well, we're running, and she laps. I just happened to notice that she runs pretty fast, seeing as her dick is tucked between her legs."

"Please tell me her nephew, Jeff, isn't in your class," Dianna said, as she tensed up.

"Information that would've been handy during fourth period gym class, Imperial," Charlie said, as he tossed his empty food container away. "So off to the principal I went. Old Deus was sitting in there too, for some reason," Charlie said. Josh nodded.

"He wasn't in English today. I thought he just didn't come to school. I noticed his buddy, Billy, sat alone and kept to himself."

Frowning, Charlie looked at them both, "Starting Monday, I have two weeks of detention."

"Could've been worse," Josh said, as he reached for his second slice.

"Oh, it is," Charlie assured him. "Sometime between now and the end of the year, I have to attend a sensitivity training course."

"Yikes," Josh empathized.

"Not even close," Charlie added. "Extra points if you can guess who the only LGBT instructor in this area is."

"I'll take 'who is Ms. Hatch' for 500," replied Josh. Dianna laughed and opened her bottle of water for a sip. Glancing over at Josh, Dianna winked.

"Needless to say, I've learned my lesson," Charlie muttered, while folding his arms across his chest.

"Excuse me. Would you guys mind if I ate here?" Josh looked up to see Billy standing at the head of the table. Quickly, he glanced at Dianna and Charlie, who, judging by the looks on their faces, were too stunned to speak.

"Sure, go ahead. Have a seat," offered Josh, clearing the table of all the extra trash.

"I really appreciate it," said Billy. "Hey, I know we didn't exactly get off on the right foot Monday," he said looking at Charlie. The redhead shrugged his shoulders but didn't say anything.

"Did you really outrace an avalanche?" asked Josh, hoping to get some satisfaction for Charlie.

Pondering for a second, Billy swayed his head from side to side and confessed, "Maybe I was a lot farther down the hill than I originally let on. I was the first person to head down."

"I knew it," Dianna chimed in, raising her hands in victory.

"It was all a misunderstanding. I told you it would be." Josh chuckled. He figured it was something like that, but he knew it would take a lot more than the admission of guilt to sway Charlie's distrust.

"It's just hard, traveling from town to town," Billy added. "My dad doesn't give me or Deus a say in the matter. He just tells us where we're going, and it's done. Sometimes it's short. Sometimes it's a while. Either way, it's not easy making friends."

"So you'll be here next year?" Charlie butted in.

"No, Oregon. We won't be here past the summer."

"I've got a question," Charlie asked. "Why aren't you guys in private school?"

Billy busted out laughing and slapped the table. My old man was poor as dirt when he grew up. He started Hasden Ambulance Service with two used rigs. He doesn't believe in private school. Besides, we've tried that in the past. Deus and I just don't fit in."

"What's up with your cousin?" whispered Dianna. "He doesn't look too happy, from what I've seen."

Billy looked over both his shoulders and answered, "Don't ever tell him I told you this, but nobody knows who Deus's real dad is. And his mom's all over the place. So my dad stepped in and took him away from her. It was a bad situation, and he's been a little screwed up ever since. I'm only saying this because every town we go to some poor jackass brings it up, and it's a fast pass to the emergency room."

Josh sat up and raised his eyebrows, "I'm glad you told me that."

"Hey, you're from California, right?" Billy asked, nodding at Josh.

"Yeah."

"I've been looking all over for you, Billy." Deus jumped in, sitting down with a thud.

When he did, Josh could feel the bench rise up a little on his side. "Geez this guy is big," he thought.

"The verdict?" Billy inquired, as he finally began to eat his cold, neglected pizza.

"Well, it's kind of like this," Deus put his fingers to his head like he was thinking where to start. "Oh, yeah. I got expelled." Dianna's eyes widened in shock.

"What?" she cried. "I don't think I've ever heard of anybody being expelled from here before." Billy peered at his cousin from over his slice of pizza.

"No big. We'll talk to dad's lawyers tonight." Deus issued a big grin and pointed at Charlie, who was cautiously eyeing him.

"This dude was in the hot seat too," he chuckled. "I overheard what you said. That shit was funny."

Josh watched as the pitbull let out a laugh. He had mixed feelings. He really just wanted to spend some time talking with Dianna. He kind of felt bad for her, because he knew Charlie wouldn't give them space. At least he wouldn't at school, anyway. Even though Josh didn't feel like entertaining, he did want to have more friends than just Charlie. And these guys were a pretty good start, seeing as everybody wanted to meet the two cousins.

Leaning backward and putting his hands behind his head, Charlie nodded toward Deus and asked, "What were you in the principal's office for?"

"Our second period gym teacher, Mr. Clark, was teaching us some wrestling moves. Pretty basic stuff," Deus said. "He knew I had experience, so he asked me to get on the mat and showcase some moves with him. I told him to watch out, because I didn't want to hurt him. So he pointed to the trophy case on the wall. He said half of the trophies were his, and he'd wrestled and beaten the best."

"So you wrestled Mr. Clark?" Josh asked quizzically.

"Oh, yeah," nodded Deus. "He really was as good as he

said he was. Fast too. But I wasn't about to lose to some old has-been, so I threw some Brazilian jujitsu in the mix. I put a reversal on him and submitted him with a rear naked choke."

"Get out!" Charlie screamed, shooting up like a rocket.

"Check this out," Billy said, chuckling and pushing play on his phone. Looking down at the screen, Josh could see two figures on the ground, and hear Billy laughing in the background. "I think he's had enough, Deus." The picture zoomed in on the face of the P.E. teacher, who was wide-eyed and full of desperation, as he reached towards the camera. He wasn't going anywhere though. Deus was behind him and had his legs wrapped around the teacher's torso, while he cut off his air with his huge arms wrapped around his opponent's neck.

"Go to sleep, old man," whispered Deus into Clark's ear, as the gym teacher's face turned blue. Then he went unconscious.

"Oh, God," said Charlie, biting his palm and backing away. "Oh, God," he repeated and walked away like he was walking off a muscle cramp. Josh watched anxiously as the redhead jumped up and down and then finally burst into laughter. "Oh, God," he repeated again, as he strolled back to the lunch table. "Today is like Halloween, Christmas, and my birthday all rolled into one. Please tell me you can send that to me. I want to use the 'go to sleep' part as my ring tone."

Billy chuckled and said, "Give me your digits, bro. It's all yours."

Josh grabbed his phone and typed:

I'M SO SORRY. IT'S USUALLY NOT LIKE THIS. IF I HAD YOUR NUMBER WE COULD TEXT.

He thought about it for a second and held his breath, as he took the phone and slid it across the table towards Dianna. A smile instantly spread across her face, and she nodded. "Finally," thought Josh, exhaling, with a feeling of relief washing over him.

The shrill sound of the bell in the background broke the silence, signifying that lunch was over. Even though lunch didn't turn out the way he planned, at least there was some measure of satisfaction.

As the five of them filed towards the building for fifth period, Josh could feel his phone vibrate. Dianna sent him a text:

> WAS HOPING TO SPEND SOME TIME JUST ME AND YOU SO WE COULD TALK :(BUT HERE'S MY NUMBER AS A DEPOSIT ON FUTURE CONVERSATIONS :)

Josh put a lock on the text. He wanted to keep that one for sure. Leaning over, Josh whispered in her ear, "At least Charlie admitted to learning a valuable lesson today."

"Well, it was a pleasure, guys," Deus said, as he stopped short of the doors. Cramming the remainder of the pizza in his mouth, Billy pounded fists with his cousin.

In a muffled voice, he said, "Pick me up after school. We'll get dinner."

"Anything in particular?" Deus asked.

"I'm thinking pizza," said Billy. "This was okay, but I want better. You know me. I love pizza."

"Not more than me," chuckled Josh. If pizza were a girl I'd marry it." Charlie grabbed Josh's shoulders from behind and kissed him on the cheek.

"Don't you mean, if pizza were a guy, you'd enter into a civil union with it?" Josh wiped his cheek in disgust, as Charlie ran away laughing. Billy started howling hysterically.

Deus laughed, as he walked backwards towards the parking lot and shouted, "I love this guy. He's hilarious."

Feeling his leg vibrate again, Josh took the phone from his pocket. It was another text from Dianna:

> SADLY, DESPITE WHAT HE SAID EARLIER, SOMEHOW, I DON'T THINK CHARLIE WILL EVER LEARN HIS LESSON.

***

"Josh, supper's ready," Claire called from the bottom of the stairs.

"Finally," Josh thought, as he shut down his computer. Immediately upon coming home, Josh felt it would be a good idea to get his room squared away, which was time well spent. The place had a familiar feel to it now. He had his New York Yankees poster up next to his photo of his dad at work. On the other wall, he had a portrait that his grandmother had bought for him two years before. It was two young, black bear cubs climbing up a tree. It was really Josh's personal favorite, because it was half painted and half sketched out.

When he looked at it, he wondered if the artist ever pondered who would buy it and why. If they did, Josh figured the likelihood that a grandmother would buy it for her grandson because his nickname was "Little Bear" was probably low on the list. Now that his sixteenth birthday was coming up, he was really trying to break his mom and grandmother from using the nickname; at least in public. It was almost odd to Josh how he could love the name so much as a child, but become almost embarrassed of it in such a short span of time.

As he ambled down the stairs, taking them two at a time, he couldn't help but think to himself how he was subtly changing. The change was slow enough that he didn't notice all the time, but he could look at his face and see his facial structure was a lot manlier than it was last year. Was something within him slowly affecting his thoughts as well? It was highly evident to Josh every summer that he came here how Charlie had markedly changed, and not just in height and looks. The paranoia and general distrust that he displayed towards other people grew with each passing year. Josh could remember when he wasn't really like this. With that in mind, he wondered what changes were coming his way. And would it stop at just outgrowing childhood things, or would he be a completely different person five years from now? He hoped not. He kind of liked who he was.

Strolling into the kitchen, Josh took in the aroma of steak and potatoes. It smelled amazing. It was hard to sit upstairs and finish his homework, while he could smell the grilling his grandfather was doing in the backyard. But he fought through the temptation. Sam was cutting up garlic bread at the kitchen counter. All in all, it looked like tonight was going to be good eats.

"How was school today?" his grandmother asked, walking up with the pot of whipped potatoes. She carefully set them down next to the dish of butter on the table.

Shrugging his shoulders and taking a seat, Josh replied, "I don't know. Okay, I guess. Charlie got sent to the principal's office."

"That's not too surprising," noted Claire.

"You should meet some new people your age, honey," Sam pointed out.

"It's in the works already, mini-Mom," Josh joked. "It was nice of Claire to give you a footstool, so you could cut the bread."

"That's the fastest way to dish duty," Sam came back.

"Okay, okay. You're tall," Josh chuckled. His mom and grandmother both were in their sweats already. He wondered if they'd even left the house today. He'd noticed that, over the past four days, his mom and grandparents had been doing an awful lot of secret glances while they were all watching TV together. They also left the room at odd intervals to talk privately.

Josh didn't see the need for all the secrecy. All they had to do was ask him what he wanted for his birthday. He figured now would be as good a time as any to bring it up. "My birthday is right around the corner," Josh said slyly, looking at both the women to gauge their response.

"Yup, right around the corner," his mom agreed.

"I'm just going to throw this out there. Do you guys want me to make a wish list?" His mom shook her head.

"You already know your grandparents are giving you the Green Machine. And I already ordered your gift online and had it shipped here."

"Really?" Josh asked, surprised.

The sliding glass door beside Josh opened. The next thing he knew, Flynn was trying to jump in his lap. "Ribeyes are done," Larry announced, walking in with the hot platter of steaks.

"Don't worry. Your birthday's taken care of," Claire said, wiping her hands on the dishtowel.

"I don't mean to pry," said Josh cautiously. "But if you guys weren't having all these secret talks about my birthday, then what were they about?" Claire looked over to Sam and then Josh. The boy could feel an uneasy tension in the room. Everybody was looking at him, but nobody was saying anything. Even Larry seemed at a loss for words. Josh looked at his mother. "What's going on here?"

After a moment's silence, Claire finally spoke. "We need to have a talk, Josh." He could tell by looking at the faces of Larry and Sam this wasn't going to be a casual chat.

"Okay, lay it on me."

His grandmother paused for a second, "Your mother mentioned that, as of late, you've been exhibiting some peculiar talents."

"What the hell was with everybody lately?" thought Josh. Couldn't anybody keep a secret anymore? "You told!" he said, staring at his mother in disbelief. "I thought you said to keep this between us. We agreed that nobody else would understand. Claire walked up behind Sam, putting her hands on her shoulders.

"Don't blame your mother. If what she said is true, then Charlie knows as well. God knows who else knows." Josh could see his mother was visibly uncomfortable.

"Well, I guess we can heat these up later," Larry said. He walked over and covered the plate of steaks with tin foil before setting the plate on the counter. Claire wiped her hands on the dishtowel once more and walked past Josh, towards the living room.

"Follow me," she called back. "It's time you got some answers." Josh watched as his mother and Larry filed out behind her. He walked to the living room to find they'd all sat down in the usual TV watching positions. Larry was in the recliner. Claire and Sam were side-by-side on the couch. His grandmother was opening a box of old photographs that had been on the floor. Josh sat down on the small footstool she usually used to prop her feet up. "Take a look at these," she said, handing him a small stack of photos.

Josh looked at them all. "These look like dad is maybe fourteen. The others are maybe you, I guess."

"Good guess, but hardly rocket science," his grandmother said. "The one thing in common with them is they were all taken at the time when our power started to manifest."

"What did you say?" Josh stammered in disbelief. He had to be asleep. His grandmother would never utter something so insane.

Claire looked at him and replied, "I know it's hard to believe, but you come from one of the strongest bloodlines under the vault of Heaven. We carry within us the power to do what most people consider supernatural or miraculous."

Josh was flabbergasted. He couldn't shut his mouth right now, even if he tried. It had fallen to the floor, when his grandmother said she had superpowers. This couldn't be real. Josh looked his grandfather and then his mom, "This is a joke, right?"

"This is no joke, Josh. I'm telling you the truth. By the time I was your age, I already figured out how to leave my body while I slept, and how to make my dog talk."

"What the hell, Nana?" Josh shouted as he stood up. "Why are you doing this?"

"If you can do all the things your mother claims you can do, why is it so hard to believe other people can as well? Is there some reason you'd think you're so special? Because I'll tell you right now; you shouldn't have powers." Claire looked over at Flynn. Automatically, the terrier sprung from Larry's lap. He jumped up on the couch with a blank look in his eye. "Oh, Flynn, my little boy. You believe me; don't you?" Claire asked the dog, nodding her head.

"I sure do. I love you," Flynn answered back. Josh stared in amazement. It sounded almost like a person who was talking while they were yawning. Not all the syllables were there, but Josh completely understood what the dog was saying.

"How did you do that?" the boy asked, looking at the dog's blank stare.

"There's really nothing to it," admitted Claire, with a look of satisfaction spreading across her face. "It's a parlor trick. My will is stronger than his, as are my brain waves. It's no more difficult than switching somebody else's TV on with a master controller or overriding your car stereo with the signal from your phone."

Josh sat down, kind of dazed. "How is this possible?" he asked, shaking his head.

"I can't tell you this stuff yet. I'm sorry," Claire said, shaking her head. "All I can say is don't make plans for Friday night."

"Why?"

"A woman is coming over. She's going to test you to see what your talents are, if you have any at all," his grandmother said.

"I can do stuff," Josh retorted.

I've been watching you all week, honey. Even I'm perplexed," sighed Claire. She looked at Josh's mom and Larry. "We've all been watching you, Josh. I've never seen anything like you in all my years. You seem to create things while you're speaking."

"I know," he said, "but it's no big deal. I mean, hell, you just made your dog talk. I want to learn how to do that."

"If you knew how the universe really worked, you'd know that what you can do is infinitely harder. But what we need to do is figure out how you have powers, and what they really are. From there, we can figure if you should be trained."

"If?" Josh said in amazement. "It's obvious I have power."

"Yes, 'if,'" his grandmother repeated. "Forgive the crass analogy, but down the street there's a woman I play bridge with once a month. She has twins, a boy and a girl."

"Yeah, they go to school with me. They're seniors," said Josh.

"So if the daughter has a vagina, and the boy has a penis, shouldn't they have sex?" Claire asked her grandson.

"OOH, hell, no! That would be totally wrong on too many levels."

"Exactly. Just because you can doesn't always mean you should, Josh. I can't tell if reality is following your prompts, in which case you'd have power that needs training so that you don't hurt yourself and, more importantly, others."

"Or?" Josh added.

"Or," Claire continued, "if you're a low-level psychic, and your increased awareness is just filtering out information that's streaming around you. In that case, you won't be trained."

"Why not?" asked Josh. "Even that seems pretty impressive."

"To some, I guess. But the secrets of the universe and how it really works is a heavy burden to carry," the woman said, looking at the dog. As if in response, the dog shivered and then came to life, jumping off Claire's lap and walking back towards Larry. "The training, just like a medication for an illness, is only given once a qualified person decides that the benefit outweighs the risk. Do you understand?"

"I guess," Josh said, turning towards his mother. Josh asked, "Did you know about this? I mean Nana and dad having powers?"

Sam let out a big sigh. "Yes, Josh, I did."

"Why didn't you tell me?" Josh shouted, beginning to get angry. "All this time, you acted like he was normal. You pretended not to know what was happening to me!"

"Watch your tone, Josh," Sam snapped back, tears rolling down her cheeks. "I really didn't know what to do. What you do is different than what your dad showed me. He was the nicest, most caring man I've ever met. But he was also complicated. There were things he had to deal with that, as a wife, I really couldn't help with. I felt hopeless, Josh. And it was hard enough doing it with him. I decided that, if I had a choice, I sure as hell wasn't going to go through it with you, if I could help it. I'm not going to lie. When your abilities surfaced, the part of me," Sam said, choking on the last word, "the part that still bears the scars hoped, if we ignored it, it would just go away. But it never did," she said, shaking her head.

Josh was floored. He'd never seen his mother so hurt before. She looked at him and tried to speak, but nothing else came out. Larry got up from the recliner and walked over to his daughter-in-law, putting his arm around her. Oddly enough, all that Josh could manage was to stare. He somehow felt disconnected. It pained him to see his mom like this. At the same time, there was a fury inside of him, a part of him that wanted to scream at the top of his lungs. This was his father. There were important things about him that she had hidden. And because she did, Josh knew he had been hurt as a result.

"Why? How could you hide this from me?" He looked at his grandparents, and his mom. He knew that somehow, something had just changed inside of him.

"Dear, would you take Sam to bed?" Claire asked.

Larry nodded. "I will. C'mon, Flynn, let's get her to bed." The dog got up and followed them both, as they left the room. Josh looked back into his grandmother's eyes. He knew there was nothing but concern on her face, but he didn't feel like any more conversation.

"If you have questions, I'll answer them," she said quietly.

"I have questions," admitted Josh, sighing and looking at his grandmother. "Like what are your powers? What were dad's powers?" Josh paused, trying not to get emotional. "And how did they fail to save his life, when he needed them most?" Josh sniffled and wiped away the tear from his cheek. "How could my mom arbitrarily hide the truth, when she has memories of him, and I don't? Yes, I have questions. But I think I'd really just like to go to bed right now."

Claire silently nodded at her grandson, "I understand. I dropped a lot on you. I can't imagine how you must feel." Josh looked at his grandmother through teary eyes. He had no words. He wished he had a response. Instead, he reached over and grabbed the remote to the TV and pushed the on button. As the picture snapped to life, it was an '80s movie that Josh had seen before. He watched as a cruel, older brother taunted the younger twins, a boy and a girl. He'd just told them the truth about Santa Claus. In their living room was a TV, and on it was the old Santa Claus is Coming to Town special.

As it played, Josh looked at his grandmother and said, "I just realized how much dad looked like the young version of Santa Claus." Josh nodded to the photo of his dad in his turnouts and black boots and black belt, his strawberry blonde hair looked exactly like the figure on the TV. Claire gasped and put her hand up to her mouth. Josh swallowed. He didn't like the idea of his grandmother seeing him cry at this age, but he couldn't hide his pain. "Part of me wishes I could forget the talk we had earlier. Thing is, once you know the truth about Santa Claus, you can never go back." Josh turned around and said goodnight to his grandmother and trudged up the stairs to his room. As he did, only one thought looped in his mind, "Touché, Charlie, touché."

***

"This Cardona's place has a really good atmosphere," Bill mentioned, while he surveyed the room. It was decorated in the rustic Italian motif. Wine bottles of every genre were displayed. The smells of Italian food flooded the restaurant. What Hasden really liked was that the booths were semi-private, and it would give him and Deus some time to plot their next move while they ate.

"Why are you avoiding the subject?" snapped Deus, looking obviously irritated. Hasden folded his old liver-spotted hands and put them on the table, letting out a sigh.

"I'm thinking!" he exclaimed. "Something you rarely do, Deus." Hasden knew he couldn't blame Deus for his narrow-mindedness. Even though he was a king of Hell, he was still in the lower end of the royal scale. His dominion resided over animal attraction, brute force, and sexual perversion, which, albeit important, Hasden knew it was only a tool to winning. That's where Bill's talents came in. "That's why I'm the head of the Monarchy and not you," he pointed out.

Pouring another glass of wine, Deus, obviously angered, replied, "As the Creator lives and breathes, that boy Josh is the child of Alex Michaels."

"I know," Hasden hissed, glancing around the large dining

hall to see if Deus was making a scene. He was on his fourth bottle already, and they hadn't even gotten their pizzas yet.

"What's even worse," continued Deus, "is he can obviously bend, which is impossible. But it's obvious that, between him and Charlie, there's no contest over who contacted who for the dream. We should be calling a meeting to discuss this."

"Absolutely not," said Bill. "The last thing we need is to call a meeting, because then news of this little situation is going to spread over to the Crown. And the last thing we need here in Milton is a throng of angels."

"I see what you're saying," admitted Deus, swirling the wine in his glass, "However, this boy shouldn't be here. He's all the way from California. And to make matters worse, his grandmother is that obnoxious bitch, Claire." Hasden reached over the table, taking the bottle of wine over to his side. He shot a glance over to the bartender, as he drug his hand across his neck to let him know that the wine should be cut off. "Slow down the wine," he warned the bartender. Then, looking over to Deus, he smiled.

"I know you're worried, but Claire's relatively inactive. We haven't heard from her since her son's death."

"I'm just saying, I really can't think of anybody who gave the Monarchy more grief than that holy terror! Her son was a pain in the ass too. And now her grandson is here, and he's blocking us from doing our job. We came here to tempt the Imperial girl."

Hasden knew what Deus was saying. It was true. He looked up at the trellis system the designers had hung off the ceiling. It was elaborate. There were vines woven through the wooden trellis, and in each corner there was a thick cluster of fake grapes. He gently reached up and grabbed on to one of the grapes. Rolling it towards Deus, he said, "It's almost ironic that Milton is known for the Diana grape. It makes an incredible wine into an extraordinary wine. I can already tell this girl's no bender. She's an avatar. I could tell from the moment she didn't take the bait, like the nice clothes and the Bentley."

Deus nodded, "I agree. Every other girl at school is in a tizzy over the expensive stuff, but she's barely said one word to us."

"So this is what we're going to do," Hasden said, setting his jaw and narrowing his eyes. "We'll use the redhead, Charlie. I haven't figured where Josh gets his powers from yet, but the redhead will be easier to influence than Alex's son."

Deus looked up at Hasden. "There's a slim possibility the power came to him through inheritance, when his father died." Hasden nodded.

"I've already thought of that myself. It's possible some of Alex's powers migrated to Josh, but that usually only manifests in low-level psychic abilities. Josh can dream bend. So we know it's not that. What I'm thinking is," continued Hasden, dipping his bread in the balsamic vinegar, "for whatever reason, Josh's subconscious made the connection joining the two boys. I don't know what the dream was, but for that reason alone, Josh won't abandon the redhead. Because let's face it, the two of them are like Frick and Frack. They blend about as well as this oil and vinegar on my plate." Hasden dipped another cube of bread and popped it in his mouth.

"Josh ain't going anywhere without Charlie, and Dianna doesn't look like she'd go anywhere without Josh," agreed Deus, nodding his head. "I saw them texting during lunch."

"I did too. That's why we take our time and work our way into the group. I'll call Mahvet tomorrow and let her know we're going to be here for a little while longer. I'll have her delegate our duties to the other board members."

"You're not going to mention Michaels, are you?" Deus asked, as he swallowed down the last of the wine.

Hasden snorted, "Of course not. If Mahvet knew, she'd be here tomorrow poking her nose in where it doesn't belong. You know her history with Alex."

Deus laughed, "Yes, I do." He motioned towards the waitress, "More wine."

Hasden sighed, "Try and show some moderation." Somberly, he looked down at the red and white tablecloth. How much like a chessboard it was. "How appropriate," he thought, that it mirrored the school's colors. Because now that he knew that the girl couldn't be swayed by shiny things, he was going to have to play chess. And nobody could control the board like him.

"Who had the supreme with extra meat?" asked the waitress, holding two pizzas.

"That would be me," Deus said. He held his arms out as though, if she threw it, he would catch it.

"Then the pepperoni and mushroom?"

"That's mine," Hasden replied with a smile. This is what he'd been waiting for, and it didn't look like it would disappoint. He took a moment to drink it all in. Over the years, he had dined at some of the most famous restaurants in the world and tasted intricate concoctions that stunned his palette. Still, he had to admit that nothing pleased him like a good pizza.

"I got a question," said Deus, as he lifted the steamy slice up to his mouth. "If Josh becomes a problem, can I kill him?" Hasden thought about it for a second, as he spread open his napkin.

"I don't see why not. After all, you killed his father."

Chapter 8
Crossroads

"I can't help it!" cried Charlie. "I have restless mouth syndrome." Dianna let out a groan and shook her head. Trying to reason with Charlie was like trying to run a three-legged race with a corpse.

"All she's saying," added Josh, "is that you don't have to swear so much."

"Thank you for throwing that in, Captain Obvious. What's your next revelation?" Charlie snapped. "Maybe that, if my sister had a dick, she'd be my brother."

"Just lovely," thought Dianna. Out of all the residents of this town, how did Josh become friends with this immature chucklehead?

"Imperial," Charlie said, swiveling in the desk chair towards her. "I swear so much because it makes me happy. And I have very little in this godforsaken life to be happy about. Besides, it's not like I'm doing it to offend you."

"Whatever. It's not like it's any skin off my nose," Dianna said. "I was just pointing out that sooner or later, God help us, you will be an adult. And other adults in higher stations of life, like possible future employers, view it as an indicator of how intelligent you are."

"Cool, I can dig," Charlie replied, shrugging his shoulders. "I'm not changing, though."

"What's up?" Billy said, as he walked up.

Dianna noticed his clothes were more toned down and less flashy this morning. Today he hadn't been as cocky as he had in the past week. She wondered if it had anything to do with the fact that Deus wasn't here. Maybe he was laying low. In English, he'd strolled right up and sat down with them like he'd known them forever. That kind of familiarity annoyed her. She was far from unfriendly, but she usually kept to herself. She liked being near Josh, but with him it seemed different. It felt like she couldn't get enough of him. In fact, there was very little she didn't like about him, except for the fact that he rode the fence on a lot of issues between her and Charlie. She kind of wanted him to take a firmer stance. Dianna wasn't a big fan of being wishy-washy, even though she knew Charlie was a key player in the dream too, which they still hadn't sat down and talked about.

"Hey, did I happen to mention I went to Cardona's last night?" Billy said. as he sat down.

Josh smiled, "We're going there for my birthday coming up."

"Dude, the food there is so good," chuckled Charlie. "You better take me with you."

"If I were you, I'd start kissing Claire's ass then, because she's making the list."

"What did you order?" asked Charlie.

Billy grinned, "The pizza. I told you guys I was going to yesterday. The pizza at lunch was just an appetizer."

"Holy shit, guy," shrieked Charlie, looking shocked. "You know they have really good food there, right? Going to Cardona's and just getting the pizza is like going to a whorehouse to get a hug. There's better stuff on the menu."

"Oh, Lord," Dianna thought. "Give me strength.

Mr. Douglas sat at his desk waiting for the final warning bell, and then he moved to the center of the room. "Yesterday we finished up our study on the Civil War. You all turned in your papers, and I'm pleased at the overall results." Dianna watched Mr. Douglas as he paced the classroom. He was one of the few teachers she had that she actually wondered why he wasn't teaching at a university. "I'd like to point out one essay in particular that stood out above everybody else's. Josh, would you mind if I read a small portion?" He immediately looked up, surprised.

"Um, I guess you could read it, if you want."

"Thank you, but I just want to touch on the summary," Mr. Douglas replied. "We have a new chapter to get into." He promptly sat down on the stool in the middle of the class and held the paper up in front of him. "Mr. Michaels wrote, and I quote:

> In my opinion, it's too hard to even guess what really happened in the events that led up to the Civil War. This week, as I read through different accounts of what other people's opinions were, one theme was constant: slavery. It was a driving wedge among the Union and the Confederacy. But no matter what I read online and out of the text, I know that these are just the popular opinions of those who had a voice. So I wondered, what about the accounts that weren't heard? I can only imagine that each side felt they were doing what was right. So I won't point fingers at who was right or wrong. I will say that I'm glad that, in a time when there was open bigotry and selfishness, there was also courage and sacrifice. I'm glad that, in a time before we were famous for being the land of the free and the home of the brave, we had heroes who weren't afraid to take a stand, when everyone was ordered to sit and be silent. As a teenager who wasn't there and didn't experience these things, all I can say is America was young.
>
> I'd like to think that seven hundred and fifty thousand people didn't die on their own soil just as senseless bloodshed. Instead, I'd like to point out that, like in childbirth, America was in pain. Emotions were high, and the time was chaotic. However, at the end of those four years of suffering, the blood and tears delivered a people who were once confined and shackled into freedom. In my opinion, the freed slaves were Lady Liberty's

firstborn. I won't go into where we've been since then, because every child is fragile when it's young. There are few things that aren't threatening to a newborn. Thankfully, in my time, the African-American culture is no longer an adolescent but a strong, proud adult who is somehow different in its identity as an individual. Yet, if you look closer, you can tell that the child grew up with its mother's eyes.

That, students, is what I was hoping each of you would learn," Mr. Douglas said, setting down the paper. He looked out over all the students.

"History has been a passion of mine for a while. Unfortunately, the one thing I learned after years of study was that the more you research something you love, the more you find that the truth is a point of view. There were kings, queens, and pharaohs who rewrote history to their liking. That's where the saying of the victor writes the history books came from." Dianna looked from Josh to her teacher, and she could tell that both of them were on the same page. She wasn't surprised about Josh's paper. She knew he was intelligent, and he'd read it to her the night before.

"Josh, I just want to ask if there's anything else you want to add that may have been left out of your paper? Is there anything you learned that you didn't include?"

Josh thought for a second and then stood up, nodding. "Yes, yes, there is, Mr. Douglas. When I wrote the report, I left out how, before I did my research, I was under the illusion that slavery ended with the Civil War. I didn't know that slavery is not only still around today, but that the numbers are larger now than they've ever been."

"That's right," the teacher said, crossing over to place the paper back in the stack of reports. He leaned up against his desk. "The road from slavery was rocky, to say the least. An unknown number of slaves had nowhere to go and no job in order to feed their families. But, with a lot of effort, these things were changed. In our lifetime, we were able to see the first Black president. It may seem that, to your generation, slavery is gone; but it's not. Now, I don't mean to upset you guys. However I wouldn't be lying if I said that, while you were watching your favorite reality TV show last night, at that same moment anywhere across the globe a girl or a boy is being sold into sexual slavery. These children face a life so gruesome it's frightening. Then after they're of no more use, they're discarded. Their lives will never be like yours. I'm not making light of the subject, but bullying is the least of their problems.

"And remember, I'm not saying this to upset you." The teacher reiterated, "But you are getting old enough that you should know that we have won a victory by being who we are, living in America. But don't ever think we won the war, and our labors are over. Because they're not. After you leave high school, some of you will go to college; and some of you won't. But, whatever happens, if you stood here in this class and you heard my voice, you have an obligation to pick up the torch that I'm laying at your feet. That is, if you can. In his paper, Josh likened the freed slaves to the firstborn children of Lady Liberty. Maybe, with your help, in the future there can be many more. Now let's move on to the next chapter."

As class ended and the sound of excited teens filled the room, Josh rushed through his history book, marking down the pages he had to read for that night. "Hey, everybody, why don't we go get some coffee?" suggested Billy.

"I'm down," replied Vivian. "Maybe after that, we can all go swimming at my place. Tonight's my mom's bunko night with the girls, and my dad works late. And we have a hot tub."

"That's an excellent idea," said Charlie, grinning from ear to ear.

Standing up, Billy grabbed his book bag and said, "Then it's settled. You're in, right, Dianna?"

"I'll go to coffee, if Josh does. Other than that, I've got a ton of reading to do."

"I'm sorry, guys," Josh groaned. "I've got a mountain of homework so big I'll need hiking boots and a Sherpa just to climb it." He felt bad, but the reality was he had fallen behind in his studies after finding out about his family secret.

"Listen Michaels," whispered Charlie as he leaned in, "Don't mess this up for me. I finally have a chance to talk to Vivian. If you're my friend, you'll do this." Josh didn't want to cave in to Charlie's request, but the look on his face was desperate. Looking over Charlie's shoulder, Josh could see Dianna smiling at him.

"Come on, Josh. Just a quick coffee," she said.

"Okay. Alright," Josh relented.

"Yes!" Charlie said quietly, as he pumped his fist. The whole group gathered their stuff up and made their way to the door.

"Josh, could I have a moment of your time?" Mr. Douglas called.

"Sure." Josh answered, stepping towards the teacher's desk. "Hey, guys, I'll meet up with you. Which coffee house are you going to?"

"We're not going anywhere without you," Billy answered back. "We'll be waiting by the cars."

"Yeah, but hurry," urged Charlie, as he walked out the door.

Josh walked over to Mr. Douglas's desk and set his backpack down. "Is everything okay?" he asked. Mr. Douglas sat in his chair, smiling.

"Of course it is. I just wanted to ask you what your goals are for the next few years. Are you planning on going to college?"

"I'm not too sure, Mr. Douglas. If I do, my grandparents would have to pay for it. I don't really want to put them in that position, seeing as me and my mom are living with them and they're giving me a car for my birthday and all."

"I understand," the teacher said, nodding his head. "It's just that you're a bright student. I'd hate to see you miss out on your chance. There are plenty of grants and loans. I'd be happy to write a recommendation for you."

"Really?"

Swiveling his chair and standing up, Mr. Douglas replied, "Of course. You have a unique ability, Josh. You can take in information and make a non-biased opinion of it. I know you're interested in the fire department because of your father, and I'm sure you'd be happy there. But you also could be a great leader in whatever community you decide to live in. As great a nation as we live in, we still have poverty, people who are utterly broken, and children who are lost. To climb out of these tough times and to keep America great, we need men and women who can lead by example. I believe, Josh, that you could do that."

He was completely stunned. "Thanks, Mr. Douglas. I might just take you up on the offer."

"I'm glad to hear that. Now get out of here," chuckled Mr. Douglas, as he stroked his goatee. "Your friends are waiting on you." Josh smiled and grabbed his bag.

"I'll see you tomorrow."

As Josh exited the classroom and walked down the hall, his thoughts were centered on what Mr. Douglas had just said. His teacher was right. His primary interest in the fire department and paramedicine was fueled by his family's background. On occasion, he'd even thought of following Larry's footsteps and becoming a trauma doctor. He'd never really considered anything else.

Josh cut across campus, making his way to Gile Road, where Billy and Charlie had parked. It looked overcast, but it wasn't cool at all. He was wearing just his black tee shirt and jeans, and he was fine. Milton seemed cooler when he first moved here.

His body was either getting used to it, or it could be that summer wass getting closer every day. Just thinking of what this summer would bring made him smile. He had a new life, with new friends. Of course, there was also Dianna.

He grinned just thinking about her, and being able to do stuff this summer without being chained to schoolwork. Since he'd gotten her number, they talked only once, but texted every day. He already planned to get his license as soon as possible. Then he'd take Dianna out on a date, where he could really impress her. Josh knew that she liked him as much as he liked her. He also knew that, as beautiful as she was, there was bound to be some competition. He really didn't want to deal with that.

From the moment Josh stepped onto Gile, he could tell something was wrong. He picked up his pace, anxious to see what was going on. He could hear shouting and then a scream. "Dianna!" Breaking from a jog to a sprint, Josh cleared the line of cars parked on the road and saw Billy on the ground. Some guy wearing a leather biker vest and a white tee shirt was standing menacingly over him. Josh had never seen him before.

Next to them, Josh could see two other guys, who were both dressed the same way. They were posturing on Charlie, who had his arms up, doing his best to protect the girls. Josh dropped his book bag and ran as fast as he could towards the group. There really wasn't any time for Josh to consider the fact that he'd never been in a fight before or that he was outnumbered. All he knew was these guys didn't look like they were friendly.

Using his momentum, Josh threw his weight forward, crashing into the two guys in front of Charlie. As he did, he shoved as hard as he could. All three of them tumbled down to the pavement. For a split second, Josh could feel the ground biting through the skin on his elbow. He paid it no mind, as he shot up and shouted, "What the hell is going on here?"

"Well, what do we have here?" said the biker who was

standing over Billy. Josh could see that, other than Billy being skinned up and scared, he looked okay. "Stay there on your back, bitch. If you move, I swear I'll cut you," the biker screamed at the spiky-haired teen on the ground.

"Watch out, Josh," warned Charlie.

"Your buddy here," the biker said, pointing to Billy still lying on the ground, "cut me off yesterday. I didn't have a choice, except to lay my bike down. Dip shit didn't even stop. He just kept driving. Then when I finally caught up to him at the stoplight to ask for his insurance, his gorilla of a friend in the passenger seat flipped me the bird."

"Geez, Louise," thought Josh. "Way to go Billy."

"Watch out behind you!" screamed Dianna. Josh barely moved fast enough to avoid the fist that flew past his head. He dove forward into a front handspring, flipping over and landing right next to the bikes, just as Charlie was slammed down on the ground by one of the biker's friends wearing a bandanna.

"Well, what do you want us to do about it?" Josh screamed, as he eyed the two bikers coming towards him. Even though he was inexperienced at fighting, Josh began to feel his anger rising.

"Once we spotted the car, we figured we'd just wait here and beat the money out of him."

"Listen, guys. You can have the car. Just take off and go," screamed Billy, lying on his back, shaking.

"Shut up!" screamed the biker, turning and kicking the car door. Josh looked over at Dianna. He could see she was terrified, but she held her book bag out like she was ready to swing it at any second.

"So what do you want?" he asked again. The biker and his buddy who had just swung on Josh, laughed at him.

"Well, we really don't want this douche's money, or his car, for that matter. But we will take his girlfriends for a spin."

That was all it took. Josh could feel a rage welling up

inside of him like he had never known before. Above him, thunder crashed directly overhead. It sounded like two mountains crashing into each other. Josh looked upwards, as dark clouds rolled overhead. He dropped his gaze down and spoke. "I was really hoping you wouldn't say that, because now I'm going to have to kick your asses." He looked over at Charlie, who was pinned to the ground. Bandanna had mounted his chest and had his knees on top of Charlie's arms. Charlie was trying to buck him, but he had no leverage.

"Hey, Zeke," bandanna yelled from on top of Charlie. The girl with the book bag is the one from the newspaper."

"Well, right on, Marv. It just so happens I've got something in my pants she can heal." At that moment, Josh could feel something snap inside of him. He couldn't explain it, but he felt like he was vibrating as he stepped forward. In a guttural voice he screamed, "SHE'S FIFTEEN, YOU SICK BASTARD!" Immediately, the two bikers stopped like they'd hit a wall. Josh clenched both of his fists and glared at them filled with fury. Then they both fell to the ground, pale as ghosts.

One was lying on his side, sweating. The other was on his knees, clutching his stomach. "All of a sudden, I feel like shit," he mumbled, drooling on the ground. The sound of thunder crashed over and over, as the light seemed to dim all around them. But Josh didn't pay any mind to the fact that the sun was obscured, and the light seemed to be sucked into him like a black hole. All Josh could think was how much he hated these three men. He could feel his face contorted in anger, when he turned to the one, trembling biker sitting on Charlie's chest. He uttered, "Run, or Die. Your choice." The stunned man rolled off Charlie and quickly walked around Josh with his hands up, as if the boy were holding a gun to his head.

"Hey, man, it's cool. I'm just gonna grab my buddies, and we're out of here." Josh's eyes never left them, as they slowly made their way towards the motorcycles. The biker with the damaged bike looked horrible, but not so bad that he couldn't flip Josh off as he rolled down the street. It was only then that Josh realized he was breathing heavily and through his gritted teeth, no less. He looked up in amazement, as the darkness dispersed as quickly as it had gathered.

"It's safe. You can get up, Billy. It's over," Dianna yelled, coming up and throwing her arms around Josh. She pulled him into her. Josh's nose was filled with the sweet smell of her hair, draining what remained of the anger that had consumed him only seconds before. Josh grabbed onto her, as relief washed over him.

"Holy cow," he thought. He couldn't believe only one minute had passed between the possibility of getting beaten half to death and standing here victorious, holding Dianna.

"That was so dope!" Charlie screamed at the top of his lungs. "Oh my God, Josh." Charlie and Vivian were now in on the hug as well. Josh chuckled nervously, as Charlie grabbed him and jumped up and down.

"Okay, okay, big guy. Put me down," Josh pleaded. With his feet firmly on the ground, Josh looked at everybody. Did that really just happen? Even though she was smiling, tears continued to cascade down Vivian's face. "Are you okay?" Josh asked her, concerned.

She shook her head. "I can't process this," she sobbed. I know I should be happy because we're safe, and things could've ended badly." She trailed off, took a deep breath, and swallowed. "But I just saw something that I know shouldn't be possible." She looked up at Josh. "You said those guys were sick, and they got sick. The sky got dark, Josh, and your voice even. I can hear it right now in my head, and it won't stop." Charlie grabbed her just as she started to fall down.

"Vivian, are you okay?" asked Dianna. "Let's get her to the Jeep, Charlie." Josh watched as Vivian completely unraveled in front of him. He knew she was having a nervous breakdown. He'd seen it before. What completely dumbfounded him was that she was right. He'd never actually used any measure of power on anybody in that manner before. An involuntary shiver went up his spine, when he thought about what she said about his voice at the time when he told the biker to run. He'd said it like he was granting him some mercy. Josh, himself, wondered what would have happened if the biker had laughed and spit in his face.

"I shouldn't think of this," Josh thought, forcing the dark images from his head, as he walked towards Billy. "Are you okay?" Josh asked, hoping Billy was in one piece.

"I'm a little scraped up from hitting the ground," groaned Billy, as he rotated his right arm around to see the damage. "We were just walking to the car. Next thing I knew, this angry guy comes up, screaming how I'm a rich little pussy and what was I going to do without my bodyguard." Billy shook his head. "I didn't even have enough time to throw my hands up. He just hit me in the jaw with the side of his elbow."

"That must've been before the scream I heard. I immediately recognized it was Dianna and came running."

"It's a good thing you did," explained Billy. "Who knows what would've happened. When the guy told me to lay down or he'd slit my throat, I thought I was a goner."

"So you never looked up or saw anything?" asked Josh.

"No, not really."

"Did you know your door's dented pretty bad?"

"I saw it," Billy said, shrugging his shoulders. "I hate to be a downer, but I just remembered I have something I have to do. Apologize to everybody for me. I'm gonna have to skip on coffee."

"I don't think anybody's going anywhere but home," Josh chuckled.

The spiky-haired boy inspected his car door and frowned. "Who knows? I'm thinking I might take a mental health day tomorrow. We'll see."

"Cool. I'll see you when I see you," Josh said, as Billy got in the car and closed the dented driver's side door.

"Good. That's one less thing to worry about," thought Josh, as he walked back to the Jeep. He was surprised as all get out when he walked up. Not only was Charlie holding Vivian's hand as she laid in the passenger seat, but Dianna was sitting in the back of the Jeep, healing her. Josh had to do a double take. He'd never actually seen Dianna do this. Here they were out in public, during broad daylight.

Dianna was stroking the girl's head while repeating, "You're safe. You're fine." It was incredible how brilliant the light was. It fluctuated between white, gold, and pink, all at the same time.

"You know she's glowing, right?" Josh pointed out in a casual manner as he hung his right hand on Charlie's shoulder.

"Captain Obvious strikes again," Charlie said, smiling.

"I wouldn't have done this, but she was in bad shape," Dianna explained.

"Really, guys, I'm okay now," Vivian said, smiling. "I still remember what happened. For some reason, I really just don't care anymore though. I just want to go home now."

"Fine by me," Dianna said, jumping out of the back of the old Jeep. Josh was surprised by Dianna's resiliency. For a quiet, little church girl, she handled the past fifteen minutes amazingly well. While Vivian, who was used to being loud and the center of attention, had folded under the pressure.

"What are you thinking?" Dianna asked, grabbing her book bag.

"Thinking about it," Josh decided to sidestep the observation. "Never mind. How about you let me walk you home?" Josh asked.

"My virtue defended, and an offer to be escorted home? A

girl could get used to this,"
Dianna teased, throwing her backpack onto her shoulder.

"Hey, I'll run Vivian home. Just text me when you guys are tired of walking," Charlie said, as he fired up the Jeep's engine.

"Don't worry," Josh said, as Dianna put her hand in his. "We'll be fine," he smiled.

Chapter 9
Center of the Universe

"How do you feel now?" Dianna asked.

"Decidedly better," Josh said, looking at his elbow. "It's completely healed. It's incredible. It's not even stiff or sore anymore. Your powers are amazing."

"Not bad, if I do say so myself," she bragged. At first, Dianna wanted to lean in and kiss his arm to show that she was making it better, but she didn't want to alarm him. After all, there was so little they knew about each other. Still, they'd only just started talking. Crossing her legs on the grass, she added "It's the least I can do, after you risked your life for me."

Josh chuckled, "I still don't know what I was thinking. I've never been in a fight." She wondered what he was thinking too. Dianna had never been in a dangerous situation like that before. Those guys could have beat up the boys, or worse. Not to mention, the bikers had plans for both Vivian and her too. She didn't even want to think about what could have happened. As soon as she saw Josh, she somehow knew that everything would be all right. She had no idea he was going to do what he did. An hour later, she was still just as confused over the events. She saw what Vivian saw. In her heart of hearts and beyond a shadow of a doubt, she knew that what Josh did, he did for her. Staring into his blue eyes, Dianna knew what they were saying. She never had to be alone. She'd always be safe with him.

"Did I tell you how surprised I was Charlie protected us?"

"No," Josh laughed. "Did you think he'd run for the hills?"

"Not exactly. Although, I wouldn't have blamed him if he did. It all happened so quickly. The guy hit Billy so fast, and he just went down. I screamed, and then Charlie looked at me and called me by my first name," Dianna said, smiling.

"What? No Imperial?" Josh asked.

"Not at all. I think 'Get behind me, Dianna' is what he actually said," she chuckled out loud. "I know he's your friend, but I can't tell you how much he's annoyed me over the years. This week even more so," she groaned. "But now," Dianna said, letting out a sigh, "I think I can stand being in his presence."

Leaning forward, Josh plucked a dandelion out of the grass. He twisted it in his hand and stared at it for a second. "What Charlie said earlier was true. He doesn't do a lot of these things to annoy his friends, but I can't tell you how many times his abrasive approach towards strangers has cost us possible friends. He's just not too trusting of other people."

"Understood," agreed Dianna. "Why do you think he's in the dream?"

"I seriously don't know," Josh replied, a look of confusion on his face. This may sound crazy, but I kind of got used to the dream and the synchronicities. I just look at the whole thing to mean we were all fated to meet." Blowing the dandelion apart, Josh watched as the separate pieces floated into the night sky. "See this?" he asked her. "If you could pull back time, you'd see all these pieces converge back together on the stem. That's what I think we're doing right now. The dream was bringing us all here. And I'm sure we're all coming together for a reason."

"I could see that," Dianna said. "I hadn't looked at it that way, but I do think... I mean, I genuinely feel like I had the second part of the dream so I could identify you when you came." "Could be," Josh grinned. "I feel bad because both you and Charlie have analyzed this stuff. For me, it just blurs together. Charlie's practically made a science out of the dream. He took every detail and researched it."

"Like what?" she asked.

"Everything. The kind of trees, the flowers, and where they're indigenous to, the color of the grass. It's been an obsession of his."

"It's good that he did that," Dianna replied, rolling onto her side towards Josh. "I didn't even think of that stuff. But now that you said it, I want to know." Lolling his head from side to side, like he was weighing the options, Josh finally answered.

"I'm not sure I wanna know. Because sooner or later, won't it happen anyway?" he pointed out. "If you find out, somehow, doesn't that kinda destine you for that particular interpretation? I'd rather make my own choices. Sometimes, with all these signs, I don't feel like I really have free will. It bothers me."

"I don't know. You have a valid point. But a little foreknowledge might be what's needed. That could be the reason you and Charlie met in the first place. He might help you with something you'd normally overlook," Dianna pointed out.

"I agree," Josh said, looking around. "What is this place? I've seen it a couple times."

"Lira bandstand," Dianna replied, pointing at the wooden construct. "Every so often during the summer, they have concerts here." She looked at the vintage, white columns holding up the shingled roof. It almost looked out of place in the uniform downtown area, but she didn't care. She loved it. "It's halfway between school and my house. So sometimes, when the weather's beautiful, I'll do my homework out here. Then I just lay on the grass and write poetry."

"Not my particular cup of tea," Josh said.

"If I asked you to write me a poem, would you do it anyway?" she asked.

Flashing a broad smile, Josh said, "We'll see. How'd you get into poetry?"

Sighing, Dianna looked away. "I was having issues."

"You don't have to talk about this, if you don't want to."

"No, it's okay," she replied, nodding her head. "When my mom and dad divorced, there was a huge court battle. My dad had to sell the house and stuff. It was kinda weird for me, because I had all these emotions. And it was never just one on any given day. In a situation where I should've been mad, it seemed that I couldn't pick between sadness or any other emotion. I was getting hit from all angles. So I kind of turned to writing to sort it out on paper."

"Did it help?"

"It helped me get in touch with myself, to know myself better. But it didn't stop the bad situations from coming. My mom moved away, after she met somebody new. He was a preacher, just like my dad was. When the guy got offered his own church in Minnesota, she went." Dianna looked at Josh. "And she never came back. The phone calls became less and less. Then she started to post pictures on the internet saying how proud she was of her daughter. But it wasn't me or my sister. It was his daughter," Dianna said.

"It just hurt me that somebody so special to me could set me down like a discarded piece of clothing. I still kind of trip over it. The woman who gave birth to me just dropped me and my sister like a hermit crab leaves an old shell. She crawled into a new shell, and that became her home."

"I'm sorry," Josh said. Dianna could see the concern on his face.

"It's okay, Josh, really. I don't talk like this to many people. The poetry helped me to work through it though."

"I can relate, kinda. My dad died, when I was four. Everybody has these amazing stories about him, and I can't even remember him. My grandparents' house has pictures of him everywhere, showing all kinds of achievements and heroic feats. So I wonder to myself, what am I going to do in my life that could measure up to a man I never knew?" Dianna listened to Josh and watched as he looked up at the sky, his blonde hair falling back as he did. "I don't even know in my head the difference between what was real about him and what's legend."

Dianna got on her knees and put her arms around him. He didn't cry, but she knew he was hurting. The look on his face said it all. She thought about how different it was with Josh in her arms right now, when earlier he had been so strong. It was a glimpse of who he could be; a young man standing up to impossible odds. This was an echo of where he'd come from. A scared, lost boy, so different from the one she had seen in her dream. When she considered the fact that Josh was all these things, it made her want to cry for some reason. Dianna closed her eyes. She felt his cheek brush against hers, as he buried his face into her hair.

"I'm okay. Really, I am," Josh said, nodding. Dianna stayed sitting on her knees and brushed his blonde bangs out of his eyes.

"I'm glad I met you, Josh," she whispered to him, biting her lip. She could see the look in his eyes, and it was tearing her apart inside. She knew what was going to happen next. Josh started to lean in. He hesitated for a small second, then he brushed his lips to hers. Then he kissed her. She felt a relief so liberating, it flooded over her body. She had dreamed this would happen, and now it finally had.

Dianna melted into his arms, as Josh kissed her again, this time harder. She let go of whatever inhibitions she had, and with them any concept of time or realization that they were in the middle of town. To her, right here and right now, they were the center of the universe.

***

"Are you even listening to me, Josh? JOSH!" The boy snapped back to reality.

"What?"

"I swear, Josh," snapped Claire. "It's like you're on another planet this week."

"I'm cool, Nana. I'm cool. I just have a lot on my mind." It wasn't like he was lying. Josh did have a lot of his mind, and it was named Dianna. Quite plainly, Josh couldn't think of anything else. He quickly looked around the backyard and then checked his phone.

"Are you sure this lady's coming, because she's ten minutes late?"

"Don't worry. She'll be here," Claire said, inspecting her roses. "That grandfather of yours... When that Sam and he get back from the movies, I'm going to light his ass on fire, like the Fourth of July." Josh grinned. Larry always had a knack for overdoing the yard work. Other than the lawn that was trimmed perfectly, every bush and shrub in the backyard looked like it had just gotten a flat top haircut.

Josh looked at his phone again. He wondered what Dianna was up to. Her dad had picked her up early. They'd gone to a place called Smithfield, so her dad could preach. In sixth period, Josh had gotten the first of many road texts. It read:

> HOUDINI COULDN'T HAVE ESCAPED BETTER. WE'RE ON THE 138 HEADED TO BLUE STAR FREEWAY ALREADY.

Glancing over at Charlie's house, Josh cringed at what could be going on in that basement right now. To say Charlie was in a bad mood today would have been an understatement. It seemed Vivian had friend-zoned Charlie before they even got to her house. "She referred to me as my friend, friend like you, friends forever." Charlie rattled off, while he angrily counted on his fingers. By the time he had dropped Josh off in his driveway, Charlie looked like he could chew through nails. Chuckling, Josh tapped the top of the patio table.

Pretty soon, Larry would be pulling out the plush covers for the iron chairs. The large green umbrella in the center of the table was extended out, even though the sun was going down. Suddenly, a strange car turned into the driveway. "Nana, I think she's here," Josh boomed. Claire walked up and took a seat across from Josh. "Are you going to let her in?" he asked.

"No," Claire said, arching her eyebrow. "She knows we're in the backyard." Josh was going to ask how, but his grandmother beat him to the punch. "She knows we're back here, because I just told her."

"Now listen to me," Claire commanded, her face deadly serious. "Whatever you do, do not disrespect this woman and do not lie to her."

"Okay," Josh said. "Geez," he thought. For a woman who, as recently as a week ago, acted like he was incapable of lying, that was a pretty stiff warning. The woman walked around the house and made her way across the lawn in smooth, graceful steps. "I could've sworn Nana said this woman trained her," thought Josh. She looked like she couldn't even be in her thirties.

"Imperial Mother, I am honored they sent you," Claire said. With a smile on her face, she stood up and bowed her head.

"I just happened to be in town, child. It is good to see you."

"Weird," thought Josh. The woman was well-dressed. She looked like she was stepping out for dinner. She had on tight jeans, black pumps, and a black cashmere sweater. It was tight enough that Josh could tell she wasn't wearing a bra.

The woman held her gaze with Claire and then stepped back. She grinned from ear to ear, "My God, Claire. My Baby Claire." The woman threw her arms around Claire. They hugged, like they were old buddies recognizing each other at the mall. The woman's hair bounced up and down as she laughed.

"Nina, this is Josh."

Standing up from the patio chair, Josh stepped forward and shook her hand. "It's a pleasure to meet you, ma'am," Josh said.

She put her hands to her face, surprised. "I can't believe it's Alex's son," Nina said, looking over at Claire, who was sitting down.

"I know. They grow up so fast."

"The last time I saw you, you were still a baby."

Josh straightened up. "Really?"

"Really," she said, nodding her head. "So, I hear you might have some abilities," she said, moving to the chair and sitting down.

"Um, I guess," he said, feeling mildly apprehensive. "It's kind of hard to explain," he said, following suit.

The woman nodded, "That's what your grandmother said." Leaning forward on the table she asked, "What do you say, Mr. Michaels? Would you like to find out what these abilities are?"

"Sure. But I've really gotta ask something. I know it's uncool to even wonder a woman's age. But if you were at the hospital when I was born you couldn't have been more than ten." Claire looked at Josh in a stern manner and cleared her throat.

"It's quite all right, Claire. What have you told him?"

"Very little. I didn't know where this would go," Claire admitted.

The woman turned to Josh, smiling. "My name is Nina," she said, sitting back in the chair and twirling her copper hair. "I'm thousands of years old. For centuries, my husband and I have trained candidates on how to develop and use their powers. I can shape shift into any form I like. Sometimes I'm old. Sometimes I'm young. I usually don't keep the form for more than ten years. It all depends. I will tell you this, though. I look nothing like when I trained your grandmother. But I can recall it like it was yesterday." Nina shook her head, and long, brown hair and tan skin took the place of her copper waves and milky complexion. She was older and more distinguished now. She reminded Josh of the school librarian. A laugh escaped Claire's mouth. That surprised Josh. His grandmother rarely ever laughed.

"Look familiar?" Nina asked. Looking her way, she shook

her hair again, and it was gone. "It's a good form of defense against my enemies."

"What enemies?" Josh asked, looking at his grandmother.

"We'll address that after you pass the tests," she said, rummaging in her purse. Pulling out a short candle, she set it on the table and said, "Josh Edward Michaels, are you prepared to be tested?"

"Yes, I am," Josh replied nervously.

"I want you to stare at this candle and light it with nothing but your will."

"Okay," Josh said slowly. He took a deep breath and stared at the candle on the table. It was hard to ignore the fact that his grandmother was sitting in front of him, and Nina was to his right. For the first few seconds, he concentrated on the candle coming to life. Much to his dismay, it obviously wasn't happening. So he pretended in his head that he had a lighter, and he was lighting it himself. After thirty seconds he sighed, and shook his head. "I don't know what to say. Nothing's happening."

"It's okay. Don't worry about it," Nina said, waving her hand over the candle.

"Great," thought Josh, as a little amber spark began to grow brighter. The wick became engulfed in flame.

"Next test," Nina announced energetically. "Concentrate on the flame in front of you. See how it's the size of a quarter?" Josh nodded his understanding. "Try to make it two feet tall."

Josh looked hesitantly at the green umbrella above them. "Okay, here it goes." Glaring intently at the flame, he repeated, "Grow, grow, grow," over and over in his head. But no matter how hard he tried, the flame just wouldn't grow. He felt so embarrassed that he couldn't even bring himself to look at his grandmother.

"One final test before we move inside," Nina said. She put her hand on the tabletop, setting down a little red, toy car. "Josh, I want you to push the car to me with your mind."

"Okay," Josh thought nervously to himself, "I've got this." He closed his eyes and imagined the car was on an incline, and Nina was waiting at the bottom. He put the car on the ground and watched it take off, picking up speed. He opened his eyes. Much to his dismay, he saw the car was still in the same spot. Josh felt his heart sink. Why was this happening? He tried again, except this time he held his breath and pushed down. Josh could feel the veins on the sides of his neck engorge with blood as he screamed in his mind, "Goddammit, why won't you move?" Finally, he gave up. "I can't do it," he said, shaking his head. He put his arms on the table and put his face in his hands. He was a failure.

"He's extremely powerful," Nina said.

"I know. Didn't I tell you?" Josh heard Claire boast.

Josh opened his eyes and looked at the little car. It still hadn't moved. Glancing up, he saw his grandmother and Nina both staring at him. His grandmother was wearing a broad smile.

"He's more powerful than I'd ever imagined," Claire said, with awe.

Josh looked at his hands. "What's going on? Nothing happened." He turned to see what the women were gawking at. Nine foot tall rosebushes were the first thing that caught Josh's attention, and they were still actively growing. "Holy cow," he said, laughing. He tried to move the chair so he could check them out better. The grass was a foot and a half tall by now. Josh looked up, completely shocked. Nina smiled at him.

"It would appear you have plenty of power. You just don't have the ability to wield it yet." Josh lifted himself out of the chair and stepped onto the grass. Turning around, he giggled to himself. He'd supersized the whole backyard. Every bush needed to be trimmed. Every potted plant was overflowing.

"Josh, if you can," his grandmother asked, "try to shut it off. As it is, Larry is going to flip his lid, when he sees what is waiting for him this weekend." Josh grinned at the thought of his grandfather stepping into the backyard and shouting, "Sakes alive," or one of his other odd phrases.

Closing his eyes, Josh said, "Stop!" as loud as he could. But when he opened his eyes back up, he saw there was no effect at all. In fact, two of his grandmother's pots were beginning to crack. Josh tried to get the plants to reverse their growth. He knew it wasn't working, when one of the planters busted and the roots spilled out. "A little help here," Josh said urgently, as one of the pine branches snapped and fell under its own weight, crashing to the ground.

Claire stepped up, flustered, "Hells bells, Josh," she said, winking and grabbing his right hand. Nina took his left. Josh felt energy start to flow through him as the women chanted. Then just like that, everything stopped.

"Okay," Nina said, satisfied. "That was the first test. What do you say we move the party inside? It's obvious you have power," Nina went on as they all walked into the house and headed towards the living room. "I'd like to see you do something more up your alley though."

"Finally. It's time to bust out with some synchronicities," Josh said happily. Nina placed a small bag on the coffee table and brushed her copper curls over her shoulder.

"After being trained, you will realize, like your grandmother did, that there is no such thing as chance or coincidence. Only extremely powerful minds bring their thoughts and will into fruition. Put your hand in the bag and grab one of the tiles," Nina instructed.

Placing his hand in the velvet bag, Josh felt a couple handfuls of little tiles, about twenty or thirty. He pulled out his hand. Resting in his palm was a jagged piece of tile with a brown square painted on it. Nina took the tile and set it down. She then handed the bag to Claire, who drew out a red circle. Finally, Nina pulled out a tile with a yellow triangle on it.

"Okay," Josh said, "what do you want me to do?"

"Well, I'll tell you what I don't want you to do," answered Nina. "Don't touch the TV or the radio. Your grandmother already told me about your little knack for the airwaves, but I want to see if you can really create. Have you ever heard the word abracadabra before?" she asked.

"Yeah. Magicians usually say it, before they do a trick."

Nina smiled. "It translates to I create as I speak." Narrowing her eyes, Nina said calmly, "I don't want tricks, Josh. I want to see if you can really bend reality." Josh sat up.

"And how do you want me to do that?"

"If you're as strong as I think you are, it's already done. Now we just sit back and see what happens," she said, reaching back into the bag and pulling out a white notepad. This is one that separates the men from the boys every time. Nina grinned, "Consider this your exit exam." With pen in hand, Nina looked at Josh and placed a long, white piece of paper down in front of him. "The lottery draws in a few hours. I want you to pick the first six numbers that pop into your head and write them down."

Josh looked into her eyes. He could tell Nina wasn't pulling his leg. She really wanted him to win the lottery. Josh was a wiz in statistics, and he knew it was almost impossible. "All right, Nina, you're the boss," he said, grabbing the pen.

"Well, what do you know, Claire? The boy's a fast learner."

"I'm trying to concentrate," he yelled, over the women's laughter.

Josh wrote down six numbers, like she asked. "Very good," Nina said. "Claire, call Larry and tell him to pick up a ticket on the way home."

"Okey-dokey," Claire chirped. "With these numbers?" she double-checked.

"No," Nina said, shaking her head and flipping the paper

over, "with these numbers." Josh looked down and saw a picture of six perfectly drawn circles with no markings on them.

More than a little hesitant, Josh asked, "What are these?"

"Consider them training wheels, Mr. Michaels. These first six numbers you picked are useless. They're vestiges of numbers you heard or possibly saw in the last few hours. This little visual aid will narrow your psychic vision down just a scooch."

Josh stared for a few moments at the six blank bubbles. Then, all of a sudden, one by one, numbers started popping into his head. Josh hurriedly jotted them down and handed the paper to his grandmother, as he watched her walk out of the room. "Now what do we do?" he asked, collapsing down on the couch and looking at the TV remote.

"We have dinner, and we wait. Most importantly, we don't turn on the TV," the woman said, grabbing the remote and putting it under the couch cushion.

***

Unfortunately for Josh, avoiding all electronic devices also included his phone. He was hoping to ask Dianna out for Sunday. It was the only day he had left, after he'd already made plans with Charlie for Saturday. He'd have to text her in the morning, he thought to himself. Josh looked at Nina. They had been waiting for hours now. It was far past his mom and Larry coming home, and far past the glee of seeing his grandfather's shock when he saw the backyard.

Looking at the clock, it was hours past the arrival of the lost pizza delivery boy, who rang their doorbell. He claimed his GPS insisted that Claire's house was the delivery point. Josh invited him in and used his grandfather's Norfolk County map to find the real route for the wayward deliveryman. To thank them, he ran to his car and returned with an extra pizza that somebody had crank called in. As Josh closed the door, he triumphantly held out the brown square box and set it on the table. Claire opened the box and smirked when she saw her red circle. Nina high-fived Claire, eagerly grabbing a slice which showed off her yellow triangle, while the others all whistled and applauded.

The only thing to do now was to wait for the lottery draw. Josh stared at the clock. It was going agonizingly slow. "Jesus, Mary, and Joseph," Claire cried. "Your phone's been ringing off the hook for the past hour."

"It's not ringing, Nana. It's vibrating. And those are texts, not phone calls."

"Well who the hell would be texting you so late at night?" she demanded.

"It's probably Dianna. She's out in Smithfield," Josh absentmindedly replied.

"A girl?" inquired Claire. "Why wasn't I informed?"

"Because," replied Josh, folding his arms and yawning, "it's a relatively new thing. And stop giving me the stink eye, like I did something wrong."

"Wait," Claire said. "Is she the girl from the dream? The one your mother told me about?" Josh looked at Nina and then to Claire.

"Yes. Not that it's anybody's business."

Claire shot up like a lightning bolt hit her. It was so quick even Josh flinched. Then, slowly, a smirk spread across her face. Her eyes began to glisten. "She's the healer; isn't she?" his grandmother asked excitedly.

"For the record," Josh revealed, "I'm not caving into your nosiness. I'm only answering you because you told me not to lie in front of Nina. Yeah, she is." Claire looked directly at Nina and tilted her head.

"That's why you're in town," she chuckled, putting her hand over her mouth. "She's to be trained," Claire said, putting her hands on her chest. "And you're going to be her trainer."

Twirling her hair and grinning, the woman coyly replied, "Who, me?"

"Oh, God," Claire leaned onto the chair grabbing her chest. "Please tell me this means what I think it means."

"Well," Nina began, "I'm not a hundred percent certain, but we do live on Taylor Road." Josh watched with surprise as his grandmother jumped up and down, singing, "Yes, yes, yes!"

"I knew it!" screamed Claire, running out of the room. "Larry, wake up! It's happened. It's finally happened."

"What has her all worked up?" Josh yawned. He stood and stretched. It seemed he was getting his second wind. He automatically felt better.

"Well," Nina began, "it's complicated, but I'll try to tell you as much as I can right now. In our world, there are different energy castes. They're different in their own unique ways." Leaning forward, she took a sip of water, ruffled her hair up and continued. "The dream benders are gifted people. They've been present since the dawn of time."

"How can you be so certain?" Josh asked. "I've never so much as heard the phrase before this week."

"I know, because I was there," Nina answered wryly. "Their bloodlines cover every part of the globe. Part of my job is not only to train them, but to keep track of them. Your family's not only the most capable, but also one of the strongest bloodlines in this part of the U.S."

"Each family has distinct gifts they excel at: telekinesis, telepathy, healing. The stronger bloodlines seem to have multiple talents." Smiling, Josh lowered his head. In some form, he was still embarrassed to find out that Nina not only knew Dianna, but lived with her and was going to train her.

"Why are they called dream benders, when it seems to be such a small portion of what they can do?"

"Funny you should ask that," Nina replied, "because your grandmother's main talent lies on the astral plane. In all my years, I've never seen somebody who took what was taught to her and then made it so much her own. She developed her own techniques, as well as her own style of psychic warfare."

"My grandmother, Claire, did?"

"Yes. In her time, Claire was one of the Host's most powerful agents. We'll get into who I work for later. Claire can create whole dream worlds in full color, without a trace of a flaw. She can bring people into that dream, and she can cast them out. But this skill, which most dream benders exhibit in one degree or another, is not why these individuals are called dream benders. They earned the name because the reality we live in is actually God's dream."

"UUUMM," Josh said, raising his finger.

"No questions, Josh. You'll be taught all of this when you start your training. I'm not here to teach you. I came here to test you. I'm sorry, but I don't make the rules," she emphasized. "Above the dream benders are the avatars, who were chosen by the Creator to guide civilization, depending on the current needs of human evolution."

"How come the benders can't just do it, if they have powers?"

"Quite plainly, Josh, they just don't have the capacity. They're human, and that humanity drags them down. Some benders develop narcissistic traits. They can exhibit domineering spirits, crushing those around them. Still, others have visions of helping humanity, but their spirit is smothered. So when they try to take on the task, they just fall short. The avatars, on the other hand, don't contain the mental impurities the benders have. Their sole existence revolves around their spiritual mission. They're the Buddhas, the Christs, the Mohammads. They live and die serving humanity."

"So what does that have to do with my grandmother just freaking out?"

Nina nodded her head and paused for a second, looking hard at the boy, "It was prophesied a long time ago that two avatars would come, each being one half of the other. Between the two of them, they would have the power to save the world from the brink of destruction. These two were to come from specific bloodlines. Yours was one of the prophesied, but it was also said there were signs to accompany it. Your house is on Deerfield. Dianna's grandmother was called Little Deer. Dianna lives on Taylor Road, and your grandmother's maiden name was--"

"Mariole," Josh said, with a confused look on his face.

"Don't interrupt her, Josh," Claire said as she and Larry stepped back into the room. "Well, at least she seems to be back to normal," thought Josh.

"There was a time in our history," Nina said, "when people based their last name on their trade, like Carpenter or Bowman. The strongest of the benders took the names Taylor and Smith, not because it was their occupation, but to let others know they had abilities. Not only was the bearer of the name extremely powerful, but they could wield that power with exceptional skill. Your family comes from the Taylor bloodline. For protection, when they arrived in America, they changed their last name to Mariole. In French, it means fool."

"What for?" Josh asked.

"Protection, of course," Claire said, sitting down. "We came to America for a fresh start. And it worked." Josh looked over at Larry, who had Flynn tucked under his arm, like a sleeping baby. Larry flashed him a broad smile, and then he looked to his wife.

"Hand me the ticket, dear." Claire grabbed a lottery ticket off the table and handed it to him. Josh watched as Larry trudged to the kitchen with the sleeping dog.

"Poor guy," thought Josh. Claire was a natural night owl, but Larry tended to be in bed by 9:00.

"So you see, there is a chance that these two young avatars may be you and Dianna. You're both exceptionally gifted," Nina finished.

"Congratulations, ladies and gentlemen," Larry said, shuffling into the living room. "You are $33 million richer." Josh's eyes bolted open, as the shock of adrenaline hit him. "Can I go to bed now?" Larry asked.

"Of course, dear," Claire said, blowing him a kiss.

"Good night, love," Nina shouted, without turning around.

"Hell yeah!" Josh screamed, staring at the ticket. This was the answer to everything he'd ever dreamed of. He felt almost like he was outside of his body, as he watched Nina and his grandmother embrace.

"Most powerful," he heard his grandmother say.

"Extremely powerful," Nina replied, as they laughed and hugged each other.

"Oh my God!" Josh repeated over and over. He knew exactly what he was going to do. He'd buy a huge house for his mother and him. Josh pumped his arm in victory. "Yes!" he screamed. He spun around, bouncing up and down, feeling completely avenged for every wrong that had ever occurred throughout his life. Finally, he sat back down and stared at the lottery ticket.

"Would you quit looking at that damn thing?" snapped Claire.

"I can't help it," Josh laughed cheerfully. Scowling, Claire reached over and tore up the ticket. "No! What are you doing?" Josh screamed.

Claire looked at him unapologetically and replied, "Exactly what we were hoping you would do."

Josh watched in horror as his grandmother took the small

pieces of paper into her mouth and began to chew on it. "No!" Josh moaned. "Why would you do that?" His body was trembling, and he began to feel dizzy. "That was the answer to our problems."

"Josh, look at me," barked Claire, spitting out the paper into her cup of tea. "I took a solemn vow not to abuse my powers in any way."

"Well, I didn't," Josh screamed angrily at his grandmother. "My mother and I are poor. We lost everything we had. How could you do this?" Fighting for air, Josh steadied himself in the chair.

Claire glanced over at Nina, and Josh saw the woman shrug her shoulders. "I'm ashamed of you, Josh," Claire said slowly, looking directly into his eyes. "You know good and goddamn well that you and Sam are safe in this house. And you are not poor. So don't pretend you are. This is a million-dollar home we're sitting in. And, pardon the expression, but both your grandfather and I have one foot on a banana peel."

"I'm just saying we could use the money," Josh replied sheepishly.

"We all could, but I promised a higher power not to abuse what was given to me. And by being faithful to that promise, even greater things continue to keep coming my way. Your grandfather and I don't have money because we stole it. We both went to college and worked hard all of our lives. I can't tell you all of the years I spent sleeping alone because Larry was on call at the hospital all the time."

"I see what you're saying, but you could've warned me you were going to do that," Josh remarked, still trying to process what had just happened.

"I'm sorry. I was so shocked by the news that you could be the Prime, I forgot that you've never seen any of this. But you know that, if Larry believed for a second that we were keeping that money, he would have been dancing his ass off next to you. He knows by now how this works." Josh sighed, nodding his head in agreement. "To show you that I do care, and that your Nana isn't completely heartless, I have something that, in my eyes, is worth far more than $33 million," Claire said, leaving the room She returned with the unopened box of stuff Larry had brought down from the attic. "With your powers," she said, "this should be right up your alley."

Josh's face perked up. "Like what?" he asked. Claire pulled out a multicolored cube and set it on the table in front of her grandson. "It's a Rubik's cube," Josh said, with a perplexed look on his face.

"Not just a Rubik's cube," Nina said, finally speaking.

"Your father's Rubik's cube," Claire said, finishing the sentence. "When he was younger, your dad would play with this for hours." Josh's grandmother stared at the cube lovingly. "With this, your father said he figured out half of the universe's mysteries."

"With that toy?" scoffed Josh.

"Your dad could figure it out in seconds, whether his eyes were open or closed."

"Go for it," urged Nina. "Consider it your last test of the night, before we pack it in, and I go home."

"Eyes open or closed?" Josh asked cautiously, as he scanned the cube.

"Let's go with closed," his grandmother said. "And how about under two minutes?"

"You're on," said Josh, grabbing the cube. Closing his eyes, he tried to hold the visual of the cube in his mind. He pictured which colors would be twisting, while turning the rows in his hands.

Josh heard his grandmother say, gleefully, "You have all the greens, Josh. Keep going." Taking a deep breath, Josh moved faster. His face was masked in grim determination.

"You have all the reds," Nina shouted.

Somewhere, after Nina's voice trailed off, Josh lost the image of the cube in his mind. Instead, in his head Josh saw a teen boy with strawberry blonde hair sitting alone in his room. Ever so faintly, Josh could hear the boy's thoughts. He could even feel what the boy was feeling. Tears began to flow down Josh's cheeks, as he realized it was his father solving the puzzle. Josh's hand stopped, as he gripped the cube tighter. The energy was familiar to him, like an old song.

As he listened to the boy, he knew with certainty this was his dad. He might not remember his father raising him, but he now saw the young Alex. As he thought and learned, Josh was sharing every discovery. For a split second, Josh was almost ashamed of his tears, until he opened his eyes to see both women's faces were just as wet as his.

Nina sat there motionless, looking like she wanted to speak but couldn't. Claire said, her voice straining, "Now do you see how much more valuable than gold our abilities are, and why we must never misuse them?" Josh looked down at the cube in his hands and nodded.

"Yeah, I understand. I was wrong."

"Then our business is concluded," Nina announced, tears still running down her face. "Josh, it has been a pleasure meeting you," she said. She grabbed the remote control from under the couch cushion and set it back on the table. "Somebody will contact you on or near your sixteenth birthday." Nina spoke, while smoothing her sweater and wiping her eyes. "The message will most likely come in a dream, so keep a sharp lookout."

"I will. It was a pleasure meeting you, likewise," Josh told her.

Nina nodded, "It's a shame you're not going to remember me."

"What are you talking about?" Josh said, bewildered.

"Claire, if you would," Nina said, stepping away.

Josh looked at his grandmother. "Is everything all right?" Claire stepped forward, her mouth curling into a broad Cheshire grin.

"I love you, Josh" she said, her voice overwhelmingly happy.

"I love you too, Nana," Josh said warily. Her eyes weren't looking at him so much as they were looking beyond him.

"I know you do," Claire said, nodding her head up and down as she talked. "In fact, I think you'd do anything for me."

"That was right," thought Josh. After all, she was his grandmother.

"Your only wish in this next sixty seconds is to do what I say."

"Of course," thought Josh. "She's my grandmother, and I'm a good boy. I always do what I'm told," he thought, as his head began to nod along in unison with his grandmother's.

"You're going to forget that Nina was ever here. You have no memory of her." Josh nodded. What she was saying made perfect sense. "You did not win the lottery. It never happened. It was just a dream you had and nothing more. Henceforth, you will not access or even entertain the idea."

Josh nodded again, although he could have sworn it was real. "The lessons, the morals you learned today are all that remain. And they were taught to you by me, your loving grandmother." Josh dropped the cube and staggered back, blinking his eyes. He felt like somebody had hit a large bell on top of his head. The vibrations rang in his ears, shrieking at him and telling him what to do. Raising up his hands, Josh tried to push the vibrating energy off of him.

"I don't know how, Nina, but he's fighting me."

"Who's Nina?" thought Josh. "If I could just get these ripples of energy to shut up." Grabbing them with his mind, Josh sent off his own vibrations to negate them. "There we go. That should do the trick." Looking back at his grandmother, Josh saw a strange lady with copper hair walking towards him. She didn't look amused.

She stamped down her left foot, leaned in towards him and yelled, "S L E E P." Josh watched, confused, as white light seemed to come right off of her body in slow-motion, jumping out at him. Then his legs folded, and he could see the ceiling rising up as his head hit the rug. The last thing Josh remembered thinking was, "Why would that strange lady do that?" He just wanted to make his grandmother happy.

"Oh, Lord," Claire groaned, putting her hand to her forehead. Nina turned towards her in disbelief. "Did you see that?" Claire chuckled.

"He's fifteen, and he's already stronger than you." Nina walked across the room and looked back at the young boy lying on the floor. "Will he be okay over there, or do you need help?"

"Oh, he'll be fine," Claire said. "I'll be up another few hours yet, watching TV. If he's still asleep, I'll put a cushion under his head."

"My God, you're horrible, Claire."

"Not at all. It won't kill him, and I certainly can't carry him over my shoulder later. Speaking of over your shoulder, where's your over-the-shoulder-boulder-holder?" quipped Claire.

As Nina walked up to the front door, she laughed to herself. She'd forgotten how blunt Claire could be. "They look great, don't they?" Nina said, cupping her breasts with both hands. "It's part of the test now."

"You're kidding," Claire gasped. "Since when?"

"Just the past twenty years or so. Since we're short on staff, this is mandatory for all male candidates. Anybody who stares for more than three seconds is automatically considered too immature for training."

"I can see that," Claire said, as she opened the door.

"Doesn't sound too much like the Creator though."

"You're right, agreed Nina. "Metatron is actually steering the ship right now. The demons are in an uproar over it."

"I can imagine," Claire agreed. "I have a question. I know it's unorthodox, but is there any way I can start training Josh, just to give him a leg up?" Nina shook her head.

"You know I'd let you do it, if I could. You're an outstanding preceptor, but your grandson isn't a bender, Claire. He's an avatar, at the very least, and quite possibly the Prime. Anything you teach him, other than history, could clash with the watcher's lesson plan."

"Okay," Claire said, nodding her head.

"I'm serious, Claire. This could be the end game, and your grandson could very well be the quarterback."

"I understand."

"Good night, child" Nina said, smiling.

"Good night, mother," Claire said, bowing her head.

***

Hasden looked down at the nearly empty bottle of gin resting on his bare thigh. It was originally cold, when he'd started drinking. It was also full. But now it was tepid and running low, just like his time here on Earth.

He sank further into the leather chair, his sweaty boxer shorts refusing to move with him. Most of the room was dark. The only illumination was the dancing of the flames in the fireplace. Hasden polished off the bottle and cracked open the new one. There was something about gin that reminded him of who he really was. It made him feel mean. Being a demon, he knew he had a mean streak a mile long. Every now and then, he noticed that he no longer just killed for sport though. Since being on Earth, he'd adopted a new policy of hearing the victim out. He loved listening to them scream and beg. It gave him more pleasure then just slaying them. Hearing the sound of the key in the lock, Hasden braced his eyes for what would happen next. Light shone forth from the doorway, as Deus removed his coat and placed it on the rack.

He stood there for a second, taking in the image. Hasden looked around at the five hookers strewn across the room, not a damn stitch of clothing among them. "Shut off the fucking light already," Bill roared loudly.

"Having a little company over, are we?" Deus asked, creeping in slowly, like a lion on the prowl.

Hasden ignored the question, launching straight into one of his own. "Where the hell have you been?" he snarled. "I haven't seen you since Wednesday night." Deus shrugged his shoulders.

"I went to New York for a few days. What's the big deal? Did something happen?"

"I don't know," Hasden said, his voice laced with venom. "Maybe I'm just pissed off because I paid three bikers to kick Josh Michaels' ass. Instead, what I got was not only proof he had powers, but that he's stronger than we previously thought." Deus's face glared at Hasden in the dark, the firelight accentuating his demonic features.

"How strong?"

"Nothing big," Hasden replied sarcastically. "He just manipulated the weather. Then he played the hired help's nervous system like he was Charlie Daniels playing a goddamn fiddle. Hope you had fun in New York, asshole, because that's the last vacation you're taking for a while," he screamed, as he hurled the bottle against the far wall.

"Understood," Deus replied coldly. "So you think Josh and Dianna could be the Primes?"

"Oh, I know they're the Primes," Hasden shouted fiercely. "Nobody has this kind of power at their age. And this whole horseshit scenario has the Creator's paw prints all over it. The only thing I can't figure out is how Josh has powers to begin with."

"Maybe God's cheating," Deus suggested.

"Have you heard yourself lately?" Hasden snarled. "God doesn't have to cheat, and you know it."

"I'm not saying like he's cheating, but what if he was letting somebody else cheat and just wasn't doing anything about it?"

Hasden thought about it, "It's improbable but not impossible."

Deus walked over to the couch and looked at the unconscious girl lying there. He stared longingly at her naked body. Then using his index finger, he dragged it up the girl's ankle, up to her hip, and kept walking. "It's possible God knows about our ace in the hole."

"I already considered that. She's safe. I'm almost certain of that. If he knew we'd have angels crawling so far up our asses, we wouldn't be able to shit them out if we had dysentery. I have a new project for you, Deus. Tomorrow we're inviting Josh and Charlie over. My new tactic is, if you can't beat them, join them." Deus grinned back, the flames of the fire reflecting in his eyes.

"If it pleases His Infernal Majesty, then it pleases me."

***

Walking up the driveway to the house, Nina still couldn't believe that tonight went so well. A crazy smile found its way to her face every time she thought of the teen boy. He was more powerful than even she had dared to dream at this age.

The only discouraging thing she noticed was that his powers seemed to be almost entirely mental, which could be a liability on the battlefield. But there were two years where his watcher could train him. He had from sixteen to eighteen to learn. If tonight was any indicator, she knew he'd learn quickly. The power was there. He just had to learn how to use it.

During the time they are being trained, the only way a demon can attack either Josh or Dianna would be if one of them openly challenged the demon. Gauging by how smart the two of them were, Nina didn't think that was too likely. The only danger she anticipated was that, in this critical time, the demons were allowed to tempt the Primes. She knew that Dianna was solid, but she couldn't help recalling the look on Josh's face when Claire destroyed the lottery ticket. It could possibly be his Achilles heel, but it seemed that he'd learned his lesson.

Another thing that added to Nina's ecstatic mood was seeing Claire after so long. She was easily Nina's favorite student out of the last five hundred years. Going through the front door, Nina noticed the lights in the house were on. "What a gentleman Ramon is. He parked in the garage," she thought to herself. "Dianna, I'm home," Nina shouted, strolling into the kitchen.

"Guess again, Blanca," an agitated voice slurred in response.

Nina stared in disdain at Ramon's oldest daughter. She looked drunk and upset. Nina could see her mascara was smeared. The girl sat at the table, defiantly, with her spoon in the last of her sister's yogurt. "Ramon and Dianna are in Smithfield."

"Yeah, I know. I didn't need you to tell me that," Cammy said, not even bothering to look up."

"Whatever," Nina said. "I'm not here to get into it with you. I've had a perfect day, and nothing you say is going to bring me down." Nina walked past the woman and opened the refrigerator to get a bottle of water.

Cammy turned to Nina with the spoon hanging out of her mouth. "I'm not here to visit, Nina. Scott kicked me out. I need to move back here for a while." Shaking her head, Nina stood up and slammed the door to the refrigerator so hard she could hear all the condiments fly off the shelves.

"OOOH, 11:59," Cammy said. "You were so close. In retrospect, I guess you could say it was ALMOST a perfect day. My bad."

Chapter 10
X

"Oh, God, please dim the sun down just a bit, so I can sleep for another hour." Glancing over at the alarm clock, it read 9:02 am. That was a lot later than Dianna usually slept. Then again, she wasn't expecting to get home at 1:00 in the morning.

They had gotten home to find that Nina had left all the lights on, which was odd. She was usually fastidious about things like that. Stretched out in bed, between the warmth of the covers, Dianna thought about Friday night and tried to sort through her mixed feelings. She'd never been so happy and sad at the same time. The evening started with her father preaching. It was absolutely awesome. It literally caused her to smile just thinking about how happy he was last night. Then, in a turn of events, Sister Beverly was brought up on stage to testify about how God had moved through Dianna on Easter morning. As soon as Beverly took the pulpit, things kind of went a little sideways. She didn't just speak openly about Easter, but she dropped a bombshell on the congregation. She revealed that not only were her eyes healed of her glaucoma, but, according to her doctor, she didn't seem to need insulin for her diabetes either.

Dianna couldn't believe how quickly the night changed after that. The next thing she knew, people were coming up to the stage, asking to be healed. By the end of service, she'd laid hands on forty-two sick people. She felt a profound sense of accomplishment and satisfaction helping these people. It was like nothing she'd thought possible. After service was over, the pastor of the church invited them to dinner. If she thought she was tired then, she had another thing coming. Dinner turned into a three hour conference call with most of the neighboring congregations. It turned out that Pastor Kato was commuting thirty miles to the church in Milton, so he pitched an idea.

He thought that, since both Dianna and Ramon had the summer off and since they were in high demand, it might be possible to pair them up with a music group and go out on a road tour. She didn't have all the particulars yet, but the projected ticket sales based on the past few weeks' attendance would pay off their house and build a brand-new church for Pastor Kato near his home, which would allow Ramon to take the reins at their church. It was too good to be true. Dianna was completely overjoyed, but she didn't want to count her chickens before they were hatched.

She just hoped that, if everything fell into place, Josh would understand. Right now she didn't even know if she could go a week, let alone a whole summer, without seeing him. But this was Ramon's opportunity of a lifetime. He could barely pay the mortgage on the house during the summer months as it was. This was a chance to pay off the house in full. It was like a dream come true.

Taking a deep breath and stretching, Dianna sat on the edge of her bed. One thing was for sure. If last night was any indicator, life on the road was going to be tough. The food she ate was horrible. Standing in front of the mirror, she checked out her reflection. She had to admit she was pleased with the way she looked. After a whole summer of breakfast for dinner and chicken fingers and mozzarella sticks, she wondered what she'd look like when she came home to Josh.

Picking up her phone and scrolling through the messages, she saw that she missed two texts from last night. One was from her sister and one was from Josh. "That's odd," she mused. She must have missed it while she was napping on the way back. The girl winced as she read the first text:

SCOTT KICKED ME OUT. NEED TO COME HOME ASAP

"Oh no," Dianna thought, crossing the room quickly. She swung her door open and almost crashed into Nina, who was sitting outside her bedroom door.

"What's going on here?" Dianna whispered, confused.

Nina looked like she hadn't done a thing all day. Her copper hair was in a bun, and she was sitting cross-legged on the hallway floor in her pajamas. "Shhh," she put her finger to her lips. "Your dad and Cammy are fighting," she said, in a hushed tone.

Dianna took a seat next to Nina and sat up against the wall. The hallway opened up to the vaulted ceilings, which led to the family room below. With the way they were shouting and the acoustics in the room, she was surprised she hadn't noticed when she woke up.

"How many times do I have to say I'm sorry, Ramon? Seriously. Let it go already."

"How can I, Camille? You're sweating alcohol out of your pores you smell like a wino off the street."

"I was at a party. That's what you do, dad. I got drunk. Get over it."

"Camille, I can call Scott. I can talk to him and smooth things out."

"Don't bother, dad. It's over. He caught me making out with one of his coworkers."

"Jesus, Camille!" Just hearing Ramon say that word made Dianna cringe. Her father rarely ever raised his voice, and he almost never swore. "You threw away a perfectly good relationship for another guy?" The room below fell deadly silent. Curious as to what was going on, Dianna started to rise up, only to feel Nina place her hand on her thigh, holding her down. Nina shook her head in protest, holding her finger to her mouth.

"It wasn't a guy, dad. Her name is Melissa. It's been building up for a while now. We usually just casually flirt, but at the party things kind went too far. I love Scott. I do. And if I wasn't so drunk, maybe I wouldn't have acted on the impulse. But

I did."

"Why do you do this to me?"

"You know what, Ramon? The thought of hurting you never really entered my mind last night. I'm an adult and I have my own life now. This isn't new, and you know it. I've dated women on and off since junior high."

"I know," he answered sternly. "I'm not questioning your sexuality. I accepted that a long time ago. I'm talking about the poor choices you make."

"Do you really care, dad? Or are you just rubbing my nose in it? I agree. Scott was a good guy. Out of all the people I dated, he definitely had his act together. I screwed up. What part of that bothers you? I've lived across town for a year now, and you've only come over like four times. And every time you did, you'd throw the same conversation to Scott. It's like a script. You start with asking about work. Then you move onto the sports stuff. It's not like you and Scott hung out, or you even wanted him to be your son-in-law. Admit it, you liked Scott because he kept me under close supervision."

"And what's wrong with that?" Ramon yelled. "That's why we couldn't have you living here before. You're a bad influence on Dianna."

"Please, Ramon, I hate to burst your bubble. Dianna is my sister and I love her. I'm no more of a threat to her than you are."

"What the hell did you just say?" Dianna brought her knees up to her chest and laid her head on Nina's shoulder. It sounded like the gloves were about to come off. "Did you just say I'm a bad influence?"

"Listen, dad. I'm just saying that, at my age, you were rebellious too. You told your daddy to kiss off and turned your back on your culture and the old ways. On top of that, you didn't get caught kissing someone else while you were drunk. You had a full-on affair, which had a direct effect on me and my sister. The

Bible asks why are you pointing out the sawdust in the other person's eye, when you have a plank of wood in your own? Or don't you remember? Maybe I do smoke and drink, but I learned a few things growing up as a preacher's daughter. And one of them was that I can get to Heaven just as easily as you can."

"Camille, I'll admit I've made my mistakes. But I've changed. I walk a better path now."

And I'm happy for you dad, but you taught me that our greatest of deeds are as dirty rags before the Lord. And we all fall short. None of us is worthy. So spare me that 'I go to church now' spiel. I'm not a kid anymore, dad. And I hate to put you in this position, but I have nowhere to go. I'm just asking for you to help me, if you can. I promise I won't do anything to negatively influence Dianna."

Dianna gripped Nina's flannel pants and waited for her dad's decision. "Okay," Ramon declared, "but you smoke outside, and the old swear jar goes back in the kitchen. I don't care if you are an adult, we don't swear in this house."

"Okay, I can live with that."

"That's not all," Ramon replied. "Come and go as you please, but nobody sleeps over here."

"That's no problem. I'll try not to be here too long."

"It really doesn't matter," Ramon's voice echoed off the second-story walls. "It looks like your sister and I may be gone all summer. Nothing's been ironed out yet. It may be just you and Nina here, unless she decides to come with us."

Dianna's head slid off Nina's shoulder, as the woman bolted upright. To say the look on her pale face was stark shock would be an understatement. Nina stood up and motioned for Dianna to follow her down the hall. Once inside, she silently closed the door. Then she exploded.

"What in God's name is your father talking about?"

***

"I'm not saying I don't like them," Charlie said, focusing on the basketball hoop installed above the garage door. "I'm just saying I don't understand them." Taking aim, Charlie tossed the basketball towards the backboard, cussing as it bounced off the rim.

"Coming from somebody who read all four books and saw the movies, I gotta go with the books," said Josh, as he grabbed the ball and dribbled.

"What don't you get?" cried Billy, standing at the edge of the driveway. "It was a crystal-clear premise throughout the whole series."

"I know," Charlie replied. "I'm just saying. The girl in the movie is fine as hell. She could get with anybody in town, and she narrows it down to a dead guy and a dog. And I don't get it." Josh chuckled. The only reason they'd gotten on this topic was Billy had revealed that Deus's middle name was Damien, like the Antichrist. So he sometimes referred to him as Deez, instead of Deus Damian. Josh, in turn, told the story of how Sam came up with Josh's middle name, Edward.

"Charlie, my man," said Billy, grabbing the ball and giving it a bounce, "You're dense. Read the books again." With that, he launched the ball.

Josh watched as the basketball swished in yet again. "Geez. Does this guy ever miss?" he thought. He wouldn't be playing so lousy today though, if his shoulder wasn't so sore. He'd woken up on the living room floor this morning and had no idea how he'd gotten there. Claire said he'd stayed up watching TV. When Larry got up, he was sleeping on his arm with the TV still on.

This Saturday, it was supposed to be just Charlie and him. They wanted to go see a movie, but Billy dropped by to look at the handouts from class on Friday. Next thing Josh knew, they were caught up in a game of horse, and the two of them were getting schooled.

This had been going on for two hours now, but Charlie refused to give up until he won a game. "Okay, one more," Charlie said, dribbling the ball in the driveway.

Josh checked his phone. Dianna had sent:

IT'S ON. I HAVE SUNDAY AFTERNOON FREE. LET'S GO OUT.

A smile crept across his face. He was glad they'd get some time to hang out before school Monday. He texted back:

HOW ABOUT 2PM? WE'LL GO FOR COFFEE.

"I hate to interrupt boys, but I need to pull out the car," Larry said, hitting the garage door opener.

"Where ya goin', Papa?" Josh figured it had to be someplace nice. He was wearing a tux.

"He's taking these fine ladies out to dinner," Sam said from behind Josh. He turned to see both his mom and Claire were dressed up in dinner gowns.

"Nice," said Josh, kissing his mother's cheek.

"Hello, Mrs. Michaels," Charlie said, spinning the basketball on his index finger.

"Hello, boys," she replied, smiling.

"Oh, mom, this is my friend Billy from school." Billy waved silently and smiled.

"Don't wait up," Claire said, doing a double-take on Billy. "Larry's playing at the event center tonight."

"What a bummer," thought Josh. He had heard his grandfather play the violin, but never in front of an audience and never playing in a group. He usually performed solo.

"Right on, Papa. Break a leg," Josh said, wishing his grandfather luck.

"Thanks, I'll need it," Larry answered, slamming the trunk on the Audi. "It's going to be a packed house tonight."

"Hey, red," Claire barked as she was getting in the car. "I know it's hard because you're all thumbs, but try to watch the windows." Josh chuckled at his grandmother's remark. His friend had only broken two windows, but Claire continuously rode the boy's ass every time she saw him. Charlie didn't say anything, but Josh noticed the ball was now spinning on his middle finger.

All three boys watched as the blue Audi backed out of the garage and onto the street. As it drove off, Billy turned his head back to Josh. "So what are you guys planning for tonight?" Snatching the ball off Charlie's finger, Josh gave it a bounce and took a poorly-aimed shot.

"Well, we were thinking of seeing that new horror flick downtown."

"Uh, not anymore. It's getting dark," cried Charlie. Billy shrugged his shoulders.

"Dude, are you for real? Nighttime's the best time for scary movies."

"I can't. Josh knows this. My imagination is way too vivid to watch anything supernatural after 6:00 at night."

"It's true," Josh concurred, bouncing the ball on the driveway. "He won't even watch the Thriller video at nighttime, if he can help it."

"Suck balls, Michaels. I'm not that bad," the redhead said, turning to Billy. "But seriously, I have a ratio. Anything scary has to be followed up by a comedy or animated TV show for double the duration."

Billy sat down on the grass and plopped one leg over the other. Josh could tell by the skeptical look on his face that he either didn't believe him, or he thought Charlie was crazy. "So, let me get this straight. You have a mathematical equation to combat your fear of imaginary shit?"

"Pretty much," Charlie said, nodding his head in agreement, "Don't get me wrong. I know that this stuff isn't real, but that won't stop my mind from playing tricks on me at 2:00 in the morning, when I'm alone in the basement."

Josh chuckled, seeing the confusion on Billy's face. "Allow me to demonstrate," Josh said, firing off the basketball and sinking it in the hoop. "Charlie, would you like to watch The Exorcist?"

"Why, I'd love to," he politely answered back. "However, I shall require no less than four hours of Comedy Central or two Disney movies directly afterwards."

"Oh my God," Billy exclaimed in disbelief, while shaking his head. "You guys are killing me."

"You laugh, but it works. And it's foolproof," assured Charlie. "The only thing that really blows for me is, when I'm hit by a commercial drive-by, I'm not prepared for those. Like, I'll just be chilling, watching my regular shows, minding my own business. Then all of a sudden, I'll hear the four scariest words in the human language: BASED ON ACTUAL EVENTS." The teen's face became a mask of worry. "Like, screw that shit," he said, throwing his hands in the air. Josh knew he shouldn't be laughing, but he couldn't help it. He knew firsthand that his friend had little to no control over his brain's impulses.

"So I'm looking for my remote," Charlie said frantically, "but I can't find it.
The announcer's like, 'See the movie people are calling spine tingling.' Some douchebag nobody cares about says he'd rather stick his dick in a live beehive than be that scared again. And now," screams Charlie, "on the screen, there's a guy watching TV in the dark on a couch. And behind him is this four-year-old with wet hair, wearing a dirty nightgown. But she's not standing on the ground. She's just hanging out on the ceiling, glaring at him. The worst part of it all is this guy doesn't look anything like me, but still I'll turn around just to check what's behind me on the ceiling."

Billy laughed and hung his head, "Why?"

"Because I can't help it. My imagination pops up like an unwanted boner at school." Charlie folded his arms in front of him and trumpeted in a deep voice, "Who hath summoned the genie of the lamp?" Returning to his own voice, he continues, "And then it starts nudging me in the back of my mind, that voice saying 'it's time to play.' So I cave in by turning on the lights."

"Why can't you trick yourself by saying it's daylight outside?" asked Billy.

"My brain won't listen, "Charlie replied. "Like, I can take off and go to the bathroom and then fold some wash. No sooner do I sit back down, then the show cuts to another commercial. But this time, it's the front of an old house, with the lights flickering. Little kids are singing in the background." Josh hated that visual. He didn't scare easily, but there was something about demon-possessed kids that gave him the chills. As if on cue, the redhead began skipping around the driveway, while chanting, "La la la la." Charlie was all in now. "Some news hound writes he was so goddamned frightened that, if he had a vagina, he would've joined a nunnery and never come out again."

Charlie started pacing furiously, easing into his manic rant, "And now my imagination is saying, 'Hey baby, c'mon. Just the tip. I swear I won't go any farther.'" Josh watched in fascination as Charlie started grooving and thrusting his pelvis on the poor sycamore tree that was planted next to the driveway. But the skinny teen was far from over. "Even worse still, there's always the scene where the house has killed the whole family; and just the seventeen-year-old daughter is alive. She's terrified out of her mind. I'm silently thinking, 'Run, bitch, run!' But she falls instead. She's just screaming, 'Oh, God. Help me, Jesus!' And I hope Jesus is going to save her. But then the announcer's voice breaks in and says, '"Faith crushing,"' writes Who Cares magazine, 'four stars.'"

Billy stared at the teen for a minute in absolute amazement, and then he chuckled, "You need medication, bro. I mean, I hate to say it, but your brain shouldn't be doing this stuff."

"I am on medication, jackass, but I'd like to attend school and graduate. So I use it sparingly. If I used the dose my doctor prescribed, I wouldn't be able to make it through basket weaving 101."

"And he's like this all the time?" Billy asked, looking slightly concerned.

"Oh, yeah," Josh confirmed, nodding his head. "He's just getting started." The spiky-haired teen stood up and shook his head.

"Negative, Cochise. I totally can't abide by that. You," he said, pointing at Charlie, "go get your anti-anxiety med and meet me at the car."

"I got some on me. What do you got planned?"

"Well, as much as I'd like to sit here and listen to you rack up frequent flyer points towards your next nervous breakdown, there's girls, and lots of them, at the movies."

"Okay, I'm down. Let's do it," Charlie said, shrugging his shoulders. Somewhere in the back of his mind, Josh knew this was going to be a big mistake. He smirked at Charlie anyway.

"I'm down. Let's do it." As they walked off towards the car, Josh chuckled and said, "Why do I see energy drinks and The Little Mermaid in our future?"

***

"That movie was so intense!" howled Charlie, stepping down into the basement. Billy warily scanned the cement dungeon.

"I can kind of see what you were talking about earlier," he remarked. "The lighting isn't so good in here." Josh was actually glad they went out for a change. It was fun. As soon as they arrived, they ran into classmates from school. Josh waved to acknowledge he knew them. After they waved back, Josh thought that would be it.

Billy, however, strolled right up and started up a conversation, like he'd known them his whole life. One conversation just flowed into another, as more and more people stepped up to chat. Even though they'd made it to the theater with plenty of time, it became apparent to Josh they weren't going to make it to the 7:45 movie. Thirty minutes later, they still hadn't gone anywhere near the ticket counter.

Josh could admire that part of Billy. He didn't seem to have rules or a plan. He just did whatever he wanted, and it was fun. By 9:45, they scrapped plans for the horror movie and went with the new Star Trek. It was worth it.

"We should rent Star Trek next week," Josh said, throwing his black Converse on the table. "I didn't see it when it first came around."

"What? Do you live under a rock?" asked Billy.

"Big Star Wars family, you don't even know," Josh informed him.

"Say no more, bro. We got the same thing in our household. I grew up strong and proud on all six episodes. But since Spock lives in Milton, we owe it to the community to rent Star Trek."

"I agree," Charlie said, swiveling in his computer chair. "I'd like to point out that Star Wars Day is coming up May 4th. It's only fair that, if we watch Kirk and Spock, we should also throw in a Jedi here and there as well."

"I'll do you one better," the spiky-haired teen said, placing his hands behind his head. "Next Friday, Star Trek. Saturday, we move on to Star Wars. We'll watch them all through the month of May."

"I'm down with that. I think it's a good idea," said Josh, as muffled electronic tones began to flow from Billy's pocket.

"Hold on a second, text message."

"Holy cow," Josh winced, both his hands leaping to his hoodie pockets.

"What the hell, Michaels?" laughed Charlie, as Josh tapped a finger on his keyboard, bringing his phone to life.

"I didn't turn my phone back on after the movie," Josh answered, hitting the power button.

"You really turn your phone off?"

"Yeah. I don't like knowing I have a text. It makes me feel obliged to answer it." Josh wasn't too worried. He'd texted Dianna good night before they went into the movie. He waited as the phone came to life. Immediately, texts began popping up. Josh stared, speechless, as he read what they said:

> I'M HEADED BACK HOME TO GET YOU. LARRY WAS JUST RUSHED TO THE HOSPITAL.
>
> WHERE ARE YOU? ANSWER YOUR PHONE.
>
> CALL ME.
>
> LARRY FRACTURED THE HEAD OF HIS FEMUR. FELL OFF STAGE. GOING BACK TO THE HOSPITAL. WE'LL TALK WHEN I GET HOME.

"Oh, no," he said, his hands shaking. "I'm in so much trouble."

"What's wrong?" Charlie asked, coming over to him. Josh handed the phone over and watched his face change with each text he read. Looking up, the surprise on Charlie's face was too hard to hide. "Dude, your grandfather actually broke his leg."

Chapter 11
Gemini

"I'm so sorry I missed our date on Sunday," Josh said, apologizing. "Since we couldn't hang out, I decided to write a little poem for you. Don't read it 'til you're alone tonight," he said, handing it to Dianna. This was just one of the many apologies Josh had been doling out over the past thirty-six hours.

His memories of that Sunday, spent at the hospital, were dark indeed. Sam was absolutely pissed at him, even though he'd explained the mistake. And Claire seemed to be standoffish as well. He knew why. For all intents and purposes, it looked like he may have carelessly spoken Larry's injury into existence.

"Thanks for the note. But how could I be mad at you? Your grandfather was hurt. You don't have to apologize," Dianna reassured him, taking a seat at the lunch table. Josh opened up his milk carton and took a sip. He never really thought he'd feel so relieved to come to school, but it was a lot better than the uncomfortable glances he was getting at the hospital.

"So what actually happened?" she asked, placing her hand over his. He could feel her energy calming his nerves and soothing him. It was something he really needed right now.

"Well, my grandfather plays violin. Nothing professional. But, every now and then, he does events like Rotary Club, Elks, stuff like that."

"Sounds like fun," Dianna said, laying out her sandwich.

"It is, or so I've heard. I've never seen him play in the group because they usually serve alcohol at those events. Anyways," continued Josh, "he was setting up on the stage. It must have been dim or something because he lost his footing and fell off the stage."

"Oh my God, that's horrible."

"Yeah, he was in a lot of pain. But there was a guy there who used to be a medic. He called 911 and took care of him until the ambulance arrived." Josh tried as hard as he could to repress the guilt that seemed to keep popping up in his mind over the past two days. He'd already disappointed Dianna once. He didn't want to heap today's lunch on it as well.

"I hope he gets better," Dianna said, obviously concerned. "I could always go with you to the hospital and kind of help," she said grinning.

"I thought of that. But seeing as he's in the care of doctors and nurses at the hospital, I don't think it would go over too well if the healer girl everybody's been speculating about, showed up at the hospital and then Larry just hopped out of bed and did the Charleston all the way to the elevator."

"Good point," Dianna said. "I happened to see another article about me the other day in the paper. It was called The Easter Miracle."

"Not bad," Josh said. "I thought the real Easter miracle was me moving here."

"I'm gonna kick your butt," she cried, slapping him on his shoulder. Dianna shook her head, "I swear. You're such a dork sometimes."

Taking a bite out of a sandwich, Josh grinned. "I try." He definitely felt better. It seemed like Dianna just chased away all the negative feelings. "I seemed to notice that the event was bashed pretty hard by the mainstream media."

"Yeah, they made a list of most of the healings and attributed them all to placebo effect, which is good for me," she said. "I don't need that kind of hassle."

"So what did you do yesterday?" Josh asked.

"Well, after I went to church and got your text, my sister hijacked me. We went to the lake."

"That sounds way better than my day. I'm jealous."

"Don't be," Dianna said, her expression kind of grim. "We were having a good time, and then these guys came by in their boat. They were nice enough. Except this one guy had a bottle of tequila, and he was annoying. Every five minutes he'd ask us if we wanted a shot." "You didn't have any, did you?"

"No, but I think that, every time he offered, my sister did. Finally, I had enough. So I started talking about my sweet sixteen birthday coming up. All of a sudden, they kinda didn't want to hang out anymore," she chuckled.

"So you guys broke out and went home?" Josh asked.

"Not exactly," Dianna replied. "I went home. My sister said she wanted to stay because they seemed nice."

"Of course, they seemed nice," Josh shook his head. "They wanted to get in her pants."

Dianna chuckled again, "Thanks for telling me how the world works, but I have a black belt in fending off male advances."

"That's what I've heard," Josh said, biting into a carrot. "But you never can tell."

Dianna laughed, "I appreciate your concern, but I've been knocking down fools ever since the girls made their first appearance." Josh's eyes followed her hand straight to her breasts, like a dog following a laser pointer.

"Nice," he said, his face suddenly getting hot.

"You're blushing," she teased. "I hate to make it worse," she smiled. "If you want to know a secret, the adjective nice barely scratches the surface."

Josh hung his head and groaned, "You're killing me."

"Am I trippin', or was Dianna pointing at her cans?" Charlie said, laughing and throwing his tray down next to Josh.

Popping out from behind him, Billy countered, "I distinctly saw that myself." Josh's gaze followed Billy, as he rounded the table and took a seat next to Dianna, opposite him and Charlie.

"I can only guess what the conversation was," Charlie said,

popping a chicken nugget in his mouth. "So, Josh, after we finish college, and you been properly baptized, this could all be yours," Charlie said, pointing at his chest.

Billy broke into fits of laughter. Then, in his best female voice, he said, "And after we've been married for a few years we can have sex with the lights on. The sky's the limit."

"Really?" Dianna rebutted. "Is that the best you can do? Because I'll tell you right now; I'm not half as inhibited as you think I am."

"Calm down," Charlie said, grinning. "We're just teasing. Take a chill pill."

"If you guys just toned it down a bit, you might actually get girlfriends of your own."

"Tone what down?" Charlie asked, chewing with his mouth open.

"Girls like finesse," she said. "They want to be romanced."

"And what am I supposed to do about that?" groaned Charlie.

"Well, you can start by remembering that every girl in here is someone's daughter," she snapped, crossing her arms, "and maybe somebody's sister."

Charlie popped another nugget in his mouth, grinning to himself. "And, hopefully, she's not somebody's brother post-op." Josh chuckled and shook his head.

"Honestly, Dianna, I don't even know why you try."

"See, my boy knows that it's a lost cause," Charlie said, stuffing a handful of french fries in his mouth all at once.

"Whatever," Dianna replied, shrugging her shoulders. "You can tell us all later about how great detention was."

"Oh, shit!" Charlie cried. "I forgot about that." His smile turning to a scowl, he pushed the tray away, suddenly in a foul mood.

"You okay?" Josh asked, concerned by the sudden change

of mood.

"My parents still have to schedule the sensitivity training course, and I haven't even told them yet. They're going to kill me for this."

"I wouldn't worry about it. Things aren't that bad," Billy said, dipping his french fries into his ketchup.

"Yeah? Name one thing that I have to be happy about right now?" Charlie challenged.

Billy stared at Charlie with a blank expression on his face, obviously caught off guard. The boy shrugged his shoulders and shook his head. "I don't know. Jesus loves you?"

Snorting, Charlie hunched his shoulders and replied, "No, Billy, Jesus loves you. You drive a Bentley and hang out with hot chicks that wouldn't be caught dead near me. I drive an old, rusted out Jeep. In all likelihood, I doubt Jesus even likes me."

"If you say it, then it must be true, bro. But I just want to tell you that it's all a matter of perception. If you think your life's good, sooner or later, it is."

"I don't know about all that stuff," Josh said. "I love my grandfather. Look what happened to him."

"Don't shoot the messenger. I'm just trying to lighten the mood, you guys. Gettin' back to hot chicks," he said, turning to Dianna, "Who was that knockout with you at the lake yesterday?"

Dianna turned to face Billy. "My sister. You were at the lake?"

"Yeah, kinda. Our house is off the water. Deus thought it was you. We weren't pervin' or anything, but we had to get the binoculars just to make sure."

"Yeah, that's my sister," Dianna said.

"Well, Deus almost had a heart attack when he saw her. How old is she?"

Dianna shook her head. "Sorry to disappoint you, but she's six years older. I doubt she even dated sixteen-year-olds when she was our age."

"That's kind of what I thought you'd say."

"Wait a second," Josh butted in. "Billy and Deus have both seen you in a swimsuit. I've gotta say, I'm a little jealous."

"Don't worry. I've got your back," Dianna winked. "I took photos at the lake."

"I am, without a doubt, the luckiest guy in the whole world," Josh said, smiling from ear to ear.

Chapter 12
The Disciple

"Take me where I want to be," commanded Claire. Even though her voice reverberated with authority, she didn't quite feel it. She took one final look, as Larry lay sleeping in the hospital bed. Then she rose through the roof and up into the sky. She didn't even bother looking back, as the earth fell away beneath her. Claire's mind was troubled. She wasn't here to sightsee. She was on a mission. It had taken quite a bit of effort, but Claire had pulled enough strings to meet with the top brass of Division.

Glancing off across the blackness of space, Claire looked towards the sun and the neighboring planets. Earth was so beautiful but definitely not unique, as most people believed. She had figured out, even without training, that this earth was only one among millions of other earths. Each galaxy had its own earth, moon, stars and sun, moving with breathtaking precision.

All these elements were neatly contained and stacked on top of each other, like little magnetic steel balls. She could still remember the day when the Archangel Michael revealed to her that the Creator didn't just preside over the multiple galaxies, like she had originally thought. The truth is that with the millions of galaxies, with all the untold numbers of people inhabiting them, their combined sentience is God.

Each universe, though infinitely large to a human, was nothing more than a nerve cell; a building block in the mind of the Creator. Claire shuddered just thinking of how miserable that job must be. It required omniscience, as well as omnipresence, at all times. And not only were there the visible worlds, but also the hidden ones in the bandwidths between. Slowing her assent, Claire sent out her consciousness, commanding, "I am a child of God. As he created, it is my divine right to do so as well." Her energy pulsed out in ringlets from her spirit self, flooding the empty space, shining and coalescing until...

    Claire opened her eyes and she was in New Orleans. "Not bad," she thought, admiring her dress. It was high-fashion, in midnight blue material with black lace at the end of each sleeve. The corset-dress laced in the back through dozens of eyelets. And it flowed out, gently touching the lush, green grass below. "Now," she said, straightening the black bow resting in front of her cleavage, "I do believe I have a meeting to attend." Walking towards the large plantation, Claire drank in the beauty around her, while infusing it with her will. As she got older, she found this particular talent got stronger and stronger. In her youth, Claire had been far too impetuous to pull this off. Though what she lacked in skill, she made up for with raw power. Nowadays, there seemed to be a balancing of the two.

    As she walked along the moss-covered oak trees, Claire listened to the birds, as they called out in unison to each other. Every detail was bursting to the seams with vitality. Her subconscious, in turn, was animating that vitality with even more detail. Drawing closer to the two-story plantation, Claire saw that the architecture was exquisite. The white columns out front offset the black iron balcony outside of the master's quarters. She wondered if God took as much pleasure in fashioning out the solar system as she did in creating this simple setting. Or was he too heavily burdened with his responsibilities? Like most artists, the Creator had helpers. And that's where Division came in.

    She knew that some people still referred to it as Heaven, and even she had at one point. Yet she knew it wasn't a final resting place. Division headquarters stood on the boundaries of time. Ultimately, God knew that somebody would have to maintain the integrity of this massive machine He created. So He created two completely opposite races of beings; the angels and the demons. The Angelic Branch he named the Host, and the

Demonic Branch he called the Monarchy. Both acted under God's authority. In every universe, they were the backbone of order. Without them, there wouldn't be any balance. It was one agency, with two branches. From the day she was first trained as a dream bender, Claire had operated in the employ of the Host. She earned herself quite a reputation, and it was only by that reputation that Claire could request today's meeting.

Walking under the shade of the tall oak closest to the luxurious home, Claire saw that her guests had already arrived and were enjoying tea at the small patio table. "Well, hello, Claire. You look stunning," Metatron said. The Director of Division took her hand in his and lightly kissed the top of it. He was immaculately groomed, as always. His short beard of brown hair was flecked with distinguished gray. "I believe you know my companion, Michael," he said, gesturing to the angel on his right.

"I do," Claire enthusiastically replied. "Michael, my darling, you look positively--"

"Heavenly?" Michael interjected, arching his eyebrow and grinning. The tall angel leaned over and kissed Claire on the cheek. His jet black locks brushing her face, as he did. Then, sweeping her up in his muscular frame, he sang her name and whirled her around. "Baby Claire," his voice chiming like a bell.

She laughed as Michael set her down. "Unfortunately, I'm no longer the little girl I used to be," Claire said, pointing at her gray hair.

"You don't see what I do," the archangel said, sitting down.

Pulling her dress to the side to have a seat, Claire bowed her head and addressed them both. "I see you're without your wings."

"Well, of course," Michael said, pointing to their clothes. "These britches are hot enough." Claire smiled at the fine two-piece suits her mind had fashioned for her guests.

"I do apologize," she said, offering her fan.

"Very elaborate, Claire," Metatron commented. "The details of the house are extraordinary. Have you ever gone inside?"

"Not too long ago, Larry and I had dinner in the dining hall, which brings me to the object of this meeting. My physical body is sitting next to Larry, who's lying heavily medicated in a hospital bed."

"I'm sorry," Metatron said softly, dipping his head.

"For all intents and purposes it looks like my grandson accidentally spoke it into existence, with powers, might I add, that he shouldn't even have." She watched Metatron and Michael exchange worried looks. Claire knew they were just talking amongst themselves.

"It's definitely unfortunate," Metatron sighed, pressing his hands together. "As much as I love you, Claire, I can't tell you everything for the sake of free will. The Crown just can't divulge certain things about your present situation. However, I will confirm your suspicions, as far as Josh being the male Prime."

"I knew it!" Claire said, covering her mouth with her hand. "That's incredible." Despite her happiness, Metatron's face still looked worried.

"Reserve your judgment, Claire. Josh will be the Dark Half." Claire's face fell, as she was filled with dread.

"How? He's so pure. There's not an ounce of darkness in him. I ... I don't understand," she stuttered.

It wasn't until she saw the angels looking around that Claire noticed the colors of the landscape were running together like an old, distorted picture. She didn't care though. The bad news was too much to handle. All around her, the landscape bled, and the flowers wilted. Claire looked down to see that she was wearing the clothes that she had put on earlier that morning.

"How can he be the Dark Half?" she sobbed. "I devoted my whole life to you. My only son, his father, died serving. Doesn't that count for anything? I gave you everything I had!" she screamed, and you tell me my grandson is the Antichrist?"

The angels sat in silence, looking at the skyline as lightning flashed in the distance. "He is not the Antichrist," Metatron said sternly, as he turned toward his angelic companion. "Michael, clean this up."

The tall angel stood up, his dark hair blowing in the stiff wind that had just kicked up. With a simple snap of his fingers, the wind died down and the brilliant rays of the sun began to break through the clouds. Claire could feel the anger leave her, as waves of hope and determination washed over her.

"Listen," ordered Metatron. "It is in situations like these, when I'm constantly reminded the myths the dream benders cling to. This isn't about good or evil. From the standpoint of human evolution, there is only complete and incomplete. Josh is incomplete, but that doesn't mean he cannot or will not change before the millennial kingdom comes."

"Please don't do this to him," Claire begged. "Please."

Metatron seemed unnerved, "Throughout time, the dream benders have always viewed the prophecy of the Prime like it's hitting the jackpot on a slot machine. A lucky event, if ever there was one, but somebody has to pay the taxes. And that somebody is Josh."

"Make her do it," Claire snapped. "What has her family ever done?"

"Don't do this, Claire," Metatron said, shaking his head. "Her bloodlines are just as strong as yours. Her ancestors on one side are Mexican, and on the other they are Spanish and Shawnee Indian. I think you know they've already given enough. She comes from a noble family that, over many generations, have paid their dues. So don't question her legitimacy."

Pausing for a moment, Metatron reached down to touch the little figure hanging from her necklace. "There are only two of these in existence, Claire. One is on your neck. The other was given to your son. It signifies uncommon valor, a trait your family has always displayed. Don't deny your grandson his right to prove his mettle."

Claire nodded. "I understand the rules. I just don't want him to hurt, is all. I can't bear the thought of what he might have to go through."

"None of the avatar's parents ever want to think about that," Metatron said softly, "but they rarely realize the avatars don't come in a golden age of happiness or safety. They come to oppose a threat and stand up as humanity's savior. These teens have to be extraordinary. The Monarchy will put them to the test, but there will be help as well."

"Everything has a reason, Claire," Metatron said, enveloping her in his energy. "I know you vehemently oppose the Monarchy, and that you favor the angels. But God does not share your opinion wholeheartedly, and you know it. This universe works on basic principles. Look at a battery. It doesn't work if it has two positive sides." Claire sighed. She knew the importance of what Division called The Prime Objective. She just assumed Josh would have the easier half. She knew that God never did anything one-sided. There is duality in everything. Claire knew the demons had just as much authority as the angels. When she was a child, she had asked her mother why God didn't stop the demons from harassing Job. Her mother never answered. It wasn't until she was older that her father pointed out the portions of the Bible where God revealed duality was all a part of His plan. At times, the Devil had strolled right into Heaven, just like he had every right to be there.

"So how does this work?" asked Claire. "Is there anything I don't know?" Metatron sat without saying anything. All Claire got were the sounds of chirping birds playing carelessly in the trees.

"Please," Michael urged his companion. "We owe her at least that much."

"This is the deal," Metatron said, stroking his beard. "There can't be any interference, Claire. The Prime Objective is built completely on free will."

"I understand," she replied.

"The world you live in is at a serious juncture. Every person who has lived, up to this point, was merely a building block on the stage of life. The Wright brothers were destined for flight, just as Thomas Edison was destined to invent the light bulb. Through their contributions, the final stage was set up. But their being here had no sway on the ultimate fate of the world. It only fulfilled their obligation to descend into matter and experience this life. The war between good and evil, and the decision of the Primes, will decide what happens to your earth. Only then will we know whether it goes to the light, or it is claimed by the darkness."

"So none of this meant anything?" Claire stammered.

"Oh, it did," Metatron answered. "But as far as the mortals and history is concerned, there has been unerring balance since the dawn of time. Whenever a great evil presented itself, nature balanced it by sending the avatars. This earth has been in balance for six thousand years. It isn't until now that the main stage is set for the endgame."

"Enter: the Prime," Michael said softly, and almost melodiously. "Two teenagers fated to come together. One is the light incarnate. The other is half light and half dark, every bit as powerful as the first. The Dark Half, as this Prime is called, has to live with both of the energies in balance and become adept at both. It is, indeed, the least desirable of the two roles."

"But only from a human perspective," added Metatron. "And deep down, your soul understands that. Just as the demonic Monarchy and the angelic Host make up the cosmic peripheral nervous system of the spirit realm, The Dark Half is what makes The Prime Objective even remotely possible. If they were both possessed of the same energy, in the same amount, there wouldn't be an attraction."

Claire sat back in the chair and relaxed. She was past the initial shock. Now she just wanted to figure out how she could make things easier on Josh. The tall angel took her hand in his and continued, "For sixteen years, the Primes receive passive, formative training from their family. Much knowledge is preserved through the powerful bloodlines. Then the children receive two intensive years with their own, assigned watcher who will teach them how to use their power best."

"Has Josh's been assigned already?" asked Claire, perking up.

Michael's face began to glow radiantly, "Yes. And he's getting the best."

"Thomas?" Claire anxiously asked, hoping she was correct.

"Yes. Nina's husband will be Josh's watcher." Claire sighed in relief. "Thank you." She'd known Thomas most of her life. He was a legend in the bending community, not only for his skills in combat but his shrewd wisdom as well.

Metatron continued, "During these two years, the children can be tempted by demons. However, they cannot be hurt or killed, unless they openly challenge an operative of the Demonic Branch."

Michael clarified, "They can be tempted by demons. However, they cannot be harmed. Inversely, they can be encouraged by the angels, but they cannot be fortified."

"UNLESS," Metatron added, holding up his hand, "unless a danger the child is not prepared for is threatening The Objective. Once the training is completed, on the eighteenth birthday of the younger of the two, all of Heaven and Hell will be let loose," said Metatron, as he looked to Michael. "The two teens will fight for their lives, as well as their love. Both of them will have to stand strong, for it is this battle that deems the fate of the world."

"What if one of them is tempted and falls?" asked Claire, fearing the answer. She couldn't help recalling her disappointment at the look on Josh's face, when he watched her grab the $33 million winning ticket.

Metatron inhaled and then exhaled sharply. "In the event that they end up on opposing sides in the battle, all is lost. The victor rules alone, with the remnant for the thousand year millennial kingdom. Unless there are two victorious Primes standing together, united, further fulfillment of the protocol is deemed impossible. Everything will be reduced to prima mater, and we start over."

Claire sat in stunned silence. "I don't understand. Why would that happen?"

Metatron nodded, "I understand your confusion. It's the same reason that a female can achieve pregnancy, but the body will purposely miscarry a genetically flawed fetus that wouldn't be viable. Without their soulmate to complete them, the Primes' subconscious will finish humanity off, as well as the angels and demons. The solo Prime's sadness and despair would devolve into madness, bringing calamity in the form of a flood or a comet or what have you."

Claire began to get nervous. How could two teens ever rise up to such a challenge? As if sensing her alarm, Michael spoke up, "But if they are victorious, civilization flourishes unhindered. They become the rulers Earth deserves. Their single offspring will one day instinctually leave at the onset of puberty, finding an uninhabited wavelength in the space in between to birth a brand new universe."

"I somehow had a feeling this all tied into the Phoenix Agenda," the woman said.

The angel smiled broadly, "Eventually, everything ties into the Phoenix Agenda, Claire. You know that. Only after the Primes are victorious and their offspring leaves, as the Phoenix, will your earth actually be inserted as a permanent building block within the brain of the Creator."

Metatron pushed away from the table and began standing up, "All of this information is highly classified, Claire. Punishment up to and including being taken out of The Book," he warned. Do you understand?"

"I do," Claire said, as she watched Metatron fade out.

Michael stood up slowly. "Are you going to be okay?" he asked.

"I have a question," Claire started, hesitantly scanning his eyes. "I've always trusted in you. In my younger years, you stood by me, making me strong."

"Every step of the way," he said, nodding.

"When I finally retired and felt the need to marry and have children, the very next man I met was Larry. I always felt that your hand was a blessing on our union, because his last name was like your stamp of approval. I'm asking, if you really had a hand in my life, please, lift that protection and, please, place it on Josh. Keep him from harm."

The tall angel stepped up, towering over her with nothing but love and compassion on his face. Gently wrapping both of his hands around hers, he said, "I love you, Claire, but Josh is the Dark Half. Based on that alone, the demons will try to tempt him first. If he falls, I have no choice but to cast him down. But if he stands strong through the temptation, just and true," he said, light beginning to blaze around him, "I swear, Claire, everybody who opposes him will know why my title is 'Michael, Defender of Children.'"

Finally satisfied, Claire nodded, "A very worthy title indeed, my old friend."

***

"11:11? Oh my God, I can't read any more," Dianna thought, as she tried to stifle her yawn. She'd just have to read the rest at lunch tomorrow. She couldn't stay up any longer. She took in a deep breath and stretched her arms. "So tired," she thought to herself.

Closing her math book, she pushed away from her desk and made her way towards the bed. She could see the poem Josh had written her sitting on her nightstand. She wondered whether it was a good idea to spoil it by reading it right now. She didn't want it to be wasted on her tired brain, but she'd been eyeing it all night, while she worked on her homework. "Okay," she told herself, "I'll read it tonight. Then I'll read it tomorrow too."

Happy with her compromise, Dianna grabbed the piece of yellow, folded paper and collapsed on her bed. Unfolding it, she saw that this wasn't just a few lines that Josh had written. A smile spread across her lips. It was a note. And she could see he'd actually put some feeling into it. Rolling onto her stomach and pulling herself toward the edge of the bed, Dianna huddled up near her bedside lamp.

As she read the page, she imagined Josh speaking the words to her:

> From the very first time we talked, Dianna, I felt the need to stroke your hair and caress your cheek. But I dare not, for fear that my forward actions would tear asunder the fragile frame that was our friendship. It is a framework I feel myself outgrowing each successive time I look into your beautiful eyes. Our first kiss is something I will never forget, because I've never in my life realized how lonely I was, until the first time I saw you. From then on, I was shackled and helpless. Only your smile, your lips released me. I don't know where the future is leading us, nor what the dream was sent for, but I'll fight Heaven and Hell before I ever step back to who I was before I met you.
>
> They say that beauty is only skin deep. But how can that be when the woman I saw that night completely

redefined the word and sang it in silence, whispering it between words? As we sat on the grass in our circle of secrecy, I was amazed as the girl that I knew opened up like a rose in the springtime and revealed the woman you truly are. Your story was a crescendo of highs and lows, but these words do little justice. Only the image that is emblazoned on my mind could re-create the hope in your eyes as you spoke of the future, or the pain, as you spoke of the past. So I've made up my mind. My most ardent intent is to do away with the past. Let us walk into the future and spread hope.

P.S. On the real, I kinda think I'm crushing on you.

Dianna rolled over, onto her back. Still clutching the paper to her chest, she smiled and thought about the words that his heart had prompted him to write. And, for a split second, Dianna thought to herself that she truly understood what it meant to be on the same page with someone. And then she silently drifted off to sleep.

***

The members of the lavishly decorated board room sat in silence, as their leader deliberated their next move. Lost in thought, Hasden sat, staring at the six foot glass case that was built into the wall in front of him. Inside of the case, a black serpent twisted its way around a piece of dead driftwood that was firmly planted in the dark stones lining the bottom. The funny part was that the glass case, and everything in it, was chump change compared to the installation cost to retrofit the wall to install it. It was insane to think that he had to go to such lengths just to obtain a simple pleasure.

"Gentlemen," Hasden announced, "we have a thorn in our side. So now we have to remove it." Pushing out the chair and rising up slowly, he locked his eyes with everybody present, all of whom were demons. "The Medical Director in section three, whom we appointed, is becoming less receptive to suggestions regarding our proposed policies. That is unfortunate," Bill said, pacing around the table. "But that's a mere infraction compared to the fact that he's being blatantly obstinate on the issue of endorsing our medical products."

"So what do you have in mind?" Deus asked, rolling up his sleeves.

"I'm glad you asked, Mr. Gregory," Hasden shouted, pointing at Deus like he was the winner of a game show. "Seeing as his father is a well-known demon, we can't just kill him or make him disappear. So this is my proposal. His biggest vices have always been liquor and women."

"Shit, I want to party with this guy," Deus said, chuckling.

"Unfortunately, from henceforth, nobody in this boardroom can go within five hundred miles of him, unless you'd like to lock horns with his father." Standing rigid, with his arms crossed, Hasden projected his will out, over the eight members in attendance. "Do I make myself clear? For all intents and purposes, this has to look like it was his own fault. Am I making myself clear?" he asked again. Each member nodded.

"There's an opening in his office for a medical tech and for a medical biller. I want them both filled, yesterday. One woman should be a plain Jane, and the other woman as exotic as possible. She should be something he can't normally have."

"I could get some ants," Deus suggested. Hasden pondered the possibility. The term ant was used to describe weak-willed individuals. It was short for "ancillary." A strong-willed demon could easily control an ant to do just about any task. He wasn't opposed to them, but it seemed the Monarchy relied on ants more than their demonic powers nowadays. It was becoming problematic. Hasden tapped his finger and looked, first at Deus to his left and then to Angela to his right. They were both at the other end of the table.

"No," he replied, shaking his head. The suggestion in their head could be traced back. "I want this clean. Find two girls and point them in the right direction. Let Mother Nature do the rest. When scandal ensues, as it most certainly will, we can have Angela anonymously tip off the press."

"The new replacement has to be a lot more receptive to suggestions. We have our new EKG monitor, the Heart Smart DCLXVI, that has to be pushed for us to show a profit. And all of our associates have to back our new Nightingale line of medications. We spent a boatload of cash sponsoring studies that suggest that, even though there are cheaper medications out there, they 'may' be dangerous." Bill smiled, as laughter filled the room, when he emphasized with air quotations around the word "may." Everybody seemed to laugh, except for Angela. She just sat silently, erasing and writing, only to erase again, in the leather-bound book she constantly had by her side.

Bill held up his hand, so the laughter would die down. "I remember the days of Sodom and Gomorrah. In fact, Deus loves to reminisce about how we had it all back then. Civilization was young. We could party all day and screw all night, sometimes four or five at a time. It felt glorious. But I want to ask you something," he said, leaning into the table to address his fellow demons. "I know we all love to talk about the glory days. But did you ever dream," Hasden shouted, "that by stepping out of the past and walking into the modern age we'd be able to fuck millions of people all at once? Now THAT'S progress." Hasden forced a grin, as applause flooded the board room. He hated to be so dramatic, but he had to set the room up for the bad news that was inevitably going to follow.

Already he could see Deus was preparing for the second half of the meeting in his usual way. He was loading up with more alcohol. "Great, looks like I'm alone on this one," Bill thought to himself. It was okay, though. He was used to it by now. Through the countless centuries they'd been together, it was apparent that Hasden was the brains and Deus was the brawn. His regent's unleashed fury was a sight to behold. He was easily twice as strong as any other demon in the room. Hasden could count on one hand the few demons at Division that could go toe-to-toe with him. Deus did have his drawbacks, but Bill always kept him nearby. Despite his obvious flaws, there was one, little fleck of gold that made Deus a worthy investment. He was fiercely loyal. And in the Monarchy, that was a hard trait to find. Having Deus by his side was what freed him up to follow all these endeavors.

Under Hasden's rule, the Monarchy wasn't just a bunch of demons tempting the humans. They had risen up to become their masters. Even so, Bill knew that every demon in the room would take his position if they could, despite everything he'd accomplished. The beast that was the Monarchy was always hungry. If unfed, it would just devour its master. That's why Hasden kept Deus in front of him at all times.

Bill straightened his black tie. "Get ready," he projected his thoughts out at his companion. Peering over, he saw Deus instantly push away his glass. "I'm glad everybody in attendance is a Monarchy associate, because we have official business to discuss. He watched, as all the smiling faces turned deathly serious. As most of you know, Mr. Gregory and I have been self-appointed to a healer out in Massachusetts." To the far right of the table, a demon stood up, his body so morbidly obese that his suit nearly touched Angela's arm next to him. Hasden noticed that she paid him no mind and continued silently checking and erasing with her pencil.

"Bill, some of the members and I would like to point out that it's been almost two months since you assigned yourselves to this girl. So far, we haven't heard a word. Although it's your right, as head of the Monarchy, to roam around to and fro, the members of this Board feel your duties lie here. And you have a fiduciary responsibility to us, as fellow investors, as well."

"Have a seat, Captain Cholesterol," Deus shouted, "or I'll take your buddy next to you, Hair Club for Tards over there, shove him up your fat ass and throw you both out that window over there." Bill looked over his shoulder toward the window.

"Does anybody else here want to push Mr. Gregory's buttons? If that's the case, I'd like to remind you that we're on the fortieth floor. Please allow me to finish." Bill shook his head and continued, "I'm sure many of you are probably wondering why Mr. Gregory and myself have not tempted the girl and found which side of the fence she falls on."

"The thought had crossed our minds," said a skinny demon, straightening his hairpiece while glaring at Deus.

"She's definitely avatar potential, but there's something else," Hasden said, carefully watching the faces of the other demons. "She could possibly be the Prime. While casing her out, we stumbled on a powerful male. Both of them come from the so-called lines." He waited while the demons talked among themselves.

"If this is true," he continued, "we only have two years until the war."

"If you knew this, Bill, why did we even have the business meeting today?" the fat demon asked. "Shouldn't we be getting ready for the apocalypse?"

Glaring at the gluttonous wretch, Bill leaned on the table, pressing his weight against the wood. "No, we shouldn't. You'll continue to helm Hasden Corp., while we sort this out." While he spoke, he continued to press down, until his knuckles were white. The sound of cracking, splintering wood filled the air. He was hoping the sound from the table would subconsciously remind all present that he would snap all their necks, if his orders were disobeyed.

Deus stood up from the table, towering over the attendees. "The girl isn't falling for the shiny stuff. The boy, as powerful as he is, shouldn't even have powers in the first place. So we'd like everybody to continue business as usual, just in case it turns out to be a false alarm. In the event that it's not, Hasden is the highest ranking demon anyway. So we'd appreciate it, if everybody just minded their own business for the time being."

"What do you mean he's not supposed to have powers? What's his name?" asked a demon in the corner. Swallowing, Hasden let go of the table.

"His name is Josh Michaels." Immediately, the lead on Angela's pencil snapped. She flinched, causing her long, black ponytail to jump. Hasden watched as her head slowly raised up.

"Little jumpy there, sweet cheeks?" glutton asked, laughing. His huge, tailored suit was trembling as his belly shook. Angela turned towards him, her eyes filled with hate.

"What did you call me?" she asked, her voice seething with resentment. Hasden could only shake his head, as he watched the black serpent slip from the wooden branch, its lifeless body dropping to the bottom of the glass case.

"Bill, call off your secretary," shouted the morbidly obese demon, who sounded frightened. Hasden pondered the look of genuine confusion on his fat face. Oh, well, there's very little he could do now. Angela took the tie out of her ponytail, letting her black hair hang free. Then, slowly, she unbuttoned her blouse. Bill watched as the white shirt slid from her shoulders, falling in a heap on the ground. Gazing at Mahvet's majestic body, he wondered to himself how many she'd have to kill before she was satisfied. As she stood there in her black leather heels, black skirt and black bra, Angela's body began to steal the warmth from everything in the room.

"Goddammit," thought Bill.

"What's the meaning of this?" shouted the demon at the end

of the table.

"You're about to find out," Hasden coldly replied, "that Hell hath no fury like a woman scorned." Angela stood, staring in a murderous rage, insanely posturing like she was about to attack the glutton.

"Get this crazy bitch away from me!" he shouted, as he scrambled to get out of his seat. Bill sat, quietly watching as the fat demon's skin flushed red to reveal his true nature, for all the good it would do him. When the obese demon saw Angela's black, feathered wings unfold, the color drained from him. "What" was the only word he could manage, before she started to drain his life force.

It looked like she'd stuck a huge straw in his chest. Spirals of dark energy swirled from his torso and into her outstretched hands. His massively bloated body decompressed, like he'd sprung a leak. Hasden watched on as the demon next to the glutton hung over the table for dear life, looking like a seasick passenger stuck on a boat, just praying the ride would end. Bill knew she'd probably kill him too. It was the effect of Death's maw that he was experiencing. Out of the corner of his eye, Hasden could see Deus was thoroughly enjoying the show, totally oblivious to the danger that was mere feet away.

As both bodies fell to the floor, there was nothing but silence, until Angela jerked to attention and screamed, "Which one of you chauvinistic good old boys wants to get it next?" The rest of the board members sat shocked, staring at the seething maniac.

"She's an Angel of Death!" cried the demon at the far end of the table. "How?" he asked, staring at her wings.

"Welcome to the new order, gentlemen," Hasden said, folding his arms. "I have a proposal for you."

***

There was nothing better than the sound of thousands of screaming fans. Josh just stood there on the stage and drank it in, surrounded by the roar of applause and lighters being lit, begging him for an encore. He'd already played through two guitar solos here, and he didn't want the city to fine the venue. So, raising his guitar up over his head, Josh screamed, "We love you, Seattle," and strolled towards the exit from the stage. Leaving the screaming fans behind him, he headed straight into the crowd, waiting for his manager in the wings. He immediately saw his manager, Flynn, was waiting for him.

"Hurry up, man. We got to get you to the party."

"Calm down. You act like this is my first rodeo, Flynn. The last two CDs went double platinum. I know what I'm doing." The crowd was thick in the hall. Josh had his manager take the lead, pushing aside the throng.

"Hey! Can you sign something for me?" a girl next to him asked.

"Holy crap. You gotta be kidding me," thought Josh, as he looked over at her. She was smoking hot.

"Sure," Josh said, smiling and taking the pen from her hand. "Do all the girls out here look as good as you?"

"No, they don't," she said, grinning. Josh took her CD from her hand. "Who do I make this out to?"

"Just sign it 'to my biggest fan, Dianna.'"

Josh signed the CD and gave it back to the smiling girl. "I don't know if you're doing anything later, but we're having a release party after. If it's cool, maybe you'd like to come and hang out." He grinned and slipped a guitar pick in her front pocket in the hopes she might show up.

"I'll think about it," she said coyly, winking at him before she turned around.

"She is too damn fine," he thought, watching her curves as she drifted into the sea of faces.

"Come on, Josh," Flynn said, leading him away.

"Don't be late," Josh called, as Flynn dragged him off.

"We need to get you some new clothes and get you out of here," the manager said, unlocking the door to the dressing room and pushing him inside. "You're going to have to wear something nice. The record execs will be there." Josh walked into the quiet room and shook his head in disgust. There on the couch, reading the back of his new CD, was a complete stranger.

"Seriously, Flynn! I thought you tightened security around here."

"Don't worry. I'll take care of it," the manager said, pushing past Josh. "I don't know who you are, man. But you need to bust out. This is a private dressing room." The older man just smiled at Flynn, thoroughly amused. He looked like one of the roadies, Josh thought, but he was older and had a beard. "What? Are you deaf?" Flynn screamed, getting on his hands and knees. "I said to get the hell out of here." Josh took a second to take in the strange sight.

"Flynn, are you all right?" The manager bared his teeth at the roadie on the couch and snarled. "What did you do to my manager?" Josh asked, confused.

"Not to alarm you," the roadie replied, but you're dreaming.

"Dude, you're bat shit crazy. Now, you have five seconds to get out of here, or I'll call security," threatened Josh. The stranger folded his hands in his lap and chuckled. He didn't even seem fazed.

"Flynn is your grandmother's dog," the man said. "Dianna is not a groupie. She's your girlfriend."

Josh threw his arms up, hiding his face. "AWWW, man." Slowly at first, memories started seeping into his head.

"My name is Metatron. I believe your grandmother told you I'd be by."

"I feel like such a dork," Josh said, running his fingers

through his hair and plopping into the seat in front of the strange man. "I don't even have a shirt on," he said, pointing to his chest. "And I'm wearing leather pants."

"Don't worry. It happens to the best of us," said the man. He was surprisingly controlled. In fact, Josh wondered how the guy wasn't laughing. He still felt like an idiot, looking at how he was dressed.

"I've come to announce that it's official. You are to be trained," Metatron said, picking up the fully-transformed Flynn. He scratched the little white dog under his collar and then set him down on the couch next to his lap.

Staring quizzically at the scruffy brown-haired gentleman, Josh asked, "So how does this happen?"

"This weekend your trainer, Thomas, will make contact with you. He'll fill you in and take it from there." Josh watched as the stranger got up, leaving the dog to curl up on the cushion.

"What can I expect?" asked Josh

"Keep an open mind, and you'll be fine," Metatron said, smiling. "This world isn't what you've been led to believe. But don't worry. I have complete faith in you. It's pretty obvious," he flashed Josh a smile, "that you're ready to rock."

Chapter 13
The Siege Perilous

"Happy birthday, brother," Billy said, placing the card on Josh's desk in front of him.

"Hey! Tell him the card's from me too."

The spiky-haired boy laughed, "Oh, Deus signed the card too."

"Dude, you're an ass," the large teen said to his cousin.

"Half the gift card's from me," Deus said.

"Thanks. I appreciate it. You guys didn't have to get anything for me though."

"What good's having money, if you can't spend it on your friends?" Deus said, smiling and taking the open seat in front of Josh. Josh noticed that the expelled teen had been a lot better since he came back. It had been almost three weeks now, and there wasn't one problem with Deus. He was as nice as pie. Josh didn't know what the lawyers did to get him back in school, but Charlie should have hired them.

"Hey, thunder guns," Charlie called from behind Josh's back. "It's a good thing you got Josh a gift card, because if you gave him cash, he'd just give it to that bum out in front of the mini-mart."

"Leave the birthday boy alone," Dianna said, sitting in the desk to the right of Josh. "How do you feel?"

"Little tired," Josh replied. "The bird woke me up bright and early again." Reaching across the table, Josh grabbed her hand. "I can't believe there's only another week and a half of school."

Nodding her head, Dianna frowned, "I know. I'm not looking forward to leaving you here for three months." Josh preferred not to think about that. He was floored, when she told him about the road tour. He really couldn't blame her though.

They were getting their house paid off. Most people could only dream of a situation like that.

"Even though we'll be apart," he pointed out, "I'll text you every day. We can also talk on the phone as much as you want."

"And," she said, winking.

"...I think I can manage a picture, too," Josh said.

Smiling, Dianna reached over and gave him a quick hug. "That's my Osito." He just grinned and shook his head. She knew her nickname for him made him self-conscious, but Dianna used it anyway. Josh leaned in and kissed her on the cheek.

"I don't know why I told you my old nickname."

"Because," the girl said, as if the answer was in doubt, "you're totally helpless against my female powers."

"It must be," he thought, because there was very little he wouldn't do just to see her smile.

"Gag, you two. Save it for after school," Charlie said, looking annoyed. Personally, Josh didn't know what his friend was complaining about. If anything, he'd made out like a bandit. All he had to do was endure ten more days of this. The skinny teen nearly had a seizure, when he heard Dianna was going on tour. Josh knew there'd be plenty of stuff to do with Billy, Deus, and Charlie, but he could easily live without them. Dianna was a different story. She'd be taking off June 24th and would be on the road until Labor Day weekend.

Josh sighed, "Pretty soon you'll be sweet sixteen."

"Yep. June 21st. Right around the corner. It's kinda cool we're both Geminis."

"If you guys are cool with it," Deus horned in, "how about we have a double birthday on the last day of school? It'll be Dianna's birthday that night anyway."

"I don't know," she replied hesitantly. "We're getting up bright and early that Saturday and picking up the RV. It's going to be a big day of packing and a lot of shopping."

"Come on. It'll be fun. Besides, it's the last night we can all hang out together. Don't you think you guys deserve it?"

"I know. It would definitely mean a lot to me," Josh said, smiling.

"Alright, I suppose," Dianna said slowly. "If you guys are gonna twist my arm."

"Sweet," the big teen said, immediately standing up. "Listen up, everybody," he shouted. "The last day of school me and Billy are throwin' a birthday kegger at our house for the two Geminis. There's gonna be a DJ and a bonfire out by the lake. More details to follow."

"Wow," Dianna said. "News spreads quickly around here."

"My pleasure," said Deus. "Now you owe me and Billy a dance."

"Okay, deal."

"Oh, and tell that fine ass sister of yours that she's invited too," the boy said, hanging his tongue out of his mouth.

"Somehow, I don't think you know what you're getting yourself into."

"Neither do I," boomed a voice from the front of the classroom. All the students whipped their heads towards Mr. Douglas's desk. "Before we finish World War II and begin review for the final, I've a question for Mr. Gregory. Your father will be at your party, correct?"

"I don't think that's any business of yours," he replied, folding his arms defensively. Josh could feel the tension that had suddenly sprung up between the teacher and his student. Apparently, nobody had sent the memo to Mr. Douglas about Deus's absent father.

"It is my business," Mr. Douglas assured the student, standing up from his desk as the warning bell sounded for class to start. "Especially, when a student in my classroom announces a kegger."

"Let me rephrase that," Deus said, his voice dripping with sarcasm. "What goes on after we leave the school is none of your goddamn business." All of a sudden, Josh's whole body went on high alert. He noticed every student in the classroom looked like they were going to jump out of their seats and run. Was Deus insane? The two stared at each other for a few seconds. Finally, Mr. Douglas sighed. "Grab your things, Mr. Gregory, and follow me to the principal's office."

"Whatever. I don't see what the big deal is. Me and you just disagree."

"I partly agree, Mr. Gregory, but we'll let the principal decide." Josh watched as Mr. Douglas grabbed his keys from the desk and began to walk towards the boy, who already had a smile of victory on his face. "I'll be back in three minutes. Until then, Ms. Imperial, who is my first period TA, will watch the class," the teacher announced.

"If it's alright with you," asked Billy, "can I read my report on courage from earlier? I feel it ties in with the topic of World War II." Josh could tell, from the look on Mr. Douglas's face, that he wasn't in the mood for any further distractions. He yielded to the spiky-haired boy, as he escorted the other student from the room. Billy grinned, as the door shut slowly.

"We don't want to hear that report again," groaned Charlie. "It sucked the first time, in English class."

Josh nodded in agreement. Their homework was supposed to be a report on what one trait the student felt was most important. Billy picked courage, but the whole thing sounded like a pitch for his dad's company. Listening to the other students protest, Josh guessed he and Charlie weren't alone in the opinion.

"Calm down, everybody," Dianna interjected. "It's only for a few minutes."

"It's okay," Billy said, not looking the least bit offended. Crossing the room, he began scribbling on the dry erase board.

"I've got something much better." Mildly intrigued, Josh watched as Billy wrote the numbers one to nine and the letters of the alphabet on the board.

"I'd like to share a hobby of mine," announced Billy, smiling enthusiastically. "Throughout the ages, some of the greatest philosophers clung to the notion that numbers and letters could reveal our true nature. Skeptics say it's a lot of baloney," stated Billy, frowning. "They say it can't be proven, but I am of the belief that those nay-sayers are minimum-wage magi compared to Plato, Aristotle, or Socrates." Josh glanced over at Dianna. He could tell she'd already heard enough and was going to put an end to this.

"Since it's Dianna and Josh's birthdays, I decided to use the numbers and letters to prove why you guys are such a good match for each other. If it's okay with Dianna, of course."

Dianna nodded, looking mildly intrigued. "As long as this is just for fun."

"Of course," Billy said. "Step up here, you two. For those of you who don't know," announced Billy, "the Gemini are the twins. They are truly one half of the other. Like most twins, there's a special bond that connects them."

Billy pointed at the letters on the board and then at the number two and said, "With your twin by your side, you're never truly alone. You guys should hardly ever disagree, because in the end you're of one mind. Yet you're different enough that you constantly entertain each other." Turning to the board, Billy wrote down Dianna's name and interpreted with the corresponding numbers. "What's your middle name?" Billy asked Dianna.

"Alexa," she said, seeming almost embarrassed.

"Good," Billy said. "And what time were you born?" he asked.

"12:40 pm."

"Interesting," thought Josh, as the spiky-haired teen quickly added up the numbers.

"Definitely a rarity," Billy said, looking surprised. "All of your information equals 777. Those are the numbers of the Creator." Josh chuckled. Seeing Dianna smile, Billy continued, "Not only that," he said, "if you add them together, it's twenty-one; your date of birth. And that reduces to the number three, which symbolizes The Trinity."

"Definitely appropriate," Josh thought.

"And this is interesting," Billy said, his face looking puzzled. "You were born on the day of the summer solstice, when the sun is at its absolute strongest. Plus, you were born at a time when the light was at its peak for that day."

"Was there any doubt?" Dianna said, winking at Josh.

"What a little braggart," he replied jokingly, as he turned to Billy.

"You already know my middle name is Edward. And I was born a little after midnight, at 12:03 am." Josh was pretty surprised how well Billy knew all this stuff. He'd never put much stock into this before, but he had to admit the numbers for Dianna were spot on. Maybe in the future, he wouldn't give his mom such a hard time when she read her horoscope in the paper.

The room was overcome by gasps. Josh heard Charlie mutter, "Holy shit." Looking up at the board, Josh saw the reason.

With a confused look on his face, Billy said, "You were born at the darkest time of the night, and all your numbers are 666." Josh's mind began to reel as he stared at the numbers.

"You must have made a mistake." Billy did the math a second time, mumbling to himself, as he shook his head.

"It can't be right," the boy said. Finally, giving up, Billy said meekly, "I'm sorry Josh. Deus's middle name might be Damien, but that's just a coincidence. According to this, you're actually the Antichrist." Josh staggered back. A pit was beginning to form in his stomach. All around him he could hear the whispers of the other students.

"It doesn't mean anything," Dianna said, grabbing the eraser and quickly rubbing until all the evidence was gone. Even though it was off the board, Josh could still see the numbers in his mind.

"Well," Billy said, shrugging his shoulders apologetically, "it looks like you guys really are one half of the other. For Josh, the uncomfortable feeling in the classroom was unbearable. Everybody was staring at him. Then suddenly, the door swung open. A woman walked in, startling everybody.

"Hello, everybody. My name is Mrs. Gran, and I'll be finishing the day out for Mr. Douglas." A handful of girls, all surprised to see their Home Ec. teacher, squealed in approval.

"Billy, can I talk to you outside?" the teacher asked. Josh watched, as they both disappeared out the door together. He didn't have any classes with the teacher, but he knew she was very prim and proper. He'd heard she had gone to an all-girls finishing school in England that specialized in manners. Billy returned with a look of surprise on his face. He quickly grabbed his backpack and left without a word.

"If everybody would take a seat, we can begin our review," the teacher said, sitting on the stool where Mr. Douglas usually sat. Josh walked back to his desk, wondering what could have happened. "Billy mentioned it's your birthday, Mr. Michaels," the teacher said, opening up the class textbook.

"Yeah," Josh replied, feeling miserable.

"I hope it's a memorable one," she said politely, as she thumbed through the pages.

"You have no idea," he said, faking a smile.

***

"You didn't have to swing on him!" Hasden barked. "What

the hell were you thinking?" He gripped the steering wheel, as he made a hard left, trying to beat the light. The tires squealed, as they took the turn.

"I don't know. Douglas just wouldn't let it go. He kept eyeing me. I thought for a split second he might attack me."

"You know you're delusional, right?" Hasden asked, nodding vigorously. "Nobody's going to believe that he did anything of the sort. Hell, even I don't believe you."

"Well, it doesn't matter either way," Deus replied. "He sidestepped, and I missed." Shrugging his shoulders, Hasden nodded.

"Yeah, I saw the lockers as I left school. It looked like a goddamn sledgehammer hit them. There's no way they're ever going to let you back on campus."

"I'll make it up to you," he said, sounding like a child. "I can go home and watch after Angela until the bonfire on the last day of school." Hasden thought about the proposal. With Josh and Dianna turning sixteen soon, their watchers would be popping up. If anything went down, Deus was his backup. Hasden didn't think the watchers were all that powerful separately; but, together, they were dangerous. Rolling into their driveway, he hit the brakes and watched as Deus flew forward with the momentum.

"Look at me," he said. "I need you here. Even if you're not in school, I need you to follow up on all the other plans we have. Remember?"

"Oh, yeah," Deus said, getting out of the car. "Aren't you comin', Bill?"

"No. I need to sit here for a second. I need to think," he angrily replied.

"Okay, I'll call for dinner," Deus said as he walked away.

Hasden sat there for a moment in the silence of the car. Then he finally screamed, "You know what? I just really don't give a shit anymore." Of course, he knew it wasn't true. But why did it seem like he was constantly cleaning up after other people? Deus was thousands of years old. Yet, like most demons, he acted the same way he did when he was freshly created. Just like the Bentley he was sitting in, the demon still had new car smell.

Hasden, on the other hand, had grown. He'd changed. He remembered when the world was new. He killed quite often back then. He actually really enjoyed it, until he found that he also liked to play with his prey. It was a thrill to hear them beg, for all the good it did them. While he was continually adapting to the changing times, it seemed as of late, that with each challenge he overcame, the world would throw something new at him. He sighed, as his phone lit up with a text:

CALL ME. MAHVET

Bill hoped everything was okay, as he hit the dial button on his phone. "Hey, are you okay?" he said, trying his best to sound like he cared.

"I just want to say I'm sorry for flipping out the other day, and that I've calmed down."

Hasden was relieved. She sounded a lot better. "Look, I know it's tough, but we're going to get through this together. I need you to know that I'm by your side, but we need to keep you away from the other demons. They can't be trusted."

"Is that why I have to stay in my room?" she asked.

"Yes," Hasden answered. "At this point, we can't trust anybody. Not even Deus."

"I kind of was wondering. Maybe I could come out there and stay with you guys for a while?"

"We're coming back for the weekend," announced Bill. "We can talk about it, when you're better."

"Okay, sounds good. I'll see you when you get here."

Bill ended the call and exhaled, having dodged a major bullet. This is exactly the kind of bullshit he was talking about.

Before Angela came along, he basically had the world on a string. Now things were haywire with her crazy-ass mood swings. He shook his head, marveling at the predicament. As much trouble as she was, he couldn't get rid of her, either.

More valuable than Deus, she was definitely his ace in the hole. If he couldn't tempt the Primes over to his side, and for some reason it came down to war, he had a little surprise for the angels; and her last name was Mahvet. Of course, when the angels finally saw her, they'd be shocked as all hell. And those who could figure out who she was, wouldn't call her Mahvet. They'd refer to her as Lilith. It seemed like only yesterday that they'd first met.

Back in the beginning, she was just an incredibly beautiful good time girl, looking for fun. She would get with just about any demon around. But even though she was sleeping with other demons, Hasden knew she belonged to him. Lilith's appetite for sexual escapades was only rivaled by her lust for power, and Hasden had that in spades.

After a couple hundred years, she wasn't just drop dead gorgeous. She was gorgeous and extremely smart. She had a list of suitors a mile long, and each one of them thought they were the only one who was trading her intel for sex. It didn't take her too long to piece together all the secrets of Heaven, magic, weapons, you name it. And she was willing to share that knowledge.

It was well known among the demons that Lilith was consorting with the other tribal kings, but they really didn't give a rat's ass. The Creator, however, didn't find it too amusing. He enacted a new policy, stating that anybody caught with their hands in the cookie jar was going to get it. Even with that threat, Bill's buddy, Samael, decided he'd risk it. He was terminated from the Monarchy on the spot. The worst thing was that Bill had to do it. He figured nowadays Samael had to be somewhere living in the U.S., or maybe Europe. He was still immortal, but completely powerless. Hasden shuddered to even think what that must feel like.

After the Samael incident, God decided to fix Lilith's wagon. He had a strict free will policy for humans. So he gave her what she'd always wanted. He made her immortal.
He gave her wings and shipped her off to the Department of Death. Bill chuckled, when he thought how God had outsmarted her. She immediately found out there was a no cohabitation law. The Angel, Demon, and Death sectors of Division weren't allowed to live with, much less have sex with, the other departments. It must have been hell, because for a girl that loved sex with angels and demons, she quickly found out she couldn't have either. After she passed probation, the Creator promoted her preceptor and left her to run the Department of Death all by her lonesome.

Every once a while, Hasden would see her on earth after a natural disaster or something large scale. She really hadn't changed. She was still super friendly. Once in a while, they'd run into each other at Division and reminisce. The last time he'd seen her, Hasden wasn't too surprised to hear that Lilith wasn't as lonely as he had thought. She'd taken a liking to a dream bender named Alex Michaels.

Every now and again, there'd be a dream bender strong enough to actually see and speak to Death. The Michaels' family was incredibly strong. Whatever happened to lead her to believe Alex was into her, Hasden didn't know. Maybe it was just the centuries of loneliness. What happened next was legend around Division. Lilith confronted Alex and threatened to kill him and a girl he was seeing at the time. It was a blatant abuse of her power. Michaels was fit to be tied, not to mention wasting away, because she was obsessing over him. It seemed to be the end for Alex. Then his mother, Claire, found out. Claire was none too pleased. She was happily married and retired, but she wasn't about to let Death have her only son. Claire slapped Lilith so damn silly that she couldn't think straight.

After all was said and done, Lilith's energy was so screwed up that Metatron had to put her back together, practically from the ground up. That was the last anybody saw of her. She kind of became a recluse, until a few years ago. That's when she showed up on Hasden's doorstep, talking crazy and sporting one hell of a tan.

Bill looked into the car's rear view mirror and smiled. For the most part, the demons could change their looks, but rarely did. The one thing they did change though was their wings. They just weren't necessary anymore. So most Division employees just tucked them away. But when Lilith showed up on his front doorstep, naked as a jaybird, sporting a full set of wings, he knew something was wrong. After a lot of effort, Deus and Bill had gotten Lilith's head straight enough to piece together what had happened.

She was at a multiple homicide, collecting up the souls and deleting their names in her journal. It was nothing unusual. It was a routine run. Suddenly, she noticed a power surge. She knew the energy because it resembled hers. She followed the signature to Nevada. Somewhere, out in the cold, empty desert, Lilith found an unconscious angel. She was shining like a star and throwing off a tremendous amount of energy. Unsure what to do, Lilith crouched down next to the naked form and tried to scan her biomatrix. Immediately, she knew that the form wasn't from this realm. Yet the visitor was miraculously like her in almost every detail. She even had similar memories, but she had somehow become deranged.

Delving further into her psyche, Lilith saw one of the last memories was of an epic battle with a blue-skinned god, and then nothing but an eternity of mind-shattering pain. Lilith frantically tried to break the psychic bond, but the other angel wasn't allowing her to disengage. The next thing she remembered, she woke up on the cracked desert floor, confused and all alone. But somehow, she could hear the alien dialect echoing in her head. Not knowing where to turn, she came to the only person she thought she could trust.

It didn't take too long before he'd wished that she had darkened somebody else's doorway. She proved to be a handful from day one. One minute, she could be laughing hysterically, for no known reason. Then she would begin to cry, without a word. This went on for months. It was almost to the point where he was about to give up on her. But he didn't. Maybe because of his perseverance, Lady Luck had not only smiled on Hasden, but she also got on her knees and did a few favors.

It seemed that, over the few months Lilith was living with him, everybody he'd hated was ending up dead. At first, he couldn't quite figure it out. Then it became obvious that his new house guest was the culprit, when one of the deceased was a fellow immortal. Before her strange encounter, Lilith was just as powerful as any other demon or angel all by herself. But now she was infinitely stronger. He had no idea what had happened out in that desert, but somehow one of them must have consumed the other. To hide her identity and keep a short leash on her, Lilith became Angela Mahvet. At first, he was worried that the Host or Metatron was going to find out and show up. He still shuddered to think of what they would do to him. More than likely, he'd probably end up like Samael, stripped of all abilities and authority.

Hasden had a theory, though. Nobody was coming because, firstly, she was doing her job. Everybody who had ever been born or had died, was recorded or erased from the book by her own hand. It wasn't always immediately, but there is a margin of error for everything. Her job was no different. Secondly, he suspected the main reason their dealings went undetected by Heaven was because Metatron just couldn't find her. Even though Metatron was the Creator's second in command, he wasn't omnipresent; and he sure as hell wasn't omniscient. Only God could pull that off.

Metatron did have access to the All Mind, but Hasden had a sneaking suspicion he was continually posing the question in the wrong phraseology. He was asking where Lilith was, but Lilith no longer existed.

Opening the car door, Bill slid out and stood in the sun light. As always, it instantly made him feel better. Thinking about the whole day's situation gave him pause. He was the head of the Monarchy. He wasn't usually swayed by emotions, but he had a lot on his plate. It looked like the end of the world was drawing near, and he was in danger of being found guilty of harboring a fugitive angel. The next few years would reveal if he would crush Heaven, or, like Samael, become an outcast. Hasden had never been a fan of the unknown, and now was no exception. As long as he had control of Mahvet, he could tip the scales. It made him laugh with glee, when he thought about the look on Michael's face, or the rest of Division for that matter, as he released his two-headed pitbull, Angela, on them.

"Soon," he thought, nodding his head. Until then, he'd keep her under wraps. He had Primes to deal with.

Chapter 14

"Oh my God. Shut up already!" thought Josh, shoving his head into his pillow to drown out the chirping. Didn't this bird have Saturday off? This was the final straw. He'd had enough. Later today, he'd grab Charlie. Together they would cut that damn tree down. Sitting up, angry but still dazed, he threw off the covers and rolled out of bed.

Quickly, before he'd have a chance to change his mind, he switched into his running pants and sneakers. Since the annoying bird was quicker than his alarm clock, over the past month, Josh had taken up jogging to start the day. He'd found a park, where there were quite a bit of man-made obstacles that he could practice parkour on. It really freed his mind up. Today he needed it more than ever.

After his birthday on Tuesday, he'd really tried to let the whole numerology thing go. It was stupid, and it couldn't be proven. For some reason though, he couldn't help it. His mind just kept wandering back to those numbers: 666. He didn't understand it. He gave money to homeless people, and he was constantly helping everybody out. Shouldn't that count for something? Josh threw on his red "bite me" tee shirt. It had a picture of a smiling computer on the front of it. Checking his looks in the mirror, he ran his fingers through his hair and then headed out the front door.

Finally hitting the pavement and breaking into a jog, the boy waited until he was at the end of the block to find a good pace. Josh wondered if Dianna was up right now and if she had any plans. Sundays after church were kind of their days to hang out. As of late, it seemed that her sister was just about as needy as Charlie was. Every Saturday, Dianna had plans to keep Cammy occupied. Every Saturday, Charlie had mapped out in advance what they were going to do. Today, though, Josh didn't know if he felt like he could deal with the redhead's brand of humor. Last night, he called Josh the Prince of Darkness. It was all he could do not to come unglued.

Jogging into the park, Josh picked up the pace. There were a few morning joggers. For the most part though, the large expanse of freshly-cut grass was empty. He ran over to where there was a small cement table and dove towards it. Using his momentum to land on his hands, he then sprung forward, vaulting off the table and landing on the other side.

"That's pretty talented," Josh heard a deep voice say from behind him. He turned to see a man sitting all by himself at the table he had just jumped.

"Thanks," Josh said. He was certain there was nobody there when he attempted the move.

"Why don't you sit down for a bit?" the man asked.

"Nah, that's cool. I'm fine." He hated to sound stand-offish, but he didn't know this guy. Josh wasn't getting a creepy vibe or anything, but the stranger was bigger than he was. He looked like he'd either just come out of the military or prison, and Josh didn't plan on finding out which. He headed off in the other direction and shouted, "Have a nice day."

"Metatron wants to know when the next tour date is scheduled," the man shouted back.

Josh slowed down, and then stopped. Looking over his shoulder, he stared towards the man sitting at the table. "Am I..."

"No. You're not dreaming. Come on over. My name is Thomas, by the way." Josh had wondered when this was going to happen.

"I was expecting somebody older."

"Well, as long as you were expecting me to be White and balding, two out of three isn't bad," Thomas said, chuckling. Stepping up close, he looked even more imposing.

Josh hadn't noticed before, because his hair was shaved so

close, but you could definitely see the crown of his head was smooth. "Are you military?" Josh asked.

The man smiled, "Yeah, something like that. I do training for Division," he said, holding his right hand out.

"Pleasure," Josh said, noticing the firm grip. "So how does this work?"

"I teach. You learn. Pretty simple and straightforward," Thomas grinned. Then Josh noticed his grin faded as his eyes became intense. "So prepare yourself inwardly for what is about to take place," Thomas commanded. Josh felt a small tingle travel down his spine and then back up, causing him to involuntarily shudder. And then it was gone.

"So, at this point, what has Metatron told you so far?" Thomas continued casually, as if nothing had happened.

"Not really anything. My grandmother's given me some background."

"Ah, Baby Claire," Thomas said, in a pleasant tone.

"You know my grandmother?" Josh asked, surprised.

"Oh, I know her all right. My wife trained her, and I trained your father. They were all great field agents in their teens."

"My grandmother?" Josh shot a skeptical look at Thomas.

"She wasn't always an old lady. She came to Division at sixteen, the same age as you are now. But enough about her, I'm here to orient you." As he said this, the man's eyes narrowed. "My official title is watcher. I've been training avatars for God knows how long. I'm going to teach you about the universe, its rules, and how to develop your powers. More importantly, I'll also teach you how to use them in a fight."

Josh nodded. Inside he felt nervous, almost queasy. He hadn't expected this to take place out in the open.

Pulling up his camouflage shirt sleeve, Thomas pointed to the tattoo on his left shoulder. "Do you know what this means?" he asked.

Josh looked at the half-black, half-white circle. "I think it's the yin and the yang, right?

"Exactly. It's the opposition and balance between light and dark. The symbol in itself is just a representation of the laws that are present in the physical, but it also applies to the spirit. For an eternity, the light energy and the dark energy have been attracted to each other. But, because of their polarities they can't experience one another. However," Thomas added, resting his hands on the cement table, "somewhere in the electricity between the dark and light, within the magnetism between them, a sentience was born."

"The Creator?" asked Josh

"Yes. Very good, Josh. Since the light and the dark couldn't know each other in the spiritual plane, they crossed over into the physical plane. That's one of the myriad of reasons for all of this, because this world isn't the only one. There are millions of galaxies, all inhabited with their own angels and demons. All have their own Primes. Some of the worlds are old and established. Some are new and barely starting out. In some, people live in water. In some, they live in the air. They're all separated and overseen by Division or Heaven, whatever you want to call it for now. If you could see this mass of connected universes from the side, it resembles a Tao or a mirror image of what you would see in the spirit world.

"Division headquarters sits just outside of our time stream, straddling the physical and spiritual realms. And it's from there that we operate. Heaven is just the way station between the physical and the other side. The Creator is present as the sentience of the two. He is the sum part of all the knowledge in every one of these galaxies. There's nothing under the sun that He didn't create."

Josh shook his head. "Why? Just so we can come here and hang out?"

"No, not really. We came here so we could play a sort of a game. On the other side is absolute knowledge and truth. We voluntarily throw that off and come here so that the dark and the light can manifest as one, but this is just part of the physical side. We're actually something of a perpetual motion machine. Every birth, every death is just like the sodium/potassium pump that causes your heart to beat and generate bioelectricity. In the spirit world, the energy descends and comes into matter fresh and new. At the end of its time, it goes back just, like a cosmic lava lamp. It's the same principle. The souls crossing over the membrane create even more energy. The reality you see, to some extent, is just a bioelectric facsimile of the Creator's dream.

"Each reality is self-contained, just like the very cells in your own body. The bandwidth between this universe and the next is patterned off the phospholipid bi-layer. It's semi-permeable. The only things vibrating high enough to leave this reality are God or the victorious Primes, who are just an emanation, or representative of the Creator. At some point, their child can as well, but for an altogether different purpose. Even the angels and demons are trapped in this reality."

"So what do they do?"

Thomas looked slightly shocked. "What? You've never heard of angels and demons?"

Josh shrugged his shoulders, looking flustered, "Yes, of course, I have. I just figured, since everything else was so far-fetched, there'd be some weird explanation for them too."

Thomas shook his head, "No, but the demons will kill you, no questions asked, if you don't learn this stuff by the time of your eighteenth birthday."

Josh folded his arms, surprised by the seriousness in the watcher's voice. "I don't see the reason for all this. Why can't I just be the Prime and everybody gets to be all happy?"

"Because you're coming here and falling in love was just a small part of the deal. If," Thomas started, "and it's a big if, if you make it past the war in Heaven and you're considered strong enough to mate with the female Prime, she will birth what's called the Meta or the Phoenix, who will spawn a new galaxy. You forget where I said that God is present in everything. The physical world we're living in, as large as you think it is, is merely a nerve cell in God's brain. He's constantly building and rebuilding, and he doesn't use half-ass weak material. That's what the demons do. They test you. And if you suck in any way, shape or form, you either get better, so you can eventually defeat them, or you get iced. Then we try again. These thousands of years of history don't even amount to seconds in the life of the Creator. He's outside of time. Even though he wants us to persevere, nobody passes just for showing up to class."

Josh tried to swallow, but his throat was increasingly dry. "It sounds harsh," he said.

Thomas eased up and smiled. His frame relaxed, and he lowered his shoulders. "Listen, Josh, I've been teaching avatars since time began. Each one is different. So I'm trying to adapt my style to your generation. So I'm sorry if that sounded rough. I really do sympathize with you, but we're backed up against a wall. Your generation is totally different than what I'm used to. A thousand years ago, you knew when trouble was at your back door because it showed up in battle gear, with swords drawn. You could always tell who your enemy was. This age is a little different. Today people smile and compliment you, while they plot your downfall.

"Take a look in nature, Josh, and you'll see I'm right. Only the strong survive. The runts of the litter die off if there's not enough food. But that's a lesson for another time. I want to get back to you. Pretty soon you and the female Prime will be the majority stakeholders of God's power in this reality, stronger than any demon or angel."

"Whose God are we talking about, exactly?" Josh asked.

Laughing, Thomas shrugged his shoulders. "Everybody's.

All these concepts are the same, but different. Just because you call those things on your feet shoes and I call them loafers doesn't negate what they actually are. The energy is the same. Each avatar just interprets it differently. For example, the Bible says God is inside and outside time, right?" Josh nodded. "I told you about the Creator and Division. The Greeks and Romans explained it in their own way, so that they could understand it. Other people did the same. 'He sees you when you're sleeping. He knows when you're awake,'" Thomas sang.

Josh tilted his head, "Santa Claus?"

"Kind of," Thomas replied, smiling. "It's your brain. It consists of three parts; your conscious, your subconscious and your unconscious. It's the microcosm to the macrocosm."

Josh shuddered, as he realized what Thomas was trying to say.

"Everything you've done, everything you've ever said is recorded. The times you've lied or if you've ever stolen, your unconscious sees it, processes it and weaves your destiny as a corrective measure so that you can learn. If you're an asshole you're going to get it sooner or later. One of its many functions is to act as a spiritual iris, letting in more spiritual light. It's constantly keeping score, like a cosmic debit card. And if you think it can't, I'd like to remind you that, while you sleep, your brain is powerful enough to fool your body in every way, shape, and form. It can stimulate you to have a wet dream, without any physical contact. You can wake up crying, believing your brother, who you knew in every detail, just died. And yet you're crying over a brother that you don't actually have. That same subconscious can wake you up a minute before your alarm clock, even though your consciousness is totally oblivious.

"This goes way deep, Josh. I'll help you, but you have to listen. I can sense your apprehension. I can only teach and advise. I can't make your choices or intervene for you. Along with that, I can fight in the battle with you, but not for you."

"What happens if you do?" Josh asked.

"If I break my sacred vow to uphold free will, then I lose my life."

Josh thought about everything the watcher was saying. It sort of made sense. Some of the concepts, like reality, he'd have to put on the shelf for later. "And there's no way I can tap out?" Josh asked.

Thomas shook his head, his face looked worried. "I'm afraid not, Josh. This reality is a team effort. We all had our parts to play, and now you have yours."

"Can I just point something out?" Josh said, rubbing his temples. He was feeling somewhat overwhelmed by the enormity of the whole thing. "I don't mean to sound ungrateful, but I just found out that I'm going to have to fight for my life to get married and have a kid. That's something other people do all the time, with little to no effort. Yet for some reason, you referred to it earlier as a game."

"I know what you're saying, Josh, but remember; it's a trade-off. These people don't have the power you do. It's proportionate. You have the power of millions of souls. In return, you have to carry the burden." Thomas scanned the park to make sure nobody was near and then continued, "I'll stop calling it a game, if it'll help. But I'd like to remind you of a few things. After living your whole life in Santa Cruz, you just moved to a town called Milton. The writer Milton is famous for writing a book called *Paradise Lost*, a tale of man and woman losing their Heavenly estate and leaving without a fight. How befitting they should have a chance to reclaim it for a showdown between the forces of light and dark and in a town of the same name. Maybe it's just coincidence. Do you know who grew up down the road from this park? Milton Bradley, the father of American board games. His crowning achievement was a game called Life. The stage has been set, Josh. All I want to know is will you play your part?"

Drawing a deep breath, Josh sighed. This wasn't what he expected to learn. If Thomas was right though, and the fate of the world was up to him, he had to go for it. "I'm in," Josh answered. A smile immediately crept onto the large man's face.

"You made the right choice. Take the week to digest the things I told you, and we'll meet here again on Saturday." Josh stood up and shook hands with the watcher.

"Could I ask you one last thing?"

"Anything," Thomas said, dusting off his black running pants and camouflage tee shirt.

"One of my friends did my numerology for my name and stuff, and everything came out to 666. I'm freaking out about it."

"Don't worry. It's not that big of a deal," Thomas replied.

"Not that big of a deal?" Josh said, flustered, "666 is the Antichrist."

"Listen," Thomas said, placing his hand on Josh's shoulder. "You watch entirely too many movies. The number 666 signifies that you are imperfect or incomplete, as opposed to 777, which is divine perfection, or 888, which symbolizes the Holy Spirit. We can work past this. In fact, with training, you can change the numbers."

"And you're sure of this?" the teen asked nervously.

"I won't lie to you, Josh. You have a tough role. It's called the Dark Half. You have two energies within you, and it's up to you to decide which one is going to dominate."

"So Dianna is light?" Josh asked.

"Yes. But you are half light energy and half dark energy, which from my perspective, makes you more like God than she is. But we'll get into that later. Right now all you need to know is that being different is a big part of what attracts people to each other." Thomas grinned at Josh and began to walk away. "Don't worry. I know what I'm doing," he called back over his shoulder.

"That's great for you," thought Josh. He was even more confused than before he came here. All the watcher did was give him more stuff to think about.

Chapter 15

"Hmmm, what to do?" thought Josh. He'd been sitting in the backyard most of the afternoon, thinking of the things Thomas had told him. There was a part of Josh that really wanted to be enthusiastic about the things he'd just been taught. The other side of him, which was rational and statistical, told him he didn't have a snowball's chance in Hell. It seemed God had purposefully placed him on the losing side of a battle.

The only upside of the day was when he got to talk to Dianna earlier. It made him smile to hear how happy she was. The smile was short-lived though, because when Josh asked what they were going to do on Sunday, Dianna reminded him that Sunday was Father's Day. She would be busy, so she couldn't go out with him.

To Josh, Father's Day had always been like salt in an open wound. Losing a day to be with Dianna just made it worse. The holiday was a painful reminder that he didn't have a father. So his mom created a tradition where she would take him out to dinner, and they would have their own celebration. Each year she would tell him a little story about his father that he hadn't heard before. Their ritual gave Josh something to look forward to on an otherwise distressing day. But this year, with the move and new friends and all, he had totally forgotten until Dianna reminded him.

He remembered one Father's Day, when he was seven. He had been so down on himself that he broke into tears. Sometimes he couldn't help it. He just felt lost without his dad. As soon as Josh began to cry, Sam put her arms around him and sang a song she always sang when he had hurt himself playing, "You are my sunshine, my only sunshine. You make me happy when skies are gray. You'll never know, dear, how much I love you. Please don't take my sunshine away." To see his mother's loving gaze, while she sang that song, always seemed to make him feel better. Now it had been years since he'd heard Sam sing it.

The ironic thing about the song was now he had his own sunshine. It was Dianna. And for whatever reason, whether he liked it or not, God was taking his sunshine away for the whole summer.

"Hey, dick face," Charlie said enthusiastically, stepping from between the trees and wearing a smile on his face.

"Oh, please, not now," thought Josh.

"Where have you been all day, man? I've been texting you."

"I know," Josh replied, as the redhead took a seat on the patio chairs, slinging his long legs onto the glass table.

"I've had a lot to think about."

"I can understand. It's been a long week. The last thing you need is to be alone in your head. And since Billy and Deus are in California for the weekend, I figured it'd be nice to roll old-school tonight at my place. A little pizza, some video games, and get this," Charlie said, reaching into his pocket with a broad grin on his face.

"Tequila?" Josh said, surprised.

"Yeah, buddy," Charlie howled, shaking the miniature bottle in front of his friend's face.

"Where'd you get that?" Josh asked, his curiosity aroused.

"My dad just came back from a business trip. He says they help him sleep. Usually, he'll leave a few stashed in his suitcase. But this time, there was a gold mine."

"So you found them by snooping?" Josh said, grinning.

"Yeah. Totally."

"You just don't ever learn; do you?" Josh pointed out.

"Nope," Charlie chuckled. "I totally don't. And as a result, this Saturday night is gonna be off the hook."

"I can't," Josh said, shaking his head. "I've got some thinking to do."

The redhead put the bottle back in his pocket. This doesn't have anything to do with the numerology/gematria thing from Tuesday; does it?"

"Yeah, kinda," Josh admitted, trying to hide the worry on his face. "But there's other stuff too."

Charlie looked shocked. "Why on earth would you waste a precious commodity like a Saturday night pondering shit that's outside of your control?"

Josh rolled his eyes, "It's not that easy."

"Yes, it is, Michaels," Charlie exclaimed, pointing his finger at Josh. "We've both known from day one that you have powers that defy logic. Tuesday just confirmed it."

Josh nodded his head, "Yeah, but I'm worried about the possibility that I could be the Antichrist." Charlie busted out into laughter, grabbing his sides. "Great," thought Josh. "He's the one person I trust with this type of stuff, and even he thinks I'm crazy."

"There's no ifs, ands, or buts, my friend. You are the Antichrist, but there's nothing you can really do about it."

"No, I'm not. And there's a huge chance that I can avoid this."

Charlie shook his head skeptically. "Ever since Tuesday, I've been researching the whole numerology thing. You wouldn't believe the stuff I found."

Shrugging his shoulders silently, Josh let out a sigh. He really didn't want any of Charlie's conspiracy theories. But if he didn't talk about it now, his friend would just hold onto it and save it for another day.

"This stuff is ingrained in who you are, and it's not stuff that you can control," Charlie pointed out.

"And you totally believe this?"

"The shirt you're wearing," Charlie said, pointing at the computer. "I don't know if you're aware, but 'computer' adds up to 666."

"What?" Josh said, confused. He wore this in front of the watcher and Thomas hadn't said anything. "Dude, seriously," Josh said angrily. "I'm not down for a bunch of horse shit you lifted off some conspiracy theory web site."

"I'm just saying. You put the shirt on today, but did you buy it?" Josh thought about it.

"No. Sam did. I got it for my birthday last year."

"Good to know," Charlie pointed out. "The poster in your room, who bought that?"

"Which one?" Josh asked. "New York or the Fox one?"

"Both," Charlie said grimly. "New York adds up to 666. The F, the O and the X are the sixes in numerology too. And the car you drive that your grandfather gave you, the one we call the Green Machine or the Dragon Wagon."

"Yeah, what about it?" Josh asked. "It's my grandpa's old car."

"Both names. The Green Man is Satan. The dragon, of course, is a no-brainer. And the car is a Deville. The goddamn word is written right on the dashboard. I mean, check it out. There's even more. I wrote a list."

"No!" Josh shouted. "No more." His ears were practically ringing he was so pissed off.

"I'm not saying this to make you mad. I'm just saying it to point something out," Charlie said, pulling his feet off the table and leaning in closer. "Josh, all this stuff is outside of your control; your birth date, the shirt your mom bought. Your mom loves you. The car. Your grandfather's the nicest person I know, besides you."

Josh tried to dial his anger down a notch. He knew deep down inside Charlie meant well. "I don't know what this all means," Charlie said, leaning back and throwing his feet back on the table, "but goddamnit, we started this together, and we're gonna finish it together." Josh smiled. He knew he couldn't tell Charlie what was going on, but it was good to know he could depend on him.

"Get your boots off the table," snapped his mom's voice through the screen door. Both Josh and Charlie jumped involuntarily at the woman's command.

"Hey, I hate to do this," Josh said, "but I really can't hang out tonight. I'm just not in the mood."

Charlie's face looked completely crestfallen. "Come on, man. It's Saturday." To Josh, the boy's face looked like a little kid who'd just dropped his ice cream cone. Just then, the screen door slid opened, and Sam stepped out into the backyard.

"I'm going out for a while. I'll be back later," she said, putting in her earrings. "I left money for you on the table. Josh was surprised. She was dressed nicely, and it was not to hang out with Claire. He'd never seen her like this.

"What did you do to your hair?" Josh asked.

"Oh, I just came from the salon in town. I got my nails done too," she said, holding them up.

Josh began to feel the ringing in his ears grow into a loud roar. It took a second, but he realized what was going on. "Are you going on a date?" cried Josh, incredulously. He could hardly believe what he was seeing.

"Not exactly," Sam said, nervously.

"With who? You don't even know anybody here."

"Well, if you must know," Sam admitted, "I'm going to the movies with the guy who helped your grandfather."

"The medic?"

"He used to be, when he was in the military. Now he's a detective. His name is Richard Shin, and he's really nice."

Josh couldn't say anything. He knew this day would come eventually. He just wasn't ready for the sight of her so dressed up. It was obvious she was going out of her way to impress this guy. He nodded his head at her.

"Have fun," Josh finally managed to shout in a hoarse

voice.

He watched his mom disappear into the house. She never wore jewelry because his dad had hated it. In retrospect, he guessed that just didn't matter anymore.

"Did you see the shoes she had on?" Charlie giggled. "Holy cow. Those were some first rate--"

"If you know what's good for you," Josh interrupted, "you won't finish that sentence." Josh held out his hand in front of Charlie, as he tried to wrap his head around the fact that his whole world was turning completely upside down.

Charlie placed the tequila in his friend's hand and backed off like an animal trainer leaving meat in a cage. Eyeing the amber liquid in the pint-sized bottle, Josh sighed. He really didn't want to do this, but he just couldn't deal with all this shit anymore. Cracking the top, he swallowed down the small bottle, wincing as it burned its way down.

"This might actually work out good," Charlie chuckled.

"How's that?" replied Josh, beginning to feel the effects of the tequila.

"There's no way they're going to let me into Heaven," the redhead replied. "So if I'm going to Hell, it's good to have friends in high places." Josh really couldn't tell if Charlie was kidding or trying to be serious. "And, hey, look on the bright side. Technically, you're the son of Satan. I say, when we get where we're going, we shake him down. At the very least, he owes you sixteen birthday presents, a puppy, and a bike."

Josh snorted and shook his head. "Ya know what? I don't even care anymore."

Chapter 16

"Today has to be the best day of my life," Dianna thought, looking up at her dad standing on the stage. It gave her a certain sense of pride, knowing that he was trusted enough to be leading the Father's Day service. Ramon would be taking the pulpit, as soon as the singers were done with their set. Until then, Dianna waited in anticipation. Nina stood on her right side. It was funny sometimes watching Nina pray. When she really got on a roll, she seemed like she was in another world. Dianna admired that. Maybe she'd try it sometime.

"This place is kinda creepy," Cammy said. "How long do we have to stay?"

Shooting her sister a glare, she put her finger up to her lips. "Shhh" she whispered. Cammy was finally in church, after all these years. "Who would have guessed it?" thought Dianna. It was definitely the cherry on the top of Dianna's sundae. Of course, just as Dianna suspected, Cammy was turning heads wherever she went. To say that her skirt was short would've been an understatement. "Oh, well," Dianna sighed to herself. She was just happy her sister came at all.

The only way Dianna's day could be any better was if Josh were here with her. She could recall the actual change in his voice when she'd reminded him it was Father's Day. He sounded upset. She would make it up to him though.

"Thank you very much for the beautiful song," Ramon said to the choir. "Aren't they great?" The sound of applause immediately echoed off the large, vaulted ceiling of the church auditorium. Opening her eyes, Nina smiled and elbowed Dianna's arm.

"I know. I'm excited," Dianna said, taking off her small, black shrug jacket. She loved how it looked over her black sleeveless dress, but it was getting too hot to wear now that summer was getting closer. She had never given it much thought, but Nina had commented earlier that, between the sisters, it looked like a stripper and a librarian were going out to brunch. So after today's service, the girls were headed out to do some shopping for new clothes.

As the lights dimmed, Dianna crossed her fingers and silently thought, "Hit it out of the park, dad."

"I want to thank each and every one of you," Ramon said. "With the days getting warmer and warmer, I know there are other places you would rather be. My oldest daughter, Camille, is here today," he said, pointing into the crowd. "She usually spends her summers at the lake or the beach, but today I'm happy to say that she is here with us. It makes me so proud to know that she chose to be with her family. So I wrote this just for her." Ramon shuffled his notes and waited for the lights to dim. Then he began.

"The Spirit of the living God is like a wave of water. Its breaking surf flows over and around us. Its momentum can pick you up and carry you effortlessly. But take care. The Spirit leads you where it will. It cannot be controlled. By attempting to do so, it slips through your fingers, passing you by and leaving you in its wake. For those who seek, the Spirit reveals hidden treasures. But no matter how large the revelation, the Spirit, like the ocean, cannot be fully understood. No matter how deep you descend into it, you have that much further left to go."

Dianna closed her eyes, listening to the calming voice of her father. She wanted to lose herself in prayer, like Nina had. "Those who claim to understand God," Ramon continued, "are likened to a fool watching the tide roll in. They only see that which is manifest; and they judge with the naked eye, never realizing that these waves are but the smallest extension to a body that blankets most all of the world." In her mind, Dianna could see herself standing on the flat, wet sand, admiring the rolling waves of the ocean.

"Eventually, the most hardened materials give way to the gentle touch of even the smallest current. The Spirit's touch on our life is no different. It washes over us, sculpting and cleaving that which is weak, leaving only the strongest and noblest traits. It's only a matter of time. And time itself is but a servant of an infinite God." In her vision, Dianna watched as the tide rolled out swiftly and then rose up towards her, rising higher and higher.

"For those who hear and believe," nodded Ramon, "I have this to say to you. The promise of the Spirit is for everyone. And like a wave of water, you can freely ride upon it, through all of this life and into the next." Dianna felt the massive wave of water wash over her, completely lifting her up and infusing her with an energy that was electric. She could hear the roar of--"

"Move!" Nina screamed. Dianna felt herself being jerked, and she fell over into Nina's arms just as a shower of glass fell around her.

"What the heck happened?" screamed Dianna. The whole auditorium was nearly pitch black.

"You didn't see that?" Cammy said, holding on to her sister's arm. Suddenly light flooded in, as the church doors opened. "I take it you didn't hear the massive feedback from the speakers?"

"No!" Dianna thought. She hadn't, but now she knew what the roaring sound was. "Where's dad?" Dianna asked, feeling a touch of panic.

"He probably went with the chaplain to reset the breaker box," Nina said, guiding her in the direction of the double doors. Squinting, as she walked out into the sun, Dianna lifted her arms up to shield her eyes.

"What went on in there?" Dianna asked. Nina looked at Cammy and then back at Dianna.

"You don't remember anything?" Nina asked, nervously, narrowing her eyes in disbelief.   "No, honest to God," the girl answered.

"You know the light that usually comes from your hands when you heal people?"

"Yeah," Dianna said, meekly.

"It covered your whole body," Nina said, smiling.

"Oh, no," Dianna gasped, suddenly noticing that everybody was looking directly at her. "Why?" she moaned. "Not again."

"That was the best church service ever," Cammy said out loud. "My favorite part was when the speakers went wild with crazy feedback, and then you arched your back and released the energy. I actually felt it as it blew past me. It was insane."

"Do you have to broadcast it to everybody, Cammy?" Dianna was absolutely mortified.

"What are you talking about? You rocked the place so bad you blew out half the light fixtures and knocked out the power. It was the coolest thing I've ever seen."

"Is everybody okay?" Ramon asked, emerging from the darkness inside.

"I'm sorry, dad," Dianna said, hanging her head.

"I'm sure everything will be okay," he assured her. "It just looks like some of the electronics are fried. An electrician is on the way," he said, hugging her. "I'm just glad everybody's okay."

Dianna shrugged her shoulders. "I guess I should watch what I'm doing from now on."

"Why?" Nina said, smirking. "What's the worst that could happen? All of a sudden, everybody who was in there mysteriously lives a happier, longer life?"

"I didn't think of it that way," the girl replied, feeling a little better.

"I just wish I had my camera on Ramon's face when the lights blew," said Cammy, with a sly grin. Ramon laughed, over exaggerating the look of shock on his face.

"Not as priceless as when Cammy stepped into the church,"

Ramon added.

"Totally," Nina agreed. "When we all walked in, Cammy stopped short of the door and poked her head in. I guess she was worried there was a force field on the door."

"Or like it was a trap, and God was waiting for her inside," Ramon said, as the two began to laugh together.

"Check those old fogeys out," Cammy said, pointing to Ramon and Nina. "While you were in your trance and the lights blew out, Ramon yelled 'Would somebody call POPCORN so I can reset the time on the VCR.'" Dianna laughed, as Cammy hobbled around like she was using a cane.

"No, I did not," Ramon said, walking up and throwing his arms around his daughters. "Best service ever," whispered Cammy.

"Best Father's Day ever," thought Dianna, as she leaned into the first family hug the trio had shared in years.

Chapter 17

"Hell's bells, Josh Michaels. Have you been drinking?" Josh looked over at his grandmother. She looked exceedingly surprised, but not as surprised as the other two people in the kitchen. Sitting at the breakfast table was his mother, and next to her was some guy he'd never seen in his life. He looked half Asian.

"Yeah, I had a tiny bit," Josh lied. He and Charlie drank more than their fill, and he was definitely regretting it right now. He couldn't recall most of the night, but Josh did remember Charlie vomiting up most of what he drank around 4:00 in the morning, crying at 5:00, and then finally passing out around 6:00. Josh, however, never fell asleep. For some bizarre reason, he just couldn't. So he basically sat in the dark on the couch, while Charlie slept. Now it was 10:00 in the morning and he felt like a raw nerve, suspended somewhere between a complete stupor and brilliance.

"What are you doing here?" Josh asked, possibly a shade louder than he'd intended to.

"My name's Rich. I'm a friend of your mom and your grandmother," the man said, in an animated manner.

"I see," Josh said, stepping through the door and into the kitchen. He noticed his mom was now on her feet.

"Where did you get alcohol, young man?"

"Same place you got coffee. Somebody thought I might need it and brought it over," he said, glaring at her.

"Charlie did this?" Claire asked.

"Yeah," Josh said, his anger rising in his throat. "The only difference between Charlie and Rich is Charlie didn't come over here under false pretenses, and he didn't intend to screw me. So do I have to ask again, Rich? Or are you going to tell me what the hell you're doing here on Father's Day?" he shouted angrily. He could see his mother's eyes pleading with him to stop, but it was too late. He yelled louder, "And another thing, don't tell me you were just in the neighborhood, Rich, because I'll take long odds you don't live in Milton."

The man's eyes flew wide open, and he stiffened up, "I'm sorry. He's right. This was a bad idea," he said, pushing in his chair and backing away from the table. "I should go." Sam got up and followed him out of the room, apologizing. Once they were gone, Josh was overcome with a spinning sensation. He was feeling lightheaded, and his fingers were tingling.

"I hope you're happy," his grandmother said, getting up from the table. "That man has been at the hospital looking in on Larry every day since the accident. Josh hung his head in shame. His grandfather was pretty much getting worse with each passing day. At first, he was feeling fine and recovering. Then he caught pneumonia. Then, to add insult to injury, he developed blood clots from being immobile so long. Claire had him removed to a convalescent hospital. It seemed like every week he was going back and forth into the emergency room.

"I'm sorry. I didn't know," Josh said, shaking his head.

"Richard comes by the hospital and chats with Larry, giving both me and your mom a chance to come here and shower." Sam stepped back into the kitchen.

"How dare you?" she said. Josh thought he'd die just from the look alone, and the icy tone in her voice was more than he could bear.

"I'm sorry," Josh apologized, thinking a little bit clearer, as the adrenaline was leaving his body.

Tears streamed down Sam's face, as she stared at her son. "I don't know what has taken a hold of you lately. I know you're mad. Maybe that wasn't a good idea on Richard's part, but you have no right showing up here drunk off your ass and ordering grown-ups around!"

"I'm sorry," Josh repeated, looking at the floor.

"Look at me, Josh!" Sam screamed. "I've lived my life for you. When your father died, I was crushed. But I had to move on because you depended on me. Because of that, I haven't dated anybody. For years, I've been alone. So don't I get to have friends too? When we came out here, I left my social network behind, Josh. My best years are behind me. I'm an unemployed, single mother. I don't have any prospects. You can't even begin to understand how scary that is. So stop being so selfish."

Josh watched as his mom stormed out of the kitchen. He knew she was right. She deserved to be happy. He had enjoyed a good life so far, and it was all due to the sacrifices that she made on a daily basis.

"So are you going to tell me what's wrong?" Claire asked. Josh shook his head, still stunned by his mom's reaction, and sank down into the chair his mother had just been in.

"I've been under a lot of stress," he muttered.

"Welcome to the club."

"No, I mean a lot," he insisted. "Ever since before my sixteenth birthday, God seems to think I'm some kind of cosmic piñata. I just can't take it. I've got Charlie's conspiracy theories on one side, and your tales about some interstellar secret society on the other. Between the two, I'm beginning to lose my mind."

"Grab a hold of yourself, Josh. When I was your age, I was just as confused. Later on, I found that all the trials and tribulations I faced had a purpose. When I was a grown woman, I used the lessons that I learned to raise your father. And, believe me, that, in itself, was tough."

"I guess," he replied. "I just can't understand why God's so hard on me. I'm a good person."

"I know," Claire said, grabbing her grandson's hand and giving a sympathetic squeeze. With all her heart, she wanted to tell Josh about everything the angels had told her. She would even fight on his behalf, but she knew it wasn't allowed. Instead, as he rested his head on the kitchen table, she silently stroked his hair and thought to herself, "Please, Josh. Please fight back."

***

By the light of the pale, full moon, Dianna could see her surroundings. It wasn't that there was much to look at, just tall grass, as far as the eye could see. Every now and again, there was an occasional tree. She was looking for a particular one: an oak. In fact, it was the oldest of its kind. Navigating her way towards the eldest of the majestic trees, she contemplated the beauty of the grass. Each time the wind gently blew, it caused rhythmic patterns in the field. The moonlight reflected differently every time, as the sea of grass swayed back and forth.

It was a secret song only for her to hear. The wind blew once again, and this time Dianna noticed just how naked she truly was under her pale, white nightdress. Suddenly, she found what she was searching for. There it stood in front of her, the mighty World Tree. Dianna hurried up to its base and took the book from under her arm. She had been secretly writing it for what seemed to be a lifetime. But now, it was finally ready to be unveiled. Unwrapping the leather ties, Dianna looked out upon the swirling patterns of the field.

Everything from the moon's position to the direction of the wind told her it was time. The patterns all said so. She quickly opened the book to reveal the loose pages of all shapes and sizes, each a snapshot of her indomitable will. Dianna rejoiced, as she gave the contents a parting glance. Then she held up the open book towards the moon. A rush of wind blew from the east, caressing her body like she hadn't nary a stitch on. The gown ruffled with the wind, as it lifted up the book's pages. Up and away, the separate pieces floated out, drifting carelessly in the wind, rising up, until Dianna called them all home by name. She called every, single one of them individually, as they made their way back towards her. The woman reached her hands out to the night, spreading her fingers and seizing the energy that was around her, bending it to her will.

Reining in the papers, she forced them into a swirling whirlpool of jumbled thought. The force of nature blew the papers in a tight circle and then sent them up over her head in twin columns. Then, they curled down, shuffling together to land on her outstretched right hand. Into the book cover fell the pages, from the last to the first. As they did, she read them all in the space of the few seconds it took to transpire. Finally, the golden front binding fell on top.

"Complete perfection," she thought to herself, admiring the result of her long labors. Dianna stood silently, until her eyes caught a glimpse of a small light off in the distance. Tucking her book under her arm, she watched as the light grew bigger and bigger, coming to rest in front of her.

"How can I help you, angel?" Dianna said pleasantly.

"I've come with news," the angel replied, bowing. Viewing the angel with more than just her eyes, she could tell the messenger was just and true. He radiated gold light from his beautiful face, which wore the faintest trace of a beard that climbed its way up his jaw to join his thick brown mane of hair.

"Have you a name?" she asked

"I do. I am Metatron, and I've come to announce that you are to be trained."

"Very well then," Dianna said, taking the book from under her arm and bringing it to her chest. "I look forward to it."

"Not half as much as we do," Metatron replied, his lips spreading into a triumphant smile. "I see you've written a book. Does it have a name?"

Lifting up the golden book, Dianna held it out towards the

angel. "I will call it The Book of Life."

The angel beamed, sending rays of light out through the nighttime sky. "I can't wait to read it, my queen. I'm sure it is a work of art," the angel said, bowing before her.

Dianna jumped with a start and opened her eyes.

"Get up!" demanded Cammy, pointing at the alarm clock next to Dianna's bed.

"What?" Dianna said, looking around her room and rubbing her eyes.

"We're going to be late to the party. Get your ass out of bed."

Swinging her legs over her bed, Dianna paused. The details of the dream flowed out of her head, and her memories of the day filtered back in. Now she remembered. Her sister had recommended she take a nap, before they went out to the birthday party. "Can you hand me my clothes, Cammy? My tee shirt and jeans are hanging off the chair, next to my desk." Cammy shot Dianna a look that could only be described as intense disapproval.

"I know you're not planning on wearing the same clothes you wore to school today." Dianna shrugged her shoulders, still disoriented from the dream. "Totally unacceptable. You're my sister, and we both have to look good. Follow me, and hurry. We have to leave before Ramon and Nina get back from their party."

"That's right," Dianna thought, standing up and following her sister to her room. Ramon was at the end of the year dinner the bus drivers had on the last day of school. According to Nina, after turning the keys in at the end of the day, all of the off-duty bus drivers had dinner at Cardona's. After the meal, wine glasses in hand, the drivers would say a toast to another year successfully completed. They would all swallow down the glass of wine, washing away all vestiges of the year's worth of bad memories. The cussing, the drama, the back-talking teenagers, it was all forgotten with one symbolic glass. And if that didn't do it, more glasses of wine followed. Apparently, it usually took around four or five glasses to do the trick.

In Dianna's opinion, she thought it was a good idea. She had seen how some of her classmates treated the people who drove the buses. It was one of the reasons why she preferred to walk home from school. Another reason was because Ramon was known as one of the stricter bus drivers in the district, and she really didn't want to hear about it from the other kids. Hopefully, this year's dinner would last all night. According to Nina, they got better and better every year.

"I hope there's lots of single guys there," Cammy said, as she picked through her closet.

"According to Billy," Dianna replied, "some of his dad's friends are going to be there. They're all supposed to be filthy rich," she yawned, trying on the dress her sister handed her.

"Filthy, huh?" Cammy said, her face lighting up. "Just stand aside and watch how dirty your big sister can get."

Chapter 18
6+6+6

"Next time, remind me to bring a pack mule," Charlie said sarcastically.

"I'm with you on that." Josh wondered to himself how many people were at this thing. They'd parked so far away, he didn't even know if they were in the same neighborhood anymore.

"Do you think I should have brought my yearbook with me?" Charlie asked.

"Not even. You'd just lose it." Josh had considered buying one of the extras, but he had plenty of pictures of the people he liked. Plus, he barely knew most of the other students. Once he decided not to buy one though, he'd regretted it. He had to explain to at least a hundred people why he didn't have one.

Apart from seeing Dianna, he kind of wondered why he even went to school at all today. All the exams were over, and they really didn't do anything but sit around and talk. The only thing that actually got accomplished was Josh put the finishing touches on a bracelet he'd made for Dianna. It was patterned off his grandmother's wedding ring, which was exceptionally detailed, almost like her Saint Michael's necklace. Josh knew there was only one other necklace like hers, and it was hanging around his neck at this very moment. The only problem was that he had absentmindedly left the gift in his gym bag, and he had left that in his locker at the gym.

Josh had hoped to get a quick workout in before the party. Instead of changing his clothes, he had ended up texting Charlie for twenty minutes about what to wear that night. Seeing the time, he just grabbed his keys and left. Now he was kicking himself in the ass. He had planned to give the bracelet to Dianna tonight, because tomorrow she'd be way too busy.

"Geez," this place is humongous," thought Josh, as the boys walked onto the front yard of the house. Billy's dad must have paid a fortune for this place. It was right next to the lake. The long, white, two-story home was dressed in reddish-black, brick exterior, with white columns stretching from the ground to the roof.

"Maybe we should knock on the door," suggested Charlie.

"I think we can just walk around the side. Follow the music," said Josh. He knew this was probably the first party Charlie had ever been to, even though he would never admit it. Josh would try his best to walk him through it. The boys walked around the right side of the large house. From all the discarded beer cups and more than a few couples making out, Josh could tell the party was in full swing. Coming around the corner, Josh thought he'd seen the worst of it, but he was wrong. His jaw practically dropped to the floor, when he saw the anarchy in front of him.

The backyard was two levels. One was landscaped and went to the lake, where Josh could see that there was a large group playing near the water. There was also a patio off of the house that led to a tennis court, which had been converted to an outside dance floor. The sun hadn't even set, and it was already bursting at the seams with people.

"Dude, I'm in Heaven," giggled the tall redhead. "Our whole school has gotta be here."

"Along with a few other schools, I'm guessing," added Josh. "Let's find Dianna before the sun goes down." He grabbed his phone, hoping she had hers on vibrate. Josh touched his cell phone to see he'd already missed three texts from her. It was just so loud he just couldn't hear them. "She's over at the dance floor," Josh yelled to Charlie, whose eyes looked like they were going to pop right out of his head, not that Josh blamed him. A lot of the girls were only wearing bikinis, having migrated from the lake over to the tennis courts to dance. With the sound of the house music blaring in his ears, Josh scanned the courts and found Dianna. It should have been difficult, but she was one of the few girls who was actually dressed. "Over there!" Josh yelled, as he started to make his way over to her.

"Wow," Charlie said, checking out Dianna. She was wearing a tight, black skirt, with a blue shirt that was open in the back.

"You look great," Josh said loudly, moving in to kiss her. He noticed her lips tasted really sweet, and she didn't smell like she normally did. It was a different perfume. Josh took a step back to get a better look at her. He was slightly stunned, when he saw the lacy black bra across the middle of her back.

Dianna immediately looked like she was embarrassed. "I had this crazy dream. Then when I woke up I was totally out of it. So I let my sister dress me. I didn't really want to wear this, but it was probably the most acceptable top out of her whole wardrobe." Josh nodded in approval.

"You look great. It's not like it's inappropriate. It's just out of character," he chuckled, noticing that Charlie was still staring. "I kind of feel self-conscious in my red tee shirt and blue jeans. If I knew all these people were coming half-naked, Charlie and I would've just worn shorts," he said, grinning.

"Holy shit, man, check that out in the corner," Charlie shouted. Looking over, Josh thought he might have seen just what his friend was talking about. In the middle of the dance floor, amidst the bouncing mass of bodies, there was one girl, who was practically commanding attention. She was perfectly tanned and, in Josh's opinion, physically flawless. The white dress she was wearing left little to the imagination. From best as he could tell, she was kissing one guy, while his friend freaked her from behind.

"What a shameless whore," Charlie screamed out loud, his eyes as big as saucers.

"That's my sister!" Dianna shouted, glaring back at him. Josh glanced over at Dianna. She was so mad, you could fry an egg on her forehead.

"Okay," Josh said, taking a step back. He was determined not to catch any of her wrath.

Charlie chuckled, "Definitely bodes well for you, if that's where Imperial is headed in a few years." Josh could only shake his head at his friend, as Dianna stormed out onto the dance floor and grabbed her sister by the arm.

"Dude," Josh said, staring at the redhead in disbelief. "Do you always have to say every thought that comes into your head?"

Charlie nodded, "Hells, yes. It's part of my alter ego. During the day, I'm a mild-mannered teenager. At night," he said, stepping forward with his hands on his hips, "I'm TOO-MUCH-INFORMATION MAN." Josh grinned in his friend's direction.

"Well, hopefully, your alter ego can keep a lid on it. If you screw up my night, your new power's gonna be invisibility."

"Follow us," Dianna screamed, walking between them, with her sister trailing behind her. "It's way too loud here." Without question, the two teens followed the girls, as they made their way from the dance floor. It was dusk, and Josh hadn't even seen Billy or Deus. Looking out on the mass of people, Josh knew they could have been anywhere. The girls walked them all the way over to the landscaped side of the house, which was fine by Josh. It was entirely too loud to talk over at the dance floor.

Dianna turned his way and introduced the girl in white. "This is my sister, Camille."

The girl leaned forward and whispered, "It's Cammy. Nice to meet you, Josh."

"The pleasure is all mine," he said.

"Amazing," he thought to himself. Side by side, you could easily tell they were sisters. Both had the same features, especially their eyes. The only difference was that Dianna's were kind and gentle. Cammy, on the other hand, while more petite and slightly shorter, looked like she was ready to kick someone's ass. She gave the impression that, if you stared at her too long, it would be your ass.

"Damn, Dianna," Cammy said, smiling. "He is one hot little guero." Josh chuckled. He'd heard the Spanish term for white boy more than a few times back where he was from.

"I told you," Dianna said, kissing Josh. "He's my Osito."

Cammy laughed out loud at both of them. "My God, that is so super cute. But why Little Bear?"

"It's a childhood nickname. My mom gave it to me," Josh said, feeling embarrassed.

"You're older now though," she replied. "Maybe you could just be Oso. That means bear."

"Oh, we already tried that," Dianna replied, disdainfully. "But old Charlie here started calling Josh 'Assho.' So we changed it back."

The three of them glanced over at the redhead, who shrugged his shoulders. "What? She can give you a nickname, but I can't?"

The look on Cammy's face told Josh all he needed to know about what she thought of Charlie. "I have an idea," she said. "We'll give Charlie a nickname. How about Payaso? It means friend of bear."

"Hey, that's pretty cool," Charlie replied, starting to smile approvingly. "I think I kind of like that. Do you ladies want any drinks?"

"We're cool," Josh said, pointing to Dianna and himself. "I'm not looking to drink tonight."

"Nothing for me, Mr. Payaso," Cammy replied sweetly.

Watching, as he strolled off obliviously, Josh held his opinion until he knew Charlie was out of earshot. "Okay, spill it," he demanded, folding his arms and looking into Dianna's eyes. He figured Cammy would reveal it, if he asked, but he knew for a fact Dianna wouldn't lie. Glancing over at her sister, Dianna began to giggle.

"It sort of means idiot."

Josh couldn't help but laugh. "Well, at least it fits," he thought.

"It also means clown," said the older sister. "Where'd you meet that rooster-looking dork anyway?"

"He's the neighbor kid. He just sort of latched on to me."

"Liar!" shouted Dianna, putting her arms around him.

Josh threw on his best innocent face and asked, "Why? What am I supposed to say?"

Cammy narrowed her eyes down. "I know about the dream. She's my sister. She tells me everything. And for your sake, Josh," Cammy said, grinning, "you're going to need superpowers, if my dad ever catches you holding my sister like that."

He could feel himself blushing, "Yeah. I'd be pretty pissed off too, if she was my daughter."

The girl snorted, her face changing from sheer amusement to seriousness. "No, Josh, Queen's English and shit, my dad will end your life."

"What?" Josh shouted, surprised. He looked over to Dianna, who was nodding in agreement.

"Like kill, kill?" Josh asked, looking for clarification.

"What is happening in America, when most immigrants I know speak better English than well-educated white kids?" Cammy said jokingly, shaking her head.

Josh knew that, to a certain extent, this had to be an over exaggeration. Cammy dressed pretty racy, as Claire called it, and their father didn't seem to have a problem with that. Surely, he couldn't be that overprotective.

"She's the baby of our family, and my dad is super protective. Anyway, it's good to see my sister actually has a weakness. I was beginning to wonder," Cammy said, as she winked and began walking away. "I'd better make my way back to the dance floor. I'll talk to you guys later. Those guys I was dancing with had their own record label. So tonight might be my lucky night," she called, over her shoulder.

"I have a question," asked Josh, looking at Dianna, as her sister walked off. "Have you seen Deus or Billy tonight?"

"Nope," she replied, throwing her arms around him, "and I don't care." Josh was waiting for her to move in and kiss him, but she stopped short. "Oh, no," she whispered. "Charlie's back, and he looks pretty angry." Josh looked and saw Charlie next to a folding table that was full of alcohol. With a bottle of champagne in his left hand, he was poking his right finger in Cammy's chest.

Without a word, Josh spun and sprinted towards his friend. If he could get there quickly enough, he might be able to avert disaster. Hopping the hedges in front of him, he took a few steps and leaped with all his might, side-vaulting not only the next set of hedges but the make-shift table with the alcohol on it. Coming down into a roll, he came up behind his drunk friend, yanking the bottle out of his left hand.

Charlie jumped, startled that anybody was behind him. "What are you doing?" he slurred, already sounding buzzed.

"I'll take care of this," Josh said to Cammy.

"No, no!" Charlie screamed, swinging his arms around aimlessly. "This dirty hooker called me a name in Spanish. So I'm going to give her one in return."

"Don't," Josh ordered. He could see this night being cut short by his friend's stupidity and Cammy's temper.

"What's your problem, Josh? You don't even know this girl." Josh could see Dianna had already come up behind Cammy and had her hand on her sister's shoulder. "Whatever happened to bros before hos?" Charlie asked, swaying back and forth. "I thought you had my back, but it doesn't surprise me, Michaels.

You were raised by women. And you've obviously been brainwashed by them, too."

"That's enough, Charlie. He's just being a gentleman," Dianna said, holding onto her sister.

"Bull, Dianna. Stay out of this. You don't see the way his grandmother bullies his grandpa, and everybody else around her. Between her and his mom, it's no wonder Josh acts like a Santa Cruz hippie-brainwashed-mama's-boy."

Josh glared back at Charlie. This was exactly the kind of stuff he hated about alcohol and parties. "You're drunk, Charlie. You don't know what you're saying. Go cool off, before you get your ass kicked."

Charlie shook his head, like he was stunned or confused, "Whatever, traitor."

Josh watched, as the boy turned towards the house and staggered off aimlessly. Grabbing his phone, Josh sent a text to Billy:

> IF YOU SEE CHARLIE HE'S PISSED AND DRUNK. HE COULD USE A COUCH TO LIE ON FOR A WHILE UNTIL HE SOBERS UP

"Dude, you totally jumped that table," shouted the stoner next to Cammy. Josh looked at the guy and then looked at the table. He hadn't thought about it at the time. Not only did he jump from the sidewalk clearing, over a table with all the bottles on it, but there was a bush behind the table. It looked like an impossible jump. It wasn't a world's record, but it was strong work. Especially considering he was wearing blue jeans and had no warm-up.

"That calls for a shot," Cammy said, grinning.

"That's the second time you've jumped in front of a bullet to help me, Josh. A girl could get used to this," Dianna said, wrapping her arms around his neck.

"I'm glad you're keeping score. But seeing as I can't be

with you all the time, I wanted to give you something to wear, while you're on the road this summer." Josh smiled, as he reached back and unclasped his necklace. Just the sheer look of amazement on her face told him beyond a shadow of a doubt, this was the right thing to do. He knew that his family would flip out, if they found out he'd given his necklace to Dianna, but he really wanted her to have something of his when she was away. Since he had forgotten the bracelet in his locker, this was his only option.

"Are you sure?" Dianna said. She was completely floored. This was his father's necklace. "I don't know what to say."

"Just say thank you," he said, as he fastened it. He stepped back to see how it looked on her. "It's not originally what I had planned to give you, but Saint Michael is the patron saint of heroes. Hopefully, he will keep you safe, while you're on the road. When you come back, I'll trade you for what I originally had planned to give you."

"It's a deal," she said, grinning, as she tucked it inside her shirt. "You might be a mama's boy, but you're my mama's boy. I wouldn't have it any other way." Josh slid his left hand around Dianna's hip, and then gripped the shot of whiskey Cammy had handed him. He knew he said he wasn't going to drink, and he didn't want Dianna to think less of him. On the other hand, he didn't want to let Cammy down either.

"I'll just do this one shot," Josh said, kissing Dianna on the forehead.

She shook her head. "All right. As long as it's just one. I don't want you to make a fool of yourself."

***

"Calm down. You're not thinking straight," Charlie thought to himself. It was almost a half hour since he'd come in the house, and still he couldn't seem to let it go. At least he found it easier to think here. As soon as Charlie hit the patio, the spiky-haired boy came out and routed Charlie to his room.

He had Charlie take a seat, leaving him with a bottle of water and some aspirin. Even if Billy hadn't said it was his room, Charlie had a sneaking suspicion that he could've figured it out. The room was very modern. It had every convenience. And even though he saw the Kindle on the desk by the door, Billy also had a large book stand filled with some interesting reads. Most of them were on military strategy. Charlie had never heard of the majority of them, but there were two books that he had read. One was *The Prince*, by Machiavelli. The other was *Art of War*, by Sun Tzu. He'd read them both cover to cover. They were quintessential reading for the world's elite. These books were, for Charlie, just another piece to the paradox that was Billy Hasden.

Billy was super rich and could do anything or go anywhere he wanted, but he preferred to hang out with him and Josh. Plus, despite having a veritable treasure trove of books on forcibly conquering people and situations, Billy was one of the biggest pacifists Charlie had ever met. "I don't know how he could read any of these anyway," Charlie thought to himself. The lighting in the room was horrible. Billy only had one lamp, and although it looked expensive, it seemed to only have one setting, which was barely enough to light the entire room. Taking a look around, he noticed there were high-tech gadgets everywhere. "I wouldn't expect anything less," Charlie thought. "Kid's a Richie Rich. I wonder if he even knows what half of this stuff does, or if he just buys whatever he sees?" One thing Charlie definitely had to admit though was Billy had style.

Except for his white carpet, the room was all done in shades of red and black. Charlie was no designer, but he was willing to bet there were no other teenagers in Milton that had a black satin bed with a hand-carved cherry wood portrait of a crane hanging above the headboard. "That must have set him back a couple of bucks," he thought to himself.

Walking over and parting the black curtains, Charlie took in the view of the patio. It was getting dark. The light of the sun had been traded for tiki torches and party lights. After a few minutes of searching, he could see that Josh hadn't gone too far. He was on the patio, with his arms around Dianna. Charlie didn't dislike Dianna. She was cool, but he wouldn't mind backing over her sister with a Sherman tank. That was for sure.

Cammy's problem was that she was too good looking for her own good. He had a feeling that, everywhere she went, guys fell all over her and just smiled and nodded to everything she had to say. His mom had told him all about Cammy's type. They live in their own, little world. He smirked, when he thought of Dianna's sister standing next to one of those signs they use to greet travelers. "Welcome to Disillusionment. Population 1."

Even though he felt justified for yelling at Cammy, he felt ashamed and guilty over snapping at Josh. Charlie knew Josh really didn't deserve it. Then again, it wouldn't have happened, if he wasn't always playing Captain Save-a-Ho all the time. It was one of Josh's traits that he found particularly annoying.

"Feeling better, are we?" Billy asked, as he walked in the dimly-lit room.

"A little," muttered Charlie, as he continued staring out the window.

"Looking at anything in particular?"

"Not really," answered Charlie, shaking his head.

"Really?" prodded Billy. "So if I looked out that window, I wouldn't see Josh and Dianna playing kissy-face?"

His expressing turning to stone, Charlie closed the curtains and turned to face Billy. "So? It's not like I was staring at them. I just wanted to see what he was doing."

Billy sat down on his bed and grinned. In the dim light, his face almost seemed to flicker between utter joy and sheer pain.

Charlie wondered what it was the boy found so amusing. "You didn't take your medications today; did you?" he asked.

"No," Charlie replied, leaning against the wall. "I knew I was going to have a few tonight, and the alcohol messes with my meds. So I said screw it."

"Is that why you came into the house?" asked Billy.

"I guess," Charlie replied, shrugging his shoulders. "It's weird how my thoughts are when I'm off the meds, but the thing with Josh caught me off guard."

"Why's that?"

"As long as I've known him, Josh has always been super fair in everything," Charlie said, folding his arms. "Nobody knows that more than me. So even though I felt like I was in the right, if Josh says I should cool it, maybe there's something I didn't see."

Billy chuckled and shook his head, "Have I ever told you how much you utterly amaze me?"

A small amount of skepticism clouded the redhead's face. "Is there some reason you should?"

"You're a genius," Billy said. "Even when you're off your meds, you know your judgment's impaired. So, like a bat flying in the dark, you use your friend's input as your marker. It's almost like sonar."

"I hadn't thought of it like that," Charlie said, smiling. "Speaking of, I'd almost need sonar to navigate this room. Why's it so dark in here?"

"Oh, that. I just prefer the dim lights. It helps with the migraines I get. Sometimes that and medication is all I need."

"Harsh. I didn't know you had a medical problem. When my older sister used to live with us, she'd get them. They can ruin your whole day."

"It's pretty tough. I'm not gonna lie," Billy agreed. "Not only do I suffer from the migraines, but I'm also OCD."

Charlie's eyes lit up. "Get out! Me too. Every time I walk

down the hall, I have to count the paintings or the pictures."

Giggling, Billy nodded to the floor, "I'm even worse than that. Did you see my carpet? It looks like somebody vomited all over it." Charlie looked down at the floor. He must have been trippin'. He could have sworn it was white. Now that he looked directly at it, he could see there were brown and black flecks in it. "My doctor recommended it," said Billy, standing up and cruising over to the window. "If I have regular white carpet, I tend to pick it clean of anything that doesn't belong there, like lint from my socks, crumbs, other stuff like that. Getting this carpet was painful at first. But after a few weeks, I got used to it. Now I could have two pounds of lint on the floor, and I'd never know."

"I should try that," the redhead thought to himself.

"You know, I'm a lot like you," Billy said, peering out the window. Charlie peeked out the other side. In the crowd, he could see that Dianna was now on the dance floor, dancing with her sister. Josh was patiently standing alone, on the edge of the tennis courts. Glancing over at Charlie, Billy leaned against the wall. "Josh is a very special person. I don't have to tell you that, though. You grew up with him. There's only one other person like him in this universe, and that's Dianna."

"I know," Charlie answered, his eyes glued to the window. "It's almost like they were made for each other. And you know what? I'm happy for them."

"That's pretty selfless of you, considering that, if Josh gets his happy ending, you're going to have to go back to your old life. When Dianna gets back, you'll be confined to the solidarity of the basement, with nothing to look forward to but late-night TV and lame chat rooms."

Charlie narrowed his eyes. "That would never happen."

"I wouldn't be so sure. He does whatever she asks. Now that you and her sister have had it out, she might not want you around."

Almost instantly, Charlie could feel it was a little harder to breathe. Leaving the window, he walked over to the computer desk and sat down on the black rolling chair. "It's not that bad," he said, wringing his hands reflexively. "I can still hang out with you and Deus."

"I love you like a brother, but we're leaving at the end of summer," Billy reminded him.

Charlie immediately looked over at Billy, who was leaning against the wall by the window. In the dimly lit room, he couldn't tell whether he was smiling or scowling.

"Suddenly, I don't feel so good," Charlie admitted, putting his hand on his chest. He could feel a panic attack coming on. He'd had a million of these before, but this one was different. He really couldn't breathe as well as he normally did. No matter how much he tried to talk himself down, he was breathing faster and faster.

"Don't worry," Billy said, as he walked into the bathroom. "I have something that might help."

Gripping the arms of the chair, Charlie sunk down as low as he could go. He felt like he was strapped to a rocket, and it was taking him farther and farther away, from the safety of the ground. "Please, don't let me pass out," he thought frantically.

Billy walked up with a pill bottle in his hand. Shaking two white capsules into his palm, he told Charlie, "The stuff you usually take will alleviate the symptoms of your anxiety, but this stuff will do that and make you feel happy." Charlie grabbed the water, his hands shaking like a leaf.

"What are these?"

"Don't worry, bro," Billy smiled. "This stuff makes everything better. I like to call it "Fuckitall.'"

***

"This is wonderful! I feel so free," thought Dianna, as she danced on the platform next to her sister. Ever since Cammy got her out on the dance floor, it seemed like every guy in the place was asking them to dance. It was such a hassle that her sister suggested that they go where no guy could follow. She was a little nervous at first, being up on the small stage in front of a crowd. But after Cammy helped her up and everybody started cheering her on, she figured "what the heck?" The school year was over, and it was her birthday today. She had every right to let her hair down for a bit and celebrate. She'd earned it.

At first, she had some misgivings about the party. However, it was her last night to see Josh and Cammy, before she took off on Monday. It was almost unfair that the two people she cared so much for should come into her life, only to be taken away for the summer. But the efforts she put out on this tour would make life so much easier.

"Shake it, sister," Cammy screamed, bumping her hip against Dianna's. Dianna was glad to have some time with her sister. They needed to re-bond. She was glad Cammy was keeping everything cool tonight. She even had her back, when Dianna said she wasn't drinking. Dianna couldn't help but smile. She felt a familiarity, dancing out here with her sister under the moon and the stars. It was close to the feeling she got, when Cammy would play with her when they were younger. It was a feeling she thought they'd never share again, after Cammy left home. Yet here they were, dancing the night away.

As the song ended, she hugged her sister. "I love you, Camille," Dianna said, her face beaming with pride. "I'm gonna go spend some time with Josh now."

"Go for it," Cammy reassured her, kissing Dianna's cheek. "Are you sure you don't want a birthday shot?"

"I'm sure," Dianna said. You know I don't drink. Stay away from those two guys from earlier. They're up to no good."

And with that, Dianna hopped off the platform and started to make her way off the dance floor. Just then the DJ switched to a slow song. "Perfect," she thought. If she was fast enough, she could finally get Josh to dance. Squirming through the crowd, Dianna slowly made her way to where she had last seen him.

"Looking for me?" Deus said, from behind her. She turned to see he was just wearing board shorts.

"I'm sorry. I'm looking for Josh. You wouldn't know where he is; would you?"

"I got a better idea, birthday girl. Why don't you come dance with me? Besides, you promised. Remember?" Dianna sighed, in aggravation. Technically, he was right. But she didn't think he was actually going to hold her to it. Looking around, she couldn't see Josh anywhere. Since the song was already part way through anyway, she might as well get it over with.

"Okay," Dianna said, frustrated. The last thing she wanted to do was cause a scene or appear ungrateful.

"Good times," Deus said, smiling. "You won't regret it."

"Goddamnit. Not again," Josh screamed in his head, as he watched Dianna walk onto the dance floor with Deus. He only stepped away for a minute to go the bathroom. "Whatever," he thought angrily. "I guess that's what I get for using common decency." For the past hour and a half, Josh sat back and watched as people he was sure didn't know Deus or Billy basically used every hedge, bush or dark area as a urinal. Maybe if he would've pissed on the ground, he could've caught Dianna before Deus intercepted her.

But instead, his conscience got the best of him. Of course, it bit him in the ass. He knew there was really nothing to be mad about, but he just couldn't help it. He was quickly beginning to realize that this party wasn't the best way to go. He hadn't seen Charlie since earlier. Even though it was great getting the seal of approval from Dianna's sister, Josh felt like he would've preferred a quiet night out, instead of all these shenanigans.

Hell, anything would have been better than watching every guy in the place hit on her and Cammy. The worst thing was a lot of these guys were grown men, and they were totally shameless about it. It would be a miracle for him to make it through the night without getting in a fight. It was hard to watch Dianna go out on the dance floor. He knew it was his own fault for never learning how to dance. When Cammy dragged her out, he wasn't surprised to see a few songs turn into a half an hour. So he passed the time by the bar and had a few more shots. What really pissed him off was that the two guys, who claimed they owned their own record label, were following the sisters around the dance floor like heat-seeking missiles.

"I should really just ask Dianna to leave with me, when she gets off of the dance floor," he thought to himself. After all, it was their last night together for three months; and he was watching it waste away from the sidelines. Nodding his head, he decided to send her a text and tell her they should leave. He immediately froze, when he reached into his pocket and realized there was nothing in there but his car keys. "What the hell else could go wrong tonight?" he groaned.

***

"Oh my God," Dianna thought, filled with shock. "I am so dead." She'd barely finished dancing with Deus, when she saw Nina standing on the edge of the dance floor.

"You'd better get your ass in the car, pronto," Nina said, "before Ramon finds you." Her voice was stern, as she pointed towards the front of the house.

"What are you guys doing here?" Dianna asked, dreading the answer.

"I could ask you the same question," Nina replied. "Aren't

you supposed to be at a birthday party?"

"Oh, yeah," Dianna said nervously. "About that, it's a lot bigger than we expected."

"Walk!" Nina ordered, nodding her head in the forward direction. Dianna did as she was told. "Where's Josh?" Nina asked, with her hand pushing on Dianna's back.

"The last time I saw him, he was by the dance floor," Dianna said, cocking her head to look behind her. "What made you think Josh was with me?" she asked. As soon as they got to the front yard, Nina spun Dianna around and grabbed her by both shoulders.

"I know Josh is here. You wouldn't come here unless there was a reason. You've never lied to me before, child. Don't start now," she warned.

"Okay," Dianna stuttered. "I won't. I'm sorry. It was wrong of me. But I didn't come here to do anything, other than spend some time with Josh."

"Believe me. Nobody understands more than me. When I met my other half, Thomas, I knew then and there I'd storm the gates of Hell just to be by his side. But your dad and Josh will meet someday. I can assure you that. The question is whether you want that to be tonight or in the future, under better circumstances?"

Dianna didn't even have to think about it. She knew the answer.

"If Ramon sees Josh," Nina said, "he'd immediately forbid you from seeing him again." Crushing sadness enveloped Dianna, as she looked at the front of the house. It was a no-win situation. She'd give anything to kiss Josh goodbye, but she just didn't have that option right now. She'd just have to wait, until she could text him.

"How did you find us?" she asked.

"Your sister's been posting pictures all night," Nina said, with her arms folded. And you're tagged in them. Your dad saw the pictures, and he had a fit. We located you because our cell phones are linked through the tracker app. I told Ramon when we got here to go find Cammy, and I'd find you. I wanted to prepare you."

"Prepare me for what?" Dianna asked, walking towards the car.

Nina sighed, "Your father is going be furious, like you've never seen him before. Watch your sister though. This isn't her first rodeo."

Chapter 19

Alone on the patio, Josh sat, drinking his whiskey and water, filled with anger and bitterness. He had tried to keep his head up. He really did. Earlier, when Cammy offered him a shot, he knew it was a bad idea. He really didn't want to drink. Especially after the hangover he got with Charlie a few weeks back. It just wasn't who he was. Josh not only swore off tequila, he'd promised himself to never drink like that again. But here he was, almost as if fate was forcing him down a path he was unwilling to travel.

Josh glanced at his watch. It was 1:00 in the morning. It was almost laughable how he'd previously regarded the black watch he'd gotten for his birthday as merely a decoration, that is, until tonight. He usually used his phone to see the time. But after searching for an hour and a half and retracing every step he'd taken, he'd called it quits. It wasn't like him to quit, but he was tired of this. It was just one more setback in a series of bad occurrences since his birthday. He was trying desperately to keep from losing it. That's when he realized that he hadn't seen Dianna or her sister in all the time he was looking for his phone.

After that, he'd walked aimlessly for the better part of two hours. Back and forth he went, from the dance floor to the lake and over to the house. Again and again, he soullessly wondered. He kept bumping shoulders with drunk people. He avoided conversations with them, even though he knew they really just wanted to wish him happy birthday again. He just couldn't manage a conversation in the mood he was in.

Josh didn't know why he searched so long. He knew, after an hour went by and Cammy was nowhere near the dance floor, they had to have left. That's when he noticed the two record big wigs were nowhere to be found either. Still, after that revelation,

Josh continued to trudge around for about another hour, hoping to get a glimpse of either the girls or his phone.

Finally, he sat down next to one of the handful of small fires scattered across the backyard. The pit was about a football field's length from the house. For the last hour, Josh had been fighting off thoughts of the possible scenarios of what could have happened to Dianna. Not entertaining the disgusting things that she could be doing right then was a form of denial that took all his efforts. But the more he drank, the more his mind gave way to dark images of her giving in to the sexual advances of the two despicable jackals who were hounding her. He could practically see Cammy talking her into it. Shaking his head in disgust, Josh took down another mouthful of whiskey. He shook his head and thought to himself, "To think I sided with Cammy over my best friend." Charlie was right. He called it, from the beginning of this godforsaken night. And, like an idiot, Josh hadn't even seen it. Now he was alone.

Perching his elbows on the lawn chair, Josh sat in bitter silence, swirling the contents of the red plastic cup. It was odd to him how closely the fire symbolized how we felt right now. At one point in the party, he'd fantasized Dianna would give in to him, and they'd finally go all the way. He didn't really think she would, but he never imagined the night would end up like this. The realization that she could have so easily left, purposefully without saying goodbye, was burning him and eating away at his insides.

His heart ached so badly in this moment that he could barely believe it. And, just like the wood in the pit, Josh knew tomorrow there'd be nothing left of his heart but white ash. If he could just find his phone, he could text her. He'd even thought of calling her from inside, but he couldn't remember her number. It was stored in his phone, so he never dialed it.

The party was winding down now. The DJ had packed all his stuff up an hour ago. Most everybody that was left had moved into the house. Josh could hear the music, but he just couldn't find the drive to leave his chair. Given his mood, it was probably better that he just sat here by himself.

"So this is how it happens, huh, God?" he asked out loud, not caring if anybody heard him. "This is how I become the Dark Half? You take me, kicking and screaming?" He knew that his cosmic role in all this had to have some bearing on how tonight played out. For the past two weeks, Josh pondered how somebody, as nice and as thoughtful as he was, could end up being the Antichrist. Now he could see it. It was all so simple. After sixteen years of being gentle and mild, God would break him. He just had no idea why. That's what was so confusing to him. He had to be the most under qualified person for the job. Surely, out of the whole world, there had to be a million people better suited for this than him. But somehow this was happening to him, whether he liked it or not.

The worst part was that, every time he tried to get back up and be his usual, cheery self, more stuff would be heaped on him. Josh shook his head, angered at what he was being put through. He felt like somebody had set off a road flare in his chest. He didn't know what he was waiting for. He could just leave. He had only stayed this long because there was a part of him that had held out hope that Dianna would somehow show up and take away his pain. Maybe Cammy had gotten sick, and Dianna took her home. Josh would believe anything that he had to, if she'd just come back. The more he sat, the more he realized that it really wasn't going to happen though.

And that's when the question entered his mind. Just how far was God willing to push him? The thought filled Josh with despair, considering how low life might take him before he was ready to be the Dark Half. Even scarier, would he ever know happiness in this lifetime again? Could it really be that, at sixteen, his best days were behind him? Josh swallowed down the last of the whiskey, his mind racing. He angrily threw his cup in the fire. "This is bullshit," Josh shouted, standing up. He just couldn't shut his mind off. He wanted a break from the visions of Dianna in his head.

What was happening to him? Silently, he paced back and forth, as the flames of the fire twisted into a funnel and then fell back down, crackling and snapping. How and when would this all end? He cringed, as all these unknowns flooded into his head. Was it really possible that he could decide his fate, like a regular person? Could or would more stuff happen, seemingly coincidentally, like tonight? Rubbing his temples, he laughed to himself, like a madman. In his wildest dreams, he never thought tonight would end up like this. If he was destined to be the Dark Half, there would be plenty more nights like tonight. That was for certain. What if he didn't do it? There were alternatives. He could...

Josh stopped pacing, as he realized just what he was thinking. The only way out of this was if he killed himself. He thought about it for a second. How, at sixteen, could his only two options be to become the Antichrist or to kill himself? What the hell had happened to him? "I'm losing my mind," Josh said to nobody. "I can't take this anymore." That's when he felt it. The tension in his body increased, and his anger flared. Josh tried to fight it, but the fury within him was building. He had absolutely no strength to hold back, "Oh, God, please don't do this!" Josh screamed, as his head began to pound.

Throwing his hands out to brace himself, Josh staggered backwards. He knew there were bushes and trees behind him. He just didn't know how far away they were. Everything seemed to fade into the distance, as the nape of his neck tightened up. "Stop this!" Josh commanded, with all the authority he could possibly muster; though that wasn't much. Everything snapped back into focus. Josh wobbled on his feet and made his way towards the lawn chair. As he reached down, almost in slow-motion, to grab a hold of it, his vision became blood-red. Blinking and looking at his hands, he was amazed to see that he was literally seeing red, almost like every other band of light was shut off. And then it hit him, like a bomb blast.

The fury washed over him like a backdraft. Josh tried for a split second to fight it off. Then he let go, as wave after wave of pure hatred poured over him. The energy pulsed off of his body rhythmically, with each beat of his heart. He felt nothing but hate. Deep within him was a dark yearning for everybody to feel exactly what he felt. Opening his arms to each side, Josh flung back his head and screamed more malevolently and animalistic than he'd ever imagined a human could. As he did, he felt the fury leave him. It felt like a hand had reached in and pulled it out of him somehow, or like he had vomited it up. Whatever it was, Josh's reality snapped back into focus; and his vision was normal.

The image that greeted him wasn't though. His eyes widened in horror, as the small, crackling fire he'd been sitting next to for the last hour had grown upwards several feet. Its fiery body was spinning, with the force of a tempest. He rolled out of the way just in time, as it swung over to where he was standing, flailing about like a blind worm searching for its mother. Awestruck, he realized that his fire wasn't the only fire doing this. All of the small fires had birthed their own fiery serpent. Even the giant bonfire next to the lake was stretching out towards the night sky.

The ringing of screams filled his ears, as the hordes of people disbanded and fled for their lives. The backyard had become a mad house of frantic drunks, scrambling to climb over one another. Besides the one next to Josh, there were two others up near the house, on the patio. Amidst the screams and his own terror, Josh decided he had to take a stand. This wasn't the time for the circus to come the town. He had to deliver. In desperation, he reached out and imagined he was strangling one fire and pushing the other down, back into the fire pit. Whichever method worked better, he'd use on the rest.

He tried to force the fires downward with all his will. Unfortunately, just like the magically growing plants in the backyard, Josh found that he couldn't stop the process. Admitting defeat, he dropped his arms and did what any rational person would do in that situation. Josh turned around and ran the other way.

***

"Holy crap. Did you see that?" Bill asked, with absolute glee in his voice.

"Hell, yeah," Deus replied, high-fiving him.

"You were right. This was definitely the way to go." Bill clinked his beer bottle to Deus's, as he looked back on the scene in front of him. They hadn't been able to see what Josh was up to. As they didn't want to enter the scene, they got up on the roof. And, boy, was he glad they did. The fireworks were spectacular from up there.

"And like a scared child, the great and mighty Prime runs off into the night," Bill said, dramatically swinging his beer around. The sounds of screams had died down. He noticed they'd been replaced by the shrill cry of fast-approaching fire trucks. Fortunately, they wouldn't be needed. Hasden was the head of the Monarchy. He could easily keep his property from burning down. In fact, if it wasn't for him, the place would have gone up minutes before. But fire was his specialty. He would, however, need a hand taming the energy Josh had infused the fire with.

"Well, Deus, what do you say we clean up this mess that Mr. Michaels started," he said, as he pushed himself up. He hated to admit it, but the tiles on the roof were a lot harder than he thought. He really didn't mind sitting up here, but he didn't think about the fact that he couldn't set his beer down on the slanted roof. "Oh, well," Hasden said, tossing the bottle of beer off the roof and into the pool.

Taking Deus's right hand in his left, he felt the raw power of the other demon link with his own. Together, as one, they flooded the backyard with their will, imposing it on the thrashing serpents of fire. While every demon had his own, special talents that set him apart, Hasden's powers were as vast as his stock portfolio. He could do everything well, but Deus was not as diversified.

He was the King of Lust and Perversion. If Hasden ordered him to, he could have extended his aura, influencing everyone in the party towards a full-scale Roman orgy that would make Caligula proud. Today, however, was not about that. Hasden had need of another talent of Deus's, which was invisibility. Hasden had him follow Josh most of the night, waiting for the time he'd finally laid his phone down. Just now, Bill needed his friend's sheer strength to boost his already incredibly strong-willed mind.

It was risky business, dealing with an elemental. You had to obey one simple rule; once engaged, your will had to be stronger. Whatever memory the other caster, whether angel or demon, had used, yours had to be that much more vivid. It also had to be the opposite, if you wanted to snuff it out. The difficulty in this, Bill knew, was not only that Michaels was the Prime, but he was also the Dark Half. From any angle, he was stronger than Dianna, based solely on the fact that Dianna would never have to battle the angels. She would inevitably unleash her light against the darkness, and let the chips fall where they may.

Michaels, though, could channel either, depending on his proficiency. And seeing as he unleashed this with fury, that meant Hasden had to use the opposite; which was pretty much outside a demon's realm, but only marginally. He couldn't conjure up love. He could, however, manage happiness and joy. That could backdoor fury on a lot of wavelengths. Once his will was properly placed, Bill opened his mind to Deus and thought of one of the most magnificent spectacles he'd seen in recent memory. It was right before they'd come to America, in fact. He and Deus were on vacation in Australia, when they heard that a volcano was getting ready to erupt in Indonesia.

He remembered it like it was only yesterday, but it was 1815. When the top blew off of Mount Tambora, ninety-two thousand people were killed, sending every one of their confused asses straight back to the Creator. It restored Hasden's faith in nature and filled him with joy, because he had grown increasingly weary of the angels continuously boasting about how the children of Adam were continuously overcoming nature's setbacks. That year, as America and Europe felt the effects of what was called the year without summer, Hasden joyously flipped a strong, stiff middle finger to his angelic haters and told them all to kiss his asshole. Bill opened his eyes and snuffed out what was left of the fire.

"Is it all gone?" Deus asked, looking around the backyard.

"I'm pretty sure it is," Bill confidently replied, sinking back down onto the roof. "But it took both of us to do it," he said, feeling the drain on his power. "It would probably be a good idea to mark our territory, by posting our sigil's at the four corners of the property, just to keep all unwelcome energy away."

"That was a boatload of energy," Deus said, narrowing his eyes. "This kid is going to be dangerous, when he learns to use his power. Should we really be playing with him like this?"

"Don't worry," Bill said, grinning. "We've done this a million times before, and you know how it goes. Some jobs are like walking in and turning on a light switch. Some are like dismantling a bomb. Thanks to the info we gleaned from this party, we know Michaels' only knows how to instinctively use his powers. And, like most humans, he can only tap into his darkness, which plays to our advantage. I have a sneaking suspicion that Josh is about to find out that the human mind is a dangerous garden. Maybe we can't kill him. If we play our cards right, we won't have to. He'll off himself."

***

Running by the light of the moon, Josh made his way back, towards where he thought the car was. His legs burned, as they pumped harder and harder. "Thank God these houses weren't tract homes," he thought, or he'd be lost by now. It was late. Most of the cars were gone by now, leaving only the unique homes to go by.

Josh didn't even want to think of the implications of what just happened. He was running completely on adrenaline, and he just wanted to get as far away from this hellish night as possible. Slowing down to a walk, Josh surveyed his surroundings. He couldn't tell, at this point, if he was even going in the right direction. The cacophony of noise around him wasn't helping either. Ultimately, he wasn't even sure if the sound of sirens was coming towards him or going away from him.

One thing he knew for sure was that the sound of howling dogs in the background was unnerving. Of course, Josh knew that dogs howled whenever they heard sirens. Josh also knew, with absolute certainty, that the canine wails started directly after he unleashed his own primal scream. Looking at the house in front of him, he noticed a statue that Charlie had made fun of on the way in. It was just a boy peeing, but it had sent the redhead into hysterics. Josh ran over to the statue and tried to imagine driving in to the complex, but he couldn't. His brain was completely fried.

"Well," he thought to himself, "it's got to be one of two ways." Josh ran off down the new street, where he saw two familiar sights. One was the Green Machine. The other was Charlie, flat on his back and sprawled out on the hood.

"Heeeeey, buddy, you're alive," Charlie said happily, propping himself up on one arm. "I'm SO glad to see you," he said enthusiastically.

"Are you high?" Josh asked, walking up to the car and trying to catch his breath.

"Dude. Words cannot express how good I feel right now. I'm telling you. I actually feel like I'm in a warm glove."

Josh didn't have time for this. He had to get the boy's happy ass in the car and get out of here immediately. "Are you able to get in the car?" Josh asked.

"Sure," the redhead said matter-of-factly, swinging his legs off the car and sliding off. Josh looked at the scratches left in his friend's wake.

"Whatever," he thought. Josh had much bigger problems than that to deal with. Sliding into the driver's seat, he slid the key into the ignition. As soon as he heard the passenger door slam, he pulled away from the curb. They were off. He didn't want to spend any more time here than he had to. Scanning the houses, Josh tried to plot his way out, with Charlie emphatically stating how great he felt over and over.

"I lost my phone at the party. So I can't GPS us out of here," he said trying to keep his eyes on the road. "Get your phone and try and find our way out of here."

"Hold on," Charlie said, smiling. Josh didn't know what was making the boy so happy, but he desperately needed some right now. "It says it can't locate," Charlie said, grinning through half-closed eyelids."

"Goddamnit. That's impossible!" Josh snapped angrily, trying his best to watch the road. "I saw when you flipped it on. You had four bars."

"Dude, check it out," Charlie said, handing it to him. Josh could see he was telling the truth.

"Why is this happening?" he mumbled, realizing his

adrenaline was fading. Now his buzz was coming back. He'd found his way to a main street out of the neighborhood, but he didn't know where the freeway was.

"I don't want to trip you out," Charlie said, quietly bumping the back of his head on the seat's headrest, "but there's a cop behind us."

As calmly as he could, Josh looked into the rearview mirror. It was coming up on them like a rocket, with its red and blue lights on. "Oh, geez," he thought. "This is all we need. Please don't let me get a DUI. I haven't even had my license for a month." Josh calmly pulled off into the next street and pulled over. It occurred to him, if he hadn't hoped he was dead earlier, he surely would after his family found out about the DUI. Amazingly enough, the cop car continued to speed past. Josh breathed a partial sigh of relief, saying, "I'm killing the engine and shutting off the lights. I'm drawing the line. Maybe Dianna left the party with some other guy. I might really be the Antichrist, seeing as I just burned down our friends' backyard and quite possibly their house. But I am not getting a DUI," Josh said, shaking his head emphatically.

"Dude. You burned down Deus's pad?" Charlie asked, amazed. "He kicked the gym teacher's ass, just for assuming he was a better wrestler than him." Putting his elbow against the window, Josh rested his head in the palm of his hand. He already had a mountain of things he'd rather not think about.

"What the hell are we going to do?" he groaned.

"Don't sweat it," Charlie said happily. "What street are we on?"

Josh opened the door and stepped out. "It's Wilson Way," he said, in a hushed tone, looking in the car.

"Cool, follow me," the redhead said, looking at his phone and getting out of the car. "And grab your sleeping bag out of the trunk," he added, as he walked off, down the dark street.

"Sure thing," thought Josh, looking at his friend and

shaking his head. "All of a sudden, your phone works?" he noted sarcastically, as he popped the trunk and grabbed his overnight bag. It was the one thing he'd used more than anything else, since he rarely stayed at home anymore on weekends and was always at Charlie's. Trotting towards the bouncing light, Josh finally caught up to him at the end of the block, as the drunk redhead was making a left.

"Do you know somebody here?" Josh whispered, checking out the houses. He noticed they were all uniform, older homes with nicely landscaped yards.

"No, I don't know anybody. But I'm using the shady economy to our advantage," Charlie said, still grinning. "This way," he pointed and staggered off. Josh followed him past five more houses, until his friend started walking up one of the driveways.

"You stupid ass. Where are you going?" Josh hissed, in Charlie's direction. The house's lawn was a different shade than the other lawns. By his guess, even in the moonlight, it looked dead. There were weeds everywhere. Josh looked around for his friend, but he was gone. "Charlie?" he whispered into the darkness.

"Come on in," the boy said, as he swung open the front door with a huge smile on his face.

"Dude, get out!" Josh said in astonishment, not believing what had just happened.

"No," Charlie giggled. "Come in," he nodded and opened the door wider. Looking around warily, Josh checked to see if any of the neighbors' lights had turned on.

"Oh, well," he thought. He'd already obliterated a dozen laws tonight. He might as well add breaking and entering to the list. Timidly poking his head into the house, he slipped in and closed the door.

"Follow me," Charlie's voice said, out of the blackness of the house's living room. Josh walked towards the bouncing light, trying not to trip on anything that might be hidden in the all-encompassing darkness. Immediately, his nostrils were filled with a foul smell. The place smelled like the owners had a dozen cats and they had pissed on everything. Josh tried to block the odor out, but it seemed to be overpowering his senses.

"Where are we?" Josh whispered. The light of Charlie's phone turned upwards to his face.

"Don't worry, man. This is a foreclosed home. I looked it up online. There's another one four blocks from here, but there was no lock on the gate," Charlie said, sounding excited. "I thought I'd have to break the window with a rock and your sleeping bag, but the side garage door was open. So I just walked in. Turned out the front door was the only door that was locked in this whole place." Josh shook his head in the dark.

"This is still illegal," he said, worried.

"Yes, it is," agreed Charlie. "But it sure as hell beats going to jail because you're drunk and I'm high on somebody else's prescription meds." Josh definitely couldn't argue with that.

"We'll just stay away from the windows," his friend said. "If anybody shows up, we run. We've got a lot better chance of making it here with no cops than if we we're just sitting in your car. And our chances are infinitely better of getting away from this house than your car."

"True," Josh agreed out loud, hearing the words echo off the empty rooms. He edged his way towards the wall, wondering to himself why an empty room just seemed to do something to your voice. The echo sounded so hollow. Dropping the sleeping bag and sitting down, he reached for the ties that kept it rolled up.

"Don't spread it out," Charlie said, as he lied down, resting his head on one side and casting his phone's light to the empty side for Josh. Once Josh was situated, he turned his phone off. Josh didn't say anything. He lied opposite Charlie, so that they each had half of the rolled back up bag to prop up on.

"Dude, what happened earlier, between me and Cammy, I'm really sorry about that whole thing."

Josh suddenly felt like he'd been kicked in the chest. Not because Charlie apologized, but because, when he thought of Cammy, it made him think of Dianna. And he really didn't want to do that right now. He just wanted to force it out of his head.

"It's cool," Josh replied, his voice cracking. "So you said the pills you took made you feel better?"

"I can't even begin to describe it," Charlie said happily, into the darkness. "Do you know how it feels when you wake up in the morning and you're kind of awake, but you could easily fall back asleep? And your blankets just feel soft and incredibly good?"

"Yeah," Josh answered. He smiled just thinking about it.

"You're all content and happy. Even if your mom was in the kitchen cooking a fantastic breakfast you just don't want to leave the bed because you're afraid of breaking the sanctity taking place between your mattress and your covers..." Josh silently nodded in the dark. He hadn't slept like that since he lived in Santa Cruz, thanks to the bird outside of his window. "Well, if you understand that feeling, then you'd have just a glimpse into how good this feels."

"Really?" Josh asked, lifting his head up from the sleeping bag.

"Do you want some? Billy gave me a whole bottle of the stuff."

Seriously considering it, Josh weighed his options. Even though he'd grown up in a pretty liberal household, they never took medicine, unless they really needed it. On the other hand, if he thought about Dianna again tonight, he'd definitely flip out.

"Yeah, you know what," he said, "go ahead and give me some. Even if it helps me to ignore the strange smell in here, it'll be worth it." He stared into the darkness. Having only just said the words, a part of him felt like this was the wrong choice. He just needed an escape. Besides, he told himself it was just safer for everyone, if he was in a good mood. Who knew what could happen, if he lost his temper again?

"Here you go." Charlie turned on his phone. The light shone down on the palm of his hand. Taking the pills and the phone, Josh made his way to the bathroom and swallowed them down with what little water he could stomach from the sink. Just the one swallow of stagnant water probably had more metal in it from the unused pipes than he'd ever had in a lifetime. Sitting down on the porcelain toilet, Josh shone the light towards his face and stared into the mirror. "What the hell is happening to me?" he thought, shaking his head.

"All better?" Charlie's voice asked, from somewhere in the dark.

"We'll see, Josh replied, gingerly laying his head down. He sat in the bathroom for about fifteen minutes, but he couldn't feel anything, except the effects of the alcohol. So he decided to go back into the living room. "Hey, let me ask you a question," Josh said, switching the topic. "Do you think God is harder on certain people?"

"I guess," replied Charlie. "I mean, look at me. I wouldn't say my life is jam-packed with goodness. Why do you ask? You're not still tripping on the number thing; are you?"

"Not really," Josh lied. Even if he wanted to, he couldn't tell Charlie about the stuff Thomas had told him. "I just feel like, since my birthday, my life is changing. And in every instance, it seems like God's being unnecessarily harsh. I don't know what for. I mean, what good can come from hurting me?"

"I don't know," Charlie said. "I'm not a child therapist. But I would like to point out that Vader chopped off his son's hand, and he still turned out pretty damn good."

"That is radically significant," Josh said, chuckling. "I'll have to consider that the next time I'm having a bad day."

Chapter 20

Silently creeping in his front door, Josh tried to make a beeline straight for the stairs to his room. He needed sleep in the worst possible way. Looking back on the night now, it all seemed like a blur. He didn't remember much after the first thirty minutes after taking the pills, except that he felt extremely euphoric. Then he nodded off.

In the morning, Josh was woken up by the sounds of Charlie vomiting in the toilet. The house that had been so dark last night was now brighter than Josh would have liked. In the light of day, Josh could tell exactly how dirty the foreclosed home really was. The floor was absolutely filthy. It was obvious that the previous owners never wiped their feet, because there was dirt smudges all over the carpet. Either that, or they weren't the only two people who were sleeping there. The thought caused chills to run up his spine. They'd never even locked the doors. What if somebody had been upstairs the whole night?

Charlie was sweating, like he'd just run a marathon, and looked like hell. Truth be told, Josh didn't feel all that great either. It was just a lot of aches and pains that he assumed he'd gotten from sleeping on the floor. He remembered they were just about to leave, when Charlie had to go the bathroom again. This time, it was diarrhea. And since there wasn't a shred of toilet paper in the place, Josh and Charlie left the house four socks lighter. It was an embarrassing experience that he never wanted to think of again.

"It's okay now. I'm home," Josh thought, silently sneaking down the hall to his bedroom, which was not only safer but infinitely cleaner. He could only breathe a sigh of relief, because the ordeal was finally done. Josh closed his door and took a look at his soft bed. It was a welcome sight, if ever there was one; especially after waking up on the floor of an old, abandoned home.

That's when he heard it; the insanely loud bird that had been a thorn in his side ever since he moved here. "Why now?" thought Josh. He was certain he hadn't heard it, when he trudged up the driveway. Shaking his head in disgust, Josh headed out of the room and down the stairs, taking them two at a time.

He was thoroughly over the inconvenience. What was the world coming to, when you couldn't even sleep in peace in your own room? Josh knew exactly what he was going to do. He'd knock the nest out of the tree with a rake and let the ugly, brown bird figure it out for himself. Walking through the back door, he shielded his eyes from the bright sun.

"Well, how lovely of you to join us," Sam said, in a sharp tone. Startled, Josh flinched like he'd shocked himself. He wasn't expecting anybody to be out here.

"Have a seat," Claire said, in a stern voice, pointing to the chair next to her.

Blinking his bleary eyes, Josh looked at both his mother and Claire. They were sitting at the backyard patio table having coffee. It was a tradition that started when Larry had entered the hospital but had stopped when he was moved to the nursing facility. "Is Papa okay?" Josh asked, as he took a seat on the padded chair.

"He's back in the hospital for his irregular heartbeat," Sam said quietly. "The doctors are afraid he might develop more clots, so they took him in this morning." Josh nervously looked at his mother and then his grandmother. They definitely looked disturbed about something, and he didn't know what. He'd already told them he wasn't coming home last night, so that couldn't be it. He wondered if they had heard of the fire last night.

"We need to have a talk," Claire said, staring directly into his eyes. Looking away, Josh glanced over at his mother, who wasn't saying anything. It was odd for him to see Sam in such a passive role.

Folding his arms in a defensive posture, Josh replied, "If

I'm in trouble for doing something, then my mom and I usually talk it out."

"I know how your mother handles things," Claire said, smiling like a cat that had just caught a canary. "However, after you were tested, we decided that, while your mother would handle her arena, I would handle any matters she was unfamiliar with."

"And what's that?" Josh asked impatiently. He really just wanted to go back to bed. Was that too much to ask for?

Claire stared at him with her piercing blue eyes and then rested her hands on the table. "Is there any particular reason why your watcher invaded my dream earlier this morning to tell me you were a no-show at the park today?"

"AHH! Damn," thought Josh, his stomach tightening into a knot. "I'm sorry. I forgot."

"Do I have to remind you that you're the Prime?" Claire said, a measure of disbelief in her tone. "You're one of the most important people in this universe, but you have to be properly trained."

"I don't mean to sound disrespectful, but I don't know if I believe a word he said," admitted Josh. He could see the look of shock and dismay on his grandmother's face. In essence, it was true though.

"I met with Thomas last week, and he was a nice guy. But easily half the stuff he said sounded so far-fetched, and I can't deal with that right now."

Claire raised her eyebrow. "A nice guy? Josh, our neighbor is a nice guy. Thomas is an immortal and the highest of the elders. He has your best interests in mind."

Josh shook his head. "I don't know about that. My whole life has become a burning hell since my birthday. Despite meeting with him last Saturday, nothing's gotten better. If anything, it's gotten worse. So, if you'll excuse me, I need some sleep, so I can finally figure out this tangled ball of yarn that used to be my life."

"I'm sorry," snapped Claire, shaking her head. "Are we inconveniencing you? Because this conversation is not over."

"God, would you shut up?" thought Josh, the nausea from the drinking and the pills was getting worse. And the bird's loud, continuous chirping was hitting his head like a jackhammer. "Please, can we do this another time?" he moaned.

Claire looked absolutely bewildered. "We most certainly will not!" she shouted.

"Shut up!" yelled Josh abruptly. "I don't want to hear your voice anymore!" he screamed, pushing away from the table. "Your voice is like a knife in my head right now." Both women's faces were contorted into shocked expressions, which made him immediately regret the tone he had just used. But he couldn't hold it in any longer. He was sick, hurt, and sleep deprived.

"I'm not taking this shit any longer," Josh said in a low, even tone, trying his best to compose himself. "I spent the better part of last night entertaining thoughts of suicide because I don't know if I can do this. And every time I start to feel even marginally better, something comes along to drag me back down. So you'll have to forgive me, if I'm a little agitated." Spinning around in the chair, Josh pointed at the tree near his window and screamed, "You can shut up too!"

The sound issued from his throat wasn't his at all, but a low, guttural growling that startled even him. What surprised him even more was the shrill sound of a red-tailed hawk cry overhead, right before it dove straight into the tree with lightning speed. It happened so quickly, Josh's eyes could barely catch it. It wasn't so much the body that Josh saw, but it was the knife-like talons and the razor-sharp beak meant for ripping the flesh of its prey. Josh stood up, bathed in the silence that had instantly engulfed the backyard. It was over so quickly. There was no battle, no contest, just the ruffling of branches. Then the hawk burst from the tree, lifting itself up on spread wings with the limp form of the lifeless

Brown Thrasher clutched in its sharp talons.

Turning back to his grandmother, Josh said, "If you feel so compelled to flap your jaws about something, why don't you fill my mom in as to who the Dark Half is? I haven't had a minute to think since my birthday. I just want some sleep. Seriously."

Claire and Sam sat speechless. Josh didn't know if it was his defiance or the hawk. Really, he couldn't care less. If he didn't lie down soon, he was going to fall down. Ears ringing and eyes blurry, Josh spun around and headed towards the house.

"Hey, Michaels," shouted a voice from behind. The sound hit his tailbone and vibrated its way straight up to Josh's skull.

"What?" Josh snapped, spinning on his heel to see Charlie emerging from the pine trees.

"Good news," the boy said, in an enthusiastic manner. "Deus found your phone, and he says you didn't burn the house down last night. So they're having a pool party at 6:00 pm. We're invited." Josh grinned as the women's faces changed from shocked to absolutely floored. He took a second to process the information.

"Pick me up in six hours," he yelled, as he staggered off towards the house. Right now there was only one thought in Josh's mind, and that was sleep. He desperately needed to seek shelter from the harsh reality of life through sleep.

Chapter 21
7+7+7=

Sitting with her knees to her chest, Dianna rocked back and forth, as she silently prayed for guidance. She needed a sign from God to ease the pressure she'd been under for the past few days. As she continued to subconsciously move back and forth on top of the red picnic table her father had put in the backyard, she looked up at the sky. The sun was going down, and she still had a ton of stuff to do to get ready. "Please be my rock, Lord. Send me a sign that everything will be all right."

Satisfied that her prayer would be heard, Dianna looked one more time at the backyard. She'd already put the barbecue away in the garage and set the timers for the lawn. She'd put all of the gardening tools away and set all the potted plants near the edge of the lawn, where the sprinkler system watered part of the concrete. Everything looked good.

Dianna let go of her legs and let them hang down off the edge of the red table. Even in her blue jeans, she could feel the splintering edge of the wood poking through to her legs. After all the yard work, her jeans were just about as dirty as her white cotton tee shirt was. Kicking her tennis shoes back and forth at random, she checked her phone. There was a new picture of Nina and Ramon at the mall in Boston, that her dad had just sent. They were headed to buy Ramon some new ties to spruce up his wardrobe.

She had sent Josh a dozen texts on Friday night and a voicemail Saturday afternoon. He'd never even responded. It was obvious that he was upset. She knew he had every right to be, but she didn't like the silent treatment. As much as she'd avoided thinking about it, she missed his kiss.

Springing off the table, Dianna walked towards the fruit

trees that lined the fence. She'd keep busy in order to keep the tears at bay. It occurred to her on the ride home that there were a lot of her classmates who'd planned on having sex at the party that night. She definitely wasn't opposed to it, but she'd never really thought about it either. Having powers made that type of stuff all the more complicated. Dianna was used to sticking around with Nina and Ramon, but, because of the dream, she always had a feeling that Josh would eventually show up in her life. Now that he had, he was all she could think about.

Still, she felt like they should wait to have sex. After all, they just turned sixteen, and Dianna just didn't feel ready yet. There was no doubt that he was the one. When the time came, she'd do it without hesitation. Cammy had started this process in Dianna's head, bringing up the topic on the way to the party. When Dianna told her sister that Josh wasn't like that, Cammy chuckled and said, "That's what you think." And now Dianna was overcome with doubt. What if Josh did something at the party after she left, without telling him? What if he'd met somebody else, who would have sex with him? These thoughts filled her mind all day yesterday.

Just as Nina had predicted, Ramon read them the riot act for half an hour, while they sat on the couch in the living room. Dianna vividly remembered that, every time her father said how disappointed he was with her, it felt like she was being whipped. It felt so bad to know that she'd hurt somebody she loved. Given the choice, as much as it hurt her, she'd do it all over to be able to see Josh again.

The most surprising part was how right on Nina was about Cammy's experience with Ramon. Dianna couldn't believe how casually she parroted the words, "I'm sorry," "I know," and, "I'll never do it again," over and over, like she was reading from a script. Amazingly, Ramon hadn't threatened to kick her out that night. Everything was good between them Saturday, too, because they were so busy picking up the RV, shopping, and packing.

Today, though, at Sunday morning service at church, Cammy tagged along, as a good will gesture. Things were going smoothly. That is, until one of her sister's coworkers came up after the service and told her that her boss had seen the photos she'd posted. Half the company, who was linked to her group, had seen them as well. Some of them didn't like the poses or the finger gestures. One complaint came from a woman who worked in Cammy's human resources department, who asked if half the people in the photographs were even old enough to drink. Her friend warned her that, when she came in on Monday, her boss was going to give her the choice to quit or be fired.

Staring at the fruit trees against the fence, Dianna checked her handiwork from earlier. The beautiful orange and lemon trees that she and Ramon had planted together last year looked horrid. Everything that was beautiful about the trees was lying in a pile on the ground, waiting to be thrown away. She hated to trim them so short. They had dropped a ton of fruit, and she didn't want spoiling fruit to attract vermin. "Oh, well, next summer they'll be beautiful again," she thought to herself. "I might as well throw this stuff away." As she walked towards the garage, she was surprised to see Nina exiting the house, wearing a serious expression on her face.

"Hey," Dianna said, stopping. "You're back already? I thought you were at the mall."

Nina cracked her knuckles and smiled, "I was. I just thought I'd come to see what you were up to."

"That's odd," Dianna thought. "Quit playing," she said, confused. "The mall's a thirty minute drive from here. I just got a picture from dad, and you guys were walking into a store." Dianna glanced to see if Ramon was peeking around any of the corners of the house to surprise her. Nina shrugged her shoulders, causing her hair to bounce.

"I didn't drive. I ran. It was faster."

The odd comment caught her by surprise. "Is this a joke?" Dianna asked, waiting for her father to jump out and start laughing.

Stepping towards her, Nina shook her head, "No, my child. This is not a joke," she said, vanishing, only to reappear behind the girl. "This is a sign."

A chill ran up Dianna's spine, as she turned to face the woman. She could faintly feel the breeze from Nina passing her, just now hitting her hair. "Metatron sends his regards," the woman said, nodding towards the clouds above.

Dianna stood completely frozen, shocked by what she had just witnessed. Narrowing her eyes, Nina's voice began to vibrate, "Now, Dianna Alexa Imperial, prepare yourself inwardly for what is about to take place."

Dianna felt a tingle go up and down her spine, as fragments of the dream from Friday trickled into her head. She didn't know what to think. Her housemate had just run from another city within minutes to tell her that an angel actually heard her prayer.

"UMM, should I bow or something? I don't know what to do."

"Don't worry," the copper-headed woman said, her voice filled with glee. "The formalities are over. Come here, my child." Nina threw her bare arms around Dianna, and the girl's nose was flooded with the smell of Nina's rose-scented hair. As surprised as she was, somehow she'd always suspected Nina was here in her life for a reason. Now she knew it was true. "You have no idea how long I've waited to say those words to you," Nina smiled.

"I don't know," Dianna said nervously. "Probably three years, I guess. What is this about?"

"You having powers is no accident. I'm actually here to teach you how to use them more effectively and in their many expressions. I'm sure this will come as a shock. I'm an immortal, and I've been waiting for the coming of the Primes for thousands of years."

"What?" Dianna asked, her jaw dropping. "I don't understand," she said, shaking her head.

Nina motioned towards the table. "Sit, child, and I'll tell you a story as old as time..."

***

"I'm serious," Billy screamed at the group. "I have trouble meeting people."

"That is such horseshit," Charlie said, laughing. Josh chuckled and hung his head back, carelessly listening to the water roll up on the lake shore. It felt great being here with his friends, having fun. This was definitely the good life. He didn't have a care in the world right now. Today, after swimming in the pool, they'd gone out to the lake for a few. Then, just like yesterday, they had a grand feast. He had to admit, Billy definitely knew his way around the grill, and he loved to show it.

Last night's bonfire started with more pills and booze, and they'd been rolling with it ever since. He noticed that Billy had tons of people who would show up throughout the day. Billy never called them friends. He referred to them as his associates. These people never really stayed too long either, Josh noticed. He took a deep breath of the night air and smiled. It smelled like freedom.

Casually, he took a momentary glance at the three women sitting across from him. He had no idea who they were, but they definitely filled out their bikinis perfectly. He couldn't understand it. Billy's place was like a way station for beautiful people. They just dropped in, said hello, chatted for a while, and then took off. There wasn't one person here who was left over from yesterday's pool party. Hanging his head back again so he could see the stars, Josh listened to Billy and Charlie playfully argue with each other.

It seemed like the oxy cured Charlie's social awkwardness.

"I want to hear that you have difficulty making friends about as much as I want to hear another half-cooked story about how dancing saved the reality show contestant's life," Charlie groaned.

"Thank you," Josh said, relieved. "Out of the army of singing shows, how many contestants do I have to listen to who say how singing brought them back from the brink? Don't get me wrong. I'm sure it happens, but these shows are driving it into the ground. It's not fun anymore."

"I'm not saying I don't meet people," Billy said, as the fire settled down. "I just don't have many true friends."

"Hey, guys," shouted Deus, carefully walking down the cobblestone path to the fire. Josh could see that he had on his usual red 32 sleeveless basketball jersey and board shorts. He was also was carrying a bottle of his favorite scotch.

"And he finally shows up," Billy said sarcastically. "I'm glad to see you. I didn't know the Betty Ford Clinic had a work release program. Where've you been all day?"

"Me and some friends had family game night," Deus answered, smiling ear to ear. "I was having a few drinks at this girl's place, and she showed me her candy land. But it was looking like too much of a risk. So I left with her friend. We went out to the truck, where she sunk my battleship."

Billy stared at his cousin incredulously. "Really? Are you sure she didn't get a load of your connect four and say sorry?"

"OOH, burn!" Charlie shouted, stomping his feet on the ground. Josh chuckled, as Billy and Charlie exchanged high-fives with each other. The girls giggled.

"Whatever," Deus mumbled, sitting down in an empty chair. "I don't have to prove my sexual prowess to anybody here."

Billy snapped his head back, like he was shocked. "When your ass gets off the couch. This guy bases his whole weekend off

Animal Planet. He could have the cure for cancer or know who shot Biggie and Tupac, and be headed out the door, but if baby polar bears are on TV, the whole night's a wash. He'll sit down and make plans to get a pizza delivered. After that, if you throw baby orangutans or wolves into the mix, he'll end up sleeping on the couch all night."

Deus grinned and took a long draw off his bottle of scotch. "So? You're like that with the History Channel."

"I'll admit to a few times, but you're the reason we never go out. I shouldn't have to P.T. Barnum your ass off the couch, like a sideshow barker. I'm serious, the spiky-haired boy said, looking at the group. And he always asks the same thing," Billy said, red in the face from laughter and slapping his knee. 'Well, who's going to be there?' Like I'm the goddamn Census Bureau." Josh laughed and shook his head. Everybody around the campfire was busting up. Surprisingly, Deus was being a good sport about it.

"Keep on laughing, you pill-popping idiots," Deus chuckled, while shaking his head. "You think you're funny because you're all high. Either you're about as funny as a hot poker to the pee hole, or I'm just not drunk enough to understand your brand of humor."

"Deus, my friend," Charlie said, standing up from his chair. "You definitely are not drunk enough. Now gather in, everybody, as I tell our next story. It's an epic tale of two friends overcoming all odds. I now present to you the story of Grabit and Tug."

Josh grinned as he watched Charlie go into one of his highly illustrative masturbatory adventures. And as the girls' faces turned to disgust, it only made him laugh harder. He had a feeling this was going to be one hell of a summer.

***

"So the angels and the demons share that one trait?" Dianna

asked.

"Kind of," Nina said, "but in different ways and for different reasons. They're both fascinated by numbers. So whatever they read, they count the letters, consonants and vowels and try to figure them out. It's neat to watch. They're just geared for magical thinking, and they see signs in everything. You can use it to your advantage, too. It comes in handy, if you're being chased by an agent of the Monarchy. Just throw a handful of sugar or sand over your shoulder, and it'll buy you the second or two you need to get away."

Scooting forward on her bed, Dianna grabbed her pillow and held it to her chest. Both Nina and her were in their pajamas now. They'd been talking on her bed for hours. She just couldn't get enough. Sitting up straighter, Nina grabbed her copper-colored curls and tied them back with the blue band that was sitting on her wrist. Then she continued, "The angels and demons are basically the same. They're like two brands of truck that are built on the same chassis. They both have two hearts. Their minds, while the same as humans, have no restrictions. So they can access its full potential. It's the same with their genetic code. They can access all their enzymes and can reconfigure them as they please."

Dianna furrowed her brows in concentration. "If I really wanted to, could I control them, as the Prime?"

"I don't know about that," Nina replied cautiously. "Theoretically, yes, you can. I've seen avatars do it, but it's highly dangerous for you," Nina said, pointing at Dianna. "I wouldn't. It's not worth the effort. After you turn eighteen, the angelic Host will follow your every command unquestioningly. They're very loyal. A demon, however, will attack you just like a wildcat would attack a human that had raised it from birth, whether it's hungry or it just thinks you're weak. It's in their nature. They don't care whether you're the Prime or not.

"The angels build up humanity. They KNOW that the

humans are the key to the Creator's plan, because of their ability to choose. The demons test and tear down humanity. They THINK that the humans are genetic inferiors. They don't see this reality the way you do. Where you see people, a demon only sees pawns. They view them as pieces in a game that they are continuously trying to win. In their eyes, they feel that Metatron is a clown. The Prime is nothing more to them than a one-trick pony."

"What?" Dianna cried. "Why would they think that?"

"We'll get into that later, child," Nina said, putting her hand on Dianna's leg and squeezing. "Today's just your first day. It's just an intro," she said, chuckling.

Dianna nodded in agreement. "I just have one more question that's bothering me."

"Your faith," Nina said, smiling.

"Yeah, kind of. I mean, I know there's different faiths and all that. Are any of them right?"

Taking a deep breath and looking into the girl's eyes, Nina replied, "They all are, child."

"How? I don't understand."

"You don't have to. All you need to know is this; everything came from God. There's nothing created that didn't come from the Creator. On this earth are different people, with different spiritual beliefs. It's supposed to be like that. Think of it like this; in my veins flows the blood that keeps me alive. Your blood is made up of different constituents, just like our spiritual world. There are red blood cells, white blood cells, lymphocytes, platelets. They all have a different purpose," Nina said, shaking her head. "But at no time do they ever point out to each other that they're different. They just perform their function. That's harmony.

"The religious institutions know that the love and praise that they send off is the lifeblood of the universe and the Creator. When they attack each other because of their differences, it causes disharmony. All these separate religions were part of the original plan to begin with. It's just the lifeblood of the Creator. Besides," Nina said, "haven't you ever noticed that the most gifted preachers rarely ever use scripture? Your father included."

"It makes sense," Dianna said. "But wars have been fought between religions. Countless lives have been lost. These people hate each other."

"Hate is a strong word," Nina replied. "It's more of a misunderstanding between them that was purposely put there by the Creator. To understand this, I'd have to explain to you how duality works and how the friction between opposites creates energy. Because, ultimately, that's what this earth does is create energy. Our earth is just a cog in a machine so grand I can barely understand it myself. That machine is only one half of the whole."

Nina sighed, taking the girl's hands in hers. "I hate the theory part so much. It's super boring. It's best to get it out of the way first, and then we can get to the interesting stuff."

Dianna got up off of her bed and stretched her legs. "What time is it?"

"Past your bedtime," Nina said, giving her a hug and kissing her on the forehead. "Go to bed," she said, as she headed towards the door. "We're going to have a long tour ahead of us, and it all starts tomorrow."

As Nina slipped out the door, Dianna threw her arms up and ran in place. She was overcome with joy that Nina was going to be her trainer. They were best friends, and Nina had helped Ramon raise her. This was better than she could have ever hoped. She looked at her phone. It was 12:34 in the morning. She was hoping to get a text from Josh, but tomorrow would be another day. According to Nina, Josh and Dianna were meant for each other. No matter what happened, in her eyes, she had found him once. She could do it again.

Dianna slid off her blue sweats and let them slip to the floor.

It was just too hot, even with the window open. Keeping her Red Sox jersey on, she slid in between the sheets and began to think about the big day ahead of her. This was the beginning of a bright, new future for the Imperial family.

***

"Early to bed and early to rise," thought Josh, as he rolled off the leather couch. His bare feet definitely felt the chill of the black marble floor. He took a look at his phone. It was 12: 34 in the afternoon. "Man," he thought, "this is getting out of hand." They'd stayed another night, without going home.

Silently stepping over to Charlie's pants on the leather recliner, Josh stuck his hand in and fished out the pill bottle, stealing a couple of the oxy for himself. It was Monday afternoon on June 24th, and he was a new man. There were absolutely no problems at Casa Hasden. It was just fun and games all day, every day. He'd definitely needed it. After the first half of the weekend being a disaster, this was a blessing. Josh realized, for the first time in his life, that he'd never truly lived. But sooner or later, he would have to sort out his problems with Thomas and apologize to his mom and grandmother.

Flicking his thumb across the phone screen, he checked his texts. They were all from Sam, asking if he'd come visit Larry in the hospital. "No more Dianna," Josh thought to himself. He shook his head and popped the pills in his mouth, swallowing them down with an old beer from last night he'd found sitting by the leather couch. "This is stupid," Josh thought to himself. "I should really just text her. After all, what's the worst she could do? Not answer?"

"I was wondering when you were going to wake up," Charlie said, as he strolled into the house. His swimsuit was dripping all over the floor. The redhead walked straight to his pants and grabbed the pill bottle that had just been in Josh's hand.

"Want one?" Charlie asked.

"Yeah, sure," Josh said, grinning. "Hey, what time did you get up?"

"I don't know," Charlie said. It was still dark. Billy and Deus were up playing poker, so I joined them until it was light. Then I went out to the pool. I've been between there and the hammock by the lake all morning."

Josh caught the white, instant release pill that Charlie tossed him and pushed it into his pocket. He noticed himself that sleep was a distant memory. There was just a series of taking too much oxy and then nodding off. Standing up, he ran his hand over his bare chest. He'd slept in his jeans for the past two days. He really needed to change his clothes.

"Hey, why don't we all run into town and get some clean clothes and visit my grandpa?"

"Billy and Deus are already in town," Charlie replied. "They said they had business to attend to."

"They're sixteen," Josh said skeptically. "What kind of business could they have?"

"I don't know, but I hope it's just code for picking up more pills, because I'm almost out."

Josh jumped off the couch and threw on his red tee shirt. "That stuff's got a be expensive as all hell."

"It is," confirmed Charlie. "Billy's dad has so many connections in the medical industry that he practically gets it for free, though."

"So you comin' or not?" Josh asked.

"Nah. I'm just gonna wash my clothes here. They have a brand-new invention just down the hall called the washing machine. You should try it," he said, grinning.

"What about going downtown?" Josh asked, hoping his friend would just cave in.

"No way, dude. I remember the last trip we took, and it was bad enough," the redhead said, with a sour look on his face. "What a cruel-ass joke that was," Charlie said, looking confused. "You come into this world babbling and wearing diapers, and you end it the same way. What kind of shit is that? I'm going to tell you something, Michaels. If I ever get that way, you have full permission to force-feed the muzzle of a gun in my mouth and turn the lights out."

"C'mon, it wasn't that bad," Josh said, taking his keys out of his pocket.

"Not that bad? Compared to what?" asked Charlie. "Larry was stuck in bed, pretending everything was okay for your benefit. But I noticed he didn't have much to say, when his roommate crapped his pants and just laid there like nothing happened."

Josh chuckled. "That was kind of uncomfortable," he agreed.

"Or better yet, Michaels, what about the lady down the hall, who kept screaming for help over and over? Tell me that wasn't a plate full of unsettling, with a big, fat cup of creepy. The worst part was the staff at the place acted like it was just another day at the office."

Josh was sorry he'd asked. "It's cool, man. I just thought you'd want to go downtown is all."

"I'll go, if he's in the hospital. I have your back, Josh. But I don't ever want to go to that place again. I mean, I know getting old happens. It's a part of life, but it's still disturbing. Like I was saying earlier, I played poker with Deus and Billy, something I guarantee you that every guy in the convalescent hospital has done at one point in his life. In fact, I bet, if you asked, there's guys in that place that have done phenomenal shit, like robbed a bank and then snorted blow off a hooker's ass."

"I guess," Josh said, heading towards the door. "It's not like they weren't young once."

"Exactly!" screamed Charlie, as he pointed at Josh. "How do you ever go from that to bingo? That's what I don't like about that place. You were there, Josh. There was a group of fifteen people bouncing a goddamned balloon around the room, like it was a volleyball. And if that's what the future has in store for me, I'll gladly pass on it. I mean, geez, Josh. Larry was a trauma doctor. He's seen everything imaginable. Now the high point of his day consists of getting somebody to wheel him up to the window, just so he can see what's going on outside. And I say screw that."

Josh thought about what his friend was saying. "Sooner or later, Charlie, we all get old."

"Not me, Michaels. I ain't havin' it."

***

"Things always seemed so different when the tables were turned," Claire thought to herself. Having been a nurse her whole career, she'd started a million IVs. Yet, for some reason, she just couldn't get used to the sight of seeing them flowing into the arm of the man she loved. There wasn't a room in this hospital that Claire hadn't been in, from delivery to surgery. None of them were as scary as the room she was in now. After twenty years, she'd never once sat down in one of these bedside chairs. She was beginning to find it was a sobering experience. This was not the way that Claire had planned on spending her summer day.

It hurt just to remember that the arm with all the IVs running into it was the same one Larry would throw over her, when they watched TV or went to the movies. It was also the one he wrapped around her body while they slept. Claire took a look around the room. For the most part, it was an ordinary, white hospital room. She'd had to raise hell with the staff, but they finally moved Larry to a private room. She felt like they both hadn't slaved away in an ER half their lives just so her husband could wind up dying of a secondary infection he'd picked up from his roommate at the hospital.

Larry had been brought in Friday for his irregular heart rate. Claire wasn't too surprised when the doctors had found even more blood clots in his legs. So they surgically inserted a catheter with a filter into the main vein of his abdomen, to make sure none of the clots would make it to his vital organs if they ever dislodged. Claire was in pretty good company when Sam was around, but she'd just sent her to get some coffee. Now the only things that were keeping her company were the sounds of the IV pumps and the beeping of the cardiac monitor mounted to the wall.

Somehow she knew this day would come. It had always been in the back of her mind. Larry was a decade older than her. She was twenty-six, when she'd finally decided to retire from Division and search for a new career. After getting her degree in nursing, she met Larry, a forty-year-old doctor, who had just gotten out of the military. In her eyes, he was everything she'd ever wanted. He was tall, handsome, and soft-spoken. At the time, his age never mattered. After he had hit his sixties, even though her mind knew that this could happen, her heart wouldn't let her believe it.

"Knock, knock," came a sarcastic voice. Claire immediately turned her attention to the door. It didn't sound like anybody she knew. Sitting still, she reached over and grabbed the EKG monitor wires connected to Larry's chest. Just one tug and they'd come off, setting off the alarm and calling half the nurses on the floor into the room.

"Don't even think about it, Claire, or I'll burn this whole ward down just to spite you."

Claire thought about it for a second and viewed her options. Finally, she sighed and let the wires fall from her hands, composing herself. She looked back in the direction of the two teens, but she knew that what she saw and who they really were didn't match. The woman knew there was only one entity on this planet who would ever be so brazen as to whip out his brass balls and disrespect her like that.

"Let me guess," Claire said, putting her fingers to her chin. "His Infernal Majesty," she said, pointing at the spiky-haired one, "and his usual bitch maid, Asmodeus. Now what do you want?" she asked, motioning to the big one with the red 32 shirt on.

Hasden threw his right arm out and caught Deus across the chest, stopping him in his tracks. "Please don't let her push your buttons." He smiled, turning back towards her. "It's been a while, Claire."

"No, actually, it hasn't," Claire said sternly, funneling her will into her gaze. "You're the boy who was in my driveway the night Larry got hurt. And you," Claire said, curling her lip up, "you were the big, dumb demon I thought I saw and had to do a double take. But you were gone by then."

"I am a king of Hell," Asmodeus snarled. "I will not be mocked by you, human."

"Sorry. I just call them as I see them," Claire said. "And I'm not the one with my personal number written on my shirt."

Hasden looked over at the white basketball jersey with the big red number 32 on it. "I swear, Deus," he said, shaking his head, "you just really don't give a shit anymore; do you?" Turning back to Claire, he said, "They truly don't make them like you anymore. You know, we're a lot alike, you and I."

"Do us both a favor," she answered sharply, "just drop the Jungle book, trust in me bullshit, and tell me what you want; so I can banish you guys." The spiky-haired demon nodded, realizing she wasn't going to drop her guard.

"The ever-so-proud Baby Claire. Have it your way," Hasden said, with as much disdain as he could muster. "The years have not been kind to you." Turning towards the bigger demon, he asked, "When you look at her, Deus, what do you see?"

"Nine, ten, a big fat hen," he sang, glaring at her.

"Me, too," he replied, folding his arms across his chest and grinning. "Strutting around, clucking and preening her feathers." Bill locked eyes with her and sent his will pouring into the room. "Who knew the bastard descendants of angels and demons could rise to be so proud?" He watched and smiled, as he saw the woman clench her jaw. It gave him great pleasure to see her squirm, after all the trouble her family had caused the Monarchy. "You're a smart girl. It probably didn't take you too long to figure out where the dream benders really came from."

"Such a hard lot in life," Deus said, through his clenched teeth. "Daddy's second best. Exceptionally gifted, but not good enough to be an avatar."

"True," agreed Bill, turning back to Claire, who was still sitting in the chair with her hands folded.

She nodded slowly. "The avatars are God's chosen. That may be true. But if he didn't have a plan for us, we never would have existed."

"I'm sure you're right, Claire. That's incredible faith you have. You know what? I'm willing to bet, that like most people who have faith, once you've figured out where the benders came from, you never asked which blood line you descended from; did you? And I'm willing to wager money that Michael never threw out an answer. But I'll tell you right now if you'd like to know."

"No. That's quite all right," she quietly replied.

"That definitely took the wind out of her sails," Deus pointed out. "And here I thought I was going to hear some high and mighty speech about how your grandson was going to be humanity's savior."

"I know," Hasden chuckled. "The prophesied one from the bloodlines."

Claire shook her head and stood up, stretching her fingers out. She could feel her energy flow through her. While the demons had been taunting her, she was building up her bioelectricity, preparing to engage them. She still didn't know what they were here for, but she knew they were here illegally.

"You're in violation of at least two cosmic laws," she said, energy crackling from her fingertips. "Approaching my grandson, the Prime, before his sixteenth birthday, and using powers of concealment on my property, when you weren't invited."

"I'll give you that," Hasden sneered. "Seeing as Nina has had her hand firmly planted up the Imperial girl's ass for the last three years, somehow, I think Division will let the Monarchy slide on this one."

Just the mention of the two names caused the hair on the back of her neck to stand on end. She didn't like the fact that the two demons knew Nina's whereabouts. Technically, they couldn't touch the teen; but they shared no love for the Imperial Mother. There had to be some reason why they were staying away from her.

"You still haven't told me what you're here for. But if it's a fight you want, I think you both know I'm not afraid of you. I've taken on Death herself, and I beat that little hussy's ass. I'll take you out just as easily." Claire put her force of will behind the threat, hoping they'd back down. Much to her dismay, Deus cracked his knuckles and stepped forward, resting his hand on the foot of Larry's bed.

"Face it, Claire. You were hot shit back in the day, but that was when you were young and had nothing to lose. Even when you took on Death, you did it for your son. You can maybe take one of us, but definitely not both of us. So just listen to what Hasden has to say."

"Thank you," Bill said, his eyes turning as black as coal. "I have an offer for you, Claire. That hussy you so elegantly referred to, recently received some major upgrades. Maybe she couldn't have your son. But mark my words, when Josh crushes the Host and assumes the throne, she will sit by his side as his queen."

Claire gasped, horrified at what he'd said. She knew the Monarchy never acted on such threats, unless they already had an elaborate plan in motion.

"Do you know what day today is?" Hasden snarled, his voice laced with venom. It's June 24th. In Canada, it's St. John the Baptist Day."

"How befitting," Deus added, "that the queen has asked us to serve up your head on a silver platter."

Claire took a step backwards and looked at her husband, unconscious and medicated in the bed, unaware of how much danger he was in at this moment. "I found out a long time ago how I die, and it's in my sleep. So tell me what you really want."

Bill cornered the bed, blocking any hope Claire had of escaping. He locked his cold, uncaring eyes on hers and spoke, trying to mask his absolute hatred for the woman in front of him. "Here's the deal. We can't have you meddling in your grandson's affairs. Not this time. And you're right. You do go in your sleep. However, I want you out of this equation. So a massive stroke is going to disable your brain right now. If you don't interfere, you have my solemn vow as the Director of the Monarchy that I won't kill your husband and a third of your old coworkers, when we leave here."

"Think about it, Claire. There's a ton of flammable gas in this building," Deus added. It won't be pretty," he said, shaking his head. "The people who do live, will be horribly burned."

Claire backed away, tears filling the corners of her eyes. She'd never expected something like this. Reaching over, she grabbed Larry's thumb with her left hand and gave it a little shake. "I love you," she said, as hot tears streamed down her cheeks. This isn't what she wanted, but Claire knew what had to be done. In the end, it was the only thing she was ever really good at; saving other people's lives. Raising her eyes to meet Satan's, she nodded her head in agreement.

"I promise it will be quick," the head demon assured her.

"I just have one question," she said softly.

"Go ahead," the Prince of Darkness replied impatiently.

Claire opened her mouth, and the sound that crossed her lips faintly sounded to Satan like a bell or chime he'd once heard long ago. "If you had a family member," Claire said, looking at both the demons, "and you wanted to take them somewhere special, wouldn't you agree that the beach would be the perfect place? Or maybe a lake?"

Hasden stared, puzzled by her vacant stare. She looked like she'd already checked out, but she was still talking.

"We always loved the water. Josh practically lived in it," she absentmindedly continued.

"PREPARE YOURSELF INWARDLY," Hasden screamed, mockingly reaching for her head. And just like that, Claire Michaels was gone.

Chapter 22
Titanium

"Like this?" Dianna asked, unable to hide the excitement in her voice.

"Yes, child. You're doing great." Dianna watched the multicolored flame, as it enveloped her left hand and then spread up her forearm.

"How does it feel to you?" Nina asked. The woman was within arm's reach of Dianna, cross-legged on Ramon's bed. It was tight quarters in the RV's bedroom, but this was the only place where they could train without being bothered. Luckily, driving the RV kept Ramon from seeing the secret training going on in the back. Dianna knew he would flip, if he saw what they were doing.

"It's weird," she said. "Even though it looks like fire, all I feel is a little tingle."

"It takes that appearance because that's the form you feel the most comfortable with," replied Nina.

Shifting her arm, Dianna watched as the flames touched her pink cotton tee shirt. She'd wondered if her clothes would burn, but they didn't. "I don't understand. It's not the form I would've chosen. It reminds me too much of Hell and people burning."

"This isn't fire," Nina said calmly. "This is your own bioelectric energy being augmented by your spirit. It's only taking the appearance of a flame." Reaching out, Nina touched the girl's arm. "See, no burns. Maybe seeing it reminds you of images you remember from the Bible, but these images are only residue in your brain. The fear you feel when you read about Hell causes your adrenaline to spike, which in turn is one of the main ingredients that cements a memory in place. This was how primitive man learned. It was a constant cycle of adapting and overcoming, trial and error. It took a steady appetite of fear to remind him what was dangerous and what wasn't."

Dianna listened intently to her mentor's voice, consciously stopping the flames just short of her face. Nina continued, "Today's world is no different. If you ask your friends what their most vivid memory is, it's always something tenuous or exciting." Dianna felt the RV hit a bump in the road. As she slapped her left arm down to brace herself on the bed, she noticed the flames instinctively went out.

"Sorry. I must've lost concentration," she said.

"Probably not," Nina flashed a smile at her. "Your conscious will continually draws on the memories I was just talking about. You still think the fire should burn, so you consciously put it out before touching the bed."

"Why would my power take this form then, if I think it's a hindrance?"

Nina leaned back against the corner of the cabinets that formed part of Ramon's headboard. "Because, child, your conscious is limited and only brings up what it can easily recall. Your subconscious, though, is infinite. It remembers all the other parts of the Bible that didn't scare you, like God appearing to Moses in the burning bush and his people being led through the desert by the Spirit of God that appeared as a flaming column."

"I'd forgotten about that," Dianna said. "But, how?"

Nina shrugged her shoulders. "It's a big book. And a lot of it is dry. Have you ever read the Bible? Or do you just go off what the pastor says?"

"I've read as much as I could," Dianna admitted. It was true. She hadn't read the whole thing. A lot of it was confusing to her.

"Don't worry," Nina chuckled. "There are very few people I know who have read it cover to cover. It's important to know that just listening to a sermon doesn't give you a clear picture about who God actually is, any more than standing in a garage makes you a car. Yet, despite this, somehow people, throughout the centuries, have gone to extremes like war and genocide, being swayed by only a handful of Scriptures manipulated by only a few individuals.

"For instance, when the Bible says all men are created equal, it's stating a basic fact of energy. But the outward expression of the populace is different; some are smart, some not so much. Some are seemingly gifted physically, and some aren't. What they lack, when stacked up against the other person, they make up for in another area. And while their conscious might envy that other person's ability, the subconscious knows it doesn't amount to a hill of beans in the grand scheme.

"When you pass on, your body is just a vehicle you drove. Everybody's soul is equal, because we were created that way. It's the same as taking two stereos that both have the same energy flowing out of them, but the soul of the person got to pick how they wanted the equalizer set up. That's all it is, and that's all it ever was. I'll go into it in greater detail, when we talk about the sympathetic and parasympathetic systems and the endocrine glands."

Dianna sat attentively, trying to take in the day's lesson. If anything, the ride certainly wasn't boring. Not to mention, she was glad to have this time alone with her friend, even if that friend was her newly-appointed watcher, who was sent to instruct her.

"Your subconscious runs your body effortlessly, and it has limitless access to knowledge. An example would be the strange cravings of a pregnant woman for things she usually doesn't eat. Her subconscious is sending them to her, because it knows what building blocks are needed for the baby that the mother can't consciously see. Even fortunetellers," Nina said, "aren't really being guided by the Spirit. Their subconscious already knows, having read the person's energy, what's in the immediate future for the person. Pretty soon, you're going to find that I can hand you a deck of cards, and you'll be able to either pick or shuffle the ace of spades to the top of the deck. It's all a matter of concentration and being able to access that ability, which takes some time; but it can be done"

"I'll take your word for it," Dianna said, chuckling. "I get the feeling you're right. What I want to know is how you know this?"

"How do you not?" Nina replied, widening eyes and giggling. "We live in a society, where the smartest man in the world is bound to a wheelchair. Autistic children, while not fitting our standard definition of normal, can outplay computers at chess. Some can even use their minds as efficiently as a computer to memorize every phone number in a telephone book. It's just a trade-off. Because it's like I said before; we are all created equal."

Nina stretched her legs out and yawned. Dianna could tell the ride was getting to her. The RV, as huge as it was, obviously wasn't nearly as big as their home, and they were still adjusting. "You know the dream benders I told you about?" Nina said, craning her neck. "They're highly gifted, but there are drawbacks."

"Do you think my grandpa might've been a dream bender?" Dianna asked. Her father had never called him that, but he definitely fit the bill.

"Oh, I know he was," Nina replied confidently. "You come from a very strong bloodline. Your powers are altogether different, and so are mine. The dream benders have access to a human's latent abilities. The mind can do awesome things, if it is properly trained. Unfortunately, when they use their abilities, it draws on the body's reserves. Their metabolism can only produce so much energy. The hormones it takes to get their minds to do these things comes with a price. The human body works on balance. If there's too much of one hormone, that means there's not enough of its opposing counterpart. So they deal with a lot of emotional problems. Some live in isolation or have lifestyles most people don't really understand. Even the avatars, as strong as they are, almost never marry and rarely have children. They see the world as their spouse and humanity as their children."

"That makes sense," Dianna said. She hadn't delved into any other religions, but she'd never heard of a savior who was a weekend warrior or held down a 9:00 to 5:00 job. "Will I ever have to deal with this?" she asked, concerned. Ideally, she didn't want to end up in a straightjacket just because she healed people.

"Absolutely not," Nina said, shaking her head. "As the Prime, you're the highest concentration of the Creator's presence in this reality. You draw your energy straight from the source. By the time you're eighteen, you'll be able to create at the speed of thought."

"I'm kind of liking that," Dianna said, smiling. Personally, she felt like she could take on the demon horde right now, even though she'd only been training for a few days. "I don't mean to pry, but what are your abilities?" she asked, feeling mildly intrigued. Dianna immediately noticed her mentor's face had lost its glow.

"I want to start out by saying I never meant to deceive you, child. It was not my intention, and I definitely took no delight in doing so." Dianna drew in her legs and wrapped her arms around them. She'd never really given it much thought.

"I trust you, Nina. You've been like a sister and a mother to me over the past three years. All I want to know is that you weren't faking it, when you cared for me."

"Not at all," Nina said, leaning forward, kissing the girl on her forehead and ruffling her hair.

"I mean, you haven't blatantly lied to me; have you?" Dianna asked.

"No, but I haven't been entirely truthful either. I did purposely move in with you. I suspected you were the Prime, and I wanted to keep you safe. The rules are very specific that the watchers can't actively train the candidate until their sixteenth year. Even then, we can't teach you, if you don't want to learn. The concept of free will is very important to the grand design. However," Nina grinned and bit her bottom lip, "the rules say nothing about being a housemate and watching said girl blossom into a beautiful young woman."

Dianna hung her head and blushed. "You didn't need to say that, Nina. But you can keep going, if it makes you feel better."

The woman laughed. "I only give credit where credit is due. Believe me."

"I forgive you," Dianna said, meaning it wholeheartedly.

The woman's pale face lit up, as the words were spoken. Her hair even seemed to deepen in color. "Then listen to me, child," Nina said, folding her legs, "and I'll tell you what little I can about myself. Then, maybe, by the time I'm done, if you find it in your heart, you can forgive me again."

The comment caught Dianna off guard. Nina lifted her right hand up, with her thumb bent in and only her first two fingers extended. Bowing her head towards Dianna, she dropped her hand into her lap and said, "Sometimes my name is Nina, and sometimes it's not."

The girl squinted. "What?"

"I've been many people over thousands and thousands of years. This face that you know me as is one of many I've assumed for my own protection." The woman stretched her arms out towards Dianna, and the girl gasped as her friend's skin tone darkened and then lightened. Next, her copper hair straightened out and then changed to brunette. "This is my only real gift from God. It was given to me so that I could hide, if I needed to. And believe me, I've used it many times."

Dianna shook her head in disbelief. "From the beginning of time, I've had the duty, along with my husband, to train the avatars and guide the dream benders in preparation for the coming of the Prime. And for this, I have been gifted with conditional immortality, granted that at no time do I ever interfere with your free will." Dianna tried to speak but found her throat was extremely dry.

"What if you do?" she asked hoarsely. "Then my life is forfeit, and all the thousands of years I've spent on this mission may have been for nothing. I love you, Dianna," Nina said. "More than I've ever loved any student. I've dreamed of your training and what you might be like for thousands of years. I want you to know that I promise to fight next to you during the final battle. I'll even lay my life on the line to keep you from harm, BUT--" Dianna noticed her eyes narrowing as she said, "when you face Satan, and you most certainly will, whether it's during temptation or the war, I cannot take your part. That is for you to do."

Visibly shaken, Dianna didn't know what to say. She really wished she hadn't heard the last few minutes. In her heart of hearts, she believed Nina, when she said she loved her. Everything else about this woman was a lie. To Dianna, the last three years, since the woman had moved in, were the best of her life. Those years didn't even constitute a heartbeat in Nina's life, if she was thousands of years old.

"I understand," she said, her voice trembling.

"No, child. I can tell by the look on your face that you don't," Nina said, unable to disguise her dismay. "I can't tell you enough how hard it was living lifetime after lifetime, fighting my way through the sands of time, to get to you. Not just because it was my job, but because you and I have a special bond that every watcher shares with their Prime. There are only two true watchers and only two true Primes. Our destinies are intertwined."

Dianna lifted her head up and managed a weak smile. "It's just a little hard to take in," she said.

"I know, child. I didn't mean to mislead you, but my hands

were tied. I was bending the rules just to come live with you."

"How did you find me?" Dianna asked.

Nina smiled, "The only sure way I knew I could. Through the last few centuries, it seems my husband, Thomas, and the angels have placed their hopes on any promising male who looked like he could fill the role, only to be let down time and again. I had a general idea which bloodline you might be produced from. I just didn't know which generation you'd be in, that is, until you had the dream. That week, after thousands of years, my menses switched to your cycle. Even at that age, your power was stronger than mine; but I'd expected that."

Astonished, Dianna laughed out loud. "Oh my God, you're kidding?"

Nina shrugged her shoulders and cracked a smile. "Don't tell Thomas though. He's still confused at how I was right on the first try."

"I won't," the girl grinned, and continued to laugh. "I thought maybe you'd use magic to find me."

"I did. My feminine magic." Nina laughed and rolled onto her side. Dianna couldn't help but notice that her vivid color was back, and her features were restored. Thinking back on it, she'd remembered times in her life when the woman's looks seemed to mirror her emotions.

"Let me ask you something, Nina. I thought you said the only gift God gave you was the ability to change your appearance. But what about the other day in the backyard?"

"Yes, you're right," Nina replied. "In a roundabout way, I'm arguably the second strongest being on the planet, beneath you and Josh."

"Even stronger than your husband?"

"Yes, even stronger than my husband. Even if he is the brains of the outfit," Nina said, winking. "He's a great man, with an incredible mind. I'm still twice as strong as he is, even on his best day."

Shell shocked, Dianna shook her head. "Are you kidding me? How did you manage that? I mean, didn't God create you both equally?"

"Yes, the Creator did. But," Nina said, holding her finger up, "I inadvertently impressed a group of angels. And, unbeknownst to me at the time, angels are very liberal with what they do with their energy. Afterwards, I came into a rather large inheritance, as a result of an act that they deemed as exceptionally brave." The woman smiled and rolled over. "Thomas was rewarded as well for other acts. It's just that, over the years, it has become his norm to sit in the passenger seat and let me shine."

"Where is he now?" Dianna asked.

Nina shook her head. "I don't really know. I can only assume he's teaching Josh. Usually, his mind is an open book. For some reason, over the past few weeks, he has dropped off the radar. Thomas was definitely shocked to find out that Josh was the male Prime." Dianna could tell by the look of concern on Nina's face that something wasn't right.

"What kind of shock?" she asked cautiously, hoping that her mentor's past was the only surprise she'd have to deal with her today.

"I guess you should know," Nina said, looking into Dianna's eyes. "After what was a veritable dry spell of avatars, the Michaels' bloodline produced a male, who was exceptional in every way. His name was Alex, and he was everything to my husband. We both knew his mother, Claire," Nina said, chuckling. "She was a favorite of the Archangel Michael, who is the Director of the Host. Her exploits as a bender are legendary. The whole situation was perfect. As Alex got older and his powers expanded, it was noticed that he didn't possess the faculties it took to be a Prime. And when there was no female to match him with…" Dianna noticed a faraway look in Nina's eyes as she reminisced.

"He was a phenomenal person and a true genius. We'd hoped he would at least become an avatar. But the older he got, the more we realized he wasn't really interested in that either. He was a good time Charley, and he just loved people. I personally never held it against him, but Thomas was a little hurt, because he had such high hopes for him."

"Was this Josh's dad?" Dianna asked, confused.

"Yes," Nina replied, nodding slowly. "Eventually, he met a girl in college. When they announced that she was pregnant, we were overjoyed. Both Thomas and I were in the delivery room when Sam gave birth to Josh."

"I bet Thomas was thrilled," Dianna said, grinning.

"Not really," Nina said, slowly. Everybody there was hoping for a girl. Or at least anybody there who knew that the only way Alex could pass on his powers would have been by having a daughter."

Confusion instantly clouded Dianna's face. "Josh does have powers. I've seen them for myself."

"That may be, child, but nobody knows how he got them. Because it wasn't from Alex."

***

"Can I help you?" the nurse at the desk said to Josh.

"I'm looking for Claire Michaels' room." With his stomach in knots, Josh waited, as she looked on the computer screen.

"She's in room 108." Looking in the direction she was pointing, he nodded and stepped away from the desk. He'd been roaming the halls for the past hour, trying to get the courage to finally come into the unit.

Hands shaking and heart racing, he stood outside the room, wondering if he really wanted to go in and face Sam's wrath. It was bad enough he'd flaked on visiting Larry at the hospital.

When Josh finally noticed Sam's voicemail telling him about Claire, he panicked. He knew he wasn't in any shape to get behind the wheel. So he lied. He said he'd gone to Martha's Vineyard with friends, and Charlie was too drunk to drive the Jeep.

In retrospect, now that he was semi-sober, Josh could totally see through the paper-thin lie. It seemed like a good idea at the time. Josh's phone vibrated in his pocket. He pulled it out to see who was texting him, hoping it was Dianna. It was just Charlie:

ARE YOU COMING BACK TONIGHT? WE'RE HAVING A BONFIRE.

Josh typed back:

I'M NOT

He had no idea if his nerves were doing this or if he was having withdrawal symptoms from the oxy, but it felt like he had the flu. On top of the aches and pains, he was sweating uncontrollably. Billy warned him about going cold turkey, so he'd cut the amount in half and planned to reduce that by another half tomorrow. At first, he thought it would be easy. But judging by the way he felt now, Josh had a feeling he was in for a rough week of detoxing. Taking a deep breath, he pushed on the door and walked into the room. It was a complete carbon copy of Larry's room. The only difference was it was his grandmother in the bed.

Nothing in the world could have prepared Josh for the look on Claire's face. Her eyes were open; but her gaze was cast off, like she was looking at something on the right side of the ceiling. "Oh, God," moaned Josh.

"Thank you for coming," he heard Sam say. She was vigilantly standing next to the bed rail, holding Claire's hand.

"Why didn't you tell me it was this bad, mom?" Josh said, confused.

"I told you what the doctors told me," she said, her voice barely above a whisper. In his heart of hearts, Josh had hoped that, since Claire was in a hospital when it happened, the doctors had just rapidly administered a clot dissolving thrombolytic. He hoped she'd be out in a few days' time, with only minor problems. But, for some reason, that hadn't happened.

"Goddamn," Josh said, feeling his eyes tear up. "I have to sit down." He felt like the room was spinning.

"Josh," Sam said in a hushed tone. "We have a guest," she said, pointing behind him. Dizzy, Josh turned to see Richard, sitting quietly in the corner of the room.

"I'm sorry," Josh said, doing his best to fight the waves of nausea that were rising inside of him.

"It's okay. After the military and my time with Boston P.D., I can deal with a little swearing every now and then."

"Trying his best to be civil, for his mom's sake, Josh raised his head up and smiled. "Thanks," he said. As much as it pained him, Josh turned back and looked at Claire. Half of her face was droopy because of the stroke. The vacant stare in her eyes was the worst though. He'd seen dozens of strokes on medical calls with the fire department, ranging from slurred speech to difficulty with cognition and motor function. Most of them were reversible, if treated quickly. But this wasn't the case. He'd seen that gaze before, and he knew that the woman who'd helped raise him wasn't ever coming back.

Stepping up to the hospital bed, Josh looked down at the woman lying beside him. "I'll never hear her call me Little Bear again," he said. And that's when the feeling of dread cut him like a knife, as the realization dawned on him that he could actually be the one to blame. "Shut up. I don't want to hear you anymore." The words flooded back into his head.

"No," Josh groaned, as his hands began to shake. He looked at Sam, but she immediately looked away. "Mom," Josh said, his voice trembling. She continued to look down at the floor. "Sam," Josh called to her, as tears rolled down his chin. "Please look at me."

"I have to go to the bathroom. I'll be back," she said, looking at the floor and turning away.

Josh brushed away the tears and wiped his nose, as his mother walked out the door. "No!" Josh repeated over and over in his head. "Shit. What am I gonna do?" he shouted, throwing his arms up to hide his eyes. Instantly, he could feel the sweat from his forearms all over his face. Or was it the other way around? His whole body was wet. Feeling a hand on his shoulder, Josh stiffened up.

"If you need help, I'm here for you." Josh quickly knocked the hand away, glaring at Richard. "I don't need your help!" he shouted. "What the hell are you doing here, anyway?"

"Whoa!" Richard said, throwing up his hands. "I'm not here to make you angry."

"I know," Josh said, immediately feeling sorry. "I just don't need this in my life right now."

Richard nodded. "I want to help you, Josh. I think I can," he said calmly. "Just trust me. There's a doctor outside this room. They can help."

Josh shook his head, confused, "What are you talking about?"

"The drugs. I'm a cop. It's not like I've never seen pinpoint pupils before. You're high."

"I'm not high," Josh said, noticing he had nowhere to go. "Is that where my mom went?"

"It's cool. She's really in the bathroom," Richard said calmly, taking a step towards him. "I just want to help."

"Screw that," thought Josh. He'd seen this tactic used by cops all the time on TV. "Back off," Josh commanded, narrowing his eyes to slits.

"We can totally work this out," Richard said, taking another step forward and reaching towards his arm.

"I said BACK OFF," Josh hissed, his head beginning to pound.

"Okay," Richard said, nodding. "Have it your way." Josh watched, as he started to move away. "I just want you to know that, in the future, when all this mess settles down, I fully expect to be a part of your mother's life. And I won't tolerate drug usage of any kind."

"That'll never happen," scoffed Josh. "You're not even my mom's type. You look like an Asian Mr. Rogers." Immediately, Josh regretted making the comment, but the damage was already done. Surprisingly, the look on Richard's face wasn't anger, as Josh expected, but embarrassment. He removed his glasses and ran his hands through his hair.

"It wasn't so long ago that I was your age, and I cared about the latest fashions. But when you grow up and join the workforce, you'll realize that some people can't get away with tee shirts and blue jeans."

"Josh, I think you should go," Sam said from the door. Josh turned and looked at his mom, who looked down at the floor again. He could feel the anger building within him, even though he had no idea why. This was all his fault. He had no right to be mad. What was happening to him?

"Please, Josh, just go. I'll see you at home," Sam said softly.

"I'm sorry," he said, as he slipped past Richard.

"Never happened," he heard the man reply.

Walking towards the door, Josh tried not to cry, as he took one last look at Claire in her hospital bed. "I'm sorry," he said to nobody in particular. "Why add a name?" he thought, as he fought back the tears. He owed an apology to everybody in the room.

***

Josh texted Dianna:

I MISS YOU TOO, BABE

Hitting send, he rolled off of his bed and strolled over to the window. The sun was killing him. Twisting the shades closed, he made his way back to the bed and laid down. The house was dead silent right now. He didn't even know how they'd all managed it, but everybody at Billy's place was on night schedule. Glancing over, he looked at Charlie, who was still asleep in his bed on the opposite side of the room.

Not like it was his business, but Josh thought Charlie was taking entirely too much oxy. Sometimes, when he watched him sleep, Josh couldn't tell whether the boy was even breathing or not. So every now and then, he'd launch his shoe at him. This time, Josh got up and gave him a shake on his shoulder. "Better ease up on this stuff. You're gonna knock your goddamn respiratory drive out." He wasn't surprised when the redhead didn't wake up. At least Charlie took a deep breath.

Making his way over to the nightstand, Josh tapped the last of his pills into his hand and headed to the bathroom. He took a slurp of water from the sink and stared at his reflection in the mirror. His hair was getting long. It was easily long enough to tie back. He also noticed his face definitely needed a shave. He had insane stubble growing in, but it looked great with his tan. So he had no intention of touching it.

Momentarily, Josh felt tempted to wipe his wet hands on his sweats. He took the extra step to the towel rack. He swore it made him grin every time he saw the "his and hers" towels Deus had bought for them, when they moved in here. He remembered they'd all went out and shot the cross bows to see whose name would be stenciled onto the "hers" towels, and Charlie lost.

Since Charlie was such a little baby about the whole thing, Billy and Josh took a trip downtown and found a woman who put computer images on fabric. One yearbook photo and a case of pink hand towels later, the shenanigans had begun. The look on the redhead's face was priceless. It was even better, when he threw the towel away, only to find a fresh, clean one hanging there in its place the next day.

Crawling back onto his bed, Josh rolled onto his back and checked the phone. "Damn," he thought. Dianna was really lighting it up today. Scrolling down, he read through the texts, taking a deep breath. For a moment, he thought about how great it felt; the sheer happiness he got just from texting her. Closing his eyes, Josh savored the sweet feeling, as he remembered how it felt just to hold her. The feelings the memory brought up made him feel good, almost the way he felt before he...

***

Josh's eyes bolted open to the sound of bass pumping from the backyard. The room was pitch black, except for the faint glow coming from the clock. "Oh, shit," he said, feeling for his phone. He'd nodded off again. He felt around his face. Last time he dropped the phone, it had beaned him square between the eyes. Rolling over on his right side, he could feel the phone stuck on his right shoulder blade.

"How the hell?" Josh groaned, reaching back and peeling the phone off. His thumb hit the power button, bringing the phone to life. He squinted at the bright light and shook his head, as he realized that he'd never even hit send. As he flipped through the messages, he saw that Dianna sent a text asking if he was okay. And then another text that read:

GUESS YOU WENT TO BED ALREADY. GOOD NIGHT.

Glancing at the digital clock, Josh could see it was 11:10. He responded and said he'd been out on the lake. Josh yawned and stretched. Flipping on the light, he threw on his wife beater, which he'd already worn twice in the past week, and headed towards the lake.

"What's up, you bum?" Deus yelled out, as Josh strolled up to the fire. The fire was enormous tonight. There had to be a few wooden pallets cooking on there.

"You missed dinner," Charlie said, stoking the fire. We went to Cardona's. It was off the hook." Grabbing a seat by Charlie, Josh noticed it was just the four of them and a petite, blonde girl with pigtails. He had never seen her before, but she was sitting next to Deus and staring at Josh. Billy lifted his empty bottle up to his mouth and spit out his tobacco.

"This is Phyllis," he said, pointing his bottle towards the new girl.

"Pleasure," Josh said, nodding.

She smiled back at him. "See. This is what I love about your place, Billy. You always have some of the best looking guy friends. You know I like 'em blonde and tan." Josh smiled. Thank God nobody could see him blush in the dark.

"Hey, is anybody holding right now?" Josh asked. "My bottle's tapped."

Charlie stood up and poured almost half his bottle of pills into Josh's hand. Then he turned to Phyllis. "Can I hook you up, milady?" Phyllis smiled and took two pills for herself. "My buddy, Josh, is actually taken at the moment. Maybe you'd be interested in something leaner, meaner, taller, and tanner?" Charlie said, smiling.

"Is that true, Josh?"

"It is," he replied, while he cracked open a beer.

"Yeah, but she's been on the road. Josh hasn't seen her for a month and a half," Billy said.

Suddenly, Josh noticed that Phyllis was looking at him like he was a piece of cake. "What a travesty. There ought to be a law against that," the blonde girl said. "When does she come back?"

"Labor Day weekend," replied Josh. "I think I can make it."

"So, like I was saying," Charlie shouted over the roar of the fire, "I'm single."

Phyllis looked at the redhead, giving him the once-over with her eyes. "You're not my type. I said tan. You're redder than a lobster tail."

Josh stifled a laugh and looked away from Charlie, towards Billy, who was grinning from ear to ear. It was true. He called it a tan, but the redhead was hideously sunburned from hanging out on the boat two days ago. Since then, Deus had come up with a slew of nicknames for him like burn ward, melanoma, and the husk, because he was peeling so badly.

Josh bit his lip, waiting for his friend to snap and throw an insult at the girl, but it never came. "Easy, Phyllis," Deus said, with a smile. "Give Clifford, the big red teenager, a chance."

Not able to hold it in, Josh let out a laugh. "I'm sorry, bro," he said to Charlie. "We told you to wear sunscreen."

"Well, I'm sure he'll remember to pack some for our vacation," the spiky-haired teen replied.

"What vacation?" Josh asked Billy.

"Well, if you'd come to dinner, you'd have known that we're all going to Burning Man for Labor Day weekend. We're going to send the summer off with a bang."

"It's gonna be tight," Charlie said, grinning. Josh looked over in his direction.

"You must be super high. I know you don't have the funds, and neither do I. On top of that, we all start school a week after."

"Before you go off all half-cocked, listen to me," Billy said. "Phyllis is one of my dad's secretaries. She just so happened to notice that nobody's touched the frequent flyer points in ages. It's just something that nobody deals with. I asked my dad if we could have them, and he said yes. So everything's beyond paid for."

"Are you sure?" asked Josh. "It's not like we don't take advantage of your hospitality enough, out here at the house. I'd die a thousand deaths, if you paid for a vacation just to be cool to us."

Deus took a long swallow from his bottle of scotch. "It's not like that. You have no idea how much money Bill, Senior throws around on clients and travel. It's crazy, but the old man's smart. He has everything from the fleets of ambulances to the house here on his credit card. He makes the payment on the corporate credit card and has Phyllis make sure the draft goes through and pockets the points. This trip is just a drop in the bucket." Josh looked at the lake rippling under the moonlight, while he considered if this was a good idea. It was the first week of August. He had planned on partying for a few weeks, at the most, and then detoxing for school in September.

"Please," Charlie begged. "I've never been. The tickets are always sold out."

"C'mon, Josh. We only have a month left together. Me and Billy are out of here at the beginning of the school year, so don't be a dick."

"Yeah, Josh, don't be a dick," Phyllis smirked. "I can't believe we have to force you to come along on this adventure."

"Listen to her, Josh. She's nineteen. She knows firsthand the fun times are few and far between, once you start working."

"I guess we're going to Burning Man," Josh said with a smile, shrugging his shoulders, to the cheers of his friends.

"So happy right now," Charlie said, his face practically glowing. "There's going to be millions of girls there. Who knows?" he chuckled, "I may finally give away my highly coveted virginity."

"But then you'd have to give away your current rank," Josh finished.

Perplexed, the blonde asked, "What rank? Like in the military?"

"Yes," Charlie declared proudly. "I am the Admiral of the Sock Children Liberation Front."

"OOH, yuck," Phyllis said, slowly. Josh could tell she was obviously unimpressed by Charlie's lofty position. "Is that all you guys do is drink and talk about your dicks?"

"Yes, my dear. That is exactly what we do," Deus said, leaning in to add even more wood to the fire.

"What about you?" she said, turning her eyes to Josh. "Is that all you think about?"

Josh smiled back. She was remarkably beautiful. The bonfire seemed to accent features he'd never noticed, when he had first seen her. Josh knew she was nothing next to Dianna. "Snakes and snails and puppy dog tails," he replied, reaching down and resting his hand on his junk. As if in response, Billy, Deus, and Charlie all moved their hands to their crotches to show their allegiance.

"Whatever, jokers," Phyllis said, with an amused look on her face. "But I'll bet my little red riding hood that you don't last the summer," she said, spreading her legs and dragging two fingers up the zipper to her jeans. "Especially when you meet my roommate, Angela."

Charlie's eyes lit up. "Do you have any pictures?" he said, eagerly sitting up.

"Hold on a second, burned man," Phyllis sarcastically replied, scrolling through her phone. "This is us a few weeks ago at a company barbecue. She just turned eighteen last month." Josh watched as his buddy's eyeballs almost popped out of his head. "The verdict?" Phyllis asked, taking her phone back.

"I think Dianna's in big trouble," Charlie replied, his eyes as big as saucers.

"I agree," Billy said, standing up and holding out his beer. "Coming from somebody who's actually seen her sunbathe topless, I can say Mahvet is literally to die for."

Chapter 23

Dianna took a second and stared lovingly at the picture on her phone. It was Josh in his sweats, with no shirt on, standing by the pool next to Billy. The last time they had talked, he told her they were all working out an hour a day with Deus. She had to admit his muscles were getting more defined. She was definitely glad she'd called him to find out he'd lost his phone the night of the party. It made life on the road easier to swallow, knowing she could talk to him and text him good night. They'd never really figured out what happened to the texts and voice messages she'd sent, but his phone was dead when Deus had found it.

There was a month left in the tour, and this would all be over soon. Her dad would have a new job. The house would be paid off. She could train with Nina somewhere, other than Ramon's cramped mobile bedroom. The part that really made Dianna's imagination run wild was that she would also have Josh back and things could go back to normal. Dianna laid on her stomach, facing the tail end of the RV. Her new, favorite pastime was staring out the window and watching the road pull away from her, as the cars behind them chased after the RV. She tried to remind herself that each mile was a mile closer to home.

"Roll over," her sister said, from behind her. Dianna rolled to her left, as Cammy crashed down on the bed like a redwood that had been chopped down. "So over it," she said, sounding exhausted, her face buried in Ramon's pillow.

"Over what?" Dianna asked, mildly amused.

"I'm over the four of us in this cracker box on wheels that has no privacy at all," Cammy wearily pointed out. I'm tired of sweating every night because the AC sucks in this thing. Most of all, I'm tired of Ramon trying to marry me off to every pastor's son on the eastern seaboard."

"You and me both," Dianna nodded her head in agreement. Part of her thought that was the only reason her dad had pressured Cammy into going with them, was to find a new guy with strong morals, who could do what Scott had done. The other half of Dianna knew that, although Ramon had no qualms about tossing Cammy out of the house the first time, this time was different. When she left home before, she had options, like her mother or her grandfather. This time, she had none. It was tough to get a job in this economy, and Dianna had a sneaking suspicion her dad was worried what she might be doing with her summer of free time. So he threw out the ultimatum; hit the road with us, or hit the road by yourself.

"Can we please go back to Pastor Kato's?" Cammy groaned, still looking miserable but chuckling.

"I'm all for that," Dianna said, rolling onto her left side and propping her head up with her left hand. "Did you notice that he was the only person who didn't try to preach to us?"

Cammy nodded, finally lifting her head up. "I'm not saying I'm cut out for the church life thing. If I did go to a church though, I'd pick his. The whole family was good times and laid back," she pointed out.

"I know," Dianna said, sitting up. "This last church was awful."

"What? You didn't like the spiritual Olympics?" Cammy said, grinning. Her spark of energy was returning to her eyes. Dianna watched, as her sister held a highly animated conversation with herself.

"Last night, I broke down into tears and prayed for an hour, when I thought of all the lost souls crying for God to come into their lives."

Dianna shook her head, saying in a deep voice, "Well, I prayed for two hours and cried until my eyes were bloodshot, when I thought of all the people who would wait in line for a TV for twelve hours on Black Friday but couldn't take an hour to go to church on Sundays."

Dianna smiled, as Cammy laughed at her impression. "The one-upmanship was fierce," the older sister said. "Why did Ramon take us there?" She silently screamed in frustration. "At dinner, when the girl next to me seriously asked if I thought she was anointed, I almost died."

"I know," Dianna said. In some respect, she was almost ashamed at how the group had acted. It seemed the whole congregation was trying to outdo one another. She was hoping her sister would have an honest-to-God religious experience that would bring her willingly back to church. But the last town was too hard-core, even for her.

"Oh," Cammy said, "then that one guy, when he told us that the Holy Ghost had told him to buy the one truck brand over the other, and he did; that was priceless."

"Not every church is the same," Dianna said. "Don't get whipped into a frenzy because we had dinner with a bunch of shysters."

"I know," Cammy snorted. "In some way, I feel sorry for them. You know, if I really hated them, I would've busted out with the knowledge and went all death-match on them."

"Many thanks," Dianna grinned. "Because then dad would have come unglued, and I don't want to see you have to leave." Suddenly, her sister stopped laughing and began to look troubled.

"It's not like I hadn't thought about it a million times on this trip."

"Why?" Dianna asked. "Why would you ever say that?"

Shaking her head, the girl's face became sullen. "You know for a fact that Ramon would prefer I wasn't here. And I know Nina doesn't want me here either." Dianna was shocked to hear Cammy say that. Usually, she didn't care either way what people thought. "It's nice being here with you," Cammy said, putting her hand on Dianna's. "But I can tell, every time I look at you and Nina, that I've lost any claim to the title of big sister. I'm just somebody you grew up with now."

"That's not true," Dianna said. "Don't say that. You're breaking my heart."

Cammy looked across the bed. "My heart has been breaking since the day you were born. I love you to death. Although sometimes just being around you reminds me that, no matter how hard I try, I'm nothing but your second fiddle."

Dianna shook her head. "I don't see it that way."

"Really. I was the firstborn," Cammy said. "I don't know why God made my life like this, but I've tried to escape the vacuum you continually leave in your wake. I was the favorite, and then I was pushed aside. After that, I went to the reservation to learn the old ways from grandpa. I not only found out I have no abilities, but that you practically hit the talent jackpot."

"If I could, I'd make you the strongest woman in the world," Dianna said, softly. She hadn't expected to hear what Cammy had just said. She had always looked up to her sister for her strength and fierce independence. The last thing she wanted to hear was that her sister felt inferior.

Cammy smiled, shaking her head. "I don't want to sing some song, like my life was unfair, or it was bad, because it wasn't. It's just that you don't know the pressure of what it's like to not only live in the shadow of somebody you love, but to also watch as that person fills your role with somebody else." Dianna grabbed onto her sister and held her, as tightly as she could.

"Nobody could ever take your place, Cammy. You're the only sister I have. I just never knew what it was like from your perspective. I swear."

"Ahem," Nina said, standing at the door. "I don't mean to intrude, Dianna, but we were supposed to talk about something." Dianna looked at her phone. Was it really that late? "What are we going to do?" Nina said, tapping on her watch. Dianna thought about it for a second. She really wanted to train, but her sister needed her just as much.

"I know that secrecy is important to you, Nina," Dianna said cautiously, "but I'd really like to expand our circle a little."

The watcher folded her arms. "How much?"

"Well, Cammy already knows about grandpa, dad, and me. She's never told anybody. So maybe she could know about you too," she said, shyly. Looking back and forth between the two, Nina thought about it and then nodded.

"Okay, but you're going to do something for me."

"Name it," Dianna said, overjoyed. "When we get to the next church, you're going to tell your dad you'd rather walk home than eat at another twenty-four hour diner. I need to eat a steak and have fresh vegetables."

"I'm on board with that," Cammy agreed. "If I have another mozzarella stick or chicken finger, I think I'll scream."

"Okay, how about I raise the stakes then? If we can have girl's day instead of training, I'll convince dad to sleep on the small, foldout couch. How about that?"

"Now, that," Nina said, a smile appearing on her face, "is an excellent idea. What do you have in mind?"

Dianna thought this was too good to be true. This was exactly what they needed. "How about we do each other's nails, while you tell us what it was like to be a queen. I loved that story."

"Say what?" Cammy said skeptically. "That's totally crazy."

"How about this?" Nina said, slyly. "You guys do my nails and I'll tell you what it was like to live with my husband in Egypt as Isis and Osiris. I'll even throw in the Exodus for free."

"No way!" Cammy said loudly. "I'm callin' B.S. on that one."

"Really," Nina started. "I was there. Moses was a great avatar, but no one ever called him that. We always used his solar name, Ra-Moses or Ramses."

Dianna giggled as Cammy's jaw dropped in disbelief. "I'll get the popcorn," the older sister cried, running out of the room.

"Interesting. You never said you were in Egypt."

"I was saving it for a special occasion, like today," Nina said. "And besides, I thought you'd put it together yourself."

"Put what together?" the girl asked.

"Why do you think all the famous prophets hid in Egypt, when their life was in danger?"

Dianna smiled. "I don't know, but I have the feeling you're going to tell me."

Nina nodded at the girl, "Because my kung fu is strong. That's why."

***

Once again it was amazingly silent in the house. There was no laughter or conversation filling the bright living room. There was just silence and contemplation. Josh let out a sigh, as he glanced over at Charlie, who was still completely slack-jawed. On the leather couch next to him sat Billy, wearing a look like he was deep in thought. He knew that Billy was just weighing Josh's options, given the situation.

But Josh already had a pretty good handle on odds and how they worked. And they weren't in his favor. The rising sun had spilled into the house and was now refracting off the chandeliers and glasses in the kitchen next to them. Josh thought it was funny how the light of the sun was casting illumination on everything in the room, except for the topic that they had been contemplating for the past half hour.

"Morning, gents," Deus said, coming through the front door. His hair was ruffled up, and his clothes were a mess. It looked to Josh like he'd been in a fight, but the three hickeys on his neck said otherwise. "Anybody want to hear how my night went?" the teen bragged, stepping into the room.

"I seriously don't understand how you do it," Charlie said, shaking his head. "Every night, the probability of you getting laid is better than a one-legged guy falling out of a fishing boat during a storm. How do you pull it off?"

"Lucky for me, I'm attractive enough to get them to look and interesting enough to get them to take me home. I'm just obnoxious enough that they don't care when I leave and don't call. It's a natural talent," he said, grinning back at the redhead.

"What's everybody up this early for?"

"We never went to bed," Charlie replied. "We were about to, and then Josh got this."

Josh replayed the message on speaker:

> Josh, it's your mom. When you get this message, call me. Larry was released from the skilled nursing facility, and we have him moved back in the house. We set him up in a bedroom on the first floor, and he's getting around with a cane. Even though Larry and Richard are on really good terms, we both agree it just wouldn't be right for Richard to stay over. So Richard asked me to move in with him, and he wants you to come live with us. I know it's fast, but we'd have to transfer you to the Boston school district. It would just best for all of us, if you start the school year in Boston. We're going to plan for Labor Day weekend, as long as Larry is self-sufficient by then.

Josh continued to stare at the phone, long after the message ended.

"Ouch," Deus said, sitting down on the arm of the couch.

"I guess I'm moving to Boston," Josh said, in a hollow voice. He'd heard the message five times over the past half hour, and he still couldn't believe it. Even though he could feel the familiar effects of the oxy withdrawals creeping up on his body, he just really felt no desire to feed the ever-growing habit he'd developed over the past month and a half. He knew it wasn't a good idea to let the withdrawals take a hold of him. It made him feel violently sick, like the worst case of the flu he had ever had. But he knew he had to think right now, and he couldn't do it if he was high.

"Bullshit!" cried Charlie. "You're never going back to Milton High School? What about me and Dianna?" Josh shrugged his shoulders.

"What the hell do you expect me to do, Charlie? Sam's my mom, and I'm not eighteen."

"I hear you on that one," Deus said. "That's how me and Billy ended up here."

Billy shook his head and stroked his chin. "Now, let's not be so quick to assume that Josh has to do what his mother told him. You have a grandfather, who you might be able to live with."

"It's possible, but I don't know if he'd let me. Not to mention, with the health problems he's been having, he could go back in the hospital at a moment's notice. That would just leave me with option A again and having to transfer schools. Except, this time, I'd be transferring mid-year, instead of at the beginning of the year. I've gotta say, from experience, that it definitely sucks."

"So, what?" Charlie yelled, a look of complete disgust written on his face. "Me and Dianna get to have split custody over you?" Standing up, he walked nearer to Josh. "You know you're not going to be able to drive out on the weekdays. You can't swing that with school."

"How are you more pissed about this than I am?" Josh snapped back. "I'm the one who's going to have to move again, and I don't know anybody there."

"How?" Charlie replied, his face full of anger. "Let's see. This is the best summer I've ever had. My life sucked, before the three of you moved here. I'll be damned if I'm going back to living in that dark basement without you guys."

"There's got to be a way around this," Billy said, still concentrating. "I don't really want to go off to Oregon either. We'd have to make new friends again. I'm so done with that. How about you, Deus?"

"I'm not opposed to sticking around," his cousin replied. "But you know Senior isn't gonna dig it, and we're not eighteen either. It's his money we're living off."

"True, but he might let us, if we had a plan for a business out here. He never went to college, and he certainly won't force us to go," Billy said. "If he thought we were spreading our wings to find ourselves and making our own way, he'd help us. If we put our heads together, between the four of us, I'm sure we could come up with a million-dollar idea. And then we could live life by our rules."

"I'm all about that," Charlie said, nodding. "I'll do anything to keep us all together."

"What have I got to lose?" Josh said. He really had no other option, and he didn't want to lose Dianna or Charlie.

"Great," Billy said, still staring at the floor, thinking. "We just need something to open up our minds and get our creative juices flowing."

"There's some energy drinks in the fridge," Josh suggested. "You want me to grab some?"

"No," Billy said, looking up and shaking his head. "I need something to open me up. Has anybody here smoked opium?"

Chapter 24

"I'm so happy to hear that," Ramon said enthusiastically into his phone. "I'll tell her you said hi."

Dianna watched Ramon strolling back towards them, while the three women stood shoulder-to-shoulder, seeking shelter in the shade of the RV. Whatever protection it had given from the blistering heat wave, it was minimal. It was finally the last week of the tour, and they were finishing up in Georgia. She seriously felt like laughing, when she remembered she'd thought the inside of the RV was hot at the beginning of the trip. She was completely deluded. Last night, they slept inside of the church, on the pews, because it was air-conditioned. Plus, the lightning storm overhead had them too freaked out to sleep in the RV.

"Hurry up, Ramon," Nina yelled. "It's hotter than Hell out here."

"It was true," Dianna thought, realizing her choice of shirts probably wasn't the best idea. She'd put on a black tank top, thinking it would be perfect for the Georgia weather. But she realized now that there was really nothing to catch the sweat, and the color was taking in all the heat.

Ramon walked up, sporting a mile-long grin. "What could you possibly have to be happy about, dad?" Cammy whined. "Didn't you notice your shirt's totally wet?" Ramon looked at the sweat dotted all across the white shirt, but he didn't seem to mind.

"Let's go inside and get some lunch," Ramon said. "I've got some good news." Dianna peered over at the restaurant, across the huge parking lot. It seemed a million miles away. If there was one thing she'd learned about life on the road, the RV was definitely not a house on wheels, like the brochure had claimed. It also couldn't be parked nearly as easily as a car. More often than not, they had to park on the outer fringes of the parking lot or even a few lots over.

"The heat really isn't that bad. I've definitely felt worse," Ramon said. "It's not like we're in the desert," he said, as the group headed off towards the steakhouse.

"I'm happy you feel that way," Nina replied, "but we're miserable right now." Dianna wanted to nod, but she just continued to trudge over the blazing asphalt. All three women were having PMS, and the hormonal imbalance was probably what made the last leg of the trip so hard. Dianna definitely had felt her fair share of pain over the past few days.

"I know girls," Ramon said. "When you're miserable, I'm miserable."

"And don't you forget it," Cammy groaned.

"Believe it or not, things aren't always rosy out in guy town. We have our problems, too." Dianna watched, as Cammy shot their dad a look of skepticism and anger.

"Are you kidding me? If you knew how I felt right now, you'd keep your back hair, and the occasional kick in the balls, and quit while you were ahead."

Nina chuckled, "Preach it, sister."

"I'm not kidding," Ramon said. "There's a big trade-off."

Dianna scoffed, "You're digging a hole, dad."

"Now, calm down, ladies. I'm not trying to antagonize you. I just feel neither side has it better than the other. But I do have some good news," he added, arching his back to avoid the mirror of a parked car. "One of the women Dianna healed last month at Pastor Guevara's church, the one with fibromyalgia, has an incredible story."

"I remember her," Dianna said, as she thought back to the middle-aged woman. She had pain in her whole body, especially in her joints and muscles.

"Let me guess. Another full recovery," Nina said, breaking formation to avoid a lamppost.

Ramon stopped walking. "Yes, and there's something else. She's pregnant after numerous fertility doctors said she'd never conceive."

"No way, she's forty-six," Cammy cried. Dianna was surprised as well. There seemed to be a growing list of people who claimed that not only the chief complaint they'd sought healing for was gone, but every complaint they'd ever seemed to have over the course of their life was resolved as well. Still, this was something she had never even hoped for.

Stopping to turn to her father, Dianna smiled, as genuinely as she could in the heat. "That's great news."

"It gets better," Ramon said, barely able to contain his excitement. "The church organization is already talking about another tour." Dianna shuddered, as her father's words confirmed her worst fears. Even though she had prayed frequently over the past few weeks that this wouldn't happen, she wasn't surprised.

"No," Dianna said, shaking her head. "I can't. I won't."

"What do you mean?" her father asked, completely amazed. "I thought this was what you wanted."

"It was," Dianna said, shrugging her shoulders and trying her best to ignore the heat. She'd prefer to be indoors. But, if this conversation was going to take place, it had to be away from public ears.

"What could be more important than our plan?" he asked.

Immediately, her thoughts turned to Josh. She couldn't spend one extra minute away from him, but she didn't dare say this to her father. If she told him, he'd demand to meet Josh, as soon as they got home. Dianna didn't want to put Josh through that.

"It's a lot of reasons, dad."

"Like what?"

Dianna could see that, under the perplexed look of her father, there was another emotion; hurt. It was something she instantly regretted, but she had to speak her mind. "I love you, dad, but I've learned something about myself this summer. It seems every town, every city we've been in, for every person I've healed, there's two more that seem to think they know what's best for me." Shifting her head, Dianna asked, "Do you understand how that feels? These people don't even know me. Just because we're having dinner together after church, they feel they have the right to plan out my life for me."

"They're just trying to help," her father said.

"I don't need their help, dad. But it's more than that. Just how long do you really think this can go on unnoticed, before the claims drive the medical organizations to look past their opinion that this is just placebo effect or faith healing? How long before they actually investigate this?" Her father stared in shock, unable to answer her.

"I could do so much more working as a volunteer candy striper at a hospital, healing really sick people in cancer wards or on the cardiac unit. And the best part is I could do it anonymously, with just the touch of a hand."

"But the church needs you, honey," Ramon said, shaking his head.

"Everybody needs me, dad. Sickness and old age isn't just confined to a select few."

"You put her up to this," Ramon shouted, glaring over at Cammy, catching her off guard. Much to Dianna's relief, Nina stepped up behind her and placed her hands on her shoulders.

"Get a hold of yourself, Ramon. She had nothing to do with this." Ramon glanced in frustration at the three women.

"Listen, Nina, while I value your friendship, I don't appreciate you jumping in and trying to control our family decisions."

"I fully agree," she said defiantly. "As the wise pastor I know you to be, stop trying to control your daughter's life. When are you going to realize these hopes and dreams your family is living are yours and not hers? She does all this stuff to make you happy. Dianna's sixteen, and she needs a father who can teach her to make safe, prudent, adult decisions, not make them for her."

Ramon shook his head in desperation. "You don't understand. It's what's best for her."

"No, dad," Dianna said, folding her arms. "I'm not arguing that you don't have my best interests at heart, but you know Nina wouldn't lie or try to hurt us. And my sister's important to me. I look up to her. This decision wasn't hers though. It was mine. Every day I get more and more powerful, and it's getting tough to hide. No more tours. I just can't do it anymore."

"I don't understand, but you know I'd never force you to do something you didn't want to do," Ramon said, still shaking his head. Dianna could see his eyes were getting glossy. She wanted to thank him. She didn't feel she could speak without crying, so instead she bit her lip. "You guys go on ahead," he said, nodding. "I'm not hungry anymore."

Watching her father walk back alone to the RV was one of the saddest things Dianna had to do all summer. Multiple times, she had wanted to run up to him and throw her arms around him, telling him she would do anything to make him happy again, even if it meant spending her whole life on the road. Almost instinctively, Nina put her hand on the girl's shoulder.

"Don't worry, child. Ramon just needs time by himself. Sometimes, letting go of his little girl so she can become a woman is the most intense pain a man can ever know." Dianna nodded. She couldn't imagine this day ever arriving, but she was sure Ramon was more shocked than she was. At that moment, images of her father caring for her as she grew up over the past sixteen years flashed in her mind. Nobody had done more for her. She knew that, but Nina was right. She had to start living her own life.

Strangely enough, as she turned around, Dianna noticed that by making a stand for herself, she didn't feel estranged from her father like she thought she would. She actually felt closer to him; close enough to reconsider what her father really meant by the trade-off.

***

"That's it, bitches. Bow down and worship," Hasden thought, as his group strolled through The Playa. Everywhere they turned, there was a new set of eyes. Each one was more awestruck than the last. It was Friday. Unbeknownst to the vacationers partying in the Black Rock Desert, this was quite possibly the most important weekend in the last two thousand years. By the end of this vacation, Hasden would have an idea of just how dark Josh's dark half could be, and to what depths he'd descend to claim victory in the name of the Monarchy.

The whole place was alive with costumes, art, music, and more importantly, nudity. Hasden knew that one of Josh's favorite classes was metal shop. Nobody fused art, metal and a teenage boy's darkest fantasies like Burning Man. It was the total package. Unfortunately, it also had something that Hasden hated more than anything: benders. There were hundreds of them, including the worst kind; hippie benders.

He didn't particularly know why these types of festivals brought together a veritable who's who of the bloodlines. Many of these people were powerful enough that they could even see who he truly was. Frankly, he really didn't care. He felt virtually unstoppable right now, and he knew that Deus felt it too. It was a feeling he'd never known existed, and it didn't come from a drug. It was coming from Josh. Hasden was high off of the interplay between his aura and Josh's, which the boy was using quite liberally.

He knew Josh was having a great time. Once they had hit the crowd, Josh really blossomed. He sent out his energy like feelers, searching and touching everything around him. He wasn't surprised when his fellow demons' auras joined in as well. That's what was causing the looks of shock and awe. It was the recognition that not only was the Royal Family of Hell present, but the Dark Half was here as well. And they'd all come to party.

As Bill walked, he noticed the girls were getting their fair share of looks too. All three of them wore their own costumes, just like the guys did. Phyllis had her blonde, shoulder-length hair combed back, with bunny ears on her head. The rest left little to the imagination. Her skimpy, white bikini rested over pink fishnets and white knee-high leather boots. Her pink sunglasses shielded her from the occasional sand whipping around them. She was beautiful. But next to her was Mahvet, and she was a vision.

Angela's exquisite long, black hair flowed with the wind's direction. It was exactly the same color as her bikini bottoms, which was the only clothing she had on, besides her black boots and leather demon accessory: wings. She pulled the costume piece on just like a backpack harness. Her dark, olive skin had been lightly dusted with gold glitter that covered her entire body, especially her cleavage. A booth in The Playa had spray-painted a black tube top where the girl's shirt should have been. Every guy had his eye on her, and Bill had caught Charlie gaping at the woman's breasts multiple times today.

"We should stop, so I can fill my Camelbak up," Charlie said. Hasden nodded, as the trio of Josh, Charlie and the third girl in their weekend crew, Bai, stepped off towards a group to see where they could get water.

"Holy shit," Deus said, in a hushed tone. "Did you feel that? His energy is intoxicating."

"He's definitely strong. No doubt about that. I'm in awe of how well our powers mesh together. It's like they were made for each other. I always knew that our energies would be complementary to each other's auras, but Josh is like nitro."

The big teen nodded in Josh's direction. "It's obvious his energy changes with his mood, and I'm pretty sure he's oblivious to it."

"I agree," Hasden said, regaining his composure, "but let's not lose ourselves in the possibilities. Did anybody notice the high concentration of benders here?"

Do you think it will be a problem?" Angela asked, glaring at the large group of people milling about in costume.

"Normally, no," Hasden said, wiping his bare chest with his handkerchief, to knock off the dust that had been blowing around. "It's important to remember, even though we might be the five most powerful entities in this hemisphere, we are still standing in a sea of fifty thousand people. A lot of them have abilities. So be ready for anything. If any of them get even remotely brave, you have my permission to end them, especially if they look like they're calling on angels or forming a circle."

"My pleasure," Angela replied, smirking.

"How are you feeling?" He was nervous about having her here in the same area where the alien angel had attacked her.

"I'm fine," she said, arching her black eyebrows. "I've got it under control." Hasden nodded, but he really wasn't so sure. He knew her demeanor could change on a whim. For half the plane ride over here, he couldn't tell if she wanted to laugh or scream, as she listened to Josh talk.

"Where's your roommate?" Hasden asked, referring to his PR agent, Phyllis Foster. When he and Deus decided they needed to stay in Milton, he'd reassigned her to be Angela's caretaker. He was careful not to use that word around Angela though. Instead, he'd given her the impression that Phyllis was her roommate, to better manipulate the loneliness he knew had been an ever-present part of her lonely career as a solo agent of death.

"Do you want me to go find her?" Angela asked, scanning the crowd for blonde hair and bunny ears.

"No. I have a better idea. She needs to remember we're here for work first and play second. If you would, Mr. Gregory."

"Of course," the hulking teen said. As he closed his eyes, he mentally roared for Phyllis, using her true name. "Mephistopheles, you are summoned!"

Hasden laughed, as he immediately saw the pair of bunny ears drifting towards them through the wandering people. For all appearances, Deus just looked like a big, muscle-headed demon. Hasden had found, over the years, that the raw force of his primal mind rivaled his muscular exterior. He wasn't smart, by any stretch of the imagination. He didn't have half of Hasden's wits or cunning, but he had his uses. In today's world, Hasden excelled. That was because, coming out of the dark ages, he'd taken control of the board and was now forcing God's children to play his game. At times, Asmodeus was completely useless. His talents of lust and perversion weren't necessarily needed in today's business world. But when he was sent into the game, Hasden knew his body was overflowing with raw might and an anger that was borderline murderous at times.

"You're an asshole," Phyllis screamed at Deus, while rubbing her painful temples.

"We're not here to people watch," he snarled. "So get your ass back on the clock. Hasden wants to have a word with you."

"Where the hell did you wander off to?" he scolded her.

"I'm sorry," Phyllis replied, obviously flustered. "I just noticed there are a lot of familiar faces walking around here." It didn't surprise him in the least. Phyllis was always his first choice, when he needed to tempt somebody or to make a deal. Truth be told, she probably knew three quarters of the benders here.

"There's been a change of plans," he said to the demon girl. "I'm taking you off Charlie detail, and I'm assigning that to Bai."

"Why? We already know Charlie would do anything I asked. I'm obviously the most qualified to manipulate him."

"That's true," Hasden replied, nodding his spiky hair at her. "But for some reason, Josh's energy has changed since our arrival. It's different than it was at the lake house. I don't know if it's because he's been taken out of his normal fish bowl and is now swimming in a large pond or what. But it seems he's adapting to the new environment. It could also just be the overall excitement of being in a titty-filled theme park tailored just for him. Either way, I need you by my side to help prep him for Saturday night. Do you understand?"

The blonde demon nodded slowly, her white and pink bunny ears lurching back and forth as she did. "Are you sure Bai's up to the task of keeping Charlie occupied?"

Hasden flashed his trademark evil grin, looking over at the tent that contained Charlie, Josh and Bai. "She was our backup plan to begin with," he said, looking at the petite girl in the super short schoolgirl outfit. "It's no secret Charlie has a soft spot for Asian girls."

***

"Bai is a beautiful name," Josh said, looking at the petite girl.

"It's Chinese," she replied. "It means princess. It comes from my mother. My father is a Dane, and my last name means light."

"Half Chinese and half Danish? Great mix," Charlie said, moving his way into the conversation.

"Thank you," she giggled softly. "So how do you guys like your costumes? I noticed you're all matching."

Josh let Charlie answer the question. He didn't particularly care for the leather pants that all of the boys had on. It didn't breathe as well as his blue jeans or even his sweats, but Billy assured him that they'd fit in better wearing these. And he wasn't kidding. This place was off the hook. He'd never known anything like this even existed. It was like being in a buffet for the senses. Everywhere he looked, there were elaborate costumes. Since they were in a desert, Josh was relieved that the guys had simple clothes.

He had on black leather boots and pants, with a black surgical mask around his neck that matched. He'd also thrown a black onyx ring on each hand, even though he wasn't too big on accessories. To top it off, Josh had black flames painted on both arms, starting at his wrist and going up to both elbows. Black sunglasses, a little hair gel, and a comb put on the finishing touches. He felt it gave him a distinct look that was somehow familiar, but he couldn't quite place it. Whatever it was, the women loved it.

He'd started the day with the black mask hanging down his back. Since he'd donned it more than a few times since then, he'd switched it around to the front. He was glad he had it. In a lot of ways, it was more useful than Charlie's brown aviator goggles were, which matched his brown leather pants. Josh watched out of the corner of his eye. Charlie was smiling and nodding at everything Bai was saying. He was the only person, out of the guys, who wasn't totally bare-chested. Apparently, Billy had noticed that, after all the daily workout sessions with Deus, Charlie still looked like a stick figure. He gained a little in his arms, but you could see his ribs on both sides. So he'd bought Charlie a leather vest.

"So, hey, do you have a boyfriend back home?" he heard Charlie ask.

"Atta boy," Josh thought sarcastically. Girls love men who can just get straight to the point. It never ceased to amaze him how Charlie used his advances towards women like a shotgun. He just sprayed it out everywhere. The method didn't have much in the way of accuracy, but he was sure he'd hit something sooner or later.

"Is there anything else you need?" the woman said, returning the Camelbak. "I have plastic bags to keep things dry and aloe vera for your friend over there," she said, nodding at Charlie's skin, which was getting redder as the day wore on.

Josh smiled at her. "No. My friend's always trying to teach me lessons. Apparently, he didn't learn his the last time he got sunburned. So I'll pass." He took a peek over at Charlie. He sort of felt ashamed for a second. For some reason, he felt a mean streak a mile long coming on, and Charlie had deserved this one since the first day of school. "Excuse me," Josh said, handing the water to Charlie, "I'm gonna leave you two to talk."

"Cool, bro," the redhead nodded. "We'll catch up in a bit."

Josh nodded at Bai and walked off into the crowd, towards Billy and Deus, stealing one last peek over his shoulder. "Payback's a bitch, sucka."

Chapter 25

"Oh my God. This is excruciating. I can't take the pain anymore," thought Josh, as he pulled off his boots, one by one. His dogs were seriously barking. He waited for a second, as the cool air hit his toes. "Ah, that's so much better," he thought, as relief flooded his system. After a full day of walking and hours of dancing under the stars with the girls, his feet were toast. Even through the pain-numbing effects of the pills, Josh could feel the sharp pain, as they trudged back to their group of tents. He briefly checked his white socks for bloodstains, but the only red he saw on them was the two red rings up at the top of his socks by his calves. His socks reminded him of little barbershop poles for some reason.

"So, are they okay?" Billy asked, taking a seat next to him at the campfire.

"Well, it definitely felt like they were cut up. But it looks like I'll live to walk another day," Josh said, settling comfortably into his fold-out sports chair. He'd initially thought of dipping his feet in the ice chest, when they first walked up. He could see now that wasn't necessary. "I don't know what I'm gonna do tomorrow, as far as walking in these things," he said.

"Now you know how women feel," Phyllis said, as she grabbed a chair and sat down. Josh noticed she'd quickly changed out of her bunny costume and now had on black boy shorts and a tank top.

"It's true," Billy said to Phyllis. "Leather boots are a cruel mistress. I don't know how you do it."

"So what do you think of Burning Man?" Phyllis said, turning to Josh. "Isn't this place cooler than a Harley made of tits and tequila?"

Josh chuckled, "It is pretty cool. I've never seen something so elaborate. I've been to a couple of street fairs and concerts before in Santa Cruz, but nothing big-scale like this."

"Santa Cruz boy, huh?" Phyllis said, flipping the metal tab on her soda can. "How appropriate for you that The Playa is your one-stop shop for entertainment. It's the beach in the desert."

"I noticed that," Josh replied. "My mom used to call Santa Cruz the playa all the time. I didn't know what it meant until I took a Spanish course."

"Yup. It's amazing how much this place is suited for you," Billy said, waving at security, as they drove up and slowly stopped at the edge of their campsite.

"Having a good night?" the Black Rock ranger said, hanging his head out of the patrol car.

"It's been a blast," Phyllis said, waving at the officer. Josh nodded towards him. Earlier in the day, he'd come by to ask where they'd purchased the elaborate tent set up. Josh felt like he was poking around, looking to see if they were following the rules. Although, it was true that they had the nicest set up he'd seen yet.

They had three giant tents. Deus and Billy were in one, and outside was a flag that had the Hasden company logo. The girls had their own tent, which sported a large, black pirate flag, with a pink skull and cross bones and a little pink crown on top. And then there were Josh and Charlie, who, much to Charlie's dismay, had a white flag, with Charlie's yearbook photo blown up on it, just like his hand towel he loved so much.

"Well, be safe and have a good night," the ranger said, slowly passing by. Josh sighed, taking in a huge breath of the desert air. He was glad it was cooler than earlier and that the sandstorms had died down. Staring at the fire, as it softly jumped back and forth, Josh noticed how different this place was from Milton. It was like the group had stepped into the other side of the mirror. The landscape was cruel, but the people were super relaxed. Even the little campfire seemed to be the opposite of the roaring bonfires they were used to at the lake.

"So, do you think the others will make it back?" Josh finally asked.

"Hard to say," Billy said, staring at the coals. The boy had donned a black tee shirt, but still had his dark green leather pants on from earlier. Josh had thought of switching out of his leather pants, but he just had no strength. At least, he'd managed to get his white lifeguard tank top on.

He'd never personally worked as a lifeguard. He traded one of his fire shirts to a schoolmate in Santa Cruz, who worked at the beach. Josh liked the big, red cross on both sides of the shirt. It seemed to let everybody know that, no matter what happened, he wouldn't fold under pressure.

"I'm sure the girls will be back in a few," Billy said, "after they're done dancing. Deus probably won't be back 'til morning, and we all know Charlie won't either."

Josh smiled, as the other two broke into laughter around the campfire. He looked up at the moon and rested his head on the back of the chair. Well, it finally paid off. Charlie was finally losing his virginity.

"What a dunce," Phyllis shouted. "Bai was totally into him. All he had to do was follow us out to the dance floor and seal the deal."

Josh thought about it, as he stood up and made his way to the cooler. He wasn't really sure how it happened. They were all pretty high, but somehow Charlie met a girl who was completely tore up. Josh literally cringed, when he thought of how dirty she looked. He grabbed a water and fished some oxy out of his pocket. They were rough and grainy after riding in his pocket all day, but he popped them in his mouth nonetheless.

"What I want to know is how Charlie picked Hilda Haggard over Bai," Phyllis asked. "She had a face that could cut a steak. And where'd she get those awful cornrows?"

"You mean the ones that I could smell from ten feet away?"

Billy said, poking at the fire. Josh noticed Billy wasn't too amused, when he'd asked Charlie to come back with them to camp. Charlie flat out refused, saying that he'd found his soulmate.

Phyllis shook her head. "What a complete and total dumbshit."

There was something about her, and Josh couldn't really put his finger on it. He wondered what it was that made her the way she was. For the most part, he liked the girl, to a certain extent. But there was a rough edginess to her that was tough for him to swallow. She was uncouth in a way that Josh found unsettling. He could count on one hand the number of times he'd heard his mom curse. Even though she did every once in a while, Phyllis used swear words like they were the only descriptors in her vocabulary. Billy had told him she was always like that, and it was just because she was a tomboy. But Josh doubted that. She didn't look like any tomboy he'd ever met. Phyllis was a knock-out, and she never wore anything without a designer label on it. But there was something unfeminine about her demeanor, and it went way beyond just her vulgarity.

"Why don't you teach your boy how to shake his ass?" Phyllis said, grinning.

"I don't know how to dance," he admitted. "I've never done it before. I was always too self-conscious. I guess, if you get enough pills in me, I'll do anything." Josh felt the sting of his conscious. Even though he told himself he was going to cut down the pill intake before school, the brakes had totally come off the train. He was doing double what he was taking at the beginning of the summer. It was getting worse and worse. Josh moved to change the subject, but Phyllis beat him to the punch.

"So did I lie to you about Angela?" she asked. As she did, Josh noticed her face had the most devilish grin to it. She was obviously happy to prove she was right.

"You were totally telling the truth," he agreed.

"So what do you think?" Billy said, seeming to come out of the deep fog. He looked mesmerized by the red coals of the fire.

"She's awesome," Josh said. "You were right, Phyllis, her looks are ravishing."

"She thinks you're cute. She told me so herself."

"Get out," he said, feeling embarrassed. "There's absolutely no way. She's totally out of my league, and she's two years older than me. Besides, I've got a girlfriend."

"Yeah, so you keep saying," Phyllis replied, obviously unimpressed. "But I'd like to remind you that Angela's hotter than hell, and you're never going to get this chance again. You're being totally stupid over a girl that you haven't seen in months. I mean, she's a thousand miles away, doing God knows what with God knows who."

Josh shook his head and glared at Phyllis, "I completely trust her."

"Cool," she said, shrugging her shoulders. "Just saying, the opportunity is there."

Stretching his legs out, Josh asked, "Why didn't you hook up tonight? You had plenty of chances."

Phyllis snorted. "Please," she said in a loud voice. "I wouldn't waste even an ounce of my sexual energy on any of those undeserving losers. I'd rather paddle my own canoe down orgasm creek."

"You're high," Josh said, giving her the thumbs down. "You're nineteen and hot. And you talk about sex all the time. Now you expect me to believe you're a saint?" Josh shook his head aggressively. "Not buying it. Epic fail."

The girl leaned forward in her chair and sat her soda can down next to the fire. "No, you ninny, of course I have sex. I offered it to you; didn't I? What I'm saying is I don't sleep with people I don't know in strange places."

"Why?" Josh asked. He didn't think that Phyllis had any

hang-ups about anything, given her usual attitude.

"Because I do yoga five times a week to raise and refine my personal energy. It's very important to me. So the last thing I'm going to do is waste it on some weirdo on vacation, whose energy is weaker than mine."

"What are you babbling about?" Josh said, in amazement. She made it sound like she had powers that were linked to her sexually.

"It's true," Billy said, casually looking over. "When you reach orgasm, your body throws off a measure of your personal energy. That's why it's called the little death, or le petite mort in French. Any time you orgasm, you're letting go of some of your life force."

"Life force I have other uses for," Phyllis said proudly, "like dream bending, maybe."

Josh's head popped up, when he heard the term. "What did you say?" he stammered.

"You heard me," she said coyly.

"There is absolutely no way this is happening," thought Josh. "If what you said is true, and orgasms produced energy, then Charlie's socks could transport us to Camelot and back."

"She's not lying," Billy said, calmly stirring the coals. "Sexual energy isn't the only energy, either. There's anger. It's one of the most formidable energies out there. It's the quickest to answer, and it's the easiest to sustain."

"Thanks, but I don't think I can pull off being angry all day, every day."

"Of course, you could," Billy answered, with a sneer. "It's easy, once you realize how insignificant everyone else is compared to you, and you watch day by day as their life gets easier, while you carry the lion's share of the work. Sooner or later, as you sit in the twilight of the midnight of your soul, you'll find all the anger you could ever need."

"How do you know this?" Josh asked, startled at the callousness that emerged in his friend's voice.

"How do you think I know?" Billy replied, throwing the question back in Josh's face.

"Let me ask you something," the girl said. "What do you think this life is really for?"

"I don't know," Josh said, shrugging his shoulders in the dark. He noticed that there was precious little light that the fire was putting out. It was just red embers now, but Billy stirred them, nonetheless.

After a short pause, the girl continued, "That's right, Josh. You don't know. For all you know, this world could be a prison for gods, built by gods. It could be a cell meant to hold a force so strong that they had to break it down into billions of miniscule parts. Then the warden, God, took these billions of soul bits and placed them into separate walking and talking prison cells. Finally, to add insult to injury," Phyllis leaned forward, her eyes as red as the embers of the fire, "what if the warden separated these jail cells by race, color, and religion, because he knew that this final security measure would never be overcome? It was a completely un-pickable lock. And with that done, he threw away the key."

A chill went up his spine, as Josh watched her slowly sink back into her chair. The coals were dead now, but Josh noticed Billy continued to poke at the ashes. "That's not true," Josh whispered, his mouth dry.

"Really?" Phyllis asked, her eyes continuing to glow, like the fire once had. "Can you move forward in time or go back to visit the past? Or are you trapped, just like the rest of us, forced to live every day not knowing what cruel and unusual punishment the warden has planned for you? Pushed against your will, might I add, just to give thanks to a God you've never met and doesn't intervene, as day by day you watch your loved ones get sick and die?"

Josh grabbed onto the two poles that held up the arm rests in the folding chair. He was feeling dizzy, and the poles felt like they were the only stable thing in his world. His reality started to twist, ever so slightly. He looked towards Billy, but the spiky-haired boy didn't seem to notice or care. He just continued to absentmindedly stir a fire that was no longer there. It was now dwelling in the girl's eyes. Josh watched Phyllis rise up from her chair and nod.

"You don't know a thing, Josh. You're sixteen years old, and you don't know your ass from a hole in the ground." He watched, as she crept towards him, eyeing him like a lioness creeping stealthily towards her prey. "The only sure thing, Josh, is that this world is a trap. If you view it as anything other than that, it only proves that, in fourteen years you haven't gotten one goddamn bit smarter. Because when you were two years old and shitting in your drawers, you wholeheartedly felt, with every certainty, that everything you saw was undeniably yours. But that, little man, just wasn't the truth; now was it?"

Josh tried to rise up out of his chair. He felt weak, just like he was a baby. All he could do was stare at her horrible eyes, as she panted faster and harder. Finally, when Josh began to feel like he was losing his hold on reality, Billy turned towards him. His forgiving eyes were filled with hope and compassion.

"The world isn't what it seems," the boy said, pulling the hot poker out of the fire and transforming it into an olive branch. "But I can teach you. I can show you the way," he said, as Josh pitched forward into the dark embrace of unconsciousness.

***

"I never even knew a place like this existed," Cammy said, stunned.

"Nice, right?" Nina asked. "I spent quite a bit of time in the area, and I remember when this place was still in the planning stages. Dianna was decidedly stunned by the cemetery's architecture, from the moment they'd walked in. The craftsmanship in the statues was a lot better than she expected.

"I'm not used to this," she said, excitedly. "When you said let's go to the cemetery, I was thinking like all uniform tombstones and a few trees."

"Come on, girls. You know me better than that," Nina said.

"I thought I knew you," Cammy said. "I kind of thought you were a stay-at-home square. Apparently, there's more than meets the eye."

"I'll take that as a compliment, my dear Camille."

"Since they'd gotten here, Dianna had seen just about every statue on the sprawling grounds, from angels to crosses to even a lion or two. "Hey, look over here. An Egyptian tombstone," Dianna nodded.

"Yeah, I've seen a few of them scattered around here," her sister said, pointing at another one surrounded by magnolia blossoms.

"There's a Civil War memorial on the hill, if you want to see it," Nina offered.

"Sure, let's head that way," Dianna said. "We can finish our power walk there and head back to get ready for church tonight at 6:00."

"I don't know if I'm going to make it to church tonight," the older sister said. "After this hour and a half walk, I'm gonna need a nap."

"Not even, Cammy. If you skip, I'll kick your butt all the way back home."

"Ha. You'll try. How about this? If you beat me to the top, you heal me. Then I'll go to church. But," the girl said, wagging her finger, "no powers."

"And if I lose?"

"Then it's nappy time tea for sleepy Cammy," she laughed. "And no guilt trip afterwards."

Dianna grinned. Personally, she felt the deal was a little lopsided. "I don't know. I say we consult the watcher on this one."

"This is Cammy we're talking about," Nina said. "That's about as good a deal as you're going to get."

"That's what I thought," the teen said, pushing her sister backwards and sprinting in the other direction, towards the hill.

"Cheater!" she heard from behind her. Dianna didn't know how she was going to do this. Even though she'd been training with Nina, she'd never won at anything physical against her older sister. Dianna had always used her intellect, and that really couldn't help her much here.

"Okay. I see how it's going to be," her sister called from behind. Even though she started strong, Dianna could already feel the burn from her rapidly tiring muscles. Apparently, the hour and a half scenic walk took more out of her than she thought. "I'm right behind you. Brace yourself for the failure," Cammy yelled, hot on her heels.

Racing past tombstone after tombstone, Dianna furiously pushed on, even though her body felt like stopping. Cammy had to be as exhausted as she was, and Dianna was dead set against losing the small advantage the shove had given her. Through the heavy perfume of the flowers and the dazzling scenery filled with voices of the other tourists, Dianna pushed on towards the top of the hill. It had looked so close, but now it seemed so far away. In the back of her mind, all she could hear was her breath panting frantically, mixed with her sister's, that seemed to be only fractions of a second behind.

"That taste in your mouth is failure, Dianna. Just give up," she heard her sister raggedly scream, as she edged closer.

"Almost there," Dianna thought, pushing her body faster.

At this point, her energy was gone. Now, only her sheer determination kept her going. In her peripheral vision, she could see her sister's fists pumping up and down next to hers. As she rounded the bend in the asphalt, she didn't dare look back. If she did, she knew she'd lose hope. So she pushed again.

"Hate to do this to you, little sis, but I really need that nap," Cammy said, surging ahead.

"No way!" Dianna screamed. She was giving it all she had, and was now trailing behind her sister. Dianna saw that she had only one option left. In front of them was a group of four guys walking in a group. She didn't know their age but, based on their clothes, they couldn't be more than thirty. Pouring on her last ounce of strength, she burst forward and shoved Cammy right into the group of surprised males. All Dianna heard was her older sister's dismay, as she ran and touched the monument first.

"Good job," Nina said, from the top of the hill.

"How'd you get up here?" The out-of-breath teen asked.

"Easy. While you two were running up the trail, I shot up the side through the tombstones. It was the shortest route."

"Hey, you little cheater," Cammy said, running up, slapping the monument and pointing at it. "That wasn't very civil of you."

"All's fair in love and war, Cammy. And besides, we both know you don't need any more naps."

"Not my point. You cheated."

Nina shook her head. "I wouldn't necessarily call it cheating. The only rule you stated was no powers." Dianna winked at her sister and pointed at Nina.

"I'm sticking with what she said."

"Would you have won, if Dianna had raced you on your terms? Of course. But all three of us know your strength is physical."

Cammy stared at the two of them, like they were from

another planet. "Nina, she cheated. Why are you advocating it? That's wrong on so many levels."

"Dianna," Nina said, "why did you push her?"

"Because, without my power, she's not only stronger but faster. Even having the inside turn as my advantage, she pulled ahead of me," Dianna panted, struggling for breath. "So I had to improvise."

"You're both out of your minds," Cammy said. "What kind of stuff have you been teaching my sister?"

"How to win. Believe me, if Dianna lied or used her powers, I'd be the first to take her down a notch. But you set the rules, and you lost. I'd think, at your age, you would have learned by now that the world doesn't exactly play with kid gloves. And by no means should you. Any time two people square off against each other, each one uses their own advantages given by nature to attempt to win."

"I guess," Cammy shrugged. "I just didn't know it was going to be like that."

"It's super important that you know that it's going to be like that every time from now on. Where Dianna is headed, there will be no quarter given and no restarts. In war, it's not just one event. It's a decathlon. You have to use all of your ability, strength, and cunning. Do you follow me?"

"Whatever. I still get healed," Cammy said, grinning.

"Hey, girls, were you really in that much of a hurry to see a statue?" Dianna turned around to see the four guys walking up.

"Oh, no. We were just racing to the top for a bet. And she lost," Dianna smiled.

"Right on. I wouldn't mind losing to you," the tallest of the four guys said. "What's your name?" he asked, looking at her and nodding his head. Dianna looked over at Nina and saw that all of the guys had walked into formation, like they were the Blue Angels.

"I'm Gabe," said another guy, approaching Nina. "What's your name?"

Nina looked to Gabe and smiled, "I'm only going to say my name once," she said to the guys. "So listen closely." As Nina raised her voice, "LEAVE" vibrated out of her mouth. Much to Dianna's amazement, the men's faces went blank. They nodded and just walked off.

"What was that about?" Cammy asked, confused.

"Usually, I don't ever do that, especially in public. But I knew they weren't going to back off, even if we were rude to them. They wouldn't be able to get the hint because they're ants. I just wasn't getting a good feeling off of them, and your sister's safety is my highest priority."

"Whatever it was, you're going to have to teach me that trick. It might come in handy at the club," Cammy chuckled.

"Follow me, girls. We'll go back down the hill, back on the grass, just in case."

"Are you going to tell me what that was about?" Dianna asked, looking around her and starting down the hill.

The reason I sent those guys off is because the whole group of them were ants, which is a term coined by the demons. It means ancillary. It's used to describe somebody with little to no will, who's open to suggestion. The Monarchy usually uses them to do their dirty work. A strong-willed demon can override an ant, like possession, and get them to do all kinds of things. One of their particular favorite things to do is to use their eyes as windows to track people, and that's why I couldn't have those guys hanging around you.

"How can you tell?" Dianna asked. "They looked nice to me.

Nina made her way carefully down the hill, winding through the elaborate tombstones and ornate mausoleums. "I can tell by their electrical charge. Most people, no matter what they do, will always be inherently good. But some bastards are just incredibly evil. Their polarities are opposite. For those who fell between the cracks, they came into the world without any real charge. They have a soul, but they just don't really have much of a spirit. Do you understand?"

Dianna thought about it, as she plotted her course down the hill. "Are those the souls that wouldn't pick a side in the war in Heaven?" she asked, stopping in front of a statue of an angel.

"I'm surprised you remembered," Nina said, turning to the teen. "Most churches never really talk about it, or they forget. The space where the war took place was actually outside of the time stream. And, yes, they're the one-third that refused to choose."

"So are they saved?"

"Not in the way you're using the term, no. But they are fulfilling the obligation we all had to participate in this life. These people aren't bad, but they aren't good either. So you need to watch out."

"It seems kind of silly that I'd have to worry about them, seeing as I'm destined to take on Hell," Dianna said.

"Well, actually, the forces of darkness will use these people against you. Take a look at those faces, because there'll be a gang load of them at the final battle. The ants have very little ambition or motivation. They kind of just hover in low stations in life, frequenting parties, looking for sex. They constantly crave it."

"Well, I must be an ant then," Cammy said, laughing.

"No, you're not. I assure you. If you were, you wouldn't have lasted the first leg of the race. Sex is a normal part of everyday life. Our bodies were built for it. Ants crave it because of their charge. They're attracted to extremely good or extremely evil people. They crave the energy that sex momentarily gives them, because they have no real charge of their own. In a lot of ways, they're like succubus or zombies. It didn't take too long before the Monarchy started using them to do all kinds of things."

"Why on earth would they do that?" Dianna asked. "The demons have their own powers. Isn't it just easier to do it themselves?"

"A few hundred years ago, they didn't just use them to fight or do tasks. The Monarchy also deployed them as leeches."

Cammy laughed, "I know a few of those."

Dianna agreed. "I've met quite a few too. Did they do it all the time?"

"Not really. Say there's a king, who says he's going to revolutionize the world. The demons can't have that, so they send an attractive ant to seduce him. Inside a week, the king has lost the wind in his sails, because the charge his metabolism that usually builds up is constantly being thieved away by the beautiful ant. The next thing he knows, he's continuously fighting off infections. Then he notices he's not as powerful or charming as he used to be. Eventually, he falls from his lofty position. Therefore, the problem is solved. In the end, it's practically foolproof, because love is blind. The target never sees it coming."

"What do the angels use them for?"

"Nothing," Nina chuckled. "The angels know that, every time the demons abuse their power or cut corners, nature just comes back producing stronger avatars to strike a balance between the two. But in the end, regardless, be warned that Satan will use them against you."

"What do I do though? I can't hurt them, if they're innocent. It's not fair," Dianna cried.

"Welcome to my world," Cammy said, hugging her sister. "Now about that healing..."

Chapter 26

Josh awoke on Saturday to the sounds of clanking pots and pans, accompanied by continuous laughter close by. He cautiously looked around at the interior of the empty tent. "What the hell?" he thought. How'd he get in here? Josh rolled over to see that he was square in the middle of the inflatable mattress that was neatly tucked into one of the corners, leaving room for their folded clothes. His heart began racing, as he recalled the events of the night before. Had Phyllis really revealed she was a dream bender?

Sitting up, Josh put his sweats and tennis shoes on. His feet were groaning in protest with every step he took. He could smell bacon through the fabric walls of the tent. More importantly, he could hear Charlie. Unzipping the exit flap, Josh emerged into the sunlight of the brand new day.

"Hey, what's up, buddy?" he heard Charlie shout enthusiastically. Taking a second to let his eyes adjust, Josh was surprised to see everybody was up and fully clothed. The tent city was alive with commotion, as the residents of The Playa milled about.

"Good morning, sleepyhead," Angela said, with a smile. She looked like a sight for any set of sore eyes. Josh smiled and then looked over at Charlie, who was flanked on either side by Billy and Phyllis. Charlie sat in his chair, wearing a grin as broad as day.

"How was it?" Josh asked.

"Somebody might need to call the police," the redhead said slowly, looking worried but then grinning. "Because I stabbed that poor woman with my mutton dagger." Josh let out a sigh of relief and chuckled.

"Okay," he thought. Maybe the world hadn't gone to Hell in a hand basket. Charlie reached over and high-fived Deus, as they both laughed.

"How are you feeling today?" Phyllis said, looking concerned. She was sitting casually in front of the propane grill, flipping bacon with a pair of silver tongs.

"I don't know," Josh cautiously said, staring at the raving lunatic from the night before.

"We think somebody might have slipped something in your guys' drinks last night," Bai said. "Me and Angela left the party a little after midnight and walked back to camp to find the three of you on the ground, talking to yourselves like you were out of your minds."

Phyllis lifted up her bangs to reveal a sizable knot on her forehead. "I must've hit my head when I fell." Josh couldn't believe how relieved he felt. It all made sense now. He walked over and took a seat at the empty spot between Bai and Angela.

"I helped you to the tent and sat with you for hours," Angela said sweetly. "I hope you don't mind, but I slept in your tent and kept watch over you."

Bai nodded, "Yeah, and instead of going to bed, like I so desperately needed, I got to sit with Phyllis, who thought she was going to jail for some stupid reason. And then there was mister I-can't-sleep-without-the-fire-poker." The girl pointed an accusing finger at Billy. "Poor guy was sweating all over me and thrashing about for hours, before he settled down."

"That made sense," Josh thought, chuckling to himself.

"You talked in your sleep last night," Angela said quietly.

Josh turned to the girl in disbelief. "You're kidding," he exclaimed.

"No," she said, gently shaking her head. It was at that second that Josh realized he'd spent so much time avoiding looking at Angela, because she was practically naked yesterday, that he hadn't actually seen her. He knew Charlie and every other guy in the place had probably stared at her openly for hours. For some reason, Josh had never made eye contact, because he felt like he would have been disrespecting her. But now, seeing as she was clothed, Josh had no problem truly looking at her for the first time.

"Did I say anything weird?" he asked, afraid of what the answer would be.

"Yeah," answered Charlie. "You said, how can I be down like my soul brothers, Deus and Charlie?"

Phyllis shook her head. "Why do I get the feeling I'm going to hear this guy bragging for the next year, at least?"

"Don't hate. There's enough Charlie to go around," the redhead grinned. Leaning in, Deus grabbed a piece of the sweet-smelling bacon.

"I think The Playa created a monster," he said, popping the folded strip in his mouth.

"Hey, pecker, hands off, until it's all done." Phyllis cried. "Everybody else is just as hungry as you are."

"Negative, ghost rider," Deus said. "I'm a growing boy. I need my energy, because tonight it's going down."

"That's right," Charlie said. "Tonight the man burns."

"It's going to be the best night of our summer," Deus said, smiling.

"And the best vacation I've ever been on," Charlie nodded. "I'm glad you guys brought me."

"Nonsense, bro, you're family. And when I think of the one spot I'd like to take family to, it's gotta be the beach."

Just for the slightest of seconds, Josh swore he heard the ringing of a bell in his ear; and then it was gone. Nobody else seemed to notice, but Josh saw that Deus had stuck his finger in his ear and was opening and closing his jaw. Maybe he'd heard the same thing.

"Okay, everybody," Phyllis smiled broadly, "come and get it," she yelled, taking the top of the pot off the hot scrambled eggs. Josh saw a little pillow of steam roll out right as she lifted the lid and thrust the fork in. Deus smiled and yanked the paper towel off the mountain of crisp bacon and carelessly threw it to the ground.

"Whatever," Phyllis said, grabbing a piece for herself. "To friendship and The Playa," she said, holding up the bacon. Josh leaned over and grabbed a few pieces and raised it up with everybody else.

He looked over at Charlie, who looked about as happy as a pig in mud, shouting, "To friendship and The Playa."

***

And on they marched. Josh smiled at his six companions, all showered and fed. Headed out in a horizontal line, it filled him with infinite joy every time somebody had to step or move out of their way. After a few pills, he'd finally gotten his swollen left foot back into his boot. It was a little tender at first. Now Josh was not only strolling about with ease, but he was practically gliding.

He looked at the fresh black flames that had just been painted on his forearms. He had to admit they looked impressive. But they weren't half as impressive as what was jiggling and bouncing to his left-hand side. Totally devoid of shame, he stared right at Angela's freshly painted breasts.

"See something you like?" Angela said, smiling innocently.

"More than you'll ever know," Josh said, grinning, as Bai reached across and slapped his knee. He only wished that he could bottle this feeling, because he honestly didn't have a clue how the hell he'd managed to live before this weekend.

The sounds, and especially the people, that made up this experience that was called Burning Man, all of it was more than he could have ever hoped for. Breathing in the desert air, Josh let out an involuntary chuckle, as Phyllis swung out of formation and hugged him from behind. "Life is good," he thought.

"Throw on your masks," Billy yelled, as the winds started

to kick up again. Swinging the black surgical mask around and cupping it over his mouth, Josh gave a raspy, involuntary cough. He'd gotten some dust and sand in his mouth with that last breath. Tears streaming from his face, he was unprepared as the wind hit twice as hard this time, knocking him off balance. "Shit," he thought, hacking and coughing. His black sunglasses weren't doing anything to protect him from the sand. So he wasn't too surprised, when his eyes continued to tear like crazy. Josh dropped down on one knee and rubbed his eyes furiously, as the wind continued to pick up. He could feel the sting of the sand on his bare arms and back. "I've gotta get between something," he thought. His best bet was to head for the last group of tents he saw, off to his left.

Taking slow, sweeping steps, Josh moved blindly, as the frantic bodies of the other hapless victims ran for shelter. One person bumped into him so hard, he nearly lost his mask. Now Josh didn't know what direction he was pointed in. The wind was dying back down, but Josh still couldn't see yet. He had sand in both his eyes.

Staggering over between a cluster of tents, Josh went down to the ground on his hands and knees. "Well, that was no fun," Josh thought anxiously, rubbing his eyes. He didn't think there was any more sand in them, but they were stinging viciously. Taking a deep breath, he looked around to grab his bearings. Nothing really looked familiar, and he didn't see any of this friends. Just like that, The Playa's crowd had swallowed them up. Slowly standing up, he gave another forceful cough that burned his lungs. "Come on, guys. Where are you?" Josh thought, scanning around him. That's when he saw him. He nearly choked, but Josh definitely knew the face of his watcher, Thomas, who did not look amused.

Shock gripped Josh, as the tall man with the short, buzzed hair locked eyes with him. He was only a few tents away, dressed in camouflage military gear from head to toe. With a beckoning wave, the man signaled Josh to follow him. Then he stepped away, between the tents. Josh began running off after him, calling out his name. "Thomas!" he shouted, as he turned only to see the man disappear between another group of tents. He charged forward, running faster. His feet were screaming in protest, and his lungs were burning. Josh rounded the corner of the tent to see the watcher standing next to a group of red tents. "Thomas," he said to the man as he approached. The man didn't acknowledge the teen, as he had before. In fact, the look on his face was wholly indifferent. When he opened his mouth, his voice was laced with a British accent.

"Oh, wrong guy," Josh said, shaking his head.

"I'm not Thomas," the man admitted. "My name's Hobbes."

"I'm sorry," Josh said confused. "It's just you look exactly like somebody I know."

"That's because I regularly use his form as my cover, just in case," a voice came from behind Josh. Spinning around towards the voice, Josh stood in stunned silence, stupefied, as he recognized the face that matched the voice. It was the homeless man from the convenience store in Milton.

"What?" Josh stammered.

He looked back at Hobbes, who said, "Sorry, guy. He totally does it without my knowledge. Now, if you'll excuse me, I'll guard the perimeter and let you guys have some privacy."

"It had to be this way, Josh. I'm sorry for the confusion."

"How?" Josh asked, totally befuddled.

"I'm not only immortal, I'm a shape-shifter too. It's a defense mechanism. I can't necessarily be killed, but I can be hurt. So it's always good for me to keep a low profile. Believe me. Just because I can't be killed doesn't mean that the group of demons looking for me won't give it a try. Even worse, they might imprison me. I definitely can't train you, if that happens."

Josh stared in amazement. He looked exactly the same as he had on the last day of school, right down to the leaf fragments in his dreadlocks. "Every day?" Josh asked, in disbelief.

"Every day." Thomas nodded and smiled, his dark skin creasing as he did. I don't normally live on the streets, but I spent my fair share of time waiting to see you."

"But why?" Josh mumbled.

"You're going to find," the Rastafarian said "that the less flashy you are, the less attention people pay to you. In my line of work, that's a good thing. You see it every day in nature. Practically everything has a disguise or something that's in their genetic code that protects them."

"What are you doing here?" Josh asked, wiping the sides of his still-tearing eyes.

"I've been texting you," the watcher said.

"I know. I've kind of been deleting them," he replied slowly.

"I figured as much," Thomas said. "I'm here to tell you that whatever situation you're in, whatever problems you're facing, we can work it out together. The fate of the world depends on you. Within you is the light, and it can ease all the pain and suffering that surrounds us."

"And how is that supposed to work?" Josh cried in disbelief. He couldn't believe the balls on this guy. "I can't even ease my own pain and suffering. Ever since I found out I'm the Dark Half, my life's been in a nonstop downward spiral; and you've been nowhere."

Thomas stared at Josh in dismay. "I could just as easily call you the Light Half, and it would be true. Your power's difficult, but it's also an integral key to who we are. Don't lose hope just because things aren't going your way. You haven't seen me all summer, because I can't force you to learn. And the property you've been staying at all summer is guarded by demonic sigils of the highest order."

"Sigils?" Josh said, confused. "The lake house is surrounded by demonic sigils?"

"I hate to say it, but yes," the watcher said. "One of them is the personal seal of the Director of the Monarchy himself." Josh felt the familiar anger creeping up on him. He had been duped. On top of that, last night, more than likely, really had happened. Shaking his head, Josh tried to make sense of it all. He knew the pain pills were clouding his thought process. He didn't know who to believe at this point. He really didn't like being lied to. Even if his friends were affiliates of the Monarchy, hadn't they treated him better than anybody else he knew?

"I'm sorry, Thomas, but you're wasting your time," Josh said. "I don't want to be the Prime. If I could, I'd gladly give the powers away to the first person who would take them. You're just barking up the wrong tree."

"Please, Josh," Thomas pleaded. "I know you're angry and confused," he said, stepping forward. "I wish you'd reconsider."

"I appreciate it," Josh said, putting his sunglasses on, "but this isn't for me."

"I respect your decision," the man said, nodding. "I only wish there was a way I could help you to see how important you are."

"Hey, boss, you're never going to guess who I just ran into," Hobbes said, briskly approaching them.

"Who?"

"Rose. And she requests an audience, after you're done with the kid."

"Who is Rose?" Josh asked, slightly offended that he'd just been referred to as the kid.

Thomas's face beamed, like it was the sun itself. "This is nothing less than providence. I know you're wary about the training, but please find it in your heart to get a second, impartial opinion right now."

Sighing, Josh nodded. "If it'll make you feel better, I'll go. But after that, I'm out of here."

"Done," Thomas said. "Take us to her, Hobbes."

"Who is this lady?" Josh asked, as they walked between the enormous cluster of tents. He was anxious to get the whole ordeal over with, but his curiosity was peaked.

"Rose is very wise. Her real name is Urania, and she's not just a lady. She's an immortal."

"And why is it important that I meet this Urania?" Josh asked, as he followed Hobbes through a clearing and into another cluster of tents.

"Well," Thomas said, glancing around them to see who was looking, "she's not affiliated with the Monarchy or the Host. So she has no reason to lie to you."

"Over there," Hobbes said, pointing to a purple tent with gold fringe.

Josh looked at the sign out front that said Fortunes and Palmistry. "No way," he groaned. "She's a gypsy. You gotta be kidding me."

"No, Josh. She's THE gypsy. Urania is a muse. Right now, that's exactly what you need."

"Whatever," Josh said, pissed that he even allowed things to go this far. "Let's get this over with."

"Follow me," the man said, as he parted the velvet folds and stepped inside. Josh looked back at Hobbes, who stood at the corner of the tent, expressionless. He never really noticed before, but the man had a small backpack on. In his left jacket pocket was the unmistakable outline of a handgun.

"What the hell have I gotten myself into?" Josh wondered, as he followed Thomas into the purple tent.

It was much dimmer in the tent than Josh originally expected, but there were candles casting a golden glow around the makeshift room. "Damuzi, it's always a pleasure," said a dark-haired woman wearing a scarlet robe with a hood on the back.

"You can call me Thomas," the watcher said sternly.

"How long has it been? A hundred and fifty? Maybe two hundred years?"

"Something like that," Thomas replied.

That's weird, Josh thought. Thomas was being rather standoffish. A moment ago, he was thrilled at the prospect of this woman. He glanced at the very few things inside the tent, besides the woman. There was a deck of cards on a small walnut table that was almost overshadowed by two large chairs. A mirror was positioned on a tripod behind her.

"I see you brought a friend," she said, her eyes lighting up.

"What are you doing here, Urania?" Thomas asked impatiently.

"So much for catching up with old friends," the woman dryly replied. "To tell you the truth, I'm not sure. This isn't my usual thing, but I'm dating the lead singer of the band that's headlining tonight. So I came along. Any other questions, watcher?"

"No," Thomas said, smiling. "I just wanted to see if this was a chance, planned or a synchronicity."

Rose chuckled, "Ah, Thomas, you never change. Always following the signs."

"Is there any other safer path to travel, when you follow God?"

"No, my friend. I guess that there isn't," she replied.

"Listen, Rose, I'm here so that you can tell my friend something in a way that somehow I can't."

"I see. That happens to be my specialty. Have a seat, nameless friend," she said quietly. Josh nodded at Thomas, who still stood near the entrance to the purple room, and took a seat on the chair. Josh thought whoever had carved it and stitched the red upholstery had surely passed on. It was older than anything he'd ever seen, and he'd been in a lot of houses as a fire volunteer.

"Do you have a name?" the gypsy asked, smiling.

"His name is Josh," Thomas replied.

"Well, Josh, my professional name is Rose. Seeing as you're traveling with Thomas, I'm sure he told you that it's really Urania."

"I wonder if all the immortals are like this?" thought Josh. Urania looked maybe twenty-eight at the most, but she conducted herself like his grandmother's friends would. She was fairly pleasant and seemed genuinely interested.

"It's a pleasure to meet you," he said, extending his hand. Urania went to grab his hand but instantly let go with a look of horror on her face.

"I see you have quite a bit of power," she said warily. Josh was surprised that her demeanor changed so quickly. She looked like a child, who'd just had her hand slapped.

"His last name is Michaels," Thomas said from behind her.

Urania stared quizzically at him. "Really?" she said, placing her hands on the table, palms up and instructing Josh to do the same.

"That's odd," Rose muttered, as she stared at his hands.

"What is?"

"Well, your right and your left palm don't match. They tell two completely different stories." The woman traced the lines on both palms with her eyes. "In fact, in one, your lifeline is extraordinarily short. The other indicates that you may live indefinitely." Josh glanced down at his hands. Whatever she was seeing, he couldn't see it. But he didn't like what she said about the short lifespan. He watched as the woman stood up and discarded the robe to reveal the pink, almost see-through material underneath. It reminded Josh of the dresses he'd seen in Greek history.

Grabbing the deck of cards, the dark-haired woman

shuffled them quickly and began flipping them over, four for his left hand and four for his right. Josh looked at one side. They were the Sun, the Wheel of Fortune, the Chariot, and the World. The other side read the Tower, the Hanged Man, the Devil and the Death card. Josh stared at the skull on the death card and felt an involuntary shudder go up his spine.

"This is impossible," the woman said, staring at the cards in amazement. Either you're the most beloved person to ever grace this planet, or you're the most despicably cursed individual alive," she said, shaking her head.

"Figure it out yet?" Thomas said, teasing the woman playfully. Urania picked up all the cards and shuffled them again, this time with a look of determination on her face that would not be denied. Josh watched in silence, as she carelessly threw the cards up in the air in one swift motion. As she did, she straightened up, raising her outstretched arms. Josh flinched as the cards flew everywhere. Oddly enough, the smoke from the candles gravitated towards her hands, like they were somehow magnetically attracted to her fingertips.

"Who is this boy?" the gypsy commanded out loud.

To Josh's surprise, the cards stayed suspended in the air. "Remarkable," he thought, as he watched one, single solitary card descending as if it were a feather. Back and forth it weaved through its brothers and sisters to land on the table face up: THE FOOL. He didn't know if he should be relieved it wasn't worse, but Josh couldn't help but feel instantly offended by what the card implied.

"Heavens above," the woman whispered. "He's the Prime; isn't he?"

"Yes, Urania, he is. And I need you to nudge him in the right direction."

Nodding, she sat down into the chair. Josh was surprised the vintage piece of furniture hadn't crumbled into dust. "Are we near the end already?" the woman asked, addressing the watcher.

"After thousands of years and hundreds of lives for both of us, it's finally happened," he happily replied.

"Well, Mr. Michaels, it's a pleasure to make your acquaintance," the woman said, once again wearing her smile. "May I ask who the girl is?" she asked, glancing at Thomas.

"I'm not at liberty to say," he replied, placing a hand on the back of the teen's chair.

"Throw me a bone," the woman said, sounding mildly annoyed. "I doubt I'm getting paid for this." Josh could tell by the silence that Thomas wasn't giving out any information he didn't have to. "At least tell me this," she said towards Thomas, but looking at Josh. "Is she the young girl I've seen all over the internet lately, the healer?" Images of Dianna flooded Josh's mind, making him take a deep breath in. "That's what I thought," Rose said, smiling. Josh looked up at the watcher, who was shaking his head.

"What? I didn't even say anything."

"That makes more sense," announced Rose. "You're the Dark Half," she said, smiling.

"You mean the Antichrist; don't you?" Josh said sarcastically.

"No," she said, shaking her head back and forth. "But if that's what you want to be, it's just like your guidance counselor at the school says, you can be whatever you want to be."

Josh shook his head. "You don't understand. It's not that easy. My life is a mess, and somehow I'm changing. There's a darkness inside of me, and I can't describe it. I hurt all the time now, and I wasn't like this before. It's getting harder every day to keep it suppressed."

Urania looked at Josh in amazement. "What? The opiates aren't keeping it in check?"

"What are you talking about?" Josh said, in a flustered

voice.

"Boy, I've been alive since the dawn of time. I literally held the hand of the Creator, as he put this world together. So tell me I'm stupid, and you're not high as a kite right now. Because your pupils say otherwise. Your aura says otherwise. The delay in your response, that you obviously don't notice, says otherwise as well."

Josh took his hands off the table and looked at Thomas, who nodded in agreement. "I could tell right when I saw you."

"Okay. So I party a little," Josh said, feeling the embarrassment creeping up on him.

"I'll tell you something," the woman said, tapping the fool card on the table. "If you don't stop this, it's going to lead you to the short life I saw. It might feel good right now, but I assure you, all that is about to come crashing down." As she spoke, the cards that had been magically suspended in the air began to rain down all over the table. "So what have you been experimenting with?" Urania asked.

"Just some oxy," Josh quietly said, looking down.

Urania sighed, "I see. In that case, let me explain something to you, Josh. Being a muse, I tend to hang with a rather eclectic crowd. The drug you're taking is fairly popular among them, and I've seen it cut down a lot of brilliant people way before their time. Its chemical name is thebaine, as in it will be the bane to your existence, if you don't stop. It's highly addictive."

Josh shrank back into the upholstered chair. "The universe has an odd sense of humor about things like that," the woman said, glaring into his eyes.

"I seriously need it though," Josh said, desperately. "It keeps the darkness away."

"I could see that," Rose said sympathetically. "But your needs and my understanding won't prevent your death." Josh watched as her finger drifted back to the card. "It's ever so unfortunate, but some poor fool always has to assume the mantle of the Dark Half."

"But why?" Josh asked. "It's destroying my life."

The gypsy paused for a second and clasped her hands together. "Because the Creator, back in the very beginning, many, many earths ago, found that, when two things are alike, they just didn't have the pizzazz it took to hold together. Like Adam with his first wife, Lilith. They were just companions. They weren't in love. They only had a weak bond, which was shattered by her stronger attraction to the fallen. The Prime Objective is too precious to leave to some weak attraction, and somebody has to carry the dark energy. There's no other way. Quite plainly, Josh, have you ever considered that you're the Dark Half because you're the only person who can bear it?" As she said this, Josh thought of his nickname.

Josh took a moment to consider what she had just said. It made sense, but then he shook his head. "People are getting hurt," he said, looking at the gypsy. "Both my grandparents' lives are ruined. My own mother is so afraid of me, she can't even look me in the eye. I'm serious about what I told Thomas. I don't want to do this."

"I know," the woman said flatly. "But you're not the first chosen to beg the Creator to pass the cup. He didn't do it for them, and he definitely won't do it for you. Not this late in the game." Holding her hands out, Josh was surprised, as the cards jumped into her outstretched palm, one by one. "Do you think I enjoy telling people bad news? Because I don't. But I know my purpose. Throughout time, talents and abilities have ever been present, and they're given only for a purpose. They're not passed out so you could put them in your closet, like your least favorite birthday present. To have abilities and not use them comes with the severest of penalties in any religion, order, or society. So why would you think you're any different?"

Josh sighed and sat up straight, "This is gonna suck. I can already feel it."

"That's the spirit," the woman smiled, "because I'm going to tell you something. Without the second Prime, we won't make it another thousand years. It's the fool, who decides it in every world."

Glancing over at the table, Josh saw the card of the young man with the sun over his head and the little, white dog at his heels. It looked so much like his vision. "What is it? Does it mean I'm stupid or foolish?"

"Heavens, no," the woman said, smiling. "This is quite possibly the strongest card in the entire tarot. It has the distinct privilege of being accepted as the first or the last of the major trumps. The fool is the spirit in search of much-needed experience. Sadly, its duality is hard to master," the gypsy said, winking at Josh. "The fool is young and inexperienced, but has infinite possibilities. He is capable of everything and nothing; its claim to fame and its potential curse. Some say that it's like that for a reason. Its nature is sort of like a protective mechanism, so opposing forces will underestimate him."

Josh looked up at Thomas, whose mouth curled up, into a grin. The woman chuckled, "Let me guess."

"Synchronicity," the watcher said proudly.

"In the days of old," Urania said, "the jester, or the fool, was considered the least of all who were invited into the Imperial presence. But behind the scenes, it was a little-known fact that the fool was one of the few the king or queen ever really trusted or confided in. As royalty, they knew that everybody had an angle and an opinion on what they should or shouldn't do with their power. But the fool knew that all he really had to do was make the royals smile, and he could keep his head another day. By bringing the sunshine to a weary Imperial, he filled the most valuable position in the court.

"You have to wake up and kick this addiction, Josh. Our world is broken. We're referred to as the me generation. If we can't change that name to the us generation, others will refer to us as the them generation. Only a fool would ever attempt to fix this. And only a fool can."

"But how? I can't get my powers to work," Josh said to Urania. "I start things that I can't finish. I say things, and the opposite effect shows up."

"Don't worry," she said. "We just have to figure out your instrument. Drummers drum, singers sing. Thomas just has to figure out what you do. I know it's tough, but it's just a sign of the times."

"What do you mean? Like a marker?" Josh asked.

"Sort of," the woman answered. "The two avatars never show up in a time of plenty. The Creator sends them as a response to a present evil. As to the situation we're in," Rose said to Josh, "God's asking you to not just take the noose off your neck, but humanity's as well. The world leads a lot of people into a false sense of security. Medals for mediocre achievements, competitions where everybody's a winner, and a lifetime of movies where the young hero always wins, have irrevocably damaged us as a society. The hero doesn't always win," Urania said. "I've lived enough lifetimes to know." The gypsy spoke, in a gentle voice, "I don't know how this happened to you, but you have to fight with every fiber of your being, if you're going to make it out."

"I'll give it a shot," Josh meekly replied.

"No," the watcher barked. "You will succeed. You have to." Josh jumped at the harshness of the man's voice.

Urania let loose with a hearty laugh at the teen's skittishness. "Calm yourself, young Prime. This reminds me of a story I loved so much from long ago. Would you like to hear it?" the woman asked. Josh settled into the chair and nodded. "Good. This is an old Native American myth called Rainbow Crow." The gypsy readied herself. The candles seemed to dim, until all the boy could see was her face. And then suddenly, she spoke. "It was so cold. Snow fell constantly for days on end, and ice covered the waters. None of the animals had ever seen the white snow before," she said, lifting her hands up and shooting snow from her fingertips. "At first, it was fun and exciting. As it got colder and colder, the animals noticed they would eventually all die if something wasn't done. 'We must send a messenger to the Creator, who created by thinking,' said their leader, Wise Owl. 'Somebody needs to ask him to think the world warm again, or we will surely freeze.'" Josh noticed that the woman's skin turned blue, as she hugged herself.

"The animals liked the idea. But who should they send? Wise owl couldn't see well in the day. Coyote was so easily distracted, surely, he could not be the best choice. The turtle had always been steady and stable, but he was too slow; and time was of the essence. Finally, Rainbow Crow, who was the most beautiful of all the birds, volunteered. It had large feathers that shimmered in all the hues of the rainbow, to send the bird on its task ever so swiftly." Josh smiled, as a rainbow appeared over the gypsy's head.

"Three days it took the swift bird. Straight up into the Heavens, up through the clouds, towards the moon and sun and past the stars themselves. Even though the elements were harsh and there was no place to rest, Rainbow Crow carried on faithfully, showing bravery and dedication, until finally the Heavenly palace was reached. Even though Rainbow Crow pecked on the window and cried out for the Creator, there was no answer. He was too busy creating what would be," the woman said. "So, Rainbow Crow began to sing the most beautiful song the bird could think of, hoping to awaken the Creator. It worked. The Creator raised his consciousness and greeted the lovely bird at the window. For brightening his day, he asked the bird what it wanted as a gift, to which the bird pleaded, 'please, un-think the snow, before Earth's animals freeze to death.' But the Creator told rainbow crow he couldn't do that, because the snow and ice had spirits of their own and could not be destroyed. But the Creator still wanted to help the lovely bird, so he thought up fire to warm the creatures of the earth during cold times." Josh watched flames around the woman's hands, but he saw the deeper meaning behind what she said.

"So the Creator stuck a stick into the blazing sun, which ignited it, burning with heat. Handing the cool end of the stick to Rainbow Crow he said, 'Fly as fast as you can before the stick burns up.' Thanking the Creator, the beautiful bird flew off, as swiftly as possible. It was a three-day trip back from Heaven, and the bird was worried the fire would burn out before then. The stick was very large and heavy, but that didn't deter Rainbow Crow in the slightest. Following the path of the stars, the bird flew down from Heaven. The fire got hot, as it burned ever closer to Rainbow Crow's feathers. Passing the sun, the bird's glorious tail caught fire, turning the shimmering feathers black. As the bird passed the moon, the entire body of Rainbow Crow was covered by the black soot from the fire. When the bird plunged into the earth's atmosphere, the smoke from the fire stick strangled out its lovely singing voice. Finally, the bird landed, thawing the ground and saving the frozen animals. But now, the bird was black as tar and could only caw instead of sing.

"The animals rejoiced and celebrated the arrival of fire, but Rainbow Crow didn't feel like celebrating. The dull and ugly feathers saddened the bird, as did the raspy voice. Then Rainbow Crow felt a wind blow by its face. Looking up, the bird saw the Creator descend from the clouds in a ray of sunlight. 'Don't be sad,' the Creator said. 'The animals will always honor you for the sacrifice you made for them,'" Josh was surprised to see Rose's eyes well up with tears. She continued. "'And when the people come, they won't hurt you,'" she said, looking up at Thomas. "'I have made your flesh taste of smoke. Now it is no good to eat. And your black feathers and raspy voice will prevent humanity from putting you in a cage to sing for them. So now you're free.'" The gypsy brushed a tear from her eye and continued.

"Then the Creator pointed to Rainbow Crow's black feathers. Before its eyes, it saw the dull feathers become shiny. Upon inspection, in each, individual feather, could be seen the colors of the rainbow." As tears streamed down her face, the gypsy looked at Thomas. "'This will remind everyone who sees you of the service you have been to your people," she said, setting her jaw, "'and the sacrifice you made that saved them all. And so shall it ever be.'"

Josh contemplated the meaning of the story. At first, when she'd started out, he saw the parallels between what he was going through and the large task ahead of him. As the gypsy continued however, he realized that she wasn't talking to him. She was talking to Thomas, which made the boy wonder. What could have happened in their shared past that was so harsh it could make an immortal weep?

"Thank you, Urania" Josh said. He could see in the mirror behind her head that Thomas had been brought to tears as well and had tried to brush them away with his thumb.

"I'm glad you liked it," she said. "It's one of my favorites. It was told to me by a Lenape medicine woman. I'm afraid I didn't do it justice, but I said the parts I could remember. Anyway," she said, standing up, "since I seem to have answered all of your questions, perhaps you could answer one of mine?" She smiled sweetly, taking his hands in hers.

"I'll try," Josh said, noticing her usual happiness had a touch of urgency or desperation.

"If it were up to you," she began.

"Urania!" Thomas shouted.

"Would you forgive me of the things I've done in the past?"

"You don't have to answer that, Josh." Looking down, the teen saw that the watcher's arm was across the boy's chest like a gate that Urania shouldn't pass. "This isn't how it works, and you know it!" Thomas said, his eyes filled with steel.

"My reply," Josh said, standing up slowly, "is ask me again, after I successfully achieve my goals."

The woman cast her eyes downward in shame and replied, "I guess that was the best I ever could have hoped for."

Thomas waited until the Prime had left the tent and spoke. "What in God's name do you think you're doing, Rose?"

"Exactly what is in my nature," the Muse said, shaking her head. "I'm not human, and I can't repent," she said, standing up. "I have lifetimes of sin on my back. Can you really blame me?"

"I suppose not. But I know the boy's heart, and it's possessed of a kindness that is rarely ever seen," the watcher said to the gypsy. "If he's successful you won't have to trick him. Merely ask, and he'll do everything he can to save your soul."

Pulling her robe onto her shoulders, the woman gave Thomas a gentle look. "Try not to hold it against me. I meant no harm."

"I know," he answered.

"I don't expect you'll ever switch back to your old form, Thomas. But can't you let go of the past? It's been a hundred and fifty years since he died."

Stopping at the tent's entrance, Thomas shook his head. "You know I can't do that, Urania."

"I understand, my friend," she nodded quietly and raised up her hand. "May the first be the last."

"And the last be the first," he replied, as he exited the gypsy's tent.

Josh stood outside, taking in the setting sun, until Thomas emerged from the tent. "What was up with that?" he asked.

"It's important to understand that Rose isn't human. At the

same time, she's not an angel or a demon," Thomas said, heading away from the tent. "So she will be judged at the end."

"I'd like to think, if she was bad, you wouldn't have taken me to see her," Josh chuckled.

"Well, given the choice, I normally wouldn't," Thomas admitted. "Even though she's been a good friend, I don't know where her loyalties lie. But given the signs, I figured that this was pre-ordained. It might sound a little crazy, but God doesn't always use angels or demons to do his work. To some, like my wife, Urania being here might seem like a coincidence. I'd like to think she was led here. Nina can't even stand the sight of Urania. She calls her the great whore."

"She seemed pretty nice to me, but not that nice," Josh said, with a grin.

"She definitely gets around, Josh. But understand this, Urania serves the Creator in a different way."

"Yeah? Like?"

"As a muse, she inspires people to create through art, sculpting, what have you. It's almost always by having sexual contact with them."

"Seriously?" Josh cried.

"Yeah. Don't look so shocked," the watcher said, laughing. "She's slept with thousands of men and women over the years I've known her. A majority of them have been famous rock stars."

"No wonder she asked if I'd forgive her," Josh said, amazed.

"No, that isn't it at all," Thomas said. "That's her job. She can't be punished for her function in this world, any more than the Monarchy can be punished for performing theirs. But in the untold thousands of years she's been here on Earth, who knows what she's done? The Creator sees the result of what she does as flattery. Imagine, if you will, the joy a father feels, as his son grows up and he emulates what he's seen the father do. After a while, the child no longer has to emulate. Sooner or later, he grows into the task.

Just seeing this process come full circle pleases the Creator. By creating, whether it's through art, music, or whatever the medium, it's a form of worship. So I've never looked down on her."

"Even though your wife's definitely not cool with it?"

"If it were up to my wife, Rose wouldn't have a snowball's chance in Hell at forgiveness, or anything for that matter. And that's why she asked," Thomas said. "Because deep in her heart, she knows that, as the Dark Half, you're the only person who will forgive her."

"You're kidding, right?"

"I wish I was, Josh. The truth of the matter is Dianna won't forgive anybody, when this is over."

"Why? She's the kindest person I've ever met. It's one of the most vivid things I remember from a dream I had about her."

"That may be true. But when she comes into the full inheritance of her powers at eighteen, after her temptation and the war, she'll not only possess the unbridled almighty power of God, she'll also possess his righteous indignation as well."

"If anybody's soul makes it to the Kingdom, it will only be because you asked on their behalf, and she allowed it because of her love for you."

"Allowed?" Josh exclaimed, raising his eyebrow.

"The real Heaven is the light side of the Tao. It always has been. Dianna is the representative of the light in the physical. Even though in this physical realm there is a blending of energies, this cannot and will not be permitted in the spiritual. Light is returned to the light, and dark is returned to the dark. The hell of it is the ghostly remembrance of what it felt like, and the un-easible pain of the chasm between the light and the dark. Dianna ultimately decides who gets to cross."

"But where does that leave me?" Josh asked, noticing the daylight was fading.

"That choice is up to you," Thomas replied, scanning the

crowd for Hobbes. "The last time I saw Rose, it was 1831. I was training an avatar at the time. I had such high hopes that he would change the world. He was exceptionally gifted. Everything I could have hoped for," Thomas said, with a far-off look in his eye.

"What happened?" Josh asked.

"Like she told you earlier," Thomas said, looking at the ground, "the hero doesn't always win. I'm not going to lie to you, Josh. The road to your eighteenth birthday is going to be hard. But, if you want to change your situation and the number that's associated with you, then I'll help you. Just know it's going to be an uphill climb, and there's no guarantee we'll be successful at the end. But if you care for Dianna, and I know you do, you'll make this journey with me."

Deep in his soul, Josh knew what Thomas was saying was true. But as it was, he was dancing on the fringe of withdrawals from the time he'd stepped out of the gypsy's tent. He wanted so badly just to get back to the camp and grab his pill bottle. After that, he could detox gradually.

"I can take you out of here right now, Josh. Just say the word," the watcher said.

"I know. I appreciate that, but I can't leave Charlie behind. I'd also like the chance to stop the drugs on my own terms. I heard what you and Urania said, and I agree with you. I want to fight. Just give me some time."

"All right, Josh. If that's the way you feel, it has to be that way. I look forward to your training. Be safe."

Josh could tell the watcher was conflicted, but it was the best he could offer under the circumstances. "There's something I wanted to ask. You said earlier that the lake house was surrounded by demonic sigils. Am I in danger or something like that?"

"Unlike anything you've ever known, and I'm not exaggerating. That's why I offered to take you out of here. I still will. But if you go, we don't go to Milton. We go to rehab, to get you ready for your training."

Josh nodded as he lowered his gaze. "I know. I promise I'll catch up with you soon."

"From your mouth to God's ears," the watcher said, bowing his head. "My time here is done. Be strong and safe. Remember, the Monarchy can't physically touch you, unless they're challenged." In a dazzling flash of light, Hobbes appeared next to the watcher.

"Where to?" he said, placing his hand firmly on Thomas's shoulder.

"Take us back home to Georgia," Thomas said.

"Georgia it is, boss." And with a bright flash that Josh could see started with Hobbes and then spread over to Thomas, the two were gone.

"What the heck is in Georgia?" thought Josh, walking back towards camp.

Chapter 27

"So, the angels do sing to the Creator?" Dianna asked, feeling semi-foolish about the image she'd always entertained in her mind before, of people actually singing songs night and day.

"Oh, yes, child. Continuously," Nina replied, staring at the Plexiglas wall. At all times, the auras of the created sing and worship him. It's an endless symphony of vibration, just like everything here."

"This place is awesome, Nina. You're right. This was exactly what I needed. It's better than what we had planned anyway." They'd originally planned on going for a morning run, heading out to a nearby park. Even in shorts and tank tops, it still seemed to be too hot. Dianna learned that maybe she could go for a run in Milton at high noon, but not in Georgia during a heat wave.

So the watcher decided they'd catch a cab to a much cooler climate, taking her training to a massive aquarium. All Dianna could say was she was pleased that the sun wasn't beating down on her. The air-conditioning was definitely welcome. Now they were surrounded by untold gallons of water, protected by only a Plexiglas tunnel. The water was teeming with marine life on either side and above the seemingly endless transparent arch around them.

"I thought you might need a break from the rest of the family, after all we've been through lately."

"I did," Dianna admitted. "Don't get me wrong. I love dad and Cammy. You know that," she said, pointing at a tiger shark as it swam past them. "But I think the heat and the lack of privacy is taking its toll."

"You're preaching to the choir, sister," Nina nodded to the girl. "As beautiful as Georgia is, I'm ready to go home."

"I wouldn't mind coming back some time to tour the cemeteries. That's for sure." The whole Georgia experience had been an eye-opener for Dianna. She was awestruck as she strolled through the huge Plexiglas tube, surrounded by water and sea creatures she'd never seen in real life before. It reminded the girl of how little she'd really experienced of what the world had to offer. "I know you're supposed to be my watcher," Dianna said, hesitantly. "I know you're not completely who I thought you were, but over the past years, sometimes I felt you had become like a..."

"Sister?" Nina said, grinning.

"I don't want to sound crazy," the teen said. "I've just felt really close to you, even since the time you first moved in, when I really didn't know you."

Nina stopped and leaned up against the handrail, letting the couple behind them pass. "You're not crazy, Dianna. The bond between you and I extends far beyond just friends. We were written in the tapestry, far before we ever entered this world."

"So, closer than Cammy and I?"

"Much more. My actual title is The Imperial Mother, and that's no accident. It's not a title that I bestowed upon myself, either. It was given."

"I didn't know that," Dianna smiled. It kind of makes me feel better about not knowing my mom so well. You came to our family at a time when I really needed you."

"Everything about your life is that way for a reason. All of life is an experience, and it contributes to your understanding of the world and your place in it. That way you can fulfill your destiny. It's important to remember that our consciousness only focuses so far into the future, and hindsight is 20/20. The Creator is outside of time. He sees the grand design. The watchers and the Primes in every universe bear striking similarities to each other."

"Like what? You and I look nothing alike and act totally differently."

"On the outside, maybe. On the inside, we're identical. That's why we get along so well. I'm sure you'd be more than interested to know that you and Josh aren't the only set of Geminis."

"You're kidding me?" Dianna laughed. "That's wild. When's your birthday?"

"Whoa, whoa," Nina chuckled, waving her hands. "Not like that. Thomas and I are called the Geminis or the Celestial Twins. We're the only two of our kind in the entire solar system."

"Oh, I get it. Wouldn't that have been incredible? What were the odds of us all being born near the same date?"

"Yeah, it would," Nina said, continuing down the glass corridor. "It's funny you should mention coincidences, because that's the ability that Josh and my husband share."

"Oh, really? What is Thomas like? Is he anything like Josh?" Dianna asked. She really wanted to know. If Nina and her were alike, maybe the answers could shed some light on her and Josh. Dianna already saw the startling resemblance between the two males in their need for their own space.

Nina's face brightened, "What can I say about Thomas?" she said slowly. "He's my soulmate. In a lot of ways, he's everything I'm not. But that's a good thing. Although, his power frustrates the hell out of me every now and then," she said, laughing. "He doesn't speak things into existence so much like Josh, but he sees cause-and-effect way before they happen. It almost seems that, at times, he knows the mind of the Creator so much more intimately than the angels or demons ever could."

"Not very good in a fight," Dianna pointed out.

"Oh, he kicks ass, when he needs to. He usually doesn't have to, because I've got his back," Nina smirked.

"And you definitely have abilities," the girl laughed out loud. Dianna knew that for a fact. Nina was her sparring partner.

"My abilities are strong, but they pale in comparison to what Thomas and I can do together."

"Like what?" Dianna asked.

"The watchers are soulmates. Our love is our one true

power, just like the Primes. The mere presence of it is unbearable to the demons."

Dianna smiled and nodded, "I'm kind of jealous, Nina. I was hoping Josh and I could explore our powers together and get to know each other more, but then the tour came up."

"Don't worry, child. You're young, and you have time," Nina said, throwing her arm over the girl and hugging her.

"I kind of can't wait for the whole final battle thing to be over, so Josh and I can actually have a real date."

"Don't say that, child," Nina warned, taking her arm back.

"Why?" Diane asked, shocked by her mentor's sudden change in demeanor.

The copper-haired woman looked both ways and then said in a hushed tone, "I know you care about Josh. In order to face the Monarchy and win, the two Primes have to rely on their love to persevere."

"I love Josh," Dianna said, looking down.

"That could be true. This kind of love goes far past attraction and transcends infatuation. I know you two are written in the stars, but your love has to become so much more."

"Like what?" Dianna said, shaking her head. She couldn't believe that Nina couldn't understand the way she felt about Josh, if they were supposed to resemble one another. "Didn't the dreams say it all? We're meant for each other."

"Dianna, I know this is hard to understand, but you're going to have to literally fight."

"I understand what a fight is, Nina."

"No, I don't think you do," Nina said, putting her finger to her lips. "I know your youth is your greatest asset, but it's also your downfall in affairs of the heart. Despite the dream and your powers, you can still lose. Nothing is set in stone."

"But I thought you said I had the power of God," Dianna said, confused.

"You do," Nina said, nodding. "But the Prime is not God any more than Michael Keaton or Val Kilmer are Batman in real life, and there are other actors that have played the part."

"What are you trying to say? That Josh and I could lose? There's no way."

"I already told you there are other earths, each one building and setting the stage for their Primes to experience love. Each human, who has ever lived and died on this planet, came here to live and love and in some way contribute to the age we're in right now. But they had no bearing on the actual fate of the world. For that, they pinned their hopes on you; God's representative and the highest concentration of power."

"I understand that, Nina. I'll face Satan right now, if I have to."

"And you would lose, child."

Dianna was shocked. She couldn't understand where this was coming from. "Nina, don't you have faith that I'll do everything in my power to win?"

"Of that I have no doubt. You need to realize that, when God plays chess, he isn't messing around. Division's directives and goals are specific. If we don't make the minimum, we lose. Before the Creator actually plays his queen, she will be made into a real queen, and not just by her last name." Nina pointed at Dianna.

"The knights that defend her have to embark on arduous journeys and sacrifice much in order to anticipate danger," she said, folding her arms. "What do you think I've been doing all this time? Even Josh must be tested. And we don't play until God is one hundred percent satisfied. If certain pieces are missing, we won't play at all."

"No. God would never let that happen," Dianna said, shaking her head.

A frown crept over the watcher's face, and she looked at

the ground. "Dianna, this isn't the first time this earth has played. In fact, we haven't won yet."

Dianna stared at the group of children walking past. One of them was waving his stuffed hammerhead shark at her. "What are you talking about?" she whispered.

"This earth has been used before. There have been other Primes. Just, for some reason or other, they failed. Why do you think the Bible opens up with God saying let's start over and tells Adam and Eve to repopulate the earth?"

"I don't know," the girl said, shaking her head, confused.

"I wish Thomas were here to explain this. He's the better historian. But here it goes. I don't know what happened to the other Primes. I do know that the universe functions like a well-oiled machine. It's so precise, in fact, you can practically map not only where we've been but where we're going. The earth itself was formed a long time ago. You can take a shovel and a pail and have a field day, for all I care. It'll tell you exactly what everybody knows. This earth is very old."

"Yeah."

"But the Bible is correct too," Nina said. "It says God finished creation in six days and rested on the seventh. It also says a day with God is as a thousand years, and most people forget that little tidbit. So right now, we're sitting on six thousand years of recorded history, right?"

"Yeah. Roughly, I guess," the girl said.

"Good. Now follow me. Have you ever heard of the zodiac?"

"Yeah. I mean, I've read about it."

"Well, it's based on the movements of the universe and the gravitational field they exert on each other and the human brain. The movements are called a procession, and we actually move backwards through the zodiac."

"I didn't know that."

"It's true," Nina said. "Each of the zodiac is roughly two thousand, one hundred and fifty years. The Creator made the newest set of angels and demons in the age of Capricorn, the half-goat, half-fish. I don't have the clearance to find out what happened in their age. Thomas and I were created during the time of Gemini and inserted into the time stream near the age of Taurus, when everybody was worshiping the golden calf. Then another two thousand years or so years later, we were in Egypt during the age of Aries, when everybody had rams in front of their pyramids. Then came the age of Pisces. It was conveniently heralded in by an avatar name Jesus. I'm sure you've seen the fish that people use to identify him with and know that he called himself a fisher of men."

Dianna raised an eyebrow, "You've gotta be kidding me, right?"

"No," Nina said. "As crazy as this sounds, it's true. And we're not in the age of Pisces anymore. We're in Aquarius. Every little bit about this age screams exactly what it is; it's the age of information."

"So?" Dianna said.

"You might not realize, because you didn't live through the '60s and '70s, like I did. That time opened the door to what you're holding in your hand," she said, pointing at Dianna's phone. "I'm not going to give you some sob story about how things were different way back when. But I'm being deathly serious when I say that in your hand is every bit of information that Ramon had to drive to the library and search for hours to find. And Ramon's dad might have just wondered what an answer was, but he was unable to make the trip to town because of his responsibilities. Many of the questions your grandfather pondered largely went unanswered and just became speculations."

"I understand that, Nina. But the whole six thousand year thing and where we are. What's that got to do with Josh and me?"

"Because," Nina replied, "Aquarius is the last age. If you don't succeed, then just like before, a natural disaster will take out civilization. It could possibly be an asteroid, flood, or an earthquake. It doesn't matter. But everything gets melted down to prima matter, angels included; and we start back at square one. In two thousand years, when we hit Capricorn again, we'll have new angels, new demons, new half fish, and new half goat, but the same God. Another try. It's that simple.

"The training you're about to go through is serious stuff that generation upon generation of avatars and dream benders have sworn secrecy not to reveal, to protect not only themselves but humanity as well. The general public couldn't handle these things any more than a ten-year-old should take their SATs just because they go to school. But now is the time, in the age of Aquarius; the age of information. Now that the six thousand years, or six days of creation are passed, we have until your eighteenth birthday before the war commences. And afterwards, the Creator will rest for the seventh day, or the next thousand years. After that, if all is well, the Creator will add this world into its permanent network within His brain. If unsuccessful, then it's a wrap."

"But--"

"No buts, Dianna. Save it for the archaeologist, who digs up your bones eighty thousand years from now, wondering if you're a distant relative of his race. We're building a potential part of the Creator's mind here, and he doesn't use spare parts. There are no exceptions with Him. We're in this together. Either you and Josh are worthy, and we all win; or you guys lose and we all start over."

Dianna sighed, "Can I just stick with what I know?"

"You could," Nina said, nodding. "But unless I teach you about how the world really works, you'd never be able to notice that, while we passively walked through thousands of gallons of water, we strolled past the different zodiac signs; like the water, the fish, the crab, the sea calf, the sea lion, and all the others. Our soul mates, who are our opposites, are probably actively making choices in a totally opposite environment to this right now."

"I so wish you hadn't said that," Dianna shook her head.

"The hazards of being a young god," Nina said, patting her head.

"Like, seriously, every one of them," Dianna said, double-checking, as they walked off.

"Yep," Nina said, "from the rocker wearing the vintage Scorpions shirt to the two teenage twins in front of us, who made fun of the tour guide and called her an old goat."

Chapter 28

On the walk back to the campsite, Josh tried to contemplate the situation he was in, but his brain just wouldn't work. The nagging withdrawal symptoms kept distracting him. And pretty soon, all he could think about was the intense nausea and his jittery muscles. Were his friends somehow working with the Monarchy? It didn't seem possible, but he knew Thomas wouldn't lie.

It was so hard to keep his head straight and fight off the anxiety. No sooner had his mind grasped a fact than it slipped away, and his mind wandered to the next thought. Josh reminded himself that last night truly had happened the way he remembered, and his so-called friends had tried to cover it up. But just as quickly, he remembered everything they'd done for him. The panic hit him again, like a speeding Mac truck. The thought occurred to him that he could be losing his mind. It was an unsettling thought, to say the least. He really had to get his pills, so he could ditch this feeling and think again. He could hear Charlie's voice, along with Deus and Phyllis. All he could see, when he walked up, was Billy cleaning up paper plates from dinner. The steady glow of the lantern was shining like a beacon on the picnic table.

"Hey, where's Charlie?" Josh asked, as he walked up quickly.

"Oh, they're two campsites over drinking beers. They're already dressed for the Burning Man." The spiky-haired teen glanced cautiously at Josh. "Are you okay?"

"I'm cool," Josh lied, looking at his skin under the lantern's glow. He was pretty sweaty. Inside he felt like he was dying. "When we got separated, I forgot that Charlie had the pills in his vest pocket, so I'm kind of having a hard time right now. There's some in my bag," he said. Making a beeline for the flap, he bent down and pushed his way into the nylon tent.

"Hey, there you are." Josh could smell the sweet nectar of Angela's perfume, before he realized she was completely naked. "I hope you don't mind. I needed a place to change," she said, not making the slightest attempt to cover herself up. Immediately, Josh's head began to reel. Even as bad as he felt, there was something so dark inside of him that he wanted to take her right there, without any words. He knew that she'd let him.

"What are you doing in here?" Josh asked, as his face flushed. He wasn't embarrassed in the slightest, but he could feel his face grow hot.

"Bai needed a little privacy in the girls' tent. Since Charlie was with Deus, I figured I'd change in your guys' tent. Besides, it's nothing I'm sure you haven't seen before." It was true. Over the past two days, he had seen so much flesh he thought he was desensitized to it. But one look at Angela's perfect olive skin, and Josh immediately knew he was wrong. Nothing could have prepared him for this. What he saw below her hips and between her thighs made him ache for the release her touch would surely bring.

"Are you okay, Josh?" she asked, as she slid her panties on.

"It's cool," Josh said, breaking his stare. "I just left the party favors in the room, and I'm kind of feeling it." By the glow of the hanging lantern, he made his way to his sports bag. "Goddamn," Josh thought to himself, as he unzipped his black bag. "I feel like I'm on fire right now, even though I'm covered in sweat." Right now he knew he didn't have time to take pills and wait for them to fix him. He needed something quicker, so he grabbed his little stash of opium and his pipe. "I'll give you some privacy," Josh said, looking to duck out of the tent.

"Hey, I was wondering," Angela said, from behind him. "Who wants to see a big statue on fire? If you're down, we could spend some time by ourselves and have some fun in the tent. I think we really owe it to ourselves to end this summer with some great memories."

"Let me just hook myself up real quick," Josh said nervously, his temples pounding. He really didn't want to blow her off. If he didn't get something on board, and quickly, he was going to throw up. And the heat in the tent was making it worse. Stepping out into the cooler night air and taking a deep breath, Josh packed the bowl with the sticky opium and lit it up. He took two good, long hits off the small, blue, glass pipe.

After a few breaths, he took a third long draw for good measure. Opium didn't have quite the same effects as the pills, but he'd found the effects were almost instantaneous. That made it was his usual drug of choice for when he rolled out of bed. It always counteracted the side effects and got him back into the groove.

Taking a deep breath of fresh air, Josh felt the high wash over him. The pounding in his head immediately eased off, and he began to notice the sounds of the other campsites. He couldn't hear Charlie, but he did hear Deus's loud, booming voice among the neighboring tents. Josh lifted the pipe to his lips one more time, but stopped when he heard Billy's voice.

"Hey, baby steps, big guy." Billy was sitting by the campfire, with the lantern next to him. "Come have a seat," he motioned to Josh. "I have a business proposition. Something I think will be beneficial for us both."

Right now Billy was the last person Josh wanted to talk to. He was still nervous about what Thomas had said, but he didn't want to tip him off either. So he headed over to the fire. Sinking down into his chair, Josh thought about the past few hours. He couldn't even begin to sort it out. One thing was certain though, he never wanted to feel like that again.

"So where did you wander off to earlier?" the spiky-haired teen asked with a devious smile on his face.

"I met some girls. I lost track of the time," Josh replied, rubbing his nose.

Bringing his arms up across his chest, Billy stroked his chin. "No, you didn't, Josh. You're a shitty liar. Like most people, you can't help but touch your nose after telling a falsehood. I learned that one at a manager's conference twenty years ago."

The odd statement hit Josh like a left hook. "How did you go to a conference before you were born?" he asked nervously.

"Let me guess," Billy said, flicking his index finger on his chin. "Thomas finally came out of hiding to try and change your mind about the path you're so obviously well-suited to."

"He did," Josh nodded. His pride was stinging a little from the realization that Billy wasn't just affiliated with the demons, but he probably was one.

"Did he tell you about the one true path, as he calls it? Or did he tell you about your other options? Because you most definitely have options."

"He said that I could definitely change the outcome, and I'm not necessarily the Antichrist."

"Geez, would you get a load of yourself? First of all, I never really liked that name. It's just so negative. And it's not like the Monarchy or being the Dark Half is bad. I want to remind you that you're up to your neck in tits and ass. Seriously, you might want to consider who has been better to you than me?"

"I don't know," Josh said, feeling the familiar anger and spite begin to rise within him. "Why don't we talk about what went down last night and the group lie that followed in the morning? Are any of you human?"

Billy grinned and shook his head. Josh noticed that his teeth, which were perfect before, now appeared pointy and yellowish. "No, but, technically, neither are you. And your buddy Charlie, we all know the word normal in the classic sense, definitely doesn't apply to him either."

"Why do all this?" Josh said, standing up. "The façade, the lies. None of this was real." Billy glared at him, his face a mask of shadows, trapped by the glow of the lantern on one side and the fire on the other.

"I fabricated one, big lie so that I could bring to you many smaller truths," he said, folding his hands and locking eyes with the boy. "Not to tie you down, like Thomas would and has done, but to set you free. You see, Thomas has a vested interest in you, as well as the Monarchy. He may talk a mean game, but I'll double down and let it ride that I have your back infinitely better than he does. And I think I've shown that." Josh marveled at how both sides were not as they seemed. He wondered if anybody was telling the complete truth.

"I've no doubt Thomas spoke to you of struggle and pain. That's his nature. I'll tell you a story of easy street, and it's no lie. You've lived it all summer long. I'm telling you the truth, when I say that the lake house and this summer is nothing more than the tip of the iceberg. You haven't even seen good times yet."

Josh nodded, "Go on."

"If anything, Thomas is predictable. I'm sure he painted a picture about a difficult, final battle filled with suffering and sacrifice, where you get to be mankind's savior. And that could happen. But if you side with me, I'll give you a happy ending right now, today. All you have to do is say one little word."

Josh stared into the moon hanging off in the distance. What did he really want? The words the gypsy and Thomas said had raised his spirits, but now Billy was showing him what Josh had felt at the beginning of the summer. He didn't really want all the hassle that came with being the Prime.

"I can show you a new path," Billy snarled, as the flames of the fire danced gleefully in response. I brought you here to show you a fundamental rule of energy. It manifested in the way we all felt, as our wolf pack stalked through the throngs of awestruck sheep." Leaning forward, towards the dancing flames, Billy's spiky hair resembled little horns, as he continued to speak. "I know you felt it, the indestructible feeling, when our energies were merged. I felt it too, and so did Deus."

"I don't know about awestruck," Josh said, more than a little skeptical, as he noticed a blonde child in white shirt and shorts stare in fright as she walked by.

"Oh, but they were. The hundreds of benders in attendance here saw us for what we truly were. And they were crushed by a sea of despair. Do you know why?" Josh shrugged his shoulders, as Billy smirked.

"Because hippie benders are the royal flush of losers, and they're too feeble-minded to realize it. Any one of them could be a beacon to the human race. God knows they have the right ideas and the power to make it happen. But they're too passive. They think a higher power favors them, and everything will work out groovy. After raising their energy, they almost always pollute their minds by smoking weed. And no matter how good the intentions they have are, they never seem to understand that comfort is the acid that eats away at Nietzsche's will to power. Us being here reminds them of that one, basic fact."

Billy stood with his hands pressed against each other, and then he pointed his finger at Josh. "Even you know, with just a little experience, that your anger almost burned the lake house down. And despite your valiant attempt to stop the fiery serpents, what happened?" Josh thought back to that night and how he tried as hard as he could to stop the pillars of flame and failed miserably.

"You found that desperation or urgency can't trump anger or rage or fury. You already know what the crowd of benders here can't accept, and that's why they lose. People like me continue to backdoor people like them. All they do is complain about how the man keeps them down or how things could be."

Josh nodded. "That might be, but we're at the end. So it

doesn't really matter."

Billy grinned. "Good point. But what are you going to do? Will you save an undeserving, lazy few? Look at the state of this world. Hell, just look at America in general. If you think everybody's on the same page, you'd be wrong. Millions still don't vote, but they feel justified in complaining, when things never change. Even worse, look at any rating system for TV, and the incredible number of people who religiously watch reality TV shows, especially the ones that have been proven to be completely staged. The numbers are in the hundreds of millions. They don't fucking care, Josh. Is that who you're willing to suffer for? Because I'll tell you; these people don't need a messiah. They need a master to tell them what to do. And that is the role I'll gladly give you.

"They need a king!" shouted Billy, his eyes beginning to glow. "And that king is you. Trained by me, not Thomas, who isn't even worthy enough to be the shit stain on the back of God's boxer briefs. What tribute do you think he'll pay to you as king? Nothing. I, however, humbly present you with this." Josh watched, as Billy bent down to a group of boxes by the lantern. He'd assumed they were just spare batteries. Billy sat down and took out the contents, holding it up to the light.

"In my hand, I present to you my humble tribute," his voice triumphantly rang with satisfaction. "While we were brainstorming these last few weeks, trying to figure out your hopeless living situation, I came up with my magnum opus."

"What is it?" Josh asked, his curiosity getting the better of him.

"A household kit of nasal-administered Naloxone." Josh knew from his time on the fire engine that Naloxone was a powerful opiate blocker. Many times he'd seen it given for a pill, opium or heroin overdose. Within the minute, the patient, who was near death, was now awake and breathing.

"This kit," Billy said triumphantly, "is comprised of multiple strength vials, depending on what the patient has taken, whether it's pills or what not."

"What about the withdrawal symptoms?" Josh asked, knowing that these people who'd received the drug, usually went through violent DTs.

"That's the beauty of this kit," Billy said, with pride. "Each vial has its own sliding reference wheel, which tells the user how many MLs of the medication to give, steering the overdose from the edge of oblivion but not awakening them or sending them into withdrawals."

"Fascinating," Josh whispered, "but the hospitals already have the plunger and needle version, which they use by IV. Why would they switch?"

Billy sat down with his new invention and held up one of the other boxes. "You mean this?" Opening the box, he pulled out the ampule that looked like a shot with the needle on top. "The nasal spray isn't for the hospital."

"I have the boys on Capitol Hill lobbying for the approval to release these for public use. Every clinic across America and Canada will include these life-saving devices as a mandatory measure with any opiate prescribed, whether it's for pain or whatnot. Even the pharmacies will carry it to be sold to Joe Junkie himself, if he so pleases. The profits will be staggering, and this is my gift to you. It's the solution to both you and Charlie's impossible dilemma and a key to a bright, new future." Josh was stunned by the presentation. He'd thought the three weeks of opium-induced brainstorming was basically unfruitful.

"Which brings us to the moment of truth," Billy said, his eyes narrowing down. "There are only two people in this world, Josh; those getting fucked and those doing the fucking. Which side is it going to be for you?" Besieged by doubts and contradictions, Josh tried to wade through them all. But after listening to both Thomas and Billy tell their sides of the story, Josh still felt indecisive.

"I'm waiting, Josh," Angela's voice came from the tent. Billy's eyes flashed towards the tent, and the edges of his mouth turned upward, into a dark smile.

"Last night Charlie lost his virginity to the most hideous girl I've ever seen. Her braids stunk of weed and patchouli oil. I'm sure her breath smelled just as bad, if not worse than that pit she calls a pussy. An unsavory lifetime memory of what should be a man's first time. But Charlie isn't a king, and you are. And what would a king be without a queen, Josh? And what a queen Angela could be. Just think about it. Every man in this place would kill to be in your position. Her beauty is sublime and intoxicating, and her hair smells like freshly picked flowers."

Looking over at the tent, Josh saw Angela spread apart the folds of the nylon tent to reveal her naked body. His heart began beating harder, in anticipation of what was about to take place. Angela motioned with her finger and then stepped away, back into the tent. Billy nodded towards Josh.

"Just as Angela was born on this ancient lake bed, so shall you be reborn from a boy to a man, by getting up and choosing her as your queen." In his head, Josh felt like he was on fire, which seemed appropriate. In the distance, he could see the man-made construct known as The Burning Man engulfed by flames. The cheers of the spectators rang in the distance, as they danced around the burning effigy.

On one hand, Josh knew Billy was right. He didn't want to suffer, especially for ungrateful people. And, after all, hadn't Billy taken care of him from every angle? He knew that what lay in that tent was the cause of his aching member, and it was also, ironically enough, the cure of it. But on the other hand, he'd envisioned his first time a million times, and it was always with Dianna. As badly as he wanted Angela, Josh knew that he only had one queen. The girl in that tent could never take her place.

"So what will it be, Josh?" asked the demon that was Billy. Josh knew his answer. He just didn't know how to say it. He took a deep breath and gathered up his courage.

"Excuse me," a young girl said from behind him. Josh turned to see a blonde girl in black shorts and a white tank top. "I'm looking for my twin. Her name's Diana. She was right by here. She has a white shirt and shorts on."

"Get the hell out of here!" Billy screamed, his voice seething with hatred. Right before his eyes, Josh watched as the flames rose higher into the night sky. "Well?" Billy said, standing up and dusting off his pants. "I guess I have your answer."

"I guess so," Josh said, nodding his head warily.

"Even now," Hasden said, his voice shaking with fury, "I'm surprised at how powerful you are. But I'll crush you, just like I crushed your father."

Josh stood up slowly, his vision instantly taking on the familiar reddish hue. "What did you say?"

"You heard him, you weak, worthless, pansy," Angela said, stepping from the tent fully clothed. Her face looked to Josh like it was about to crack. "What a disappointment you are," she sneered with contempt. "Not strong enough to be the messiah, but too weak to be the Antichrist." Josh watched her through his red vision, hate coursing through his veins. All of a sudden, he felt alive and ready to take on anything. "I'm going to kill your girlfriend, Josh. Then you'll beg me just to look at you." She spat on the ground.

"It's funny," Billy said, his top lip curling up, like he was a wolf. "Time constantly repeats itself, like an echo in a canyon. You aren't the first to be tempted in the desert." Josh nodded grimly, as he realized that was what this whole thing was. It was all a trap.

"There's only one man who's ever said no to Angela, and

that was your father. And we all know where that got him."

Josh glared at the two of them. He felt like he could kill them right now and wipe their stupid smiles from their faces. He looked over to the fire and felt it call for him. It was practically begging for something to consume. The only thing that was holding him back was Josh knew he had no skill at energy manipulation. There was a sneaking suspicion in his mind that he might hate these two enough to burn them down where they stood, but he might not be able to stop what he started. There was still fifty thousand innocents here.

"If what you said is true, and you caused my dad's death, I'll personally eat both of your souls. But not until I'm eighteen." Josh could hear the guttural vibration in his voice. It basically meant that it was go time. He wanted to engage them both so badly. He held back for the same reason that he suspected the demons did; neither one of them wanted to break the preset law placed by the Creator.

Josh stared at the two of them, his vision shifting back to normal. And then, suddenly, Angela arched her back and screamed, falling on the ground as if in agony. Writhing on the ground, the woman's face began to contort into a grotesque mask of pain and then back into her usual, sweet smile, while laughing maniacally.

"Oh, shit!" Billy said, falling to his knees. "Please don't do this here, Angela." Josh backed away in disbelief at the scene that was unfolding in front of him. The look on her face was bone chilling. It seemed that she was arguing with somebody who wasn't even there. Then, to his surprise, she began speaking in another language. The strangest part of all to Josh was the way Billy, who had just mere moments before acted like he owned the whole world, was now in the dust begging helplessly.

"It's going to be okay," he said, stroking her hair. "Please just hold on. Deus!" he shouted towards the neighboring tents, "get over here!" Josh had almost forgotten about the three other demons.

"Satan, help me!" Angela screamed, slamming her head backwards repeatedly against the ground and immediately switching to the other tongue. Josh tensed up, as he saw the group appear. His spirit immediately fell, as soon as he realized they had Charlie flanked on all sides.

"What the hell's going on here?" shouted Deus, as he stomped up to the campsite.

"Geez," thought Josh. "He looks even bigger and angrier than the first time I saw him."

"Dude. What's happening to Angela?" Charlie said, as she kicked and screamed on the ground. "It looks like she's trying to fight off an imaginary attacker."

"I want you to take a good look," Billy shouted, staring directly into Josh's eyes. "Look at the faces that called you brother. Because when you see them again, it will be as enemies."

"Don't you have bigger things to worry about?" Josh asked, looking at the convulsing girl next to Billy's side.

"So I guess it's a no?" Deus asked, scooping up a handful of boxes next to the lamp.

"Yeah," Billy said, still glaring at Josh. "He made his choice. He wants to do things the hard way." Emptying the boxes, Deus grabbed four of them in one hand and drove them into Angela's jerking thigh.

"Holy crap," Charlie said, astonished.

"Get over here. We're leaving," Josh yelled at the redhead. "I don't have time to explain."

Deus removed the needles from her thigh and drove them into the ground. "What do you mean, Michaels? The fun's just starting," he said with a snarl.

"Yeah, Michaels," the girls both said mockingly. "The fun's just starting."

Josh backed up towards Charlie, as Angela's twitching slowed down, and her eyelids fluttered, finally closing. As they did, Billy gritted his teeth and shouted. "The rules say I can't physically hurt you or kill you. But they don't say anything about the redheaded stepchild."

"What the hell's going on here?" Charlie said. Josh could see the confusion written all over his face.

"Run, Charlie!" Josh screamed, as Deus began heading towards them. He'd seen the look in his eyes before, in the video of him choking the gym teacher. Taking a few steps forward towards Charlie, Josh immediately saw his path was barred by Phyllis and Bai, who seemingly appeared from nowhere.

"Where do you think you're going?" Phyllis said.

He immediately felt a feeling of true helplessness wash over him, as he watched Charlie slowly back up, stammering, "I don't understand. We're friends."

Josh didn't know what to expect from the two girls walking towards him. "Door swings both ways, dipshit," the blonde said, her voice dripping with sarcasm. "We can't hurt you, but you can't hurt us either, without it being considered a challenge. So how about a friendly hug, for old time's sake?" she said. Both her and Bai wrapped their arms around him and began to chant devilishly, "We love you to death, Josh." Josh tried to pull away, but the girls both hugged even tighter. "Are you challenging us?" Phyllis chuckled. "We don't want to fight you. You're practically our half-brother."

"What the hell is going on here?" Charlie said, right before Deus open-hand slapped him in the face, sending him to the ground.

"Charlie!" Josh screamed so hard the veins on his neck felt as if they might burst, sending both girls into hysterics. "Don't do this!" Josh screamed, trying to push forward with his legs.

The girls dragged him back, chanting, "We love you,

brother. Give us a hug."

"Why are you doing this?" Charlie said, completely stunned. He was holding his face with one hand and holding out his other arm in defense, as if that could stop the giant teen.

"Why so nervous, Shaggy? Did you leave the Mystery Machine double parked outside?" Deus said, chuckling.

"I'm not trying to fight you, man. I thought we were friends."

"Friends?" the demon said, amazed. He spoke it like he'd never heard the word before. "The English language doesn't even contain characters that could express how much I truly dislike you. I'd probably need a refresher course in Hebrew or ancient Sanskrit to express how much I loathe your kind."

"What?" was all Charlie could stammer, as he cowered in fear.

"Do you know what your problem is, Charlie? It's the same goddamn problem that most teenagers have. You want to sing the blues," the demon said, reaching over and grabbing a hold of Charlie's wrist. "But you ain't paid the dues," the demon said, twisting the teen's arm and then jerking. Josh closed his eyes as he heard the sickening "crack," and his friend scream in pain.

"Oh, God! Make it stop," Josh whispered, but the screams continued.

"Remember, we love you," Phyllis whispered mockingly into his ear, as they clutched him tighter. Josh opened his eyes and saw that Charlie's right arm was horribly broken. The bone had pierced the side of his forearm.

"Now, that is a singing voice," the demon shouted proudly. "See, you're getting better already. I must be a better teacher than I thought."

Turning to Billy, Josh pleaded. "Don't do this anymore. Please stop."

Billy snorted. "Not so goddamn high and mighty now; are

you? Deus, put the cherry on the sundae. Let's get out of here before security arrives with the cops." Deus fished into his pocket and pulled out the Naloxone shot. He took the cap off the needle and stared apathetically at Charlie. Trembling on his knees, Charlie clutched his broken arm, still too stunned to speak.

"Listen up, bitch boy," Deus said, looming menacingly over him. "I'm gonna visit you every now and then out in Milton, just to help coach you on your singing lessons. And the next song I'm going to teach you is called the leg bone used to be connected to the knee bone." Josh struggled against the two female demons, his feet digging into the desert floor. But he couldn't gain any ground towards Charlie. Suddenly, without warning, Phyllis and Bai let go and side-stepped Josh.

"See ya, Michaels," Phyllis said, flipping him off, while she walked towards Billy.

Josh ran towards Charlie and Deus, hoping it was all over. But when he saw the look in the demon's eyes, he knew it wasn't. Taking the Naloxone shot with the two inch needle, he held it up like a knife. "Remember just the tip, Charlie? Well, this is for talking nonstop that Saturday." Deus swung down hard, stabbing the boy in the spine and squeezing the plunger. "Here's a sweet little gift just for you," he said, whispering in the stunned boy's ear. "And remember; I know where you live. Scary commercials in a dark basement are the least of your worries now."

Josh ran up, just as Deus sprinted off. The look in the crying boy's eyes was almost more than he could bear. "Why?" Charlie screamed over and over, looking like the pain was unbearable. "Why?" Kneeling down, Josh removed the needle, tossing it aside in the sand. He wondered the same thing. Why?

After choosing what he thought was the correct path, why was Charlie punished so severely? He collapsed down on the warm desert floor, cradling his crying friend's head, screaming into the darkness of the night, "Somebody call 911!!"

But the tents were deserted. Everybody was standing on The Playa, dancing around The Burning Man.

Chapter 29

Staring at Nina, dumbfounded, Dianna shook her head and tried to pull herself out of the fog. The light of the fluorescent RV lamps blared intensely, causing the girl to look down at the bed. "What's the matter?" the watcher asked softly. "You were crying."

Dianna looked up to see the woman standing by the light switch, with concern written all over her face. If she was really crying, she hoped that she hadn't screamed as well. The dream was so vivid that she remembered that part. "I'm okay," she quietly said, hoping her father didn't come bursting in.

"What the hell?" Cammy said, rubbing her right side. "You elbowed me in the ribs."

"I'm sorry," Dianna said, shaking her head. "I just had the worst dream. And it seemed so real. It was like I was standing right there." Nina took her finger off the light switch and crossed over to the bed.

"What was it about?" Nina asked, still confused.

"Josh was in the desert, being pushed around. I was watching it like it was a movie. I remember he was surrounded by flames," she said, frustratingly shaking her head. It seemed that the clearer her thinking got, now that she was awake, the fuzzier the dream became, like it was somehow a sliding scale. "I remember two of my classmates were there, and there were demons too."

Nina's eyes widened in horror. "What did Josh do?"

Dianna could tell by the look on Nina's face she was highly disturbed by the last part. "For some reason, he wouldn't fight them. They didn't beat him up, either. Our other friend was attacked pretty badly though. His arm got broken." Nina breathed a sigh of relief.

"And that was it?"

"As far as I know," Dianna said. The vision was slipping away, like sand through her fingers. "It was just a dream; wasn't it?"

"You can never really tell," Nina said, a far-off look in her eyes. "But you may have actually seen a passage of his life, because of the passive sleep state you were in and the intensity of his emotions. Whatever the cause, we'll be home soon, and I'm sure we we'll be able to figure out things from there."

Cammy rolled her eyes. "I've got a great idea. Why don't you get on your cell phone and ask your husband how Josh is doing?"

"I wish it was that easy, but it's not. As the only two watchers, it's not advisable to have direct access to one another when on assignment. We only contact each other telepathically."

"Are you kidding me?" Cammy said, in disbelief.

Nina shook her head. "The work we do is highly important for all of Division's plans and agendas. If one of us were caught, it puts everything in jeopardy. So we usually wait to contact each other on the astral plane, while we're sleeping."

"And you're cool with this?" Cammy asked, accusingly.

"You act like I really have a choice," Nina replied. "It's more reliable than a cell phone, and it can't be traced. I can't help it, if Thomas isn't answering." Dianna knew the watcher better than most, and she could tell the woman was being stoic.

"How long has it been since you've seen him?" Cammy pried.

"The last time was right before school broke for summer vacation."

Cammy shook her head. "I would kick him to the curb."

"I would too, if I were mortal. But I'm not. I've spent thousands of years with him," Nina replied, grinning. "A summer isn't even a few hours, when you're immortal. It's not always like this." Moving behind Dianna, Nina grabbed the hairbrush off of the miniature nightstand, dragging the brush through Dianna's jet black hair. She continued, "When we're not on assignment, we lead semi-ordinary lives. We can disappear for years on end, changing our appearances and blending into society."

"All that sounds better," Cammy said, lying on her side.

"It is. I cherish those times. Some breaks are longer than others, and then there's always the off-chance that only one of us is on assignment."

"What do you do with your free time?" Dianna asked, getting drowsy again. The memory of the dream was all but gone now.

"Sometimes I go to school. I have a couple of degrees, one in business and the other in psychiatry. Every now and then, I work. It all depends. My favorite things to do are training and testing."

"Testing?" Dianna asked, opening her eyes.

"Sometimes I test to see if a possible candidate has abilities."

"You didn't test me."

"I didn't need to, silly. I already knew you had power."

"When was the last time you tested anybody?"

The woman put the brush down on the bed. "I wouldn't normally tell you this, but I don't want you to think I'm keeping secrets from you. I tested Josh," she admitted hesitantly.

"What?" Dianna stated in disbelief. "He never said anything about it."

"That's because he doesn't remember. His grandmother wiped his mind of certain elements of the test."

"I don't understand. Why?"

"One of the tests involves winning a large sum of money, to see if the candidate could influence the fates. Josh won the lottery that night."

Immediately, Cammy's head popped up. "Say what?"

"We immediately ripped up the ticket. The test isn't really to see if that candidate can win. If they do win, it's actually designed to see how they react to the loss."

"Oh, my God," Dianna exclaimed, putting her hands to her mouth. "What happened?"

"On that part, he could've done better," Nina said. "He threw out markers that indicated that for a Prime of his power, he's surprisingly immature and possibly not ready for the training."

"But that's not true," Dianna said, shaking her head. "He's way mature."

"No, Dianna. He just excels in certain outward characteristics. On the whole, as a total package, he falls short at this point."

Dianna wondered what the woman was talking about. Josh was incredibly courteous to everyone he met. He had manners and morals that far surpassed the norm. What was she expecting from him? The watcher's stiff standards seemed to bother her, but not half as much as the fact that Nina continually seemed to be withholding information. To Dianna, it was unnerving. She was getting tired of trusting the woman implicitly, only to find there were more secrets.

"I know the tests might seem stringent, but it's for the best. The teachings we give would give a peasant the ability to become a king, so they're not given lightly. In the wrong hands, the student could bring great harm to those around them and even themselves."

"Wrong hands?" Cammy said, raising an eyebrow.

"Like somebody who can't control their emotions, particularly their anger. Once the abilities emerge, if the student isn't well-developed, their anger could destroy them bit by bit, driving them insane. Take this lamp, for instance. If the bulb is clean, it casts out perfect, untainted light. But in a person who has mental baggage, it's like the bulb has a smudge or fingerprints on it. It casts shadows instead."

"My power would never do that, right?" Dianna asked.

"Most probably not. Anger isn't your strong suit; love is. Your power heals, but Josh can access anger and hate. They burn red hot. Out of the spectrum of emotions, it can be easily held, just like worry or spite. Once accessed, if the student doesn't make an effort to change the emotion, then it's the same as siphoning a gas tank. Once started, it will flow and drain as much energy as it can. That's why people, who lose their tempers, find themselves with low immune systems. The student gets ill, which gives them just one more reason to be angry. The cycle repeats itself, until the very power that the student prized is now a curse. It destroys them and everybody around them."

Looking at her sister, Cammy said, "You know what? I take it back. I like being normal."

"Now I'm worried. Nina, is Josh in trouble?"

"It's hard to say. From what I saw, he's extremely powerful. But he doesn't know how to control it. In fact, he can't really even perform most simple tasks. However, you, child, can heal on command and control your power at will."

"You mean like this?" Dianna said, her whole body covered in flames.

"Yes, like that," Nina chuckled, as the girl switched the power back off. "You're getting much better, but it's possible that he's a lot stronger than you. His powers seem to mirror the Creator's, which is bizarre. I've never seen an avatar with powers quite like his.

"Are you talking about the synchronicities?" Dianna asked.

"Yes. If you had any idea what the odds are that events can unfold in the manner he affects them, you would know the implications are astronomical. It means that, somewhere inside of him, Josh may already know how, why, and when certain events are going to unfold. And he also has a say as to what happens."

"That's actually really good," Dianna said, somewhat proud.

She'd seen him use the power before.

"Well, yes and no," Nina replied. "In the end, Josh has to be cleaned of all emotional problems, which he's constantly in peril of just because of the way his power works. We don't know if he'll be ten different types of crazy by the arrival of his eighteenth birthday, or whether he could change the world just by one super happy event. In my opinion, he's a wildcard."

"I've got a question," Dianna asked, looking at Nina. "Have you ever messed with my head?"

By the look on Nina's face, Dianna already knew the answer. She could tell by the way the woman's eyebrows and hair darkened ever so slightly. "The absolute truth," Nina said, holding up her right hand, "is I did access one, and only one, of your memories. I only did it for your protection."

"What are you talking about?" Cammy's eyes narrowed, as she rose off the bed. "And you didn't even tell her?"

"I didn't need to. I asked for permission to enter, and Dianna's subconscious let me in."

"When was this?" Dianna asked, feeling mildly hurt.

"When you met Josh. I needed to actually see the dream to see if you were fooling yourself. To a certain extent, I have to say, your memory is somewhat selective."

"I think the key to Josh's power was embedded in that dream, which was more vivid than anything I'd ever seen. I'm one hundred percent certain that his powers are locked in his subconscious, which is what created that dream and sent it as a calling card. That he bent the space/time continuum to deliver it to you at a different time only confirms it. I suspect that he actually grafted the one dream on top of the other, so that you'd spot him based on clues that were there. For some reason, his subconscious is keeping him in the dark. I don't know why."

"Was it something you saw revealed in the dream?" Dianna questioned, shaking her head.

"There were definitely clues," Nina said, nodding, "as to who was pulling the strings. The location was key, as well as the river where he saved your life."

"The Neponset?" Dianna asked.

"It's a Native American term," Nina replied. "It means he walks in his sleep, or, basically, the sleepwalker."

***

"Hey, do you mind if I smoke again?"

"Go right ahead," Josh said, thoroughly annoyed. The curly-haired cabdriver slapped the pack against his palm. Sparking up his lighter, he cheerfully said, "Smoke 'em, if you got 'em."

"Yeah, right," Josh mused. The whole cab smelled like an ashtray, and it was playing havoc with his nausea. Somehow, he didn't think the cabbie would be too cheery if he vomited all over the back of the cab. Which, given the withdrawals he was going through, was very likely. Glancing over, he saw that Charlie had finally passed out against the door. His fresh cast was gently rocking in his lap, as the cab made its way to Josh's house.

The past eighteen hours had been a nightmare of epic proportions. It had only taken the ambulance ten minutes to show up. By then, Charlie looked like his body was in borderline shock. The Naloxone shot Deus had plunged into his spine entirely blocked all of the opiates in his system, and he was throwing up violently and sweating uncontrollably. Josh soon found that the demons had thrown his and Charlie's bags on the fire, before they left. So when he arrived at the hospital with Charlie, basically all he had was his ID and the clothes on his back. But the fun was only starting. Soon, the police showed up. As Charlie was getting treated, Josh got to play fifty questions with the detectives who basically accused him of being a liar after he gave a full statement of the events.

Apparently half of the people involved didn't exist. William Hasden didn't have a son named Billy, but there was a Deus and a Phyllis that worked for him. However, they were sixty-six and forty. They hadn't seen their teen years in quite some time. At one point, one of the detectives had asked if they'd gotten jumped trying to score heroin, because they were obviously addicts. Even at this moment, Josh could recall the laughter, when he denied being high. The detectives both read him the riot act on that one as well. It was one of the most humiliating things Josh had gone through. But that was merely the bread for the shit sandwich God would force Josh to eat that morning, because then the hospital contacted Sam and Sue. Then the ass kicking contest really began to get underway.

He was fairly certain Charlie would be grounded for life after this one. Sam was pretty upset, because they'd planned on moving today. His mom had already packed the small truck. She was just waiting for Richard to get off his night shift and get enough sleep to function. So basically, they were both in a holding pattern for Josh.

After both mothers had wired money and secured new tickets, Charlie and Josh were almost on their way. But they had a small problem, and that was Josh's withdrawals. So Charlie asked for more pain medication for his arm. The doctors sparingly gave him a few pain pills, which the redhead promptly turned over to Josh. The first thing Josh noticed was that they were piss weak and barely did anything for him. Secondly, it was obvious they weren't going to last throughout the plane ride.

Now his life was right back at square one, and it was ten times worse than before. How the hell was he ever going to get out of this? And when would the parade of tears end? Josh shook his head, remembering he'd been promised he could save the world. Yet the only thing that had happened over the summer was he'd picked up a crippling addiction. He may have felt like a king in the desert, but now it was back to reality, and things looked pretty bleak. Even worse, his phone had been in his duffel bag, and that was toast. But it was okay. The next time he saw Thomas, he was sure he'd receive some lecture on how the universe strives for balance or some shit like that. "Balance," Josh laughed.

"You say something?" the cabdriver asked?

"Sorry," Josh said, snapping back to reality and realizing where he was. He was delirious right now. He could barely hold it together. In between the desert, the hospital, and the extreme paranoia that he and Charlie both experienced on the flight home, he didn't know if he was coming or going. At any minute, he wouldn't have been surprised if Billy had poked his head out from one of the chairs, even though he knew they were on a different flight. At one point, Charlie freaked out and swore that the pilot's voice sounded exactly like Deus. He was convinced that the demon was going to crash the plane. All in all, Josh felt completely destroyed. He needed some opium to smoke, but he had no idea where to score some.

"Hey, Charlie. Get up," he said, reaching over and lightly touching Charlie's shoulder. He shot up like a Jack-in-the-Box, surprising not only the cabdriver, but Josh as well. "Are you okay?"

He sat with his eyes wide open. Josh knew the look. It was sheer terror. "I'm okay," Charlie said sharply, looking around.

"We're almost home," Josh said, in as soothing a voice as he could muster.

Relaxing, the lanky teen sunk down into the gray interior of the cab seat. "Dude, I'm trippin. Don't mind me."

"It's totally cool," Josh assured him, even though he didn't believe it himself. He was just glad Charlie had forgiven him. He knew Thomas would have a fit, if he found out he'd told Charlie all about the background of the dream benders, avatars, and the Primes. Josh really didn't care at this point. It had to be done. It was the only way he could explain why he stood by, like an idiot, while his best friend got mauled by a demon.

In the end, Josh couldn't really tell who got the better half of the deal, though. If he had the chance, he would take Charlie's part, if it would take away the constant feeling of helplessness he had been experiencing since last night. The feeling had really started on his last birthday, but Josh knew he covered it up with drugs and alcohol over the summer. After last night, it was back with a vengeance. He felt like he was spinning out of control, and he didn't know what to do.

"Okay, guys, that'll do it," the cabdriver said, as they glided around the corner. The first thing Josh saw was the moving truck, packed and waiting at the front of the house.

"Well, I guess this is it," Charlie said, looking at Josh.

"I guess so. As soon as I get a new phone, I'll call you."

"Are you really going to a new school next week?"

Josh hadn't thought about it. In fact, he hadn't thought about a lot of things. It just seemed he was hiding from the mounting pressure that life was throwing on him. The whole summer was an endless cycle of lying to himself, repeatedly saying that everything would get better and that he'd get off the oxy. But he never did. Now, here he was.

The old cab's brakes squealed, as it stopped at the curb. Josh swung his legs out of the door and was greeted by the cool Massachusetts breeze. "Finally," he thought, taking in the fresh air. It smelled so good and clean, which was good for the nausea, but did little to ease his massive flu-type symptoms.

"Hey, you okay kid?" the cabbie asked from the driver side window.

"Yeah, I'm fine," he said, while thinking to himself, "Can't anybody mind their own business?"

"It's just that it's 65 degrees right now, and you're sweating like somebody has a loaded gun to your head." Josh looked down at his red tee shirt, which was dotted with his own sweat.

"I hadn't noticed," Josh said, handing the money to the man. "I hope I'm not coming down with anything." To some extent, it gave him a thrill, when the cabdriver took the money from his hand but put it in the ashtray, wiping his hands vigorously on his jeans. A strange sense of foreboding washed over him, as he looked at the front of his house. He didn't even want to think about how pissed off Larry and Sam were going to be.

"Hey, do you have any pills stashed?" Charlie asked, as Josh stepped away from the departing cab.

"If I did, I would've told you. Believe me," he replied. Truth be told, he didn't really know. But he planned on going through his dirty clothes and his desk as soon as he made it through the door.

"Well, I really wish you wouldn't go, man."

"What are my options?" Josh asked, shrugging his shoulders.

"Screw this place. Do you think I want to stay here and wait for my blues tutor to show up?" Josh wanted to say that Deus was just trying to scare the teen, but who knew what he'd really do.

"What do you have in mind?"

"I don't know yet," Charlie said, but I'll figure something out. Maybe we could run away and join the military. Hell, I'll join the circus, if it'll take us away from here."

"What about your meds?" Josh asked. The last thing they needed was to make the situation worse by Charlie flipping out.

"I'll figure something out," Charlie said, turning towards his house. "Text me as soon as you get a new phone."

"I will," Josh replied, heading up the driveway. As he watched Charlie walk off, he wondered if he was doing all that he could for him. After all, this was his fault. And now he was just leaving to another city and leaving his friend to deal with the mess. Gripping the front door, Josh thought, "Here goes nothing." He swung the door aside and stepped in to see Sam and Richard waiting on the couch.

"Thanks for finally showing up," Richard said.

"Sorry."

"Have a seat, dear. We need to talk," his mother said, nodding to the chair across from them.

"That's funny," he thought. Something didn't seem right. He nervously walked over to the chair. "What's going on?" he asked, wiping his sweaty palms on his shirt. Sam folded her arms.

"Well, we were hoping to make the best of the daylight today, but I wasn't planning on waking up to a phone call from an ER nurse."

"I know," Josh groaned. "I'm sorry. I should've told you."

"What have you been thinking, young man? This whole summer you've been off doing whatever you want. You rarely text or call."

"I lost my phone," Josh said anxiously.

"Great!" Sam exclaimed. "This is, what, the second time in three months?" Josh nodded. He just had to accept what was coming to him. "Well, I hope it was a blast," she said, with a tinge of sorrow in her voice, "because it stops here."

"I understand." All things considered, he knew this was coming. He meekly looked over at Richard, who was literally giving him the evil eye.

"Your mother and I have been talking, and we made a decision last week. The stunt you pulled this weekend only reinforces our decision. I've suspected, since the hospital, that you've been using opiates."

Josh thought about it for a second. He knew he couldn't lie anymore. It had all gone too far. He needed help. But he'd be damned if he was giving in to anybody other than his mother. In fact, he wasn't gonna give this tool the satisfaction. "So I party. Big deal."

"Well, I hate to say it, Josh, but the party's over. You're

staying here with Larry for the night."

"What?" Josh asked, confused.

"I told you, you weren't coming into my home under the influence. And I meant it. Your mother and I are moving this stuff tonight, while we can. I don't have the vacation time to take tomorrow off. I've got to be to work tonight, and the truck has to be turned in by 9:00 am. So you can expect me to be here at 9:30 sharp. After that, Larry and myself are taking you to rehab."

"This is bullshit!" Josh yelled. "I could detox at home."

"I'm sorry," his mother said, looking highly stressed. "I really want to believe that you can, but..."

Glancing down, Josh could see Richard's hand on his mother's thigh. "Dear, we talked about this, remember?" Richard said sternly.

"Talked about what?" Josh snapped angrily.

"About your temper and your mother not enforcing the proper rules."

"What are you talking about? If my mother asked me to walk to Boston, I would do it. I don't have a problem quitting the drugs, and I can handle this on my own."

"I don't think you can," Richard countered. "You're under the illusion that you're in control, but this drug is highly addictive. I've seen it a million times. Effective immediately, you no longer have a car."

"Are you high? My grandfather gave me that car. It's mine."

"I know, but I've talked to Larry. We both agree that it's better that we keep you on a short leash. Plus, you guys never transferred title. Technically, he still owns it. Once we get you to Boston without a car, your mom can have peace of mind that you're not over here hobnobbing with the neighbor boy, who's obviously a bad influence."

"There's really no need for this," Josh shook his head.

"And from now on," Sam said, "we're getting you a basic cell phone. No internet or texting."

"I need that, though. I have a girlfriend."

"I forgot about that," she said, turning to Richard.

"Honey, it's like I said. You can't let him push you around, because he'll take advantage of you. He's been doing it all summer."

"Mom," Josh pleaded. "I'll go to rehab. Just don't take my car away."

"Time for deals is over, Josh," Richard said, in an uncaring voice. Despite the fact he knew they were trying to help him, Josh couldn't help but feel Richard was going out of his way to be hard on him. He had gotten enough attitude from the detectives at the hospital. He was probably thinking the same thing they had; he was just a junkie. But he wasn't. Personally, he didn't care for the tone.

"I said I'd go," Josh said, trying to compose himself. "Just, please. I need the car and the phone. I can't have a girlfriend and not be able to see her."

"Sorry, no deal. You've mistreated and manipulated your mother for the last time. You've known all about today for quite a while. You laughed it off, and that's disrespectful. She didn't want this, but look at what happened because she refused to lay down the law." Josh nodded his head. He just wanted this to be over with. He was tired, and he felt like he was going to be sick. Richard snorted. "It's a shame. You can tell the impact not having a father figure has had on your life."

Immediately, Josh felt like he'd been touched by a live wire. "What the hell did you just say?" Josh hissed.

"You heard me," Richard said, standing up. "Enjoy your last night of freedom, because it is your last. Now, if you'll excuse me, your mother and I have to unload the truck in the dark." Josh looked over Richard's shoulder, at the picture of his father in his turnouts, and then back to the wanna-be usurper.

Somewhere in the back of his mind, he could hear a voice in his head saying, "Do it. End this sorry S.O.B. You can take him." Josh felt his anger swell. "You want to know something, Richard? If you ever mention my father like that again, I'll end your life. And so help me God, I'm not kidding."

"Josh, stop this!" Sam screamed. "He's trying to help you. Can't you see that?"

Josh sighed and shook his head. "Well, he doesn't have to be an asshole about it."

"Like I was saying, I'll see you tomorrow," Richard said, as Sam quietly got up and followed him to the door.

Staring at his father's picture, Josh waited until he heard the door close before exhaling. He knew it was wrong, but he could feel the hate building inside him. "Ease off," he said out loud, as the power radiated off of him. Josh tried to force the image of Richard's smug face out of his mind, but he couldn't. Even though he knew he'd been setting himself up for failure all summer, he still felt like the man was trying to get one over on him. The worst part was, after a lifetime of living with Sam, she'd taken the side of somebody that she barely knew. And for that, he hated Richard Shin, whether he meant well or not. He had no right to talk to him like that. Josh tensed up, as his vision changed to the red tint that he had grown so accustomed to. "Take my car? My phone? Who does this asshole think he is?"

"I shouldn't be thinking like this," he said, catching himself. But his stomach was tied in knots, and the withdrawals were fueling his anger. Just then, Josh saw a tiny line appear on one of the pictures. And then, one by one, all the pictures started to develop the same tiny line. "Oh, shit," he thought, as he realized they were cracks in the glass and that they were growing. A large snapping sound came from behind, and Josh saw the whole living room window was splintering straight across. "Don't do this," he pleaded, shutting his eyes, as if in prayer. There was no reply, except for the sound of the wood beams in the wall beginning to buckle.

Sprinting across the living room, Josh grabbed the doorknob and was about to run, until he heard the sound of Larry's screams from the bedroom. "Sam? Rich? What's happening?" Josh had never once in his life heard fear in his grandfather's voice before. He hated to do this, but it was the only thing he could really remember. Taking what Billy had told him at the campfire, Josh spun on his heels and dropped down on his knees, flooding his mind with images.

He thought of his mother and how it felt when she smiled. He thought of Claire and how it felt when he was eight and she had told him how his father was named Sugar Bear, and that's why they called him Little Bear. And even though he could hear his grandfather's screams from the bedroom, Josh blocked them out and imagined how proud he was to sit in the front seat of his grandfather's green car, as they drove to get ice cream. He could feel the wind in his face and his hair blowing around, when Larry used the master controller to raise and lower Josh's window. And then it was gone. The hate, the surging power, and the sounds of the house's impending doom, were gone.

Josh opened his eyes and saw his grandfather standing in front of him. He was propping himself up with a cane. He looked so fragile and thin, unlike the image Josh had just seen in his mind. Looking around him, he could see the damage to the glass was done permanently, but hadn't gotten any worse. The house had been spared. Getting up slowly, Josh dusted off his knees.

"It's going to be okay, Josh. You'll see." Even though the man in front of him looked markedly different, there was no mistaking his kind tone and gentle nature.

"I love you, Larry. I don't know if I've said that since I was a little boy, but it's true," Josh said, as a tear rolled gently down his cheek.

"I love you, too," his grandfather replied.

Josh nodded silently. "I know. It's because I love you I'm going to say goodbye right now, while I can. Because I don't know what the future holds for me. I want you to be safe, the way you made me feel when I was younger."

Turning his back, Josh grabbed the door and walked out. The last word he heard his grandfather say was, "Wait," as he shut the door.

Chapter 30

"So let me get this straight, Michaels, and don't get me wrong. I like your first idea, but this second one's kind of weak."

"Trust me. I'll make a few calls and score some heroin for us to smoke," he said, looking at Charlie, who he hoped could adequately steer the Jeep both with his non-dominant hand and under the influence of narcotics.

"We'll find a better abandoned house in a nicer area. Over a few weeks, we can just reduce the dose, until we're clean." Having split the rest of Charlie's newly-filled prescription pain pills, Josh felt a lot better. He wasn't sweating anymore. For the most part, he felt normal. "Once I'm clean, I'll resume training and take the demons out."

"What about Deus?" The redhead said, sounding concerned.

"If we happen to run into him, I'm pretty confident I could knock him on his ass, if he's by himself."

"That's funny," Charlie said sarcastically. "When I opened the door, the flight of stairs into the basement seemed to knock you out."

"Get a grip. I was in full withdrawals. Now I am strong, like Russian bear," Josh said, grinning. Scrolling through Charlie's contacts, Josh looked for anybody, who he even remotely thought could score some drugs. Even if they only knew a small time dealer, that person would know where to get heroin.

"It doesn't look like school's jumping off this semester," the redhead said, switching his hands to steer with his cast.

"I wasn't going to school anyway. Per Rich, I was going to rehab, because I'm a naughty boy. But there's no way I'm doing it on his terms. He can kiss my donkey horn, before I move to Boston with no car and no friends."

"Any leads?"

"I have it narrowed down to Nick or Amanda. Would either one of them trip, if they got a text from you asking where to score drugs?" Josh asked.

"Only one way to find out."

"Cool. Keep heading to the bank. We'll both pull out as much money as we can." Josh scrolled through to the contacts, as Charlie slowed down. Typing out the message, he sent it to both the classmates.

"Keep moving," Josh heard a strange voice say, as his nostrils were filled with the unmistakable sulfur smell of road flares.

"What's going on?" Josh said, looking up. Charlie didn't say a word, as the Jeep slowly passed by the gruesome scene. It reminded Josh of a cheap carnival ride. The road was littered with debris. There were two cars that were already being pulled off the road by two trucks, their grills both mangled masses of plastic and metal. Fear seized the boy, as he instantly recognized the small moving truck flipped over on its passenger side. And then it became apparent that the debris on the road was Sam's clothes. Jumping out of the Jeep while it was still moving, Josh's feet pounded the pavement mercilessly, as he ran towards the truck. Then he was falling... Past the rushing ground and into the abyss.

***

Josh fluttered his eyes and winced, as they were met by a light so strong and unnatural it could only be the fluorescent lighting of a hospital emergency room. He didn't know how his mind had shut it out, but there was a baby in the room next to him screaming inconsolably. The overhead speaker was right over his head, calling for Dr. Roberts to report to oncology. Somehow, though, it didn't seem quite real. He knew why he was here, but he no longer felt anything.

It was weird. It was like he just lost consciousness. He remembered falling in slow motion, like a building being demolished. Then he remembered fragments of what seemed like a dream. First, he was by the truck. Then they put the sheet over his mother's body. Next, there were police and firemen trying to pin him to the ground, as an animal roared in the background.

All the while, the pain within him burned with the fury of a supernova. But that was a distant memory now. He felt like he'd taken a red-hot branding iron to his chest, viciously burning away all that was inside him. All that was left was the dead char of what he used to be. He felt completely foreign, even to himself. The senses he'd become accustomed to weren't giving any input. The screaming child, the people in the other beds, the lights overhead, they all registered, but meant nothing to him. In fact, if the building went up in flames right now, he honestly didn't know if he'd move.

"Are you awake?" Charlie's voice came from behind him. Trying to turn, Josh noticed that he couldn't.

"Yeah," he replied flatly. His friend's tall, skinny form stepped into his field of vision, cautiously at first.

"They knocked you out pretty good."

"How long?"

"It's been about four hours," Charlie replied, staring anxiously at him. Josh struggled to move, but he couldn't. Under the sheet, he could see the thin outline of leather restraints; one on each wrist and one on each ankle. He was firmly held to the metal frame of the hospital bed. Lifting his head up, he could see the exit was right in front of him. The nurse's station was just to the right of that. Laying back down, Josh noticed the only two things in his vision were a clock and a crucifix on the wall.

"When did they put these on me?" Josh asked, quietly nodding to the restraints.

"At the scene of the accident," the redhead replied nervously.

"I don't remember."

"They thought you were on PCP, because you threw three cops into the side of the truck when they asked you to step back."

"I barely remember," Josh said. "It's kind of a blur."

"Lightning struck the water tower next to us, when they were tying you down," Charlie said. "Do you remember that?"

"No."

"I do. It was weird, because the sound the lightning made when it struck the metal sounded just like your screams, after the bystanders told the cops that Richard had just driven right into oncoming traffic." Josh had no reply, but he remembered now the woman in the car next to them said it looked like Richard suddenly jerked the wheel to avoid hitting something; except there was nothing there.

"Can you bring the sheet down, so I can see my wrists?" he asked. Reaching over, Charlie pulled the sheet down to just above Josh's underwear. He was surprised to see he didn't have some old gown on that had worn, frayed edges. He was completely bare chested. For the first time, Josh saw why his left forearm felt so cold. There was an IV flowing into him. "It must be behind me," he thought.

"I know you can't see it, but there's a serious storm outside. Do you think maybe you could shut it off?" Charlie asked meekly.

Josh shrugged his shoulders. "I wouldn't have a clue," he mumbled. But in reality, the fact was he really didn't care. He was done with all of the trouble. The power that wouldn't do what he asked, the difference between good and evil, it really didn't matter anymore. Even as he looked at Charlie, he wondered to himself why Charlie looked like a complete stranger. It seemed like the bond was gone. At least, that's how he felt. The only thing that was familiar to Josh was the hunger for pain killers, and the constant, recurring thought that, if he couldn't feed it, he'd rather just die.

"Hey, Josh, how are you feeling right now?" He looked up to see an older nurse in yellow scrubs. He could see through the ingenuous statement. She didn't give two squirts of piss what the answer that came out of his mouth was. She'd give him his meds and roll off to the next patient. "I'm sorry to hear of your loss. I don't know you, but I was trained by your grandmother. She was always proud of you. In fact, she came to my wedding and showed off your baby pictures. If there's anything I can do, just say so."

Faking a smile, Josh nodded. "Whatever," he thought to himself. "I guess now that God's taken everything worth taking, he doesn't have time to save me. But he's still got time to kick me in the balls and contradict my thoughts," Josh shook his head. He felt like even his mind wasn't sacred anymore.

As she stepped away, another, younger nurse with auburn hair walked up in blue scrubs. "How are you?" she asked.

"Peachy," Josh muttered, glancing at Charlie, who had moved his hard, plastic chair to the foot of the bed. The sliding doors behind him slid open to let in a police officer, who was drenched by the storm outside. The nurse reached over and checked his IV. Her stethoscope swung back and forth, dangling from her neck as she moved. "I'm in a lot of pain," he said, even though he knew it was a complete lie. If anything, he was totally numb.

"Really?" the nurse replied. Josh could already hear the skepticism in her voice, but he didn't care.

"Where does it hurt?"

"Everywhere, but mostly my shoulder. I think it's from when the cops threw me on the pavement," he said, smiling defiantly as the cop walked up.

"I'll see what I can do. When we started the IV, we drew blood. Your tox screen tested positive for opiates, methamphetamines, and cocaine." Josh continued to stare at her blankly.

"I'm in pain," Josh bitterly repeated. Lowering his head, he wondered where the last two drugs came from, but he wasn't surprised. They had no idea what they were smoking at the lake house because Billy was their supplier.

"Josh Michaels?" the officer said. Josh looked up. The patrol officer was completely soaked by the downpour. "My name is Officer Trujillo. I'm here to advise you that you've been placed on a 5150 for suicidal ideation. From here, you'll be placed in a psychiatric facility for up to seventy-two hours."

"What the hell for?" Charlie cried.

"For stating multiple times on scene that he didn't want to live anymore. You didn't think we'd just let him go after that; did you?"

"But he didn't mean that," Charlie said, raising his voice.

"Listen," the cop barked, "this isn't your house. There are other families and children here. I don't know where you're from. In the real world, you don't tell authority figures you're going to kill yourself and then just walk away." Glaring at the now silent redhead, the policeman continued. "Your rights as a U.S. citizen are hereby revoked for the next seventy-two hours. Since you are unfit to make adequate decisions, the hospital staff will make them for you. Do you understand?" Josh nodded slowly.

"Maybe it's for the best," the cop said. "They have a rehab center next to the psychiatric facility. With any luck, you'll find your way there afterwards." Josh laid his head down on the pillow. Apparently, he wasn't going anywhere, until a psychiatrist gave him the stamp of approval. And what was worse, if they didn't like what he had to say, they could diagnose him as gravely disabled and send him to a locked facility for as long as they wanted.

"You know it's 2:00 am, right?" he heard the officer say from the foot of the bed. "How old are you?" Josh lifted up once again to see the defiant look on Charlie's face.

"Old enough," Charlie sneered.

"Wrong answer," the wet cop said, shaking his head. "Pull out your license."

Josh was just lowering his head to the pillow, when he saw a sight that almost stopped his heart in his chest. Richard walked right past him.

"I'm here for my discharge papers."

Struggling to see better, Josh strained to sit up; but he couldn't. He was too weak. So he propped himself up on his elbows.

"Last name?" the nurse asked.

"Shin," he replied, looking at the redhead next to him, talking to the policeman. "Like the shin bone's connected to the knee bone." Josh watched as the color in Charlie's face drained away.

The cop glanced over at Richard. "Weren't you the driver?" he asked.

"Yeah, my name is Richard Shin. I'm Boston P.D."

"If I'm not mistaken, you're in custody for vehicular manslaughter, whether you're P.D. or not."

"No, I'm not," Richard replied. "Your lieutenant cleared me as accidental."

Shaking his head, the policeman walked away from Charlie and pulled out his wet cell phone. "Step over against the wall, while I make this phone call."

"Come have a chat," Richard said to Charlie, as they stepped over to the bed.

"Hello, Josh," the man smiled behind his glasses.

"Hello, Deus," Josh replied, without raising his head. It was surprising to him that, even though he felt completely dead inside, the tears still flowed from the corners of his eyes and down his cheeks. "Why?" he asked. "She was completely innocent."

"So was Larry," Richard replied, "but I jacked his shit up too. That's what I do. I'm a demon. It's my specialty." He chuckled cruelly. "Bill knew that Claire and Larry's mental defenses were way too strong. So I used your mother to follow your moves and take you down a peg or two. Her mind wasn't easy to control at first. But after we had sex a few times, it was like reading a book. And that's how we monitored everything from your argument with Claire to what color Flynn's shit was when she walked him in the morning. You see, I hate you so much, you wouldn't believe how much willpower it's taking me not to grab your pasty bitch ass out of that bed and hurl you headfirst into that glass door," the demon said, pointing at the exit.

"So why don't you?" Josh asked, almost hoping he would.

"Because," he said, rocking the shiny metal side rail of the hospital bed back and forth with demonic glee, "this is so much better." Josh looked over to Charlie, who was dumbstruck. "I bet you feel completely dead inside; don't you?" Deus said, grinning. "You want me to let you in on a little secret?" the demon asked. Josh glanced over at the half Asian, half Caucasian mask his tormentor wore. "If you were to fold out these rails flat and stand this bed up, you'd look eerily similar to the guy up on the wall." Josh looked at the hospital linen grouped between his legs, and then to the cross on the wall.

Even though a chill ran up his spine, he looked back at Deus and said, "Nope. Not seein' it."

"It gets better, asshole. After the hospital staff pulls you off this cross you're fastened to by your wrists and ankles, that nurse with the long reddish-brown hair will put your limp, medicated body in a wheelchair and walk you across the way with two male security guards. They're gonna lay you in a gray, cement construct that looks surprisingly like a tomb. There's no windows at all. And your punk ass is gonna lie in there for three days," he grinned, still rocking the bed rail. "But on the third day, after your seventy-two hour hold expires, and that heavy ass gray electronic door rolls away, you're not going to emerge victorious, clothed in rays of glory. You're going to hobble your weak, frail little body over to Howdy Doody's Jeep. Then you guys are gonna get high. Because you're a junkie, and that's what junkies do. Because they're predictable, and that's how the Monarchy rolls."

"If we stay high, there's no more singing lessons, right?" Charlie stammered.

"Oh, when I'm through with you, Charlie, canaries will line up to suck your dick, you'll sing so sweetly," the demon replied, winking.

"Why?" Charlie said, confused. "I never did anything to you."

"Because," he said with disdain, "I had to pretend to be your friend for one hundred and forty-six days. I heard you say the word 'like' ten thousand, two hundred and seventy-two times. And for that, I'm gonna take your bottom lip and stretch it over the back of your head, like a covered wagon." Charlie's face filled with dread, as the demon danced around mockingly. "'At first I was like this, but then I was like sweet, but then I was like right, and then I was like whaaa...'"

Josh watched as Officer Trujillo approached Deus with two security guards by his side. "Well, boys, it's been real. But I've got places to be," Deus said, turning towards the approaching men.

"Richard Shin, you're under arrest for vehicular manslaughter and, my personal favorite, impersonating an officer of the law."

"Oh, my," the demon said, holding out his wrists, with a smile on his face. "I guess you'd better take me into custody then."

Josh laid his head back on the pillow, his cheeks still wet from tears that he couldn't wipe away, even if he had wanted to. So to add insult to injury, Deus wouldn't even kill them quickly. He was going to torture them both slowly. The nurse walked up to the bed with a syringe in her hand. He was happy she had come with something. He was astonished by the fact that, despite everything that had happened today, there was a voice in his head that shouted, "I hope it's something strong." That's when he had the realization that either the demon would kill him or the drugs would. Even as a god, Josh was powerless to do anything about either.

"I hope that helps with the pain," the nurse with the long reddish-brown hair said.

"Actually, I seriously need to pee," Josh said. "I'd ask for a urinal. But my arms are so numb from the restraints, I don't think I can hold it."

"Okay," the nurse said, calling for one of the guards to help him to the bathroom. The guard unlocked the boy's restraints and told him to sit up slowly, so he didn't get lightheaded. Clenching his hands to bring the blood to them, he slid slowly to the edge of the bed. Gripping his right wrist, Josh ran his hand over the impression the restraints had left in his sore arm. Looking out across the ER, Josh got to see what was causing the cacophony of sound around him. There were three hospital beds along every wall in the jam-packed ER. There were people in wheelchairs in the corners. This was on top of the rooms. No wonder it sounded like a zoo in here.

Now that he was up, he could see the bed behind him. He noticed a girl, who couldn't have been more than fourteen. Her ankles were both restrained, and she held a bucket of black charcoal-looking vomit. For all intents and purposes, she looked normal, except for the black substance caked all over her chin and lower lip. Josh had a hunch she had just attempted suicide. Apparently, he wasn't the only one going through some tough times.

"What did she do?" he asked the guard, as he gingerly stepped down to the cold tile floor.

"She overdosed on acetaminophen because her boyfriend broke up with her," the guard replied. "The charcoal absorbs as much of the pills as possible, but it wasn't enough. I guess nobody ever told her that all that drug does in high doses is kill your liver. I don't see the whole point," the guard said, handing the IV over to Josh. "Sooner or later, she would just forget him and fall in love with someone else, who treated her better. All she had to do was hold on for a better day."

"Will she need a transplant?" Charlie asked, peering over the bed.

"Definitely," the guard said. "But she won't get one. I'm pretty sure trashing your liver disqualifies you from the organ recipient list. When she got here, she swore up and down that she accidentally took the whole bottle for a headache."

On his way to the bathroom, Josh glanced over at Deus. The officer was leading him out to the parking lot, when all of a sudden the demon dropped to the ground. "Man would you please leave?" Josh thought. He stared in disbelief as the cop shook him with no response.

"Code blue, emergency room. Code blue," the nurse announced into the microphone.

Josh stopped at the bathroom door. Damnit, that would place Deus in the room right next to him. Charlie sat alert as a meerkat, while he watched the policeman start CPR, pushing hard and fast. Josh knew Deus had no intention at all of going to jail. He planned on taking a nap and leaving through the morgue, quite possibly when the mortician went to take a bathroom break.

"Well, two can play at that game," Josh thought, as the nurses crowded around the lifeless body with the crash cart. Josh looked at the guard. "Hey, before you go off, I wanted to ask, when is the last time the fire department checked the fire alarms in this place?" As he spoke, he concentrated as hard as he could on the words "fire", "alarm," and "go off."

"What?" the guy said, his face a mask of confusion. "Seriously. Do your thing, so I can take you back to bed," he said, shaking his head.

"Goddammit," Josh thought to himself, as he stepped in the bathroom and turned the light on. "I swear, what a shit power," Josh muttered under his breath. How embarrassing. The guard probably thought he was a nut. Josh took a look around the bathroom, until his reflection caught his eye. He stepped towards the mirror and took a look at how hideous he looked. He still had black mascara around his eyelids, which had run from his tears. The makeup was left over from Saturday night, along with the black flames and a coat of dirt from the desert. He was completely filthy, even more so in the sticky areas where the EKG electrodes had been. He looked like a hobo and a circus clown had a baby together.

"I hate you," Josh said softly, at the image staring back at him in the mirror. "I hate you," he said again, this time louder but still almost silent under the roar of the bathroom fan. Holding his IV in his left hand, he made a fist with his right hand and hit himself in the skull, screaming it one more time. "I HATE YOU!"

Immediately, the bathroom was filled with a red glow, as the fire alarm began to wail. Josh was so surprised that he fell backwards, into the tray of urinals and pee cups. The empty containers crashed to the floor, bouncing everywhere. It still wasn't loud enough to warn the guard. "What do they put in that thing, an airplane turbine?" Josh thought, looking up at the exhaust fan. Quickly peeking his head out the door, Josh looked at Charlie.

"Where'd he go?"

"He told the other guard to watch the door, while he answered a call on the second floor. But when they moved Deus into room five, the solo guard went in with them."

"I don't know about you," Josh said, grabbing his clothes from under the gurney, "but I'm not going to the psych ward."

"I'm down with that," the redhead said, shooting up like a rocket. Josh pulled his dirty tee shirt over his head and slipped on his Vans.

"Where do you think you're going?" the fourteen-year-old said through her black mask of charcoal.

"Never you mind," Charlie said, glaring at her as he slipped past. Breaking into a full run, the boys pushed the electric faceplate on the exit. But just as Josh thought, it didn't lead out of the hospital, only deeper in. They were in a hallway now that went left or right. Josh cut left, under the red glare of the lights and screaming alarms. Running as fast as his legs would carry him, he quickly glanced over his shoulder to see the tall redhead pounding the tiles behind him.

Josh knew Charlie was a terrible runner. Maybe he'd just never had the right motivation before, because he was definitely keeping pace. He could only imagine what it would look like to somebody else, if they saw this right now. A blonde kid with makeup on was sprinting down the hall, carrying an IV bag in his arm, as if it were a football. And all the while, he was being chased by Frankenginger. Coming to the end of the hall, Josh ran up to the door and slammed up against it, only to be knocked back by stiff resistance.

"Damn," Charlie said, winded. "It doesn't even look locked."

"The magnet," Josh panted, pointing to the big square device in the corner of the door. "It's attached to a magnet." Stepping up to the door one more time, Josh said, "OPEN," aloud.

"Really?" Charlie said, as nothing happened.

"Damnit to Hell. Open the door. Seriously!" Josh screamed, pushing the door which stubbornly held to the magnet. All of a sudden, the fire alarm shut off. The hall was completely silent, that is, until the sound of the long-haired nurse flooded it like the voice of The Great Oz.

"We need security to respond to the ER for a missing patient." Josh shook his head. Well, that was it. Their goose was cooked.

"Don't stop!" Charlie screamed. "Keep trying."

Josh could hear the sound of boots running down the hall. He looked at the door and said, "Listen, I know we're not always on the same page, but if you don't unlock the damn door right now, the only thing that is certain is we'll be in withdrawals for the next three days." With that, Josh heard the magnet shut off.

"Super creepy," Charlie said, staring at the door in amazement. Throwing his weight against the door, Josh pushed through and kept running into the blackness of the windy, wet night.

Chapter 31

"See. I told you that you'd feel better," Cammy said, holding up her shopping bags like trophies and smiling. Dianna had to agree. She did feel a little better. After getting in last night during a brutal storm, Ramon had given the ladies their own thank you cards for not running him into the ground during the three-month tour. Each was filled with an assortment of gift cards to their favorite places at the mall. To Dianna, they were as good as gold, after she had worn the same five outfits pretty much over and over for the whole summer. She had already planned to go school shopping this week, anyway. Ramon had given her that money as well, with the gift cards on top of it. Swinging the bags around, Cammy bounced on the tips of her new shoes.

"How do they feel?" Nina asked, holding bags in each hand.

"Pretty good. Not like my heels, but I can't wear those to the gym; now, can I?"

Dianna chuckled. "I can see my healing powers are going to be pushed to the limit tonight." To top it off, Ramon had renewed their gym memberships and added Cammy to the family plan. She really couldn't describe how good it felt to be home and to fall asleep in her own bed, knowing the house was paid off. Ramon had already signed the paperwork. It was a done deal.

"You know what's funny?" Dianna said, looking at the two other happy shoppers, as they made their way out. "As great as it was to sleep in my own bed, I kind of had trouble falling asleep, without my girls next to me."

"It was a crazy long time until I fell asleep last night," Cammy agreed, dodging a group of kids and almost walking into the potted plant near the exit.

"Maybe we could have a little reunion tour in my room tonight," Dianna suggested.

"With a little popcorn," Nina added.

"We could try on our new flannel jammies," Cammy chimed in.

"Then it's settled. After the gym tonight, we camp out in my room." The other two cheered in unison. It lifted her spirits somewhat to have them as her support group, after Josh had stopped returning her phone calls. She thought things were a little weird. By August, he was spotty at best with his text messages, sometimes not even responding at all. Dianna noticed, by the end of August, Josh had a new excuse every day for why he couldn't call her. It was doubly upsetting for her, because she missed him so much. Sometimes on the road, he was all she'd think about. So it was hard to swallow when he hadn't responded to any of her texts after Labor Day weekend and ignored the voicemail she'd left after the bad dream. Something was definitely up, and she wanted answers.

Walking out the exit, Dianna glanced over at Nina. She had asked the watcher to send word to her husband to find out how Josh's training was going, and Nina promised she'd contact the male watcher as soon as they got home. True to her word, Nina came down for breakfast in the morning, dressed in her black blouse and blue jeans, to say that she sent off a message to Thomas to contact her. Now all they had to do was wait.

"Anything yet?" the girl asked, as they walked off towards the car.

"Nothing yet," Nina said, shaking her head. "Don't worry though, child. It will be soon. Sometimes Thomas might seem a little odd in his ways, but he's definitely not stupid. When I tell him to contact me ASAP, he knows better than to blow it off."

"I hate to be impatient," Dianna said, "but I can't help but feel something is wrong. The more we've worked on my energy and my prayer meditation, the more it seems to confirm it." Dianna stopped at the car and scanned the parking lot, while Nina fished the keys out of her purse. Even though it was storming last night, the weather was good today. The ground had dried up by midday. Just in case, she had worn her blue Boston Red Sox track jacket. As the trunk popped open, the girls all heaved their bags in.

"Oh, snap. Would you look at that?" Dianna heard Cammy say. Turning around, she saw the most beautiful dog just sitting right where she had just been. Dianna had to do a double take.

"I was just standing in that spot," she said to her sister.

"I think it's a Chesapeake Bay," Cammy said, reaching down and petting it.

"A red dog," Nina said, grinning.

"I've never seen one this pure, though," Dianna said, looking at the dog's fur. It wasn't auburn or reddish-brown. This dog was deep red and had beautiful amber eyes.

"He can't be more than two years old," Cammy pointed out, grabbing the dog's paws. "Check it out," she said, pointing out its blue collar with a red "B" hanging from it.

"Great taste in teams. He's a keeper," Dianna said, scratching the dog's back. Dianna smiled, as the dog licked her cheek. It was definitely affectionate.

"Check this out," Cammy said, showing her the back of the dog tag:

I HAVE NO OWNER. I AM FREE. CATCH ME, IF YOU CAN.

"No way," Dianna cried. "Is this a joke? Nina, did my dad put you up to this?"

"Definitely not," she replied. "I'm as surprised as you are."

"This dog is pimp, boss, and regal all rolled into one. I think he'd be a great addition to the Imperial family," Cammy said, smiling.

"You know dad has always wanted a dog," Dianna said. "And the tag says it doesn't have an owner." To her, the idea was irresistible. It was exactly what she needed to raise her spirits.

Panting away, the dog sat and wagged its red tail, looking totally content. Then, suddenly, it ran off between the cars, barking for them to follow. Much to Dianna's surprise, Nina sprinted after it, without so much as a word. Dianna could tell exactly what her sister was thinking just by the look in her eyes.

Standing up and tightening the belt around her black Dickies, Cammy screamed, "I want that dog."

"Then let's get it," Dianna said, following after her watcher. She could barely see the copper flashes of Nina's hair, as she dodged back and forth between the cars. She knew, if she followed the sound of the barking dog it wouldn't matter. They were all after the same goal. Nina was pulling away from them, and Dianna knew why. She was using her abilities to augment her strides, so she could catch up to the dog. Luckily, Dianna had mastered that trick, while they were on the last days of the trip. Releasing her powerful aura, the flames burst forward, engulfing Dianna. And then she narrowed it down, so it was only a thin, protective coating, barely noticeable to the naked eye.

"Follow me," she screamed, extending her aura to her sister. Within seconds, both Cammy and she were practically gliding on the black asphalt between the cars. It was easy. After Nina had taught her that she could heal from a distance, it wasn't too long before she'd figured out that she could extend her energy field around people.

"Woo hoo!" her sister screamed, making a zigzag pattern through the cars, leaving nothing more than a faint streak behind her.

"Watch out and stay low, so no one can see you," Dianna warned. She knew, even if somebody had seen them, they'd be in and out of their field of vision too fast to recognize who or what they were. But they couldn't be too safe. Darting in and out of the cars, she moved faster and faster. It seemed the faster she went, the faster Nina and the dog were pulling away. She could hear the red dog barking, but she couldn't see a trace of either of them.

"We're losing them, Cammy. Let's cut through the parking garage." Pushing ahead even faster, Dianna was barely touching the asphalt, as she glided over the terrain. In one quick move, she vaulted over the gate to the entrance, while Cammy dropped to her knees and slid under. "Watch out!" Dianna spoke into her sister's mind. "We're moving way too fast, and your brain can only react so quickly." But there was no reply. In fact, her sister was nowhere to be found. Shooting out of the other side of the parking garage, Dianna slowed down and stopped, waiting for her to catch up. But there was no sign of the girl.

Suddenly, without warning, her sister burst off the top of the parking structure four stories up. Arms and legs flailing wildly, Dianna gritted her teeth, as her stomach dropped. "Oh, no!" Even she had no idea how this one would end up. She'd never been crazy enough to do anything like this. Cammy's legs continued to run, as she hovered over what remained of the parking lot for the last hundred feet and then descended to the ground.

"Yeah!" she screamed, landing on her feet and taking off like a rocket, only to crash headlong into the cement trash can. Dianna cringed as cement chunks, trash, and debris exploded out in every direction. Rolling and tumbling, her sister flew forward, until she came to a stop.

"Holy cow," Dianna said, looking at the mess. Cammy had obliterated the receptacle. "Are you okay?" she asked, jogging up to her sister. She sincerely hoped nobody had seen the event. Looking straight ahead, she could see a car waiting at the light. And up on the parking garage, an older woman was peering off the top of the parking structure.

"Well, that didn't go as planned," Cammy said, dusting herself off and picking the banana peel off her shoulder.

"How about, from now on, you just follow my lead?" Dianna said. "Thank God it was Labor Day, and only the mall was open," she thought, grabbing her sister and speeding off. Dianna tried her best to expand her awareness. "Nina, where are you?" Dianna asked, reaching out with her mind.

"I followed the dog out to the train tracks. I'm in the rundown business area about a mile away from you. There's a bunch of abandoned buildings. I have the dog in my sights."

"Perfect," Dianna said, running towards the nearest exit. "Follow me," she told Cammy. Veering onto the gravel path along the train tracks, Dianna hopped onto the track itself and glided forward like she was ice-skating. After having seen Cammy wipe out, she had a pretty good idea that her power would protect her, as long as she didn't do anything extremely crazy. Since nobody was around to see, she wanted to put her speed to the test, just to see what she could really do.

Speeding ahead, the wind rippled through her black hair. She had to be doing at least 80 mph. "It feels amazing," she could hear Cammy say in her mind, as she smiled from the adjacent track. Seeing the older buildings coming up quickly, Dianna nodded towards them and jumped off the rail, with her sister hot on her heels.

"Look out for the puddle," Dianna thought, as she skirted the edge of the pool-sized collection of water the rains from the previous night had left.

"Negative, ghost rider. Watch this," Cammy said, running straight over the water, leaving barely a ripple. "How do you like me now?" she asked, sliding to a stop in front of the abandoned warehouse.

"Impressive," Dianna agreed. "But watch this," she said. "After all, why should Cammy get to have all the fun?" she thought, as she ran right up the side of the abandoned warehouse wall in front of her. Once on top, she skimmed the edges of the roof looking for Nina or the dog. From that height, she could see for miles.

"I found her," she heard her sister scream from the ground. "She's over here." Dianna made her way back to the cracked, gray asphalt and ran over to the two women. She noticed the road out here was terrible compared to the smooth, newer black asphalt by the mall. "Damn, this place is a dump," Cammy said distastefully. Dianna agreed. It was definitely run down. There was an old neighborhood a few blocks over and a liquor store with bars covering the windows. It looked like a ghost town, but people still obviously lived here.

Nina stood in the middle of the street. She was staring at a warehouse that appeared empty and an old library. Judging by the boards on eighty percent of its windows, Dianna guessed it was closed as well. "I followed the dog here," Nina said, scanning the intersection. A loud bark turned their attention to an old church. It actually looked open. At least, there were cars in the parking lot.

"There," Cammy said, pointing to the dog laying on the lawn on the side of the church. Talking softly, Dianna tried to coax the young dog.

"Do you want to come home with us and have a nice, warm house to sleep in?" Putting its ears up, the dog let out a playful bark. It was almost like the dog understood her.

"Yes, you do," Cammy said, slapping her hands on her knees. "Come to Cammy. As soon as we get you home we can give you a new tag that says your name is Drake Imperial."

"Really?" Dianna asked, putting her hands on her hips. "There is no way."

"Augusto then?" Cammy smiled.

"Can we deal with this later? Let's just catch him first." Dianna was within five feet of the prize. Then, suddenly, the dog playfully bounded around the corner into an alley, between the church and the next building. Following after it, Dianna rounded the corner, but there was nothing there. The alley was empty. "That's strange," she thought. The playful red dog was nowhere to be found.

"Where's our dog?" Cammy groaned. "I saw him run right in here."

"I did too," Dianna said, disappointed. The sound of rustling trash bags caught the girls off guard, surprising them. A homeless man sat up, looking like the girls had just woken him from his nap.

Rubbing the sleep from his eyes, he asked in a gravelly voice, "Are you guys looking for something?"

"No, it's okay," Dianna said, apologetically. "We were just going."

"What's your name?" the old man asked, picking the leaves from his dreads.

"EWW. Super unsanitary," Cammy muttered under her breath, turning to go.

"My name is Dianna."

"Hmm, Dianna means heavenly or divine."

"You're right. It does."

"Wasn't there a goddess named Dianna?" he asked.

"So I've heard," Dianna said with a grin, as Nina came up from behind her.

"This place is some sort of clinic?"

"Yeah," the man said, standing up and pulling off the wet newspaper stuck to his dirty pants. It's the Epidaurus Clinic. Half of it's a rehab. At night time, it converts to a homeless shelter."

"Do you live here?" Nina asked, eyeing the man.

"Sometimes. It depends. Tonight, I think I'll sleep in the library. I kind of like my space. It gets cramped in there, especially in this economy. That reminds me," he said, flashing a smile from under his grizzled beard, "they're hiring inside. They're lookin' for volunteers and nursing assistants."

"Right on, old man," Cammy said, nodding at Dianna. "These are the kind of people you should be helping. I'm not digging the neighborhood too much, but I could definitely use the work. If you volunteer, you could just come on the days I work. We could carpool together. After a few months, maybe I could get into nursing school."

"I guess," Dianna said, looking at the old building. It was pretty solid. She definitely wanted to see what was inside.

"Let's take a look and ask for an application."

She turned to the watcher. "Can we run inside?"

"Sure," Nina said, glaring with uncertainty at the Rastafarian. "Go on ahead, and I'll go back to the mall and get the car," she said, watching them as they went.

"Hello, babe," the man said, looking towards the ground, as if he were ashamed.

"Thomas," she said, shaking her head. Her eyes filled with tears, "My God, what have you done to yourself?" Stepping forward, she put her pale hands to his unshaven face and stared lovingly into his eyes.

"You're looking well, Nina."

"You, not so much," she said, half laughing and half crying. "Where have you been?" she whispered.

"I've been closer than you think. But, for your safety and Dianna's, I had to fall off of the grid. Come see me tonight, when it's safe. I'll tell you everything," he said, leaning in and kissing her lips gently. Nina shuddered as his familiar power enveloped her, raising her spirits up to a height she knew no other man could take her to. Only her soulmate was capable of doing this. For one brief moment, all was right in Nina's world.

Chapter 32

"The dead, they walk," Phyllis said, tipping her glass of merlot towards her blood-red lips and then quickly handing it over to the bartender for a refill. Deus smiled, as he held out his arms and spun around.

"It's true, boys and girl. Look who's fresh from the morgue. I came back to life because I heard there was a party at Cardona's."

Hasden smiled. "Come on and have a seat, buddy. We'll order something for you." He prepared a seat for him at his right side, like always. Across the red and white checkerboard table sat Bai and Mahvet. Right now, Hasden was about as thrilled as a demon could be. Of course, the weekend could have gone better. But in his line of work, he was well known for taking setbacks and turning them into golden opportunities. His team had performed so well that he figured he'd rent out the Italian restaurant for a well-deserved celebration.

"Bartender, shots," Hasden said loudly, pointing at the table. "The best whiskey you have, please."

"Lovely weather we had last night," he pointed out, as he watched Deus lower himself into the chair.

"Was he crushed?"

"Beyond crushed. He was obliterated," the hulking gray-haired man said loudly.

Phyllis strolled up to the table with the bartender's tray full of filled shot glasses. "Let me guess?" she asked. "Was the obnoxious vagina funeral there by his side?"

"Charlie? Oh, yeah," he replied, laughing. "He almost pissed himself, when he realized who I was."

"Did you know that little shit lied about getting laid?" Phyllis said, giggling and swallowing the first shot of whiskey.

"Oh, horseshit," Hasden said. "He reeked of that girl. He

practically smelled like he crawled inside of her."

"Yuck, you guys," Bai said, shaking her head.

"Oh, he tried," the blonde demon said, "but the little soldier wouldn't stand up and march because he was so high. Somebody should have told him that pain pills and raging hard-ons don't travel in the same pack."

"Who's your source?" Deus asked.

"I was looking for a bathroom on Saturday. The lines to the porta-potties were outrageous, so I was looking to cut in any way I could. That's when I spotted Charlie's hippie soulmate near the front. So I buddied up and eased on in. She said he fumbled for ten minutes, making every excuse in the book. Finally, she shut him down and told him to go to sleep."

"I'm so gonna rub this in his face the next time I see him," Deus said, throwing his right arm around Phyllis and kissing the top of her head.

Bai looked at them both and smiled, "That's funny. Luckily, none of us had to sleep with him. On another note, I still don't think it was a good idea to tip your hat to the Michaels kid," she said, looking concerned. "But you're the director, so I'm sure you have a reason."

Hasden nodded. "I thought of concealing rather than revealing," he said. "It's better that he knows what we're capable of. That way he'll think twice before crossing us, if he lives that long."

"You don't think he could've served some purpose?" Bai asked, helping herself to a shot of whiskey.

"Nah. Believe me, the Michaels family has been a thorn in my side ever since they were the Marioles, and the Taylors before that. I knew that, if he wasn't on board by the end of the weekend, he's never going to be. We can't have a wishy-washy Prime. It's too much of a liability. So it's better we put him in his place. If we didn't, sooner or later, he'd just end up believing Thomas could change his luck. And we can't have that," Hasden said, shaking his head.

"Ideally, I was looking to convert him. But Saturday's outcome will work almost as well. He's no good to Thomas, or the Host, as damaged as he is. And without Josh, I doubt the Imperial girl has the strength to keep her head above water, after we go after her. So, effective immediately, for anybody sticking around town after tomorrow," he said, looking at Phyllis and Deus, "if Josh shows his face around town, after they let him out of the funny farm, feel free to heckle the shit out of him. But refrain from attacking, unless he engages you. Vent your frustrations on the beanpole instead."

"Here, here," everybody said. Everybody, Hasden noticed, except for Angela. He looked into her heavily-medicated eyes. He was worried about her. A lot of things depended on her in the future. She was his secret weapon, and he couldn't keep drugging her up with sedatives every time she pitched a fit. If this continued, she'd be of little use to him by the time the war in Heaven came around. He needed her to be a wrecking ball, not a balled-up wreck.

"Are you okay, princess?" Hasden asked softly. She slowly nodded with the far-off look in her eyes the benzos usually gave her. "Good," he said, "because we need you to get better."

"I want to stay with you guys. I want to stay with Phyllis," she slurred.

"I'm sorry. I can't do that. But Bai's going to be your new roommate for a while, just until we get things squared away here. We have big plans coming up."

"What do you have planned?" Deus asked, swallowing down two shots at once. "Per protocol, we still have to tempt the Imperial girl, even though I get a feeling she's just going to tell us to piss up a post."

"No," Hasden shook his head, staring at the table's red and

white design. "We need to remember that this isn't personal. It's a game. For some reason, Thomas is making all his moves behind the scenes, and I want to know why. So I say we find him and rattle his cage. Then we turn our attention to the girl"

"That's an excellent idea," Phyllis said, bringing another tray to the table and setting them down. "You guys can handle Thomas, as long as I'm the one who gets to rip out Hobbes' spine and turn it into a walking stick."

"Don't delude yourself," he bluntly replied. "You're too valuable to me. Stronger demons than you have lost their ability to be useful because of him. The last thing I need is to find out that Wonder Brit teleported you into the Mariani trench and left your lower half phased into the ocean floor. Leave him to Deus."

Phyllis looked like she was going to launch a rebuttal, but it was interrupted by the welcome sight of the appetizers. "Ah, mini pizzas are here," Hasden said. It was definitely what he was looking forward to. The staff members walked them over one by one and set them on the table in front of the party, quickly walking away. He could appreciate that. He'd really hate to have to kill a staff member in his favorite dining establishment just because they were nosy.

Reaching over and grabbing his glass of scotch, Hasden stood up straight and proud. "I'd like to propose a toast," he said, smiling at every one of them. "I just want to say, from the bottom of my dark hearts, that your efforts this summer, culminating at Burning Man, paved the way for the downfall of one of the Primes." Picking up a shot of whiskey with his free hand, he continued, as the others followed suit. "You guys know I find nothing redeeming about the human race. To say I'm furious about the Monarchy being left out of the canonical Bible is an understatement. One of my biggest gripes with Adam's children is that they read what they want and only use the parts they like, or the parts they want to throw in the faces of the people they dislike.

All the while, they forget that I massacred Job's whole family under God's express authority. And I didn't do it so some snake charmer on Sunday morning TV could boast about how he orders us around, like the hired help. Because I'll slap the Brylcreem right out of his hair. The point is, there is a war coming. And I'm going to lead us out of the shadows and straight to the front lines. By the time this is over, by all I hold holy, the Monarchy will be the only thing left standing. So on this Labor Day, I'd like to say thank you for everything you've given. Your efforts are duly appreciated."

Throwing back their drinks, everybody shouted, "Here, here."

Hasden smiled over at Mahvet. "Soon," he thought. The sooner he could master the other half of her dual personality, the sooner its alien secrets would be his. It was a little-known fact that each universe was, for lack of a better term, self-contained and vacuum-packed. But it was like that for a reason. He had a sneaking suspicion the knowledge within Angela's head wouldn't only help him subjugate humanity, it would also help him ascend to the throne of God himself.

***

It was well past midnight. Thomas could tell just by the position of the moon in the night sky. Sighing, he looked out on the neighborhood from his perch atop the roof of the abandoned library. He couldn't see anything out of place in the perimeter. All was quiet. Not even the wind had come out to play tonight. For a brief second, he wondered to himself if Nina was purposely doing this, just to let him know she was pissed.

Silently, he walked over to the other side of the roof in his bare feet, paying no mind to the scattered gravel he was stepping on. The clinic was by now. It was hours past its 10:00 curfew. In the shadows of the stone masonry, Thomas could sense something wasn't quite right. He mentally went over the huge building with a fine tooth comb, asking himself what was out of place. Then he saw it. Resting in the shadows, breathing ever so shallowly, lay a magnificent black jaguar, its yellow eyes staring at him.

"Finally," Thomas thought to himself, as he stood up and cautiously waved. The big, black cat rose up from its haunches and gave the sharp, unmistakable roar that the jungle cat was known for. Sharp and full of fury, the sound echoed through the quiet neighborhood. "Oh, yeah, she's pissed," Thomas said out loud. Turning away, he walked across the rooftop and descended down the hatch that led into the library's second-story, where he was camped out. Since most all of the windows were all boarded up, he figured this was the best vantage point, if he needed to make a hasty retreat. If they happened to be human, he could just drop down a floor. If they were demon, he could escape through the roof.

The one thing Thomas knew he had over his adversaries was, even though most of them could switch their looks, they couldn't do it half as quickly as he could. And he could assume animal forms, which they couldn't. Although, it wasn't as if he worried about it too much; especially here. The current church was built on the site of an older one, and the boundaries of the holy site had extended across the street and into the building. The vibrations would be way too unpleasant for any of the Monarchy to ever come over here.

Taking the other spare candle out of his travel pack, Thomas carefully lit it off of its twin, doubling the light in the vast room. Downstairs was a mess, but up here it was nice and orderly, just like he fancied. Last night, during the storm, he'd picked up around his living space. A lot of the books had just been left behind, because of water damage from a few years back. It seemed the flat roof of the old library had terrible drainage issues.

After the roof began to leak and sag, the city shut it down.

It was sad to Thomas, as an immortal, to remember a time before the printing press. Owning books was a privilege held only by the elite. It was a status symbol. It made the statement to those who saw them that, no matter what that person thought about you, you weren't somebody who could be tricked, coerced or bullied. It let them know that the knowledge within those pages was in your head as well. If any person even attempted to pull the wool over your eyes, they would end up finding out just how much wealthier and smarter you were.

In today's world, though, even the lowest class couldn't be bothered with books. All of these were just sitting around here for the taking. "Oh, well. It was bound to happen sooner or later. The pendulum has to swing back the other way. We had a good run," he said, to the stack of books next to his sleeping bag.

The low, rhythmic vibration of the Jaguar's breathing rose up the stairs, alerting the man to the cat's approach, even before he'd seen it. Thomas wasn't too surprised to see Nina was using her old spirit animal from their time with the tribes, any more than Nina was probably surprised when he had shown up as a red dog earlier. It was one of his favorites. At the top of the stairs, the black cat stood up on its hind legs, and its body melted into the form of a woman. Standing up slowly, the dark black fur and the lighter spots of the jaguar receded into Nina's pale, naked skin. Thomas marveled at her form, which seemed to cast off its own light. Even though she switched forms, he couldn't help but notice how she walked towards him like she was still a stalking cat, her hips swaying like the animal's shoulders. Finally, the pale figure descended on her prey.

"Look, Nina, I know you're mad," Thomas whispered, "but I can explain." Putting her finger to his lips, the woman pushed him onto his back.

"Right now, I don't need to talk to the watcher. I need to

talk to my husband," she said, blowing out the candles.

***

It was surprising, Josh thought, how he couldn't see an inch in front of his face. But the pipe could find its way to his lips, as surely as the swallows migrating their way back to Capistrano. Flicking the lighter near the bowl, Josh puffed on the heroin, catching a quick glimpse of Charlie. Josh saw him on the carpet in front of the cold, brick fireplace across from him. Then, just as quickly as he'd appeared, he was gone. Josh plunged into the blackness. He held the smoke in his lungs and then slowly exhaled.

Luckily, he was right about who to score from. Amanda had come through. This morning, they'd met her at the park near his house, where Josh made his first official drug buy. Right after that, they'd found a great new foreclosed home with plantation shutters. They could turn Charlie's cell phone on, if they needed to, without neighbors getting suspicious. A screwdriver and a flip lock later, they were safely shut behind the locked master bedroom door. They weren't necessarily safe from demons, per se. But no homeless people were just going to roll through, or anything like that. Now here in the black of the room, with no sound and as high as he was, Josh truly couldn't feel a thing, which was exactly what he wanted.

He needed a break from the stimulus. He needed time to forget about the events of the summer. The heroin did exactly that. In the quiet, pitch black room, it was like being locked in a sensory deprivation chamber. At first, that seemed scary. Now, it felt almost second nature, a déjà vu of sorts. He didn't know if it was quite like being in the womb again, but there was a familiarity to it on a base level. He was caught somewhere between total serenity and panic, worried that the all-encompassing darkness might be permanent. Josh decided that this room may be dark and empty, but his imagination wasn't. So, retreating from the world, Josh filled the darkness over the waters of his mind. Instead of saying to himself, "Let there be light," Josh decided this time he'd just sink into the water. And that's exactly what he did. He just eased in and drifted away under the surface and into the depths.

***

As Nina struck the match, the flame furiously erupted from the tip, engulfing the wick and spreading light all over her naked form. "So would you please tell me why you're living on the streets?" she asked, sitting on her knees.

"Well," Thomas replied, rolling onto his back, "the synchronicities led me here and keep pointing to this one area."

"Seriously!" Nina groaned. "Besides the fact that you appeared as a red dog and led Dianna all the way over here, what coincidences led you here? And where is your Prime?"

Thomas sat up and handed the newspaper to Nina. "Brace yourself," he warned.

"Oh, Sam," Nina said, her face looking crestfallen, as she began to read out loud. "Her companion, Richard Shin, died in the ER from an aortic tear, presumably from the force of the crash."

"I'm sorry. I know you knew her a little better than me, since both you and Claire were in the delivery room when Josh was born."

"Do you think it was purposeful?" she asked, wiping a tear from the corner of her eye.

"I don't know," Thomas said. "But if you say the name fast, it sounds like 'diction.' And which demon do we know whose pet peeve is verbiage?"

"Asmodeus," Nina said, alarmed. "You're not just going off that; are you?"

"No," Thomas shook his head. "If you look at the fact that

the Hebrew letter 'shin' is 'sin,' and it's composed of three vavs. Each letter vav equates to the number six. So 'shin' is actually 666. I don't know exactly who it was, but it had to be a demon."

Nina shook her head in amazement. "So where's Josh?"

Thomas sat silent. "It's a complicated story, so let me start from the beginning. As you know, we came here for your self-appointed assignment."

"Go on," she said, setting the newspaper down, while still staring at the front-page headline.

"We were both on the same page, when Josh showed up unexpectedly."

"I agree," Nina said.

"Well, after the demons showed up, I wasn't too concerned. Given the fact that Dianna was on the internet, I figured it was just a routine check and tempt. But the demons they sent were the King of the Seventh Hell and the Director of the Monarchy."

"Satan is here?" Nina screamed furiously. "Why didn't you tell me?"

"Because," Thomas replied, "I knew you'd act like this. So I called in Hobbes, and we began to case him out. Somehow, Josh wandered onto his radar. The next thing I know, they've got sigils all over the place, and Josh has refused the training."

"So he hasn't done any training?" Nina cried, incredulously.

"No. None. We were supposed to meet for his second installment on the first day of summer vacation."

"How could you let this happen?" she cried.

"Gee, I'm sorry, Nina. While you were on the road for the past three months, eating out every night and clapping your hands to Bible hymns with your Prime, I've been on the streets trying to find mine, who basically isn't interested in the training, because he thinks he's the Antichrist. Somehow, the Monarchy got into his head. Both him and his friend had been camped out on their property pretty much all summer. There seemed to be no way I could get to him. Then we saw an opportunity. During Labor Day weekend, Hobbes and myself stole him away, so I could get him to reconsider. He was standoffish. He somehow feels he's a danger." Thomas's voice trailed off, as he considered how to proceed. He'd forgotten Nina didn't have a clue what had happened to Claire, and he hated to be the one to tell her.

"Spill it already," Nina said impatiently.

"I don't know how to say this. While you were gone, Claire had a massive stroke."

"No, it can't be. I've a bond with her. If she was in danger, I would've known," Nina said, her eyes widening in disbelief.

Thomas sighed and shrugged his shoulders. He knew this was true as well. "Something happened. I don't know how, but Josh feels that he is responsible. Now he has become even less receptive to the idea of the training or even fulfilling his role as the Prime."

"So right now he's refused?"

"No. He's on board," Thomas said cautiously. "You're not going to like this, but he followed the Monarchy out to the desert for a festival called Burning Man." Thomas watched as his wife's face hardened.

"Please tell me they didn't already tempt him, three months out of the gate."

"It looked like it was going that way, but Hobbes and I couldn't stick around. It was way too dangerous. We were heavily outnumbered, more than two to one against the demons. Since there were fifty thousand people there, the demons could have easily overwhelmed us with ants."

"So how'd you get him to change his mind?"

"Well," Thomas said, hesitantly, "as luck would have it, Rose was there. She got him to change his opinion."

"Luck?" Nina scoffed. "Let me guess. A fantastic string of events, too impossible to define, led you to the company of an immortal, who has no allegiance and could possibly jeopardize the Prime Objective," she said, fuming.

"It still worked," Thomas replied. "I did the best I could under the circumstances. Try to keep in mind that somehow you've known Dianna was the Prime for years. None of us were expecting Josh. As a result, I've been at a serious disadvantage."

"Okay, I'll admit that. I've had the easier end of the bargain. But that still doesn't explain why you're camped out in an abandoned library, across the street from a methadone clinic, or why you hijacked my Prime and led her on a wild goose chase over here." Sitting in silence, Thomas stared into his wife's blue eyes, hoping that she would put it together, so he wouldn't have to say it.

Suddenly the dawn of recognition spread across her face. "No, no, no," Nina said, sounding almost terrified. "Please, Thomas, tell me Josh isn't addicted to pain pills or heroin."

"As best as I can tell, it's pills," Thomas said, with a frown. "He didn't have any track marks on his arms from what I could see." Track marks. She hated the term. It was used by most caregivers to identify the buildup of scar tissue from repeatedly injecting drugs into a person's veins. Usually, the person would start at a low part of their arm, and over the course of their addiction, they would work their way up.

"With any luck, Josh should be released from the hospital soon. His primary care doctor should recommend him to the long-term care clinic across the street. The hospital is equipped with rehab services, but not as long-term as he'll need. I'm hoping the doctor will notice that and send him here. I know that this is bad news to you. If you had seen the aerial of the Burning Man festival and an aerial of the Epidaurus theater," he said, pointing towards the clinic of the same name, "you would know that this was meant to be. They're two sides of the same coin. This is where Josh will end up. Trust me." Thomas watched and waited, while she sat in silence, until finally she spoke.

"Thomas, I know you're bound by celestial law to preserve free will. But unless you intervene and set him straight, this reality and the Objective is lost," she said, standing up and walking off.

"Where are you going?"

"I'm leaving, Thomas, before I lose my temper. I love you to death, but you're putting me in a bad position right now."

"Why are you laying this on me? Don't you think I would rather be home with you, safe in Georgia?"

"That's not what I'm angry about. I know your feelings, and I know you mean well. For thousands of years, we've been devoted to training and sculpting avatars. Each one was molding the future, just to set the stage for the final showdown between the darkness and the light. So I'm a little upset when I come here, after you've basically shut me out all summer, to find that your Prime, who is an integral part of this world's survival, is basically worthless to us. And instead of being proactive, you're following what you see as signs and hoping for the best."

"It's what I do, Nina. You know this."

"Well, right now, it's not good enough," she said, unable to hide her distress. "Look around you, Thomas. We're in the endgame. The Monarchy doesn't seem to be playing fair. Yet, somehow, as smart as you are, you seem to be shocked by this. I'm disappointed. For all your long vision, I don't need to tell you what could happen to Dianna, if Josh can't step up to the plate." Thomas hung his head but gave no reply.

"If Josh bows out, you know this reality is a scrub. It also means that Dianna has to fight the war alone. Even with the angels at her command, the fate of the battle isn't assured. If the demons overwhelm her, they'll enslave her and physically force her to sire their children for the remaining thousand years until the earth is destroyed."

"It won't come to that, Nina. I swear," Thomas said,

shaking his head.

"Oh, you can bet your goddamn ass on that!" she cried. "If you can't turn the situation around in a week's time, I'll request that we switch assignments."

"What?"

"You heard me, Thomas. If you won't whip Josh into shape, I will. I love Dianna like a daughter. I will not let her purity be destroyed by the Monarchy. And you, of all people, know to what extent I will go to protect someone I love." Thomas nodded. He knew exactly what event Nina was speaking of. Even though it had been five thousand years, he still remembered it, like it was yesterday. "One week, Thomas. That's all I can put up with, before I step in," she said, shaking her head.

"There's always the option of conventicle," he suggested.

Nina thought for a second, considering the option. Each side had one mandatory timeout, called conventicle. Once called, both sides would leave this reality and go to Division to have the Creator arbitrate any differences of opinions, so he could balance the scales out.

"You know conventicle is the only timeout we get, and we always said we would save it for as long as we possibly could."

"I know," he agreed, "but the Monarchy is being unusually aggressive. If they're abusing their powers and bending the rules, we should stop them, before it gets out of hand."

"That may be true," she replied, as gray feathers began to grow over her pale skin, "but it doesn't mean we have to cash it in so soon." Thomas watched, as her arms became wings that effortlessly lifted her up into the air and out the hatch to the night sky.

She had a point. Thomas knew that everything she had said was true, but he couldn't abandon the signs that surrounded him. It was a secret language that only he and the Creator knew. Leaning back against the wall, Thomas drank in the silence around him once again. It was only him and the little candle that lit his way.

Glancing over at the shelves full of books, he wondered if he should formulate a plan. Every book on the far left of the room was dedicated exclusively to the great world wars. All he'd have to do is open any one of them, and they would inspire a new fighting strategy. His other option was to continue to follow the signs and hope that they led to a victory unattainable through regular means. He knew it was a huge gamble, and only a fool would face the end of the world without a plan. "What say you, old friend?" Thomas said out loud, to the seemingly empty library. In response, the little candle reached the end of its wick, plunging him into darkness.

"Well, God," Thomas said, a smile spreading across his face, "the fool's path it is."

Chapter 33

"Another night of barely any sleep," Nina thought, as she rolled out of bed. "I can't keep doing this to myself." Opening the door and stepping into the hall, she noticed that not only was Dianna's door open, but that Ramon's was too. Both rooms were empty. "That's odd," she thought, trudging down the hall to the bathroom. It had been two days since she'd seen Thomas. Ever since then, she just couldn't sleep, like something was nagging her conscious.

Flicking the light on, Nina looked in the mirror. "Lovely," she said out loud, as she noticed the puffy bags under her eyes. "We can't have any of that," she said, cupping her hands together as if they were filled with water and dragging them across her face. "Refresh," she said mentally. Then she looked back at her reflection. It wasn't her usual, vibrant face, but at least the puffiness was gone. She knew this was all tied to her mood. She had been in a funk since leaving the library, and it was all hinged on what she had said. She didn't really mean to be so abrasive and threaten to switch students. It was a hollow threat. She would never leave Dianna's side, but she had to kick Thomas into gear.

Later that night, though, as she had tossed and turned, she realized he was right. In a peculiar way, he always was. That's what perplexed her. She grabbed her toothbrush and loaded it up with a fat strip of toothpaste and pressed the on button, placing it to her teeth. What was killing her was Thomas's flippancy toward her situation. This was nothing new though, and she knew it. What made it all the more infuriating was she believed in Thomas's ability. But waiting wasn't her strong suit. She believed in action.

Her husband's path was looking for the tell-tale signs the Creator had left all over the place, as a sort of roadmap. It was like God's fingerprints. For those who could see them, they were everywhere. Spitting and rinsing, Nina flashed her teeth at the mirror and inspected them. To a certain extent, even Nina used them, but to a lesser degree. It was how she had known Josh was a shoe-in for Prime. Not only did the Imperials live on Taylor, which was Claire's true maiden name, but Claire's house was on Deerfield. Dianna's grandmother, Mary Jo, had gone by the name little deer, when she was younger. These threads were everywhere. Thomas always had to take it to a whole different level though. Sometimes it was hard for her logical side to take.

It was like what he said about the clinic. Maybe what Thomas was pointing out was true, that Burning Man and the clinic were just the flip side of each other's coin. As a doctor, Nina knew that the same was true with the sympathetic and parasympathetic systems of the body. The fiery sympathetic system burned like a sun throughout the day, and then the parasympathetic came at night and repaired all the damage that the day had done. She saw the correlation. What bothered her was when Thomas went so deep into the fabric of reality that he started to unravel even the threads themselves. As his wife, Nina had ridden the Thomas roller coaster before. It seemed to her the more interested he became with the synchronicities, the looser his grip on reality became. It was odd, because she'd seen in the past it had ebbed and flowed, and it was always tied to their time together.

When he was by her side, the man stayed firmly grounded and aspired to great heights, usually living his lives as an affluent aristocrat or sometimes even royalty. But on his own, his mind seemed to disperse. She noticed a pattern in the lives Thomas had led, and they all revolved around penance, subjugation, and slavery. She had brought it up every so often, and Thomas always dismissed it as luck of the draw. Nina suspected there was more to it than that, she just couldn't put a finger on it. It was almost as if there was an inherent self-loathing or a self-imposed exile that kept him down, when she wasn't around to pick him up. Whatever this certain malady was, it was definitely present in his Prime as well. Nina felt an involuntary shudder, as she remembered the similarities the watchers supposedly shared with their Primes. Was it also possible that the loneliness, that plagued Adam in the beginning, was still present in his male descendants all these long millennia since?

Nina wiped her hands on the blue towel near the door and strolled down the hall, towards the stairs. She could definitely hear Ramon and Cammy engaged in some heated discussion, but when weren't they? It wasn't until she made it down the stairs that Nina could tell what they were arguing about.

"Absolutely not! I forbid it, and that's final," Ramon said, folding his arms.

"What is?" Nina said, stepping into the kitchen to see both girls sitting around the breakfast table in their sleepwear.

"Just the woman I wanted to see," Ramon declared, pointing at her.

"I received a phone call at 8:00 this morning," Ramon said, "from a clinic where Camille applied for work."

"Yeah," Nina replied, shaking her head and realizing where this might be going.

"The director of the clinic told me that, since he had me on the phone, he might as well ask about Dianna as well, who had also applied," Ramon said, staring at Nina. "Of course, it totally blew me away, because I was never told about this. The best part is the director thanked me for my time and concluded with 'I'm just going through the motions, because the girls are so highly recommended.' Then he asked me how my daughters knew Dr. Nina Livingston."

Cammy shrugged her shoulders, "Sorry, Nina."

"No need to apologize," she said. "I'm happy to refer you, and I hope you get the job."

Ramon nodded in agreement. "Camille needs a job, but

Dianna is a full-time student, and she doesn't have time to volunteer anywhere but at the church."

"But I want this," Dianna said. "Doesn't my input matter?"

"I'm sorry, but not as far as this," her father stated. "We're just barely getting the church transferred over, and I need you there."

"I can do both, and you know it, dad. I'm a good daughter, and I've always done what you've asked. It's my free time. I should be able to do what I want with it; shouldn't I?"

"I would think so," Nina interjected, as she leaned up against the counter. "Work experience is an integral part of a young adult's life. She's a junior in high school. It would be good for her."

Ramon pushed away from the table. "I said no, and that's final."

"What a crock," interrupted Cammy. "You obviously didn't mind when she worked through the whole summer for you to get this house."

"Watch your mouth," Ramon warned her. "You live under this roof, but you don't have to."

"Ahem," Dianna spoke up. "My opinion's the same. And quit threatening to kick Cammy out, because she's not going anywhere."

"I hate to burst all three of your bubbles. Dianna's sixteen, and she'll do what I say."

"Just like that?" Nina cried.

"That's the way it has to be," Ramon said, defiantly. "I thought the four of us going on the road together would be a good idea. In some ways, it was. But instead of bringing us closer, like I'd hoped, somehow I ended up being the outcast. My daughter developed a rebellious streak a mile long. For the sake of the family, I kept everything together. I did my best for you girls. I gave up my room, so that you could have whatever alone time you needed to vent to each other. But now that we're back home, I'd like to point out that neither you nor Camille outranks me as head of household. I'm the parent here," Ramon shouted in Cammy's direction, "even though some people forget it."

Nina shook her head. She was hoping she could put this off as long as possible, but it looked like she had no choice. "We need to have a talk Ramon."

"Oh, really?" he said sarcastically. "As who? Nina Oleksander or Dr. Nina Livingston?"

"All of them," she replied calmly.

"I'm not going to sit here, while you stand and try to lecture me," he said, standing up.

"Feel free to do as you please, Day Star."

Ramon recoiled, as if he'd been bitten by the very word. "How?" he asked, shaking his head. "Nobody knows that name. I've never even spoken it before."

"I know," Nina said softly, her eyes deep with understanding.

Ramon turned to his daughters, "Did my father tell you?"

"No," Dianna said, shaking her head, as her sister shrugged her shoulders.

"If grandpa told me, I would have remembered. Believe me," Cammy said.

"Then how on earth could Nina know? Somebody must have told her."

"I know, Ramon, because I was fortunate enough to have been there on the day you received that name."

"There were only three people in that room; my mother, my father, and an old woman my mother knew."

"Did she look anything like this?" Nina asked, as her features shifted. Her hair became long and white. Her youthful, pale skin became creased and flooded with color. Startled, the grown man staggered back against the wall, speechless. "Relax, my friend," she said, shifting back to her familiar form. "I have powers too. It just happens that mine are a little different than yours or your daughter's. I'm a watcher, and so is my husband. I went to the reservation just to see your naming. I was Mary Jo's friend for a brief time. My husband knew your father when he was a young boy."

"Is he the one who taught my grandfather to do all those things?"

"Yes," Nina nodded.

Seemingly dumbfounded, Ramon braced himself against the wall. "But you listened the whole time and acted like you'd never heard the story," he finally managed to say.

"I hadn't," Nina insisted. "And that's why I wanted to hear it. Even though I've met your parents, it hardly means I know all their intimate details. At least now you know how I waltzed onto the reservation so easily. I was invited by, and under the protection of, your stubborn, old father. He wanted to see his granddaughter, the Chosen One, whom he knew I would train."

His eyes were as wide as saucers. Ramon turned to look at Dianna, who had thus far sat silently at the table. "Um, hi, dad," she said, smiling.

"Did you know this?" he asked Cammy, as he slowly lowered himself back down to his seat.

"Like, yeah, dad. Wasn't it obvious? You grew up in a family that had powers. Your daughter's strong enough to whip ass on a whole gang of elders, and she's barely sixteen. Of course, she's the Chosen."

Nina took a seat at the only empty chair left at the table next to Ramon, who was still eyeing her with suspicion. "You don't have to be alarmed, Ramon. I'm still the same Nina who has lived with you for the last three years."

"I'm sorry. I'm just so shocked. I feel like I've kind of been lied to, and you seem so unfazed by it."

"I suppose you have every right to feel that way. It's not like I don't understand what you're going through. It's just that I'm immortal, and I've lived hundreds of lives. I've been so many people in so many cultures, I kind of forget."

"Just how long are we talking?" Ramon asked warily.

"A long time. I'm thousands of years old. My husband and I have traveled the world many times over, teaching the different cultures information they needed to flourish in that age. And over the centuries you'd be surprised how many diplomas and degrees you can acquire. I really am a doctor, for what it's worth."

"Okay, Nina." Ramon said cautiously. "I'm trying my best to understand my daughter's special, and you're not what you seem to be. Where is this going?"

"I'm asking you, as a friend, to let Dianna make her own decisions," Nina replied, gesturing at the teen. "You're a good man, Ramon, and a good friend. But Dianna needs to grow, and you've taught her all you can."

"I'm her father, though."

"One of the best. I should know. I've known you since you were a boy, and I've lived with you for three years." Ramon winced just hearing the comment. Nina cocked her head and chuckled, "Don't get bent out of shape. When I went to visit Mary Jo and see you, it was a happy, proud day for all of us, even though your mom and dad had been fighting all morning over a dream your mother had."

"I remember my dad was angry."

Nina nodded. "Your father had come up with a grand plan of how his son, the Day Star, would lead the Shawnee to redemption. But Mary Jo already knew that wasn't your path. In her vision, you would leave the reservation and follow your own way. I know you and your father never really saw eye to eye. I'm sure you didn't talk much, but I know he at least told you about some of the things the Chosen One must face." Ramon nodded solemnly, as he looked towards Dianna.

"I care for you, Ramon. You've been a great friend, and you're everything I could have hoped Dianna's father could be. I'm proud of who you've become, but you can't teach Dianna what she needs to learn to defeat the adversary." Ramon sighed and hung his head, nodding. "Before your father passed, he knew that Dianna would face the coyote and fulfill every hope he had for you. I'm asking you to allow me to help her do that."

"I don't know," Ramon said, frustrated. "I'm her father. I've always protected her."

Nina flashed a broad smile, "Dianna, if you would." Ramon watched as Dianna got up from the chair.

"It was true," he thought to himself. Somehow, he always knew she was special. He also knew that he'd have to let her go someday, but he just couldn't. Even though he knew she was sixteen, in her pajamas she still looked to him like she did on Easter ten years ago, eager to hunt for hidden eggs. Then, all of a sudden, her whole body began to glow.

"Don't trip out, dad. It's not real fire," she said, as she burst into flames. Expecting heat, Ramon brought his hands up to shield his face, but soon saw that it wasn't necessary. Cammy's laughter echoed through the kitchen.

"Put your hands down, Ramon. There's no need to be scared." Looking around the kitchen in amazement, Ramon could see that nothing had caught on fire. Each flame coming off of his daughter was its own hue of red, yellow, and orange.

"It's incredible," he said, watching the power engulf the whole room. All the same, he felt a little nervous, as the flames touched his skin. But whatever hesitation he felt soon vanished, as he noticed that all the pain he usually had in his lower back, from driving the bus, was instantly gone. Even his knee injury from high school football relaxed.

"Your daughter will lead the Host of Heaven into the final

battle to crush the darkness. I know, as a father, you feel compelled to protect her. As you can see," Nina turned her head to Dianna, "she can protect herself."

"Check this out," she said, with a proud smile. Ramon gasped, as his daughter held her hands out shoulders' width apart, and a bolt of electricity began passing from one hand to the other. It was thin at first, but slowly became thicker.

"How does that feel?" Ramon said, reaching out his hand towards the energy, only to be stopped by Cammy.

"That's actually electricity, dad," she chuckled out loud.

"Oh," Ramon said, instantly feeling embarrassed. "It was just that the fire didn't..." He never got to finish the sentence, because he was overcome by pride. Between Dianna's hands, the electricity had split, becoming two bolts, which Dianna mentally shaped into what Ramon thought was going to be a circle.

"Come on, Dianna. Just like we practiced," Nina urged her.

The teen furrowed her brow in deep concentration, and the circle became a heart. "I love you, dad," she said, winking.

"Way to go," Cammy shouted, clapping loudly.

Nina smirked his way. "So what do you say, Ramon? Are you on board?"

"I guess," Ramon said reluctantly. "A lot of the people at the church are going to be disappointed though, when there's nobody to heal them."

"I agree," Nina said. "That's why I'm going to unlock your latent healing powers."

"Is that even possible?" he asked.

"It's well within my powers to unlock the genetic potential your mother passed to you, if that's what you want. Bear in mind, it's not as strong as your daughter's. But it's strong enough to cure just about anything."

Ramon smiled and looked at his daughters. "Well, what do you think?"

"Go for it," Cammy shouted.

Dianna nodded, "Follow your dreams, dad. Make our church proud."

"Okay. Let's do this," Ramon said, turning back to Nina.

"Okay," Nina said, cracking her knuckles and placing her hands on either side of his ears. "I never thought I'd see the day when I said this in my pajamas, but here it goes." Ramon waited in anticipation, as her hands became warm and Nina's gaze became locked on his. "Ramon Day Star Imperial, prepare yourself inwardly..."

Chapter 34
September 18th

"Mornin', space chimp," Charlie said, as Josh stepped out onto the patio. He slowly shuffled over to the diving board Charlie was lying on.

"How long have you been up?" Josh asked, sitting down on the concrete next to the empty pool.

"Don't know if I ever truly slept past 3:00 am," Charlie said, staring up at the blue sky.

"You should really watch yourself," Josh said, looking at the bottom of the sun-scorched pool. There was very little water in it, and the drop had to be twelve feet.

"I know," Charlie replied, turning his head to face Josh. "I seriously couldn't sleep last night. I kept having nightmares."

"About what?" Josh asked.

Charlie held his right arm up in the air. "What do you think?"

"Gotcha," Josh nodded. He'd had a dream about Deus, too. He was in a coffee shop with Dianna, and the hulking teen threw a bike through the front window. If he wasn't so high, it probably would've jolted him awake. Because of the drug, he was trapped in a long saga of running and Deus killing everything in the vicinity, while Josh was barely able to stay a step ahead of him.

"Every time I close my eyes, he's there," Charlie said wearily, "just constantly taunting me about singing the blues and how I haven't paid my dues yet."

"Maybe you should talk to somebody," Josh suggested.

"I am, asshole. I'm talking to you," the redhead chuckled. We're not here on vacation. We're hiding. Remember?" He sat up and placed his feet on the cement. "It's come to the point that, even when I'm awake, for some reason I'll sing the song in my mind."

As if on cue, an unwanted voice in Josh's mind began to sing, "The hip bone's connected to the leg bone."

"Gee, thanks. You're a real friend. C'mon, Josh. Share the pain," Charlie smirked.

"So what did you do all night long? Just sit there?"

"I guess," Charlie said, nodding solemnly. "I kind of had one moment, when I was caught up in a crystal-clear epiphany though."

"Really?" Josh asked, bringing his knees up. He really wished they had something to sit on, but there just wasn't any furniture. Everything in the backyard was concrete. If it wasn't concrete, it was either dead or in a late stage of dying.

"Sometime near morning, before the light came, I was laying on my back, just kind of taking mental inventory, when I remembered this freaky show I'd seen on a nature channel." Standing up, Charlie stretched towards the sky. Josh heard the pop of his back. "So anyway, these kids that were around our age were talking about how their lives were, and it was totally insane. This boy had to trek for four days, braving all kinds of obstacles, just to attend school every term. He said that he would do it every day, if he had to, just to get an education."

"Holy crap. That's wild," chuckled Josh. He wondered if Charlie's conscious was telling him something. It was the middle of September, and neither of them had set foot on campus. They promised each other they'd take a week to cut down on the drugs. Here it was, nearly a week and a half later. If anything, the amount of heroin they were smoking hadn't decreased but had increased.

"Then this other brother and sister go out and walk all over this hot as hell sandy desert area, so they can hunt. On their way, they run into a lion's paw prints. So they decide it would be better to take the long way around. So here they are, just practically bare-assed, with the sun beating down on them. Finally, they see this little gopher-looking thing, and the sister shoots it with a blowgun. And they get hella happy, jumping around like they won a car or some shit." Josh couldn't help but laugh, even though he knew Charlie was being serious.

"But they didn't win a car," Charlie exclaimed, with a befuddled look on his face. "They were happy because the family could eat that day. And because they could eat, that meant they could live to hunt another day."

"And this was your epiphany? You remembered a show you watched?"

"No, Michaels. It wasn't," Charlie groaned in frustration. "It was after that, when I realized that I don't have any of their skills or virtues. For some odd reason, I expect a life that they could only dream of. The shitty thing is, it's right at my fingertips, but unless it's given to me, I don't know if I can put forth the effort." Josh sat in silence, dreading to find out if this was Charlie's moment of clarity, or if it was, as he suspected, just the tip of the iceberg.

"If I were in their position right now, Josh, I seriously don't know if I'd adapt, grab a blowgun and go hunting with them," Charlie said, shaking his head, "Or maybe I might just curl up under a rock and wait to die."

"What? You're kidding, right? You'd just give up?"

"I'm not sure. Personally, I don't think I have it in me anymore. If the American way of life vanished, I don't think I could go on with less. There was a time I could, but now I just can't. I can barely find the enthusiasm to continue right now."

"Don't talk like this, Charlie. You're freaking me out." Josh didn't want to admit it, but he'd thought the same thing. They had been in the place over a week, and neither of them had seen a shower since coming here. At least they had a few sets of clothes though. After three days of wearing the same thing, day in and day out, Charlie suggested they sneak into their places under the cover of night and get fresh clothes.

"I guess remembering the show wasn't what boggled me," Charlie continued. "It was after, when I realized that Deus was right. I've been singing the blues, like life's hard, ever since I could talk. But even my worst day would've been a triumph for any of the kids on that show."

"Damn, Charlie, you've been up since then?"

Charlie shook his head slowly, "No." His voice threatening like he might cry at any moment. "I blazed up the pipe and nodded off and had another dream. In this one, I was being chased by Deus. But in this one, I didn't run. I walked up to him and just held my arm out."

"And what happened?"

"He broke it," Charlie said, his glassy eyes staring at his dirty, plaster cast. "But I didn't ask why afterwards, like I normally do. I just sat down in the sand and thought about how one of those kids would still probably trade places with me, if they had the chance. And if they did, I'd still probably die inside a week."

Josh pondered the weight of what Charlie had just said. He was just about to respond, when he heard the screen door open behind him. Immediately, he saw the blood drain from his friend's face, as he stood up.

"Mini-mart!" the confused teen shouted.

Josh turned to see Thomas walking towards him and felt his heart sink. "Jesus Christ. Can't this guy take a hint?" he thought to himself. "It's not what you think, Charlie. It's my watcher."

"Oh," the teen replied slowly, sitting back down on the diving board.

"Whatever you have to say, I'm not interested, Thomas."

"Just please hear me out," the man said. "I just need a minute of your time."

Charlie smirked, "Actually, after months of arguing with

him, I'm interested in hearing what he has to say."

"Josh shrugged his shoulders. "Whatever. How'd you find us?"

"I tried to locate you with my mind. As your watcher, I should be able to find you when I need to. Right now I have a sneaking suspicion you're obscured from everybody. It's unusual, but I figured you had to be somewhere. So I've been driving all over this town, looking for that ugly Jeep that's parked down the street."

"Thanks, guy," Charlie said, shooting a salute to Thomas.

"First of all, I'd like to apologize, Josh. I'm sorry to hear about Sam."

"Yeah, that was unfortunate; wasn't it?" Josh said, frowning at Thomas. On top of the dream about Deus, Josh had also had recurring dreams about the accident site. It was one of the main reasons why he was smoking so much more heroin. He didn't just want to get high. He wanted to go under to a point where he didn't think anymore.

"You might as well apologize to Charlie too, after he viciously got his ass kicked out in the desert."

"I'm actually not at fault for that. For what it's worth, I'm sorry."

"What do you mean, Thomas? You could've taken us out of there."

"I did offer to take you back to Milton, remember?"

"I don't remember that," Josh said. "What I do remember is you saying something about I might be tempted." Josh wondered how he could be so insanely pissed, but the usual red vision or throbbing temples were nowhere to be found.

"Yeah. That was one hell of a tempting," the skinny teen said, holding up his arm for Thomas to see. "You really missed out."

"You're lucky," Thomas said. "They could have killed

you."

"Lucky me, I suppose," Charlie snorted.

Josh laughed and shook his head in amazement. "Been a real hoot. Thanks for the condolences, but I don't need any more problems in my life."

"I thought you wanted to fight for your future with Dianna? The future of humanity isn't that important for you?"

"It was," Josh said, looking away from Thomas. "But I realized, in the depths of my temptation, when I found the strength to say no to Satan, there was no help for what happened, as they ripped my life to shreds afterwards. So let me ask you a question. After denying Satan, didn't I deserve better than I got?"

"I don't know what to say. I'm sorry, and I'm here to help you in any way I can. Just ask."

"I don't want your help. I know better than to fall for your line of BS again. And if I ever meet the Creator or any of the angels in this lifetime, I'd sooner spit in their eye than ask for their help."

"Please tell me you don't mean that, Josh."

"Shouldn't I? Really," Josh said, angrily. "I was offered the world on a platter, Thomas. And I walked! And what did that get me?"

"You got the chance to live and fight another day."

Josh laughed out loud. "Oh, my God. That's hilarious. You should have been here about five minutes ago, because we were just talking about something along those lines."

"I'm not surprised," he said, nodding. "Your power extends both forwards and backwards. It's a part of you." He hoped that would help. To Thomas's dismay, Josh's reply was as emotionless as his face.

"I don't care. I'm over it."

"I'm sorry you feel that way," Thomas said slowly. "I was hoping there was a bit of the Josh Michaels I used to know inside of you, but it seems the drugs have taken their toll."

"What's that supposed to mean?" Josh snapped back angrily.

"The opiates, or any drug for that matter, have a profound effect not only on your body's metabolism but on your brain's chemistry, too. It can permanently change everything, even your sleep cycles. I know you don't notice it," Thomas said, pointing at the two boys, "but you're both nothing like the way you were when I last saw you. Just say the word, and I can get you both into treatment right now."

"And why would we want to do that?" Charlie asked.

"It's obvious; isn't it?" Thomas stated, in shocked disbelief. "If not for drugs, you still seriously need therapy for the post-traumatic stress disorder you both seem to be suffering from, and that can take years of work with a psychiatrist."

"Years?" Charlie cried. "It only took a minute for Deus to beat me up. It's easier to stay high," he said, folding his arms.

"Come on, now. Don't be so hasty," Thomas replied. "If Josh continues his training and gets in rehab, he could easily heal you."

"Dude! I totally didn't think of that, my fair-weather Freud," Charlie said. "Josh, you could use your powers to fix my brain and put me back to normal!"

Josh chuckled and stood up from the ground. "Are you seriously crazy? Both of you are ignoring the fact that my powers never work right in the first place. It's a crap shoot on what they'll even do, when they do decide to work."

"But you can try," the redhead pleaded.

"Try what? Psychic neurosurgery on my best friend? I think I'll pass. As it is, my grandmother's in a hospital bed, unable to speak, thanks to me."

Thomas raised his eyebrow. "I wouldn't be so quick to think that. I'm not convinced it was you. Your power doesn't work the way you think it does."

"Come again?"

"Dianna's powers work like that," Thomas said. "She's the fiery aspect of the sun. She can call forth energy on command. Yours is a little different."

"Different how?" Charlie asked, suddenly interested.

"Josh's power is similar to mine but to a much larger degree, because he's the Prime. If Dianna is active, you are passive," he said, pointing to the boy. "You can basically do the things she does. Instead of doing it on command though, you just need some kind of emotion to back it. And I don't see you being so mad at your grandmother you could strike her down, and definitely not accidentally. Your power reaches forward and backward simultaneously, influencing events to bring your wants and needs into the now. It's a very special gift."

"What can you do with it?" Charlie asked.

Thomas paused and grinned. He looked at Charlie for a moment and then said, "Okay, I want you to think of a number between one and ten million."

"Okay," Charlie said, with a cocky smile.

"Just make sure it's not four," Thomas smiled.

"Shit," Charlie shouted.

"Or one thousand and eight."

"Dude," Charlie shook his head and looked at Josh. "A little help here." Josh chuckled at Charlie's predicament. "What are you laughing about? Derelict Dan is reading my mind like it's the Sunday paper."

"Mmmm, I doubt it," Josh said, thinking it over.

"Then how did I do it?" Thomas asked, pulling his dreads back over his shoulders.

After a moment's thought, Josh answered, "You didn't read his mind. You told him what to think."

"What?" screamed Charlie. "That's like ten times worse!"

"I'm sure that being immortal, his central nervous system is stronger and more evolved."

"Very good," Thomas said, well pleased. "That just so happens to be one of the first steps in the training."

"Yeah, and I'm sure there's no synchronicity there," Josh said, kicking his foot at the ground. "Thanks for the impromptu training, but I'd like to get back to being high with my buddy."

"Okay," Thomas said, shaking his head. "I don't want to burden you with saving the world or rescuing the girl you supposedly love. God only knows, the demons will go after her next."

Josh snorted and clenched his jaw, "Don't try to guilt trip me, Thomas. The same Creator, who crushed me like an ant under his heel, will no doubt step in and save her."

"How did you get like this? I can't even recognize you."

"I often wonder the same thing," Josh replied, unable to hide his pain. "But then I remember. There was a time when I was younger, before I came to this goddamn town. A time when it was just me and my mom, and I didn't have a care in the world. There was a feeling I had that can only be described as safety," he said wistfully. "But it's gone now," he said, his voice getting louder. "And it's never coming back," he said, gritting his teeth as if the realization had cut him like a knife.

"In fact, for the life of me, I can't even remember what it felt like. Because every time I try to think of my mother, the memory of happy Sam isn't the one that comes to me. It's always the look of fear on her face. My mother is afraid of her own child. That's how positively crippled I am, Thomas. I know you just want me to see, but I'm blind now. And unlike somebody who's been blinded, it's worse for me. At least they can remember what the light used to look like. I can't even do that."

"I'm sorry, Josh. I truly am," Thomas said, gripping the boy's shoulder. "I didn't come here to hurt you or cheat you out of the right to be mad. I'll go. Just do one thing for me."

"What's that?"

"Can I come by tomorrow and bring clean water and some food? Real food, not like the junk food I saw in the kitchen."

"I guess," he mumbled. "But no more training."

"No. I can see that, for now, you're far too gone for that. But I do hold out hope that we can get you help, when you're ready for it."

"Why are you doing this?"

"Sooner or later, these drugs aren't going to get you high anymore. You'll realize that doing them is no different than wiping your ass with the back of your shirt, after you've taken a crap. Maybe you feel clean, but now you've just got a different problem following you around."

"Well, if getting me into rehab is your aim, then don't waste your money on me."

"It's not my money," Thomas said, pulling out a roll of bills. "It's yours." Josh looked in Thomas's hand to see every bit of cash he'd ever given the man, when he thought he was homeless. "Do you see what's in my hand, Josh? It's a symbol of a higher truth."

"What do you mean?"

"I know you think the Creator's laughing at you, but it's not him that's the beast. And like your addiction, it's never satisfied. No matter what you feed it, it's always going to ask for more, raging impatiently, hurting you, and laughing while you bleed. But the Creator is kind and patient. He takes the love you send him, and he holds it until a time when you need it most. And then he sends it back to you, like rain on a dry, cracked, desert floor. This roll of money is the kindness you showed me, even though your friend said I'd just spend it on drugs. Unfortunately," Thomas said, walking towards the house, "that's exactly the reason why I can't give it back to you right now. You'd just spend it on drugs."

***

"Did I ever tell you," Charlie said, tying the tourniquet around his arm, "that I like to take one word song titles from the '80s and '90s and sing them out loud? But instead of the girl's name, I like to insert the word pizza."

"No," Josh chuckled out loud, watching his friend trying to shoot up for the first time. "Why those songs?"

The redhead heated up the spoon with the heroin in it. "I guess because that's the stuff Sue listened to, when she'd fold laundry and clean." Josh watched nervously, as Charlie put the cotton ball in the bubbling solution to act as a filter. He flexed his left arm against the rubber band.

"And you sing the whole song with just the word pizza substituted for the girl's name?"

Charlie grinned a huge grin and stuck the needle into the cotton ball. "Don't get me wrong. I'm just saying that as an example," he said. "You could just as easily use any other word, like Vivian or porn." With that said, he drew back on the plunger and sucked the fluid from the spoon into the syringe.

"Are you sure you want to do this?" Josh asked anxiously.

"Hell, yeah," Charlie said. "I'm not having jacked-up dreams tonight." Josh had hoped his friend wouldn't say it with so much zeal. Somewhere in his mind, he'd hoped Charlie's stomach had the same butterflies as he had. Nervously giggling, Josh watched as the needle pierced the biggest vein on his skinny arm. "Are you okay with doing this?" Charlie asked, calmly drawing back on the plunger to see the rush of blood, and then he pushed down carefully on the plunger.

"Yeah. I guess I'm just kind of scared," Josh replied, looking tense. "In the past, I always justified everything we did by telling myself that at least we weren't shooting it." No matter who Josh had talked to, whether it was in school, the fire department, or the hospital, everybody said this was the point of no return. After this, you were officially a bona fide junkie.

"Goodbye, Deus," Charlie said blissfully, as he withdrew the needle and slammed his forearm up against his bicep to stop the minuscule hole from bleeding.

"Your turn," he said, glancing at the half-full syringe.

"No. I'm cool," Josh said quietly. He couldn't decide whether he was working up the courage or giving himself time to back out. He was pretty surprised, when Charlie suggested they bust out the rig that Amanda had given them the first time they'd bought heroin from her.

"I'll keep an eye on you, just to be safe," Josh said.

"Good idea," Charlie said, his lids getting heavy. "It's kind of funny," the redhead said, closing his eyes.

"What is?"

"How the hell did we go from fighting the dragon in video games and shooting horse in your grandma's driveway to chasing the dragon and shooting horse in an abandoned house?"

"For the life of me, I couldn't tell you. But I've wondered the same thing," Josh answered bitterly, staring off in the distance.

"Wow," Charlie said, sliding farther down the wall. Josh jumped up and laid him on his left side. "It's cool," Charlie whispered.

"How does it feel?" Josh asked. All the teen could manage was a smile and a nod. Josh picked up the needle and syringe and placed it on the mantle of the fireplace, where nobody could accidentally poke themselves.

All of a sudden, Charlie's eyelids fluttered. "It's awesome! Remember when I said that falling asleep when I wasn't high was as hard as a midget trying to win a slam dunk contest?"

"Yeah," Josh chuckled, lying down on the carpet.

"Well, I'm a ten foot tall midget right now," Charlie grinned, with his eyes closed. Josh looked up at the syringe. He really wanted to do this before the last of the sun's rays disappeared. After it was dark, it would almost be impossible to do by the light of Charlie's cell phone. Josh put the tourniquet on his arm and stared at his veins, squeezing his fist. Somehow, he just couldn't get into it. Every time he searched for a vein, he spaced out.

Josh pulled the tourniquet off. This was bullshit. As much as he told himself he wasn't going to let Thomas's statements get under his skin, it had happened anyway. Ever since the watcher had left the house, Josh's mind kept wandering to Dianna having to fight the battle by herself. The thoughts of her falling to the Monarchy had played in his head over and over. Every time he felt the urge to get high, he'd see her face that night at the Lira bandstand, lying on her back with her head in his lap. He saw her dark, raven hair spilling over his arm in the same area where he planned to place the needle.

Staring at the syringe on the mantle, Josh felt inside him a different kind of war. It was a war of indecision. It raged within him, with all the fury of an inferno. It was between what he felt for Dianna, the girl of his dreams, and the heavy burden of his reality. And he felt the key to his shackles was inside the syringe. All he had to do was set himself free. He wondered if he could ever truly go back to who he was. Was that person already dead even? He didn't know. All he knew was that, in the current shape he was in, he couldn't save anybody. He'd only drag Dianna down into the depths of his despair, along with him, quite possibly drowning the both of them.

Chapter 35

"What an absolute shit hole," Deus said, walking through the sliding doors of the twenty-four hour supermarket.

Nodding at his companion, Hasden smugly replied, "Well, what do you expect? He's on a teacher's salary. Let's just find our friend and get out of here."

"I've been waiting to kick this guy's ass since the first time I saw him," Deus chuckled out loud, as the night manager and his female checker exchanged worried glances. Walking down the aisles, Hasden searched for his prey. Aisle five: diapers and baby food. Definitely not. Aisle four: hair care products. Highly unlikely. Aisle three: fruits and vegetables. Hasden grinned as he took a peek around the corner. Bingo.

He would have recognized the olive khaki pants and shaved head anywhere. He motioned to Deus to sneak up aisle four, so they could catch him from both sides. The thought of what was about to transpire, as the giant demon made his way up the aisle, practically made him giddy with anticipation. There was something about the thrill of the hunt that was so primal and raw. As a demon, there were few words to describe it. Seeing this sorry son of a bitch drive by earlier today was like finding a lost $20 bill in an old pair of jeans. They'd been stalking him ever since.

The only thing that was disappointing to Hasden was that it had to end here, and it was going to go down to the tune of elevator music. Whatever. He'd make do. Stepping into the aisle, he did a double take at his target. Oh, yeah. It was Douglas all right. He even had his trademark douchey leather teacher's satchel with him in the shopping cart.

These places usually had security measures, but Hasden genuinely doubted this one did. Even though it had the tilted mirrors near the edge of the ceiling, he didn't see any cameras.

Quickening his pace, he put a fake smile on and said to himself, "Showtime."

"Mr. Douglas, what are you doing here?"

The teacher spun around, genuinely surprised at first, but smiled cordially. "Billy, how are you?"

"Good, good," he said, holding out his hand. The teacher grabbed on and gave it a slight squeeze.

"It's funny, running into you here," the teacher said, pulling the sleeves of his sweat shirt up. "How was your summer vacation?"

"Good," Billy replied, robotically. He could see that Deus had rounded the corner and was headed down the aisle, straight towards them. As the teacher smiled and droned on, Hasden wondered how many times he'd fought the urge to smack that idiotic goatee off of his clueless face.

"Hey, can I ask you a question?" Billy said, leaning in towards the teacher.

"Sure, go ahead. Is it school-related?"

"No, no, it's personal," Billy replied, seeing Deus's dome rise up behind the unsuspecting man. "I never got your first name."

"Oh, it's Tom. I'm named after my father."

"That's interesting. Are you sure it's not Thomas?" Billy asked, as the surprised man noticed the large teen behind him.

"Oh, hello," the teacher said nervously.

"It's good to finally see you again," Deus said, placing the emphasis on the word "finally."

"You, too," the teacher meekly replied, noticeably trembling.

"Why, Mr. Douglas," Billy said with glee, "you don't have to worry about Deus. You're actually one of his favorite teachers. In fact, the other day, we were talking about the fact that Deus never really grew up with a father in his life. But, if he did have one, he'd want him to be like you."

"I did say that," Deus said, as he began rummaging through the teacher's cart and arbitrarily tossing toilet paper at the teacher's feet.

"How'd you like to join our family, Mr. Douglas? You can be Deus's new father figure." Billy glared in the eyes of the nervous man. "How about it, Douglas? Would you like to become a part of our family? You could be Deus's dad, which would make you my Uncle Tom." Hasden grinned evilly at the end of the sentence.

The teacher shook his head, confused. "I don't understand. Was that supposed to be racist?"

"Of course," Deus said, tossing more items from the cart. "That's good ol' plantation humor, right there."

"I don't know what you guys are talking about," the cowering man replied. "What is this about?" Hasden sighed. Looking in the mirror, he could see both employees were eaves dropping. It wouldn't be too long before they called the cops. Personally, he could do this all night, but it had to end now.

"Cut the crap, Thomas. We know who you are."

The man shook his head. "What?"

"Listen, and listen well," Hasden said menacingly. "We know where Nina is. We've known all along. We've just been waiting for you to pop your head up, so we could get a shot at you both. But goddamnit, if you don't drop the charade," Hasden said, poking the man's chest, "I swear I'll send Deus over to the Imperial house. What he'll do to your wife will make what we did to Lilith look like a heavy petting session in comparison. Now is that what you want?"

Like a serpent, Hasden stared into the man's frantic eyes. It practically sickened him. The man was so good at acting, he had no idea when to quit. Hell, they never would have figured it out themselves. But after four days of scanning the minds of ants, they saw something peculiar; a grungy, homeless man getting into the same make and model car that their old American History teacher drove. So they figured they'd pay Mr. Douglas a visit.

"I don't know what you're talking about," the teacher cried, his legs giving out. The terrified man fell back so hard, he took a pyramid of apples down with him. As the fruit cascaded down, bouncing and rolling in every direction, Hasden shook his head.

"Have it your way, Thomas. Just remember, I gave you a choice. Come along, Deus."

"Finally," the demon roared with a fierce joy. "I've got a whole diary of dark fantasies that I've been saving just for her." The huge demon grabbed the shopping cart and threw it effortlessly at the security mirror, shattering it over the employees' heads. "Clean up on aisle four," he shouted maniacally.

Hasden waited only long enough to see to which side the metal frame fell, immediately hyper-sprinting to where he knew the frightened employees would run to. "Ah, just like a rat in a maze. They're so predictable." Both employees stopped dead in their tracks, when they saw him appear out of thin air and shout, "SLEEP!" Bill smiled, as they fell to the ground like marionettes with their strings cut, collapsing into a heap against each other. "After you awaken," Hasden said, pouring his influence into the command, "you will not call the police. Instead, you will be overcome with the urge to clean this pigsty. It's filthy."

Thomas didn't know how they'd found him, but it hadn't taken too long for him to assess the situation and realize he was at a serious disadvantage. He knew he couldn't fight two demons in close quarters. He had to get them outside, where he could maneuver. As soon as he heard the automatic double doors, he dropped character and sprung up off the floor, making a break-neck run down the aisle, towards where his bag had fallen. "I guess I don't need this," he said, pulling off his black sweatshirt and throwing it down.

In the glass doors of the dairy section at the end of the aisle, Thomas could see Douglas's reflection sprinting towards him. It quickly changed, adding ten inches of height and fifty pounds of lean, toned muscle to become the true Thomas. Coming to a halt at the end of the aisle, he took a look at the face he hadn't seen in over a century. A face that, despite being his true form, had somehow become the stranger. "Good to see you again," he said, at his reflection.

Then he darted towards his bag, unlocking it, to reveal the two semi gauntlets inside. Each one was a six inch brass rod that fit comfortably molded to his closed palm, curving up over his hand, becoming brass knuckles. Thomas slid on the left one and smiled. On the bottom end was a spike, and on the top end was a smooth brass adaptor that could accommodate anything from a mace to a blade. He was traveling light today, so he pulled out the twin braided bullwhips, with razor blades woven into the ends.

As he fitted the attachments, Thomas thought about the fact that he had been right all along. He'd suspected the Imperial girl ending up on the internet would cause Nina to stick out like a sore thumb. In fact, he anticipated that the Monarchy would send demons to investigate. He just never dreamed that it would be the same two demons who seemed to love destroying the fruits of his labor. To say they had a long history of mutual hate was an understatement. He hoped they'd leave by summer. When that didn't happen, he knew he'd have to go underground for everybody's sake. And after a summer of staying in the shadows to protect his wife, there was no way in Hell he was going to let them anywhere near the Imperial house.

Charging towards the sliding exit doors, Thomas smiled, knowing that his vengeance would be released through the twin braids of justice trailing behind him. Cool wind greeted his face, as he stepped outside. Immediately, he could see the demons had dismantled Douglas's car. Pieces were strewn around the empty parking lot. The tall demon had pulled the engine block out of the chassis, hefting it over his head triumphantly.

"Ha-Satan," Thomas roared, snapping each of the bullwhips at both sides of Deus's jugular veins and cutting them both viciously. Screaming in pain, the demon dropped the engine block on his face.

"You son of a bitch!" he screamed, as it crashed to the ground. Deus gave it a kick, launching the engine towards Thomas. He rolled to the right. The huge hunk of metal crashed through the front of the supermarket instead.

"Oh, the old Hebrew names," Hasden said, smiling. "It makes me feel so nostalgic." Thomas readied the whips. He could see Deus's bloody, smashed face was rapidly healing.

"So help me, God. I'm gonna kill your black ass for that!" Deus screamed. Thomas replied by snapping the left whip as a warning to stay back.

Hasden smiled. "You don't plan on holding us back with those; do you?"

"No, Satan. I'm just going to teach you a long overdue lesson. Don't mess with my students."

The demon grinned, "Who, me?" Thomas gritted his teeth. The demon's arrogance turned his stomach. "Oh, Thomas. Please tell me you're not still holding a grudge over the whole Nat thing?"

"Yeah. Just slightly," he snarled. "What you did was wrong, and completely out of protocol. And I'll be damned, if I'm going to let you do it to Josh."

"Really?" the spiky-haired demon replied. "I hate to say it, but I already have. I'm in this bitch to win it. And I'll break anything or anyone who gets in my way. When all is said and done, Thomas, you're going to wish you were back on the plantation with your prodigy. The Monarchy's goal isn't to enslave just one race. We're gonna put a noose around the neck of the whole world."

"Not while I'm here," Thomas defiantly shook his head. "I might not have your powers, but my sight is keen and my vision is long. That's why I brought these," he said, cracking both the whips in tandem. Stepping forward, Thomas launched both whips at their faces, catching them both off guard.

"Kill him!" Hasden yelled. Deus lowered into a football stance.

"Nice bull whips, bitch. I had one back in the day too, so I know they don't work too well up close." Thomas took a low stance, as Deus charged in swiftly.

"That's right, come to papa," Thomas said. At the last possible moment, he side-flipped over the charging juggernaut and landed between the two demons. First, Thomas struck low to bring their guards down. Then he quickly spun around and swung high. Both whips immediately found their marks, wrapping the razor-tipped braids around their necks. Thomas pulled with all of his might to tighten the hold, bringing Deus to his knees. And then hitting the built-in disengage levers, he released the whips, sending Deus forward and Satan reeling back.

Thomas moved towards the larger of the two demons first. As long as he could keep him off balance, he could press the advantage. He fired off with an uppercut. Then he began to pummel Deus's body with the brass knuckles. One more hard jab in the ribs, and Thomas spun as fast as he could, backhanding the demon with the spear tip. He felt a dull crunch, as it pierced the skull. Then he disengaged the tip, leaving the demon convulsing on the ground.

"Don't think I forgot about you," Thomas turned to Satan.

"Oh, I wouldn't dream of it," Hasden growled, as he pulled the leather whip from his bloody, lacerated neck. Thomas smiled, as he saw the damage the razor blades had done. Satan shook his head, as he looked down at his shirt. It was stained red, with his own blood.

"You're fast for an old man," he said, grabbing his throat. "But in the end, you're still just a watcher, and I am the Prince of Darkness. And, quite plainly, you're surrounded by it right now. So I'd say you're shit out of luck, Thomas." With that, Thomas began to notice forms emerging from the darkness around Satan's aura. It was barely noticeable at first, except for the void of any light. The darkness quickly began to morph into the shape of two wolves.

"I have to get to higher ground," Thomas thought. Looking up, he searched for a way to get up on the building behind him. All he saw was Mephistopheles descending down on him from the roof. The shock barely registered with him. The only thing that did was the dull crack, as the baseball bat in her hands connected with his head. Then he was covered in darkness.

Chapter 36

"Is it midnight already?" Cammy groaned, as she began to clear the dinner table.

"You'd better get used to it," Nina chuckled, "because this is life on swing shift."

"It's not bad," Dianna said from her seat across from Nina. "Besides, my shifts are only Wednesday and Saturday. Dianna had to admit though, the time did seem to travel fast. All it took was a trip home and a fast meal, and, already, it was after midnight. She wasn't entirely used to waking up on a Wednesday and then going to bed on a Thursday yet, but it was worth it for the medical experience she was getting.

"Where were you?" she asked Nina, noticing she wasn't wearing her usual Pilates outfit. Instead, she had dark blue jeans and a white satin blouse with her black leather jacket on.

"The movies. I figured if it was out by 11:00, I could meet you guys here and ask how the shift went. Now that I'm back to a normal routine, I'll have to live vicariously through you two."

"It was good," Dianna replied.

"Seriously, sis? I wouldn't say it was good," Cammy chuckled, as she threw the fast food bags away in the trash. "I'd say it was a little better than last shift. Which reminds me, Nina. Have you ever heard the term, 'You're full of shit?'"

The woman smirked and nodded. "Over the past few centuries, I've heard it a few times."

"Well, me and mi hermana here came on shift today and had to call 911 for this twenty-eight year old guy, who was all constipated from his pain pills. He's in the treatment program at Epidaurus and was at his weekly drug recovery meeting, complaining of stomach pain. We found out that he hadn't taken a crap in a week." Cammy sat down at the table, with a look of disgust on her face.

"Oh, lord," Nina laughed.

"The doctor said the pills he takes do this all the time. I was just gonna have hands of light go in and cure him, but she complained it stunk too much in the room." Dianna hid her face behind her hands, while she laughed.

"That is so not how it happened, dork. My power cures energy abnormalities and deficiencies. He had an obstruction. There's a big difference."

"Whatever, Dr. Imperial," Cammy said to her blushing sister.

"You called 911 for that?" Nina cried.

"We had to. The doctor gave him enough laxative to give the whole town diarrhea for a week, and nothing happened. Besides, he was in pain."

"But at least there was a bright side. Cammy got a date Friday," Dianna said.

"I swear. You are awful," Nina said to them both.

"What? Is 911 not the number you call to have hot guys and girls in uniform delivered to your doorstep?" she chuckled.

"No, it's not." Nina laughed and shook her head. Then she slyly asked, "So did they say you guys looked cute in your medical scrubs?"

Dianna smiled. "Yes, they did, as a matter of fact. But I have to agree with Cammy, there wasn't a guy who showed up on the engine or the ambulance who didn't look insanely fit. They were hot."

"Oh, no. Not you too?" Nina said, shaking her head in amusement. "You're supposed to be there learning how to heal."

"I am," Dianna said. "But every now and then, I need a diversion. I'm beginning to notice it's a lot more stressful than healing in church."

"I know, child. Those people had a complaint you could focus on. These people are affected systemically, from their kidneys and liver to their brain chemistry. Believe me, this is good training for you."

"I know," the girl agreed. "It was definitely the challenge I was looking for, but I wasn't ready to see so many. They just flood off the streets. They're so lost, it practically breaks my heart. Which reminds me, any word from Thomas about Josh? Is he doing any better? After his mother passed, I know you told me he was having a hard time trying to cope."

Nina's smile faded, and she grimly nodded, "Thomas contacted me today, and-- AAAHHH!!" The woman screamed, clutching her head, surprising both girls.

"Grab her!" Dianna yelled, rising up from the table. The older sister was already up and gripping Nina by the jacket, guiding her to the ground. Cammy reached down to stabilize her head, but it was gone.

"Thomas is in trouble!" Nina said, painfully holding her head while moving towards the front door. Don't go anywhere. And for God's sake, DO NOT follow me," she said, looking at Dianna.

"But, Nina, I can help," the girl said, as protective flames erupted from her body.

"No, child. Please," Nina pleaded, "if you ever loved me, don't put yourself in this harm. You're not ready yet." Seeing the pain and urgency in the watcher's face, she nodded. And just like that, the copper-haired woman was gone. All that was left was the gust of wind in the doorway and the sound of exploding windows and chirping car alarms all along Taylor Road.

***

Moving at the speed of sound wasn't an easy feat, but Nina didn't have time for convenience. Thomas had taken a blow to the head that would kill an ordinary man, and time was of the essence. She knew, as an immortal, he would heal without sustaining permanent injury. But if she didn't get there soon, the Monarchy would try to take him prisoner. As she let her magic guide her to her twin, she tried her best to not think of the stories she'd heard of what the demons did to their immortal captives, like locking them in vats of acid so the skin would eat away, just as quickly as the immortals body could replace it.

"All I have to do is get there," she thought to herself. She was stronger than he was, magically, and against demons, magic was the best defense. Closing her eyes, Nina let his pain guide her like a beacon, as she began to draw the electricity from the transformers and electrical lines along the road. Breathing it in, she held it. She could see them in her sights. "Wait for it," she thought, holding the energy she had ripped. Then, stopping on a dime in front of Thomas, she released it and let it flow with her momentum.

A shower of arcing electricity struck the blonde demon standing closest to Thomas. The female's skin began to bubble, as her muscles twitched violently. She went unconscious. "Stay down and cover your ears," Nina screamed to Thomas, as she faced the bigger of the two remaining demons. Rolling forward, she came up swinging her outstretched arms together in one massive clap, sending out the remainder of the energy in sonic waves. She grinned as the back of his head blew out behind him, and he crumpled to the ground like a sack of potatoes.

"Nina," a spiky-haired demon said. "We were just talking about you." Nina stared at him. It looked like Thomas had put up one hell of a fight. The boy's neck was still bleeding, and she'd seen a spike in the bigger one's head.

"Watch out. It's Satan," Thomas cried, getting to his feet.

"Thanks," Nina quickly said, cartwheeling back to miss the black tentacles he had sent out. Jumping up as high as she could, Nina ripped more energy from the power lines. Then she finished the backflip, orienting herself to the ground. She could already see Thomas was charging at the charred body of the girl. Landing in a crouched position, she shot her left hand forward, shielding it with her right and snapped her fingers. She hoped for the best, as the white spiral of energy that shot out of her left hand hit Satan, snapping bones and exploding both of his eyeballs out of their sockets.

She'd faced Satan before. He was consummately skilled in the casting of dark energy forms. His power could siphon off a person's will in seconds. She had no intention of touching them. As his body hit the ground, with his eyes useless and blood running from his ears, she saw she wouldn't have to. He screamed in agony, clutching his face and writhing on his back. "Hopefully, that will take a while to heal," Nina thought, forcing herself up on her wobbly feet. She was drained. "We've gotta get out of here while we can," she told herself.

There was no way she could keep this pace by herself. The big one's leg was already jerking, as his nervous system began repairing itself. She began to jog towards Thomas, who was actively brawling with the female demon. Nina had hoped she'd be incapacitated by the energy surge. As it was, not only had she been hit by the wave of electricity, but the girl had a metal baseball bat that had acted as a lightning rod. Yet, amazingly enough, here she was on her feet. The burnt char was already flaking away to reveal fresh, pink skin underneath. "I can't let her recover, or we'll never get out of here," thought Nina.

"Coming in hot and to your right," she shouted. Hyper-sprinting with the last of her strength, she charged forward in a blur of motion. Nina punched forward, hoping Thomas was on the same page as her. Stopping short of colliding with the demon,

Nina threw her weight forward into the punch and felt a wetness run up the length of her arm. She opened her eyes to see the demon was sandwiched between her and Thomas. The two watchers each had a black heart in one of their hands, which was protruding from either side.

The shocked, blonde demon turned to Nina. With her face contorted by pain, she whispered, "Stupid skank," before going limp.

"Quick, Thomas. We have to get out of here," Nina said, pulling her arm from the body.

"Take my hand, Nina. We can still fight them off," Thomas cried, quickly pulling his arm out of the dead demon and casting it aside. Without answering, Nina fell to the ground, silent.

"Thomas, you sorry son of a bitch!" Satan cried, from his hands and knees. "You just killed a high-ranking celestial diplomat and one of my best operatives. You're a dead man!" the blind demon screamed. "Do you hear me? I'm gonna kill you! But first, I'm gonna kill your high and mighty wife!" On the ground, wrapped around Nina's ankle, was one of the many dark tentacles the blind demon had been sending out.

"Thomas, run!" Nina whispered, her eyes glazing over.

"Now that my ears are healed, let's hear a good, old-fashioned scream of terror," Satan said, dragging Nina towards him. Thomas winced at his wife's scream of terror.

"Nina!" he yelled, running after her, only to be struck down by a blast of vicious red energy. Searing pain wracked his nervous system, as the bolt ripped through his body. Lying on the ground, Thomas gasped for air, but his diaphragm was barely working.

"What did you do?" a voice screamed from the darkness. "What did you do?" Thomas could hear nothing but venomous hatred in the voice. Rolling onto his back, Thomas saw the large body of Deus lumbering towards him, surrounded by red waves of energy. The look on his face was a mix of rage and sorrow, as he looked up into the night sky and called out the fallen demon's name. "MEPHISTOPHELES!" he shrieked, releasing another blast of violent, red energy. This one was twice as big as the first.

"Oh, God," Thomas thought to himself, knowing there was no way to avoid the onslaught headed his way. Tucking into a ball to protect himself, he felt the energy hit him like a monsoon, picking him up and throwing him. At that moment, Thomas felt like he was trapped under a roaring train. Then he slammed back on to the asphalt a hundred feet from where he'd been. "Oh, God!" he cried in agony, as he clutched his sides. He couldn't feel his left leg, and something felt horribly wrong with the bones in his spine. They seemed to be broken or completely out of place. "Get away from her!" Thomas shouted helplessly from the ground, trying to force himself up.

The two demons circled around Nina like wolves. The realization of what they were going to do washed over him, as they unleashed their energy. It began knitting together, swirling slowly at first and then picking up speed to form a cyclone of black and red energy. "My God, they're going to try to remove her soul!" Thomas screamed to himself. Directing all of his energy into healing, Thomas tried to get up, but his body just wouldn't respond. He hoped he hadn't shattered his spine, but he could feel the mass of destroyed vertebrae. His body was attempting to repair itself. It just wasn't moving fast enough.

"Too bad you're missing this," screamed Satan, over the howl of the tempest. "Your wife's soul is about to be irrevocably ripped asunder, while you lay there like a rag doll. Would you like to see?" Thomas watched helplessly, as the creeping black vines of energy squirmed along the ground towards him. Even though Satan's tentacles hadn't reached him yet, Thomas felt he was already succumbing to despair.

"It can't end like this," Thomas thought. There had to be a way. He knew that, even if he could get up, his only choice at this point would be to run. Nina would never forgive him for risking his life. They'd already promised each other that the Primes had to be trained at all costs. The fate of the world depended on it. They already knew there was a good chance of something like this happening, though they had prayed it never would.

Gritting his teeth, Thomas tried to get up again, as the tentacles rose up over him. He could feel the bones in his back begin to slip back into alignment, but it was too late. He was out of time. As the dark matter pounded into the asphalt, Thomas exploded into a flurry of black feathers and wings, bouncing off the ground and then furiously crashing down again. He finally lifted up, with his left leg trailing behind him. Caught in mid-transition, Thomas screamed in pain, as he traveled up higher, leaving behind him a trail of blood drops and feathers in his wake. He tried his best to use the air currents, but his part-human, part-crow form was too heavy. He could feel the vortex of hate and despair that was enveloping Nina. He tried one more time to finish the transformation, but it was no use. His spinal cord was too damaged.

Hovering above the hurricane, Thomas could see Nina's body lying in the eye of the storm, motionless. He couldn't tell whether she was alive or dead. All he knew was he just couldn't leave her behind, no matter what they had agreed. Knowing that the fate of the world and the Primes rested on this one decision, Thomas descended into the black and red maelstrom of energy. It immediately felt like he'd been thrown into a blender of pain and despair. To avoid hitting the sides, he did the only thing he could do. He dove straight down, spiraling until he landed by Nina's side. Covering his wife with his black wings, he did his best to protect her, as the whirling energy pulled at him from both sides. But he refused to yield, finally transforming back into his human form.

"Nina, can you hear me?" he shouted, pulling her up by her jacket and holding her close. She gave a weak smile and nodded.

"You came for me anyway; didn't you?" Nina said, weakly.

"I couldn't leave. I tried, but I'd rather die with you than live without my other half."

"Then let the power of two become one," her voice rang like a bell in his mind. Taking Nina's hand, he lifted her up. Standing together as the storm raged around them, Thomas grabbed her right hand with his left and opened his heart. In his head, he heard his wife speak. "I am Nina, mother of many magics, but none so powerful as the love I have for my husband."

"And I am Thomas," he loudly proclaimed, "eldest of the twins. But without my other half, I am incomplete." Slowly at first, Thomas felt the energy spill forth from within him. It felt somewhat foreign, like when he'd seen his true reflection. But just as that had passed, so did this. And Thomas's heart, now one with Nina's, began to open, letting out the rose-hued light from within. Surging forth, the light dissolved the darkness. With the red and black energy giving way, he could once again see the two angry demons pouring out their energy. Yet for all their effort and strain, the light was driving them back.

"This is not death," Thomas shouted, raising his right hand towards Satan. "It is Life."

"And this is not a perversion," Nina shouted, raising her left hand to Asmodeus. "This is Truth."

Then, shouting together, they both exclaimed, "This is Love!" Thomas felt the vibration, as the last word passed his lips, and watched, as the fiery rose light flung the demons backwards.

"Enough!" Satan screamed, rising from the ground and shielding his face from the light's brilliance. "You may be able to stand toe to toe with us, but that doesn't negate the fact that you two have to stand together to pull this off."

"Yeah," Deus shouted, grinning maliciously. "And you might have the power of one, but we have the power of two. We not only know where Dianna is, but thanks to Homeless Harry there, we also know where Josh has been hiding. So it's only a matter of time." All of a sudden, Thomas realized how they'd found him. He'd made a grave mistake. As he realized this, he watched the light dwindle down.

"Sooner or later, we'll catch one of you without the other," Satan said, stepping forward. "And we will rob you of your other half."

"Seeing as Josh is the weakest animal of the pack," Deus said, advancing, "it won't be too hard to take him down. So we're still going to win."

"What do you have to say to that?" Satan sneered.

Nina looked at the two smiling demons and uttered one word, and one word only, "Conventicle."

"I love you," Thomas said, squeezing her hand affectionately. He hadn't wanted to use this, unless they had no choice. He trusted her judgment.

"No, wait!" the spiky-haired demon said. "We can talk this out!" But it was too late. A huge, stained oak door, bearing the signs of both the Monarchy and the Host, appeared next to him.

"Horseshit!" Deus screamed angrily.

"Are you sure you're okay with this?" Nina asked. "It's our only one. Somehow, given the moment, it just felt right."

"Don't worry," Thomas said. "I've learned to trust your female intuition." Faintly in the background, he could hear the wail of sirens. As the huge door swung open, and Michael himself stepped out. "Thank God," thought Thomas, relieved to see his old friend. He felt even more so to see that he was wearing his battle attire.

Michael smiled at the two watchers, as he emerged from the door. He looked over at the demons, with a distaste that was too obvious to ignore. "Attention," he announced loudly. "Conventicle has been proclaimed. Please cross the threshold in front of you. Failure to do so will result in the severest of penalties."

Chapter 37
Promises

It was relatively quiet now, except for the distant sound of sirens fading in the background. "I wonder what's going on," Dianna thought impatiently, as she sat alone in the backyard. It wasn't easy to watch Nina leave like that, but she'd resisted the urge to follow her. Now she wished that she had gone. At least then, she'd know what had happened. The past ten minutes had been a weird, emotional roller coaster, that confused her more than the events leading up to the watcher's departure. At first, she was angry, and then numb, as if something had died inside of her. But then she was overcome by a feeling of intense love, a feeling that she'd felt only with Josh. So Dianna had taken out her phone and looked at his smiling photos.

Words really couldn't express how much she missed him. Each day at school was another day that she hoped the teacher would say, "Class, we've got a new student," and he'd walk in, like he had before, with his huge smile. In her mind, she could feel the surprise, when he did the flip in class. But sadly, it had been a week and a half since school started, and she was losing hope. The worst thing for Dianna was the not knowing. She heard what happened to his mother, but he'd broken contact with her before that. If he'd at least said goodbye, she could put his memory away or start to heal. Just to break contact like this was torture for her.

And now her love, much like her life, was a mirror image of purgatory. It was neither here nor there. School was mundane, just like before. Her work at the clinic was filled with so many lost souls, that she didn't know where to begin. It seemed the love that the boy with the huge smile gave, the smile that animated her life and gave her hope, was becoming nothing but a fading memory. Dianna hoped that Josh would come back soon, so she could be freed. Because right now she felt imprisoned. She couldn't live off of a memory. She had to have the real thing. Every day, without contact from him, only made her realize her worst fears had come true.

Initially, when she'd told Josh about the tour, there was a tiny voice inside her that said he might not make it through the summer. She had forced the voice down in her mind. She'd told herself she was way too optimistic to be pushed around by doubt, and that's what she told herself all summer. But here she was, alone and confused in her backyard.

She didn't understand. Even though she'd planted the seeds of hope and desire, much to Dianna's dismay, her garden of hope had been overrun by weeds. It was just like the backyard had been, when they came back from the long tour. Looking up at the sky, she sighed. She hated to admit it. If she'd known things would end up this way, she wouldn't have left for the summer, no matter how much they'd offered her. She might have paid off the house. In the long run, she'd lost something so much more valuable. And now she wished she could do it over.

It seemed like June was a million miles away. Dianna remembered sitting in this very spot, praying for a sign. It was a prayer that was answered almost immediately. Overcome by doubts and regret, Dianna stared at the full moon. Her eyes filling up with tears, she whispered, "Please let Josh come back to me. I need him." And then she closed her eyes and wept alone in the backyard.

***

Gently, like a thief in the night, Josh slipped out through the patio door and crept into the backyard, silently shutting the sliding glass door behind him. Then, when he was sure Charlie wouldn't be disturbed, he covered his mouth with his arm and screamed into it, to muffle the sound. He couldn't hold it in anymore. It seemed the war within him was reaching a fever pitch. It felt like he was losing his mind. He knew he needed a fix bad, but the image of Dianna wouldn't let him go through with it.

The past ten minutes had been a bizarre rollercoaster of emotions. At first, he noticed that he felt angry for no particular reason. Then he felt scared, like he'd never see Dianna again. He'd tried to push the sensations out of his head. Josh figured he was just being emotional, because he was going through withdrawals. But he wasn't sick or sweating. As he sat in the darkness, wishing he could just shoot up or smoke some heroin, Josh was overwhelmed by a feeling so pure and true that it almost felt like what he'd talked to Thomas about yesterday. It was how he had felt, when he was safe and secure. It made him think of how it felt to finally kiss Dianna, after weeks of nervousness. And then just as quickly, it was gone, leaving him in the dark, with that empty feeling, like he was never going to feel that way again. He didn't know if he could deal with that.

"I need to chill out," he thought to himself, "or I'm going to go insane." He walked out onto the dead grass in his bare feet. It was hard to believe that something so alive, something that used to flourish, could be so burnt and dead, just after being deprived of one element. Josh couldn't help but wonder to himself, if this would happen to him eventually, too. He turned his head, not wanting to think about it.

It seemed odd to him how the light of the full moon seemed to illuminate things less than the sun, but it accentuated them so much more. The sun was bright, but its rays shone on everything in the same amount. Nothing really jumped out at him, not like it did under the full moon. Looking out across the backyard, it all became clear to him. The darks were darker, and that was the difference. It created a sensation within him that could only be described as fear; fear of the unknown. Under the light of the full moon, there was the potential that there was a Billy behind every blade of grass, and, off in each of the shadows, there was a Deus patiently watching and waiting.

The revelation of this sent a chill up Josh's spine. "Dude, I'm freakin' out," he said, quickly moving to the center of the backyard, where there was more light. Stepping up on the diving board, he took a look down. The pool was bright in the moonlight. Even the chemical ring around the sides stood out with a sort of brilliance. With the small amount of water still left, it looked like a bottomless pit. "How appropriate," he thought to himself.

Suddenly, a police helicopter roared overhead. "What the hell?" he thought, immediately bringing his arms up, as the spotlight blinded his eyes. "Ahh, man," he said, as he heard it trailing off. "Right in the eyes," he thought, rubbing them and blinking. Carefully, he stepped off the diving board. He could hear sirens now. "Something's going on," he told himself. It was weird. He instantly noticed that just that brief flash had wrecked his perception of the back yard. Now everything was darker and less defined. "I'd better go inside, before I trip over something or accidentally fall into the pool," he thought to himself.

Walking back over to the sliding glass door, he opened it gingerly, trying not to make a sound, as he slipped back into the house. Standing motionless, Josh waited for his eyes to adjust. When they finally did, he saw the heroin rig he'd absentmindedly left by the door. Had he somehow unconsciously done this? He pondered the idea while staring at it. Whatever the reason, the sight was too much. Once more, he felt his resolve crumble. Finally giving in, he grabbed the kit and slipped back outside. Now, more clearly than ever, he saw where he was going, as he purposefully made his way across the backyard and sat cross-legged on the dead lawn. Inherently, he knew this was wrong, but he needed it. He just couldn't fight it anymore.

It was kind of weird, but he practically reveled in the shame he felt putting the tourniquet on. And even though he knew this would only multiply his problems, he mechanically went through the same steps as he remembered Charlie doing them earlier. Every motion, every step was laced with shame and guilt. But strangely, he rushed through them all the same, like he was somebody else and he wasn't exactly doing this. It made him feel, for lack of a better term, alive. Taking a deep breath, Josh looked at his arm and lowered the needle down flush with his vein. Just like all the other times earlier in the night, he saw her face, a face that seemed to stay there, even as his eyes filled with tears, and even as he plunged the needle into his vein, sending the drug to its destination. It was done.

Almost instantly, the weight of his decision crashed down upon him. It made him wonder where his life was headed. When he got there, would she be waiting for him? From here on out, nothing was certain. He gave a quick pull on the band, letting it fall to the ground. Then he removed the needle slowly, carelessly tossing it into the planter next to him. He knew this was the fastest route for the drug, but it was already hitting him hard. He really had to get inside fast, before he crashed. He tried his best to get up but immediately fell back down, landing on his left leg. It seemed to be asleep from sitting on it. All he could manage was sliding out his right leg, before he laid back on the prickly blades, but he didn't care.

The warm feeling was beginning to spread all over him. Pretty soon, he'd be totally gone. As he lied there, Josh stared up at the bright, full moon. It was captivating. He'd never truly looked at it like this. He couldn't tell if the euphoria he felt was coming from the revelation or the heroin. Slowly, the moon's light retreated, as Josh fell further into himself than he ever had before. The only sensation he felt from the outside world was the slight tickle from his tears, as they fell from his eyes and ran down his cheeks.

"I'm sorry, Dianna," was his last conscious thought, as the hard soil began to give way to the rising waters around him. Instinctively taking a breath, the teen submerged, watching as the moon's reflection rippled above him. Then he slowly sank further and further away, into the endless deep of the abyss.

***

Breathing in a sigh of relief, Thomas made his way to the huge oak door. "How big do you think that thing is?" Nina whispered.

"Big enough for an angel and his wings," he said under his breath.

"I'm waiting," Michael said impatiently to the demons.

"Hello, Michael," Satan said with disdain. "You look rather annoyed right now."

"That's because I am," he said, staring directly into the adversary's eyes. "In fact, there's a couple of people inside, who would like you to explain why you're running around looking like you're the lead singer of a boy band and not wearing the Division-issued visage you were assigned."

Chuckling, the demon replied, "Well, Mike, you're only as old as you feel."

"Yeah, Mike," Deus chuckled. His laughter was short-lived though. As the archangel locked eyes with him, he shot his right arm out with lightning speed. The angel grabbed Deus by the shirt and pulled him close.

"My name," he said, through clenched teeth, "is Michael. I would like to remind you that it means who is like God. You would do well to remember that you are only an aspect of God, and a fairly limited one, at that." He slowly pulled the demon in so their faces were mere inches apart. "If it comes down to a contest of wills, I will throw you down faster than you can blink. Am I understood?" Holding his breath, Thomas waited for the demon to reply, but he merely glared. Not releasing the demon's shirt or looking away, Michael reached up with his left hand and drew his blade from the leather sheathe fastened to his back. Immediately, white flames danced around the blade, as he lowered it down in front of Satan's smug face.

"You guys seem to have picked up some bad habits down here. In the future, please remind your operatives who their superiors are."

After a moment, Satan cleared his throat. "I understand fully," he said, showing no emotion. "I would like to point out that, while my second in command may have a minor respect issue, they," Satan said, his skin instantly flushing a deep red, as he pointed at Nina and Thomas, "they have killed an innocent operative. So what will be done about that?"

The archangel gripped his weapon tighter. As he did, the flames burned even brighter. "We all know that Mephistopheles was anything but innocent. But I'll look into it. Now, are you guys going to cross the threshold, or am I going to have to help you?" Michael said, tapping the flaming blade under Satan's chin.

"No, Michael. That won't be necessary," Satan replied calmly. "However, don't think it uncouth of me, if I point out that someday soon I have a present I'm going to give you. The surprise will quite literally shock the life out of you."

"Is that so?" Michael said, removing the blade from under Satan's chin and slowly re-sheathing it.

"Oh, it's the honest-to-God truth," Satan said, grinning at his sworn enemy. "Come along, Deus. I guess we should get this over with." Thomas watched in amazement, as both demons disappeared into the portal.

Nina gave a heartfelt chuckle. "Good Lord, Michael, I've never seen you act like that," she exclaimed. The angel bent down, taking Nina's hand and lightly kissing it.

"I'm sorry, my dear. But as of late, it seems that force and thinly-veiled threats are all the Demonic Branch responds to. With each day, they get bolder and bolder; a sure sign that the end draws near. But enough of this," he said, smiling and turning to face Thomas. "You're looking very well, my friend."

"I appreciate that," Thomas said, "but you should have seen me a few days ago."

"He needed a shave and a haircut badly," Nina said, laughing. The woman's laughter was cut short, as the sounds of a helicopter approaching became increasingly audible. Thomas sighed, as he looked behind him. Off in the distance, he could see a large group of red and blue flashing lights approaching.

"I guess the fireworks tipped them off," Michael said. "Looks like somebody's in trouble."

"Speaking of," Nina said, looking in the archangel's direction, "is there really going to be an investigation?" she asked hesitantly.

"Not at all," Michael replied. "In fact, I wanted to say that I was impressed by the act of extraordinary courage the two of you performed. I'm going to recommend that both your powers be augmented."

"I'm honored," Nina said, slightly bowing her head.

Folding his arms, Thomas shook his head. "I'm flattered as well, Michael, but we both know it's not what we need."

"What is it you desire?"

"After this incident with the demons, it's obvious we need actual protection. They're just too aggressive."

"I agree," Nina said, watching the helicopter's search light approaching up the pavement in front of them.

"I'll see what I can do," the angel said. "We should leave."

Thomas nodded, but didn't move. Tonight's victory for him seemed somewhat bittersweet. Even though he'd done everything in his power, it seemed his student was slipping away. Looking back towards the approaching emergency vehicles, he asked, "Will Josh be alright?"

Michael's face became grim. "All I can say for certain is that he'll be alive when you get back."

"When?" Nina asked.

"Yes," Michael replied. "Metatron has already determined that, after the meeting, you will be reinserted into the time stream, at a point that's more advantageous to Josh. You have to remember that Josh has to learn what he came here to learn. His destiny lies in the Creator's hands." Thomas nodded quietly. He knew he had to have more faith in both the Creator and the boy. There had to be a plan. The signs constantly said so.

"I know you are troubled," the archangel said quietly. "When things seem their worst, look up, because hope draws nigh." The watchers both followed the archangel's gaze up to the full moon, as he continued. "Today is Thursday, September 19th. It's a full moon in Pisces."

"Is that a good thing?" Nina asked.

"Most indeed," the angel agreed. "It signifies synchronicity and intuition. Sound familiar?" he asked, smiling at the two of them.

"Not at all," Nina said, grinning and walking towards the portal. Thomas watched her, as she stopped and turned to give him a wink. Her pale skin and copper locks were flashing with the blue and red hues of the approaching lights. She smiled and said, "I'll see you on the other side, soulmate." Then she turned and disappeared. A warm feeling spread over Thomas, and it made him smile.

"You are a lucky man, Thomas," Michael remarked. "So what do you say?"

"I'm ready," Thomas said, stepping up to the threshold and walking through. The archangel held back, perched between the doorway and the night. He envied the watchers. As long as they had each other, it seemed they could face anything. He only hoped the teens could do the same. There was a war coming. Michael knew that much. He didn't know everything about the Creator's plan, but he didn't need to. As unique as Thomas was in this reality, the archangel knew that he wasn't the only one who could read the signs. Michael folded his arms and took a parting glance, as the emergency vehicles approached. It didn't take much for him to see what the Creator was saying.

"Hang on, kids. Help is on its way," he said. And with that, the dark, oak door slowly shut, and then disappeared.

Shelter O

Made in the USA
San Bernardino, CA
30 September 2013